Praise for the Novels of Carol Berg

The Soul Mirror

"A compelling and altogether admirable work." —*Kirkus Reviews* (starred review)

"Berg brings life and grace to a story of magic and politics that should appeal to the author's fans as well as lovers of Renaissance-style fantasy." —*Library Journal*

"Lavish. . . . Berg's characters return to vivid life. . . . [She] refreshes and reinvigorates the familiar trappings of epic fantasy, shaping a novel that rings true both linguistically and imaginatively. This is one to savor."
—*Publishers Weekly* (starred review)

"A novel that stakes an early claim to my Top 10 list of 2011, *The Soul Mirror* (A++) takes the Collegia Magica series to the next level with a gripping tale. . . . Magic, science, family feuds, a kingdom and maybe even a world—or at least its laws of nature—in peril, a great heroine with a superb cast, and traditional fantasy does not get better than this!" —Fantasy Book Critic

"An enjoyable otherworld fantasy that has an Age of Reason historical feel to the story line. . . . Fans will want to accompany the reluctant heroine as she learns there is much more than science in the wonderful world of Carol Berg."
—*Midwest Book Review*

"A compelling addition to the world of the Collegia Magica and you'll wait with baited breath as you follow Anne's travels into the unfamiliar world of magic and sorcery." —Bibliophilic Book Blog

"Ms. Berg's wonderful use of prose makes Anne's voice irresistible as she takes us on an incredible journey fraught with mystery, suspense, and fantasy. Incredible world building superbly translates the emotions and feelings of Anne and the court as a whole. The overall story line is quite elegant and lyrical in its ebb and flow. . . . I recommend Ms. Berg's Collegia Magica series as a must read for those who enjoy a historical themed fantasy with memorable characters, exciting mystery, taut suspense, and a sprinkling of romance." —Smexy Books Romance Reviews

continued . . .

The Spirit Lens

"In this superbly realized leadoff to Berg's quasi-Renaissance fantasy trilogy . . . Berg shapes the well-worn elements of epic fantasy into a lush, absorbing narrative."

—*Publishers Weekly* (starred review)

"Rich with vivid characters and unforgettable places. . . . [Berg] spins an infectiously enjoyable series opener that fans of thought-provoking fantasy and intriguing mystery should appreciate."

—*Library Journal*

"[An] interestingly twisted new series."

—*Locus*

"A super opening to what looks like a great alternate Renaissance fantasy. . . . Fans will appreciate this strong beginning as science and sorcery collide when three undercover agents investigate the divine and unholy collision of murder, magic, and physics."

—Genre Go Round Reviews

"Berg is entirely adept at creating a detailed and nuanced fantasy world, made all the more impressive by noting that other books she has written seem to be about other worlds with other rules."

—I Don't Write Summaries

"A genuine page-turner that should please both mystery and fantasy fans."

—*Booklist*

"Keeps the reader on edge. . . . Berg keeps the pages turning."

—SFRevu

"A nonstop ride to a superb ending that left my appetite whetted for the next installment."

—Fantasy Book Critic

"Berg is a master world builder that novice fantasy authors would do well to study. This first installment in a new trilogy, Collegia Magica, is a winner."

—*Romantic Times*

"*The Spirit Lens* is an incredibly enjoyable fantasy adventure for those who love unexpected heroes, web-worked plots, magic versus technology, and librarians with a skill for investigative spying."

—The Reader Eclectic

Breath and Bone

"The narrative crackles with intensity against a vivid backdrop of real depth and conviction, with characters to match. Altogether superior."

—*Kirkus Reviews* (starred review)

"Berg's lush, evocative storytelling and fully developed characters add up to a first-rate purchase for most fantasy collections." —*Library Journal*

"Replete with magic-powered machinations, secret societies, and doomsday divinations, the emotionally intense second volume of Berg's intrigue-laden Lighthouse Duet concludes the story of Valen. . . . [F]ans of Marion Zimmer Bradley's Avalon sequence and Sharon Shinn will be rewarded." —*Publishers Weekly*

Flesh and Spirit

"The vividly rendered details . . . give this book such power. Berg brings to life every stone in a peaceful monastery and every nuance in a stratified society, describing the difficult dirty work of ordinary life as beautifully as she conveys the heart-stopping mysticism of holiness just beyond human perception."

—Sharon Shinn, national bestselling author of *Troubled Waters*

"Valen is unquestionably memorable—in what is definitely a dark fantasy as much concerned with Valen's internal struggle as with his conflicts with others."

—*Booklist*

"Chilling fantasy." —*Publishers Weekly*

The Bridge of D'Arnath Novels

"A very promising start to a new series." —*The Denver Post*

"Berg has mastered the balance between mystery and storytelling [and] pacing; she weaves past and present together, setting a solid foundation. . . . It's obvious [she] has put incredible thought into who and what makes her characters tick."

—*The Davis Enterprise*

Song of the Beast

Winner of the Colorado Book Award for Science Fiction/Fantasy

"The plot keeps twisting right until the end . . . entertaining characters."

—*Locus*

"Berg's fascinating fantasy is a puzzle story, with a Celtic-flavored setting and a plot as intricate and absorbing as fine Celtic lacework . . . the characters are memorable, and Berg's intelligence and narrative skill make this stand-alone fantasy most commendable." —*Booklist*

Books by Carol Berg

THE COLLEGIA MAGICA SERIES

The Spirit Lens

The Soul Mirror

The Daemon Prism

THE LIGHTHOUSE SERIES

Flesh and Spirit

Breath and Bone

THE BRIDGE OF D'ARNATH SERIES

Son of Avonar

Guardians of the Keep

The Soul Weaver

Daughter of Ancients

THE RAI-KIRAH SERIES

Transformation

Revelation

Restoration

Song of the Beast

THE DAEMON PRISM

A Novel of the Collegia Magica

CAROL BERG

A ROC BOOK

ROC
Published by New American Library,
a division of Penguin Group (USA) Inc.,
375 Hudson Street, New York, New York 10014, USA
Penguin Group (Canada), 90 Eglinton Avenue East, Suite 700, Toronto,
Ontario M4P 2Y3, Canada (a division of Pearson Penguin Canada Inc.)
Penguin Books Ltd., 80 Strand, London WC2R 0RL, England
Penguin Ireland, 25 St. Stephen's Green, Dublin 2,
Ireland (a division of Penguin Books Ltd.)
Penguin Group (Australia), 250 Camberwell Road, Camberwell,
Victoria 3124, Australia (a division of Pearson Australia Group Pty. Ltd.)
Penguin Books India Pvt. Ltd., 11 Community Centre,
Panchsheel Park, New Delhi - 110 017, India
Penguin Group (NZ), 67 Apollo Drive, Rosedale, Auckland 0632,
New Zealand (a division of Pearson New Zealand Ltd.)
Penguin Books (South Africa) (Pty.) Ltd., 24 Sturdee Avenue,
Rosebank, Johannesburg 2196, South Africa

Penguin Books Ltd., Registered Offices:
80 Strand, London WC2R 0RL, England

First published by Roc, an imprint of New American Library,
a division of Penguin Group (USA) Inc.

First Printing, January 2012
10 9 8 7 6 5 4 3 2 1

LIBRARY OF CONGRESS CATALOGING-IN-PUBLICATION DATA:

Berg, Carol.
The daemon prism: a novel of the Collegia Magica/Carol Berg.
p. cm.—(Collegia Magica series)
ISBN 978-0-451-46434-7
1. Magic—Fiction. I. Title.
PS3602.E7523D34 2012
813'.6—dc23 2011032115

Set in Bembo
Designed by Elke Sigal

Printed in the United States of America

For Kylie, Madeline, and Ethan.
May you always see the magic.

ACKNOWLEDGMENTS

Many thanks to Ken Perry and Celu Amberston for their gracious insights into the world of the senses. To Susan Smith and Linda Kinsel for your most special friendship, support, encouragement, and writerly counsel, and to the whole circle of Brian, Catherine, Courtney, Curt, and Susan for keeping me honest. To my dear readers and colleagues near and far for encouragement and commiseration through the tough days as well as the fine ones. To Mother, Brian, Jerry, and Andrew for understanding. And forever to the Exceptional Spouse for patience and support above and beyond.

THE DAEMON PRISM

Dante

CHAPTER 1

30 OCET, 883RD YEAR OF
THE SABRIAN REALM, SUNSET
PRADOVERDE

"Stop right there!" I bellowed. My student's resolute little inhalation signaled her ready to bind her first complex spell. I resisted the temptation to shatter or repair the well-structured but ill-conceived little charm. She had to learn.

Mercifully, she was well disciplined. Though her will tugged fiercely against mine, she obeyed.

"Concentrate. Look deeper. A hundred thousand streams in Sabria comprise water, rocks, willows, and trout. But to draw on *this* stream's keirna—its essence—you must unearth the secrets that make it unique. You're no child swatting a fly. Misjudgment could drown us . . . or bury us . . . or turn yon pasture into a swamp." In this case, likely all of them and worse.

She knelt along the stream bank, not half a metre from my boots. Having spent most of every day for two years in her presence, I could sense her every muscle twitch, accurate signals for divining her level of confidence. It had taken her a very long time to prepare for this step, and she was very sure of herself. She hated mistakes.

"There's nothing wrong with it," she said after a few moments' contemplation. "Sealing the snag will just divert the water around the end of it, digging out the far bank a little more. I'm not blocking the water flow completely. There's plenty of leeway."

She readied herself again.

"No!" I drove the heel of my staff into the rocky streambed.

She jerked but held her ground, not yanking her hand from the water. It wasn't so easy to startle her into attendance anymore. So I assaulted her weakness with words. "Have you learned nothing? There's mud between the rocks. What color is it? What consistency? Does the sun reveal glints of metal in it? What would that tell you of the stream's origins and use? You're a woman of science. Where is its source? Has its course evolved as nature prescribes or has it been purposely altered? Your friend Simon provided you the Pradoverde land grants. If you'd studied them with half a mind, you'd know this land was once a disputed boundary between two blood families. Why?"

"None of those things has to do with a snag of twigs formed this past summer." She was so sure. So calm.

"Wrong! If you'd studied the legends of the Fremoline outcrops, where our stream has its source, you'd know there were persistent tales of gold deposits—"

"There are no gold deposits anywhere in the demesne of Louvel." I could imagine her rolling her eyes. "The rocks are almost entirely limestone. The rumors provide nothing useful to weave into the spellwork."

Breaking her prim, scholarly ways of thinking had been my most difficult challenge. It was why I had chosen this particular exercise on this particular day.

I repeated my probe of the streambed. Again, and then again, moving upstream until the muffled jar of metal shivered my staff and the razored sting of long-bound enchantment flowed up my arm. The virulence of the spell threatened to dissolve the bone. But I held the staff in place and tapped it sharply with my forefinger, my signal that she should touch it, too. She had to feel the magnitude of her error.

Her discipline held. A gurgle out of place in the rhythmic bubbling of the stream told me she'd withdrawn her hand from the water. A quiet chink, a scuff of dirt, and the release of pent power said she'd kicked aside the length of slender chain she'd laid out for her spell enclosure. Determined steps and a brush of skirts brought her to my side.

"If you'd looked deeper," I said, cooler now that I'd snared her full attention, "you'd have found a bronze casket buried here at the seventh metre past the dogleg bend—the corner of the disputed territory. This is how the one faction, intending to ensure that they alone could harvest these rumored riches, shifted the streambed to fit their desired boundary."

I could not see her face any better than I could see anything else in this daemon-blasted world. Yet, even had I not smelled her soap-scented sweat or heard the tight hiss of her annoyance, I'd have known her the moment she laid her finger on the carved hornbeam of my ancille—the moment the spells bound into my staff became instantly more useful, more lethal, faster, sharper, swollen from the inborn power she brought to any working. One would have to plumb the tangled depths of a forest's roots or the moldered residue of an ancient battleground to match Anne de Vernase's potential for magic. That she possessed a mind and will fully capable of wielding such power made her reluctance to take hold of it inexcusable.

She snatched her hand away. "A spelled artifact buried in the streambed!" Her explosive astonishment was not feigned. Nor was her humiliation. "But that changes everything . . . risks conflicting spellwork . . . unending complications . . . flood, mudflows, cave-ins. . . ."

"Even so."

"But the land grant said nothing of an altered streambed or buried caskets. How could you—anyone—possibly know of it?"

"Because I *think*. Because my expectations of devious human behavior are more accurate than those of a star-eyed aristo lady who grew up sheltered by a rich father. A blood family would never allow civil law to settle a boundary dispute, nor would they yield desired territory if their sorcery could possibly prevent it. Because when it comes to keirna, unfounded rumor can have greater significance than historical or scientific truth; thus I betook my commoner boots out of the library and into the hills and deigned to speak with a few crofters hereabouts. And because I don't allow trivial concerns to intrude on building spellwork. Magic is not a study for dabblers."

Before the words faded, I knew I'd gone too far. She whirled on me like a tornadic wind.

"My family is not trivial!"

I didn't retreat, but I did raise a shielding spell. Her uncontrolled anger could peel the paint from a wall, crack its foundation, or flatten an unwary teacher against it—only a few of the possibilities we had uncovered as we'd explored the dangerous side of her blood heritage. But again her discipline held.

"And a *dabbler*? I've heeded your every word for two years, worked your tedious exercises, allowed you to lead me to the netherworld and back, not complaining about your insults or criticisms or your stubborn refusal to heed my wishes or speak with me on topics of my choosing. I agreed to your conditions. Indeed, I no longer fear I'm going to murder someone by accident, and you've given me an understanding of the world I never imagined. But this part of it . . . working spells . . . Clearly, I can't get it right. And I was failing long before I decided to visit Montclaire."

No possible response was going to soothe her. So I spoke the truth, though it dripped brine into her wounds. "You fail because you refuse to commit yourself to the work."

"But I can't be like you, Dante. I can't pretend I have no family, no life, no past, no future. I can't wall off my heart. I can't forget that my sister was murdered or ignore my conviction that we should be studying the lore of Ixtador and the eternal Veil and the horrors we witnessed on Mont Voilline instead of these ridiculous spells. I am not dead." No one on this side of her flaying tongue would imagine that. "If you would just listen to me . . . talk with me . . ."

"Control and discipline are not enough," I snapped. "If you cannot shape your own power, you might as well be dead."

Anne was right that something was terribly wrong in between the living world and the realm of souls beyond death—the borderland pious folk named Ixtador Beyond the Veil. She believed she had heard her sister's voice after the explosive end of the de Gautier conspiracy at Mont Voilline. Dead only a month, Lianelle had begged Anne to find help for those beyond the Veil, claiming that the souls of the dead were being *leached away*. Our friend Portier's experiences of that night had convinced him that Ixtador's existence prevented the dead from moving on to whatever awaited humankind beyond mortal life—whether that be Heaven or the Souleater's realm of ice and darkness or blessed oblivion. Yet, how could we possibly remedy such an aberration in the natural order?

Anne's conviction made the problem of Ixtador real and urgent. But I had insisted she learn to control her power and develop the fundamentals of spellworking before we dealt with it. We weren't going to make any headway on such mystery without her magically capable.

My gift for sorcery was extraordinary, all the more so in an age of the world when sorcerous practice was moribund. But as I had taught Anne . . .

as I had been taught . . . one could not effectively or safely create spells while ignoring any evidence of intellect or senses. After two years blind, my memories of the visible world were becoming imprecise. Every day I failed to bind some construct correctly because I could not recall or learn a physical detail I needed.

Certainly, others could describe things to me. But temporary crutches would not solve my problem. The inevitable lay before me like a bottomless chasm. Sooner or later, I'd have to stop practicing sorcery. An assassin's knife would be a mercy on that day.

Yet I refused to take a dead man's year, enjoying careless pleasures or opening doors into rooms I could never enter. Germond de Gautier's conspiracy to upend the laws of nature had consumed Anne, Portier, and me and spit us out broken. Though we had won the day at Mont Voilline, the full accounting for de Gautier's deeds had yet to be rendered. Someone with exceptional power and well-honed skills must be ready when payment came due. Portier was in seclusion a thousand kilometres away. It certainly wasn't going to be me. That left Anne.

"Dante, wait. . . ."

"Sunset. The lesson is over." I was already tramping across the pasture to the guesthouse, though poking with my staff like some witless beggar to find the cairns she'd used to mark the path precluded the kind of dramatic departure that might emphasize my point.

The days would be wretched with her gone.

Anne left early the next morning. As her maidservant Ella and Ella's brother Finn loaded a borrowed donkey cart, I sat on the steps of Pradoverde's main house, letting the weak autumn sun bathe my cold skin and soothe the void in my gut. Every morning it was the same—a panicked sickness when my eyes opened yet again to eternal nothing.

Anne was busily instructing Finn about the care of the house, the horses, the pantry, and her herb garden. She didn't mention how to tend an irascible blind spellcaster. Not this time. She'd been instructing Finn on how to put up with me since he'd joined our household the previous year.

Ella was accompanying Anne to Montclaire; thus Finn and I would be left alone at Pradoverde. Finn was a steady, honest lad with useful skills when it came to carpentry and mechanics, but he scuttered about the place like a nervous weasel. I had learned the uncomfortable limits of my sightless state in those first months after the cursed rite at Mont Voilline, else I would have thrown him into the cart with the women.

Anne dashed past me and into the house. Her steps, ever light, raced up the stair. Doors slammed. More quick steps, as she returned.

"Almost forgot the book of poems for Ambrose," she said, as she crunched across the gravel to the cart. She was excited to go. It was her first time back to her childhood home since she'd been forced to leave it two years before, an event that roused her dormant talent for magic to the benefit of the world—and her own dismay.

I didn't plead with her to stay. She knew my arguments.

Ten years previous, a natural philosopher named Arronge had formulated a theory that the energies of objects in motion are invariant, transferred from one to another as the objects interact in the physical world. The concept translated well into the sphere of enchantments. Magical energies, the stuff of life, thought, dream, and enchantment, every bit as observable to those who had the sense for it, could not simply evaporate, either. Drained from one place, they must end up somewhere else.

If Anne and Portier were right about their experiences at Mont Voilline, then our mystery was far greater than Ixtador. The energies created by stripping the essence from human souls must be inconceivably huge, and we had not the least idea where those drained from Ixtador had gone. The universe was unhealthy, very like the shell of a diseased hen's egg, thin, brittle, and ready to shatter. Profound magic would be needed to solve the problem.

"Will you not bid me a safe journey?"

I jumped, grazing an elbow on the brick pillar behind me. Gnarled worries must have left me deaf. Unlike Finn and Ella, Anne was always careful to let me know she was near.

"Naturally. Yes."

She waited for more. But words ever eluded me. I hated her leaving. She knew that already.

Threads of her unruly hair itched my cheek. "I'll come back," she said softly. "As I told you on the day I walked into this house, we are irrevocably bound. I *know* you. I value—"

I jumped up and slammed my stick against the front-door lintel so as to get through the opening without crashing my face into the wall. Anne was naive and sentimental, forever inviting me into places no uncouth, ill-tempered necromancer belonged.

I cannot ignore my family's need. Her declaration, bound with apology, followed me indoors, voiced not in audible speech, but in the unspoken diction of the mind, a gift Anne and I shared. *Dante, I* will *return.*

Devilish perversity made me slam the door behind me. Moments later the cart clattered away, leaving me alone in the everlasting dark.

Words spoken in the aether testified clearly to the speaker's truth or lies. But Anne's present belief didn't matter. She had acquired what she most needed from our arrangement. She wasn't coming back.

NEVER HAD I IMAGINED ANY person like Anne de Vernase, much less met one. Unbelievably disciplined, yet so . . . replete . . . with exuberant life. An exceptional mind. Determined as an avalanche. Her courage in the face of true horrors would put the king's chevaliers to shame.

I had come to know her in the aether, the medium of souls, where the passions of the living are expressed in an unceasing torrent of "voices" only a few in the world can hear. From earliest childhood I had been gifted—cursed—with the ability to perceive them. But until encountering Anne, I'd never found anyone in that mad, noisy maelstrom who could hear my own directed speech, much less speak back to me in kind.

To discover that this exceptional person was the daughter of the man I believed a traitorous mastermind near overthrew me. Yet even that profound astonishment had been overmatched on the day Anne walked into this house and announced she intended to live with me, so I could teach her how to control the fearful power in her blood. Her mind raddled by an ordeal that would crush weaker spirits, she'd spoken a great deal of sentimental twaddle that day. But I had believed her serious about her magic.

Now King Philippe was engaged on Sabria's northeastern borders with a gritty enemy whose longships threatened the kingdom's precious shipping lanes, and he had summoned his demesne lords to bring reinforcements. Anne's father, the king's good friend and brother-in-arms, had survived his five-year ordeal as de Gautier's prisoner, but his bones were like honeycomb and his mind fragile. He'd never again be fit enough to fight at his liege's side. By law, the heir to his demesne, Anne's brother,

Ambrose, must go in his stead. Ambrose could likely have won royal exemption, but he had suffered his own torments during de Gautier's conspiracy and had been chafing to kill someone ever since. I didn't blame him, and I preferred the victim not be me—which had ever been in his mind. I had hoped Anne might persuade Ambrose to make other arrangements for minders at Montclaire. But she had made her choice.

34 OCET

Surprisingly enough the days passed rapidly. We had decided to fence in a paddock for the four horses Anne had acquired in the summer. Likely Finn could have done it as well alone as with me. Sightless assistants with only one good hand are rarely invaluable. But I craved physical labor, and Finn insisted he would welcome my help. I used no power of mine to probe the truth of his words.

As a boy I would have scoffed at the idea that any but a king might hold a demesne so fine as Pradoverde. Yet the main house was actually only five rooms, the guesthouse two, and the rolling terrain comprised a mere fifteen hectares—cramped by the standards of royal holdings. We had pasture enough for the horses, and a few sheep should we choose to have them. The previous owners had planted a decent kitchen garden and a small orchard of apple, pear, and cherry. To the west lay a fair expanse of open woodland and the once-disputed stream. Despite its contentious history, it was a good place. Healthy. Quiet. But for this bit of land . . . and Anne . . . I'd have been a raving lunatic. Worse than I was already.

Three days saw us almost done with the fence. While Finn mounted the gate hinges we'd forged that day, I set some simple spells on the fence, ancient charms of ward and welcome to keep the horses in and thieves, moles, and whipsnakes out.

The weather was a confusion only a late autumn day could produce: hot sun, chill air, dry, dusty, and still. The silver mage collar that bound my neck itched with sweat and grime. By the time we had hung the gate, the angle of the sun signaled dusk, and I'd no thought for anything but the barrel of beer cooling in the cellar.

Finn sluiced his head at the courtyard font and bolted for the nearby village of Laurentine to pursue a budding rapport with the tavern keeper's daughter. I carried my beer to the steps of the main house, leaned against the porch rail, and inhaled the night. The cooling breeze rustled the dying vines and grasses, stirring up scents of dust, horse, mice, and drying mint. Tree crickets trilled. The collared dove perched in the stable eaves whimpered. The horses whuffled. All that presented itself to my senses I tried to absorb. To remember. To see. Inevitably, my fingers drifted to my bracelet of thin copper.

"Oraste," I whispered, triggering my newest version of an enchantment I hoped might counter the damage to my eyes. Magic poured out of me until my flesh near caved in.

The night remained entirely black. Spitting curses, I launched my cup into the garden.

The device de Gautier had used to blind me as punishment for my duplicity had been made two centuries past, when the knowledge and practice of sorcery had reached heights never recovered after a century of savagery. Even so, my skills should have been sufficient to disentangle the original spellwork and effect a counterspell. Unfortunately, trapped in an underground vault and near out of my mind with the fire in my eye sockets, I had destroyed the cursed device. Devising a counter without access to the original enchantment would likely take me longer than I had left.

Terror of destroying my eyes altogether prevented anything but the most cautious experimentation. I had only just begun to experience any success—an occasional shadow landscape, where objects appeared as darker blotches in the dark. I'd not even told Anne as yet. Unfortunately, even so primitive a reversal required every scrap of power I could muster. And the spell failed the moment I stopped feeding it. Nights like this when I was physically and magically depleted, I could not even begin.

A sirening disturbance in the aether interrupted my litany of invective. Hooves trod the lane from the village road. Though our boundary wards signaled but one intruder, I stood and reached for my staff. I needed no eyes to draw on its enchantments, ever ready to release fiery destruction. Half the population of Merona and the entire Camarilla Magica would gleefully slit my throat if allowed the idea it was possible.

"Sorcerer?" The horseman's booming voice bounced firmly from the stone and brick. No telltales of magic accompanied him.

"Who asks?"

"Be ye the sorcerer called Dante?" No anger or hostility marred his query. Wariness, yes. If he knew aught of me, that spoke some rudimentary intelligence.

"Why should I yield my name to a stranger who refuses the same courtesy?"

Halted on the gravel, the horseman dismounted smoothly. He tethered his horse—no mountain pony or farm hack, but a large, spirited animal—to one of the oaks that shaded the lane. Firm, confident steps crossed the gravel yard. A heavy man with the slightest trace of a limp.

"Masson de Cuvier, Grenadier, First Legion of Sabria," he announced. "Honorably retired."

A tall man. His voice was almost on a level with my face. He smelled of good horse, good leather, and no spirits.

"I'm Dante," I said. "What's your business?"

"Peace." His voice broke ever so slightly, a burden of desperation surely unaccustomed for such a strong, confident man. "A fellow in Bardeu told me ye can take a dream away. Is't true?"

"It's been more than six years since I left Bardeu." That's where Portier had found me and dragged me into his investigation of conspiracy and secrets.

"But they remember you. Around Bardeu, folk claimed ye were a healer of the mind, as well as a sorcerer. One said ye'd kept a dream from killing him. So is't true or not?"

"Eradicating dreams is only possible if they're visited upon you by enchantment. Some are just the natural stuff of the mind—"

"I've heard all that. But this dream is not natural. 'Tis a plague and an abomination, and if I cannot be rid of it, I will die by my own hand before the new year breaks."

That, I understood.

"Well, then . . ." I stood aside and motioned him into the house.

CHAPTER 2

PRADOVERDE

"Dark as a tomb in here. Can't see a wretched thing!"

"A moment," I said. A twitch of my staff raised a steady warmth from a lamp Anne kept on a stool beside the stair. *Pivot. Three paces.* I laid a hand on the back of Anne's chair.

"I heard ye don't see. It's true, is it?"

So he'd talked to someone of more recent knowledge than Bardeu. "Yes. But there's no need for you to sit in the dark. Sit where you like."

He sat himself in the large chair nearest the fire. I took Anne's chair and waited for him to begin. He didn't seem shy.

"Tell me, sorcerer, have ye sight in your dreams?"

I'd told no one of my dreams or my daily horror upon waking. My frights were no one's business. But I answered Masson de Cuvier. His was no idle question.

"Yes. Every night. And every morning on waking, I lose it all over again. It's like suffocation."

"Aye. Just so."

"Tell me of your dream."

"I got to tell ye some history first. I'm a professional soldier, no conscript, no tenant summoned to service a king's liegeman. Nor am I a chevalier. I'm a common grenadier, and a cracking good one, too. I've served on every border and in every campaign for fifty-three years under three kings. I've no family save my cadre. My men don't love me, but they know what I drill into them keeps them alive. A paragon, ye might say, and so I have been.

"There've been things that troubled over the years, for certain. Men dyin' from a commander's foolishness. Enemies a man can't fight face-to-face with honorable weapons. And the people in these far places . . . some of them good people, but enemies nonetheless, some wicked folk we must treat as allies. I've seen things, too, oddments a man can't explain: some fair, some fearful. I've seen evil."

His practiced delivery suggested he'd told this story many times. Yet at the mention of evil, his voice trembled again. I waited for him to go on.

"Near twenty years ago, young King Philippe chased the witchlords from their stronghold in Kadr. We run 'em to ground like rabbits in a place called Carabangor, an abandoned fortress city deep in the desert. That ruin was a labyrinth, made ten times larger by the witchlords' illusions. But the king's alchemists devised incendiaries that allowed us to sight the difference between their illusions and the true walls, and we soon took the gates. The night fell quiet, as if all were dead.

"'Twas too dangerous to move men into the city to clean the last of 'em out. Their wicked enchantments seemed to feed on the night. But we dared not give them time to slip away or rebuild their magics. So I took a party into the city to spy out where they were hid. Five of us were on the scout, Des de Roux, Unai Focault, Benat Toussaint, a boy called Hawk, and me. Soon as we were under the walls, we split up. Des and Unai headed for the old citadel. Benat went off to scout a barracks near the southern gate. Hawk and me combed the streets in front of the gates, working our way to meet up with the others.

"It was a terrible place. Mostly rubble. Ye didn't know what ye was going to find around the next turn in the road or behind some ragged scrap of leather flapping in the wind. There was no moon, and ye dared not show a light. Ye crept along those twisty streets quiet as death, wishing ye'd left your boots behind so as to silence your steps the more. Ye'd think none but rats and fere-cats had walked there for a thousand years.

"We was a half hour in when we heard the crying—a woman or child sobbing as if the world had ended. Hawk was of a mind to ignore it. He was a hard boy, no family, no close friends among the men. Fine tracker, though. Best we had. But I'd never left woman or child crying that I could help, and said we had to look. It could've been a witchlord woman, after all.

"So Hawk and me tracked the sound to a grand place, more a temple than a house, with six great eagles stood in the front of it. A deal of the roof had caved in, so we'd starlight to navigate by. We followed that crying down and down a curved stair, past more great birds and beasts standing in the dark, till we thought we must come to the heart of the earth itself."

The grenadier paused and cleared his throat.

"We'd come to a lake down there, the water milk white, and a fog hanging over it. Stars shone so bright through the broken roof, the fog glowed like pearls. Stone paving, slick with mold, ran right up to the edge of the water, so that ye might call it a pool more than a lake, save it was so big. Some fifty metres from the bank lay an island, naught but a rock in the center of the pool. And there stood the comeliest woman I ever looked on.

"Like a willow withe she was, with ghost-pale hair, though her skin was the color of good earth and eyes black as ebony. Her hair and her white robes floated out from her in the white fog so ye couldn't tell where one ended and the other began. She called out, weeping, begging us to set her free.

"A shell boat lay moored by the bank, and Hawk moved to jump in, but I stopped him.

" 'Wait,' I told him. 'This be no ordinary maiden to be rescued. Consider if it be some phantom, planted here by the witchlords to lure us to our destruction—and mayhap our king and comrades with us.'

"Hawk glared at me in his cold way, and said I'd led us on this merry chase instead of doing what we'd come to do, so how was I to have it both ways?

"Whilst I stood there, undecided, the woman held out her hand to show a green gem the size of a plum. 'Take it!' she says to me. Though her voice had dropped and she was so far away, it sounded as if she whispered right in my ear. 'It is beyond price. Transport me across the lake and it's yours evermore. 'Twill bring you what you most desire.' "

"Hawk moved again to fetch her, but I said no. 'Twould take precious time and our duty was to king and comrades. But indeed, I feared that place more than any weapon I'd ever faced. Already the jewel plucked at my yearnings.

"Hawk shrugged it off and ran back up the stair. I called to the woman that we'd duties but would come back for her quick as might be. She wailed till my blood curdled. When we came out of that temple, we found the dawn wind blowing, the whole night gone, though it seemed less than an hour.

"We worked our way quick to the citadel. Des reported Benat had found the sorcerers' lair in the old barracks. He and Unai had gone back two hours since to bring on the assault. They feared we'd been caught in a witchlord spelltrap, as I believed we had been.

"So came the final assault, and on that terrible morn King Philippe and his friend Ruggiere, the Great Traitor who's now redeemed, wiped the plague of Kadr from the earth."

The old man stopped, breathing hard, as if he had come straightaway from that battlefield to tell his tale. Half the night could have passed, I was so caught up in it. "So did you go back?"

"Nay. Unai, Hawk, and I were dispatched right off to the occupation of Kadr. I told Des and Benat about it, quick before we marched out. Told them to have a care and take a mage if they could, to see if the woman was real or no. Years later when I saw them again, they said they'd gone no farther than the beast statues. Her wailing had spooked 'em, and they'd run away."

"Likely she was only a phantom," I said. "A Kadrian spelltrap after all."

"Ah, nay. For there's the dream, ye see. And the witchlords of Kadr be all dead and their stronghold burnt. I saw it all."

"Tell me about the dream."

"When the dream came in those first days, Hawk said 'twas 'cause we left the woman. Yet I didn't and don't feel guilty. I was right to choose as I did. But each time I see her face, she weeps and cries, and begs me come and save her. And in the dream, I row out there and fetch her away."

His growing terror near lifted me from my chair.

"Soon as we return to shore, I take that great emerald, green as moss . . . beyond price . . . and it shows me my desires fulfilled. But it has a foul heart. I look deep and see a doom unleashed upon the world that is evil beyond anything I can speak. The woman laughs, and her laugh is all wicked and all desire, and I cannot put things back right again."

"But you were strong," I said. "You didn't fall into the trap. What you dream never happened. Why is it so fearful?"

"Because I want it—that green jewel. I desire it the way a blind man craves his sight, and when I wake without it in my hand, 'tis like a suffocation."

"Twenty years on, she's escaped or dead," I said. "Assuming she existed at all." Yet spider feet teased at the hair on my neck.

"Oh, she's still there, all right. When the dream wouldn't go away, I hunted up Des and Benat. She calls to them in their dreams, too. They never even saw her, just heard her wailing, but they can describe her and the lake to me in every aspect. They hunger for the emerald, though I never told them of it. But they were both crippled up and couldn't travel."

"And you?"

"I've resisted thus far. But this year past, the dream comes every night, much stronger than before. If ye cannot take it from me, it'll drive me to Carabangor. I'll free her, then, and take her evil talisman and loose it on the world. That's why I daren't live with it longer."

There was no doubting his determination.

"What of Hawk?"

Rapid fingers slapped softly on solid flesh—his own hand, chin, or forehead. I waited, curious as to his hesitation.

The tapping stopped. "Hawk was ready to go back. I couldn't allow it."

Night's daughter . . . murder.

Needing time to assess a sensible course, I offered de Cuvier wine or beer. He refused. But I betook myself to the cellar to fill a new mug for myself.

In the years of my apprenticeship, my mentor had squeezed every spell, every book, and every scrap of magical knowledge from his far-flung web of friends and acquaintances—a granny here, a hedge wizard there, a tessila Reader too poorly educated or too drunk to work in a temple. Among this lot, two or three claimed to use Kadr magics. The Kadrites—the witchlords as they called themselves—had been a race of barbarian sorcerers who had settled in the desert country bordering Sabria and Aroth. Cruel and skilled in war, they had partnered with the mighty Arothi Empire to invade Sabria when we were weakened by the Blood Wars. From what I'd seen, the witchlords' spellwork reflected their lives—brutal and unsophisticated. Subtle work like prisoned maidens or compulsive dream sendings seemed entirely unlike them.

In my practice at Bardeu, I'd dealt with a number of compulsions caused by ill-wrought charms or potions, death curses, or the like. I'd seen naught so powerful as would drive a soldier like de Cuvier to murder one of his own, yet experience testified to some small hope I could help him be rid of it. Certainly no Camarilla practitioner would attempt such a healing. The Camarilla believed magic a strictly physical discipline, producing results that could alter physical perceptions alone. They'd name de Cuvier a lunatic to imagine ephemera like dreams compelled his actions.

The grenadier pounced as soon as I topped the cellar stair. "So, sorcerer. Can you help me?"

I shook my head. "Can't be sure. I need to be with you when the dream comes. Probe it to discover its nature. If I judge the task possible, we'll need a few days."

"No matter. Can't do naught but think of it, anyway. If I cannot be rid of it, I'll not live."

"We'd best give it a try, then."

"I'll pay whatever fee you set," he said, "sell my horse, my sword. And you'll have my undying grat—"

"Wait till I've done, and we'll settle. Stripping dreams . . . touching the mind. This is a dice game with many ways to lose that have naught to do with coin. So understand, I make no promises, save to take all good care and stop when I can do no more."

"Agreed." He didn't hesitate.

"Come back tomorrow evening, and we'll begin."

"What's wrong with tonight? To my mind, it can't be soon enough."

What was wrong with tonight? Only that it had been a long day already, and an all-night vigil at de Cuvier's bedside would not improve on it. But the tale . . . the magic . . . was superlatively intriguing. No harm in looking.

"All right, then. I'll have my . . . assistant . . . prepare a room for you." The wayward Finn, reeking of ale, had just clattered through the back door.

While de Cuvier installed his horse in our stable and fetched his kit, Finn and I dragged a bed down the stair and placed it in the middle of a barren little chamber just off the study. Finn, keeping his lips shut and muffling his hiccups as if I were too thick-witted to deduce his condition, set a chair next the bed and brought in a night cupboard, table, and lamp. I knelt and laid my hand on a glassy ring that encompassed most of the floor. As the circumoccule's magical structure took shape in my mind, I strengthened the enclosure, sweeping it clean of spell scraps and repairing blemishes in its structure caused by Anne's errors and my own fumbling.

If the grenadier's dream was caused by enchantment, then I could better disentangle it in a magically uncluttered environment.

When de Cuvier returned, I encouraged him to make all his usual preparations. He expected no problems, he said, as he was a man of regular habits, well accustomed to bedding down in unusual circumstances. "A cup of warm milk laced with brandy will put me out till sunrise."

I'd give him two hours to settle.

Once Finn had set out the posset, I sent the boy off to the guesthouse where we two made our beds. Yawning, stumbling, and giggling like a milkmaid, he'd be little use until morning.

Unfortunately, his absence prevented any useful preparation for the work. I'd written notes about the Kadr spellwork in the journals of my apprenticeship. And among my books were a bound manuscript on dreams and a text that related to gems. Emeralds, in particular, had interesting and complex magical properties. But pages were useless without eyes to read them.

I resisted slamming a fist through the wall. Instead, I paced the sitting room. Twenty steps, turn, fifteen, turn . . .

Naught remained of the night sounds I had studied earlier, save the ticking of the mechanical clock on the hearth shelf, as if time was all that was left in the world.

Anne's father had gifted her the clock. She'd laughed when it arrived, describing it as *an inducement to stay grounded in the world of scientific truth, while abiding in the countryside with a daemon.*

Five years of torture to fuel a sorcerer's power might have changed Michel de Vernase's beliefs about magic's efficacy, but the ordeal had imbued him with no love for its practitioners. His younger daughter had died at Collegia Magica de Seravain. I hadn't killed her or conspired in her murder. But I'd known of it, hidden it, in the same way I'd known of and chosen not to report a prison warder's abuse of his son, Ambrose. Those weren't even the worst things I'd done to insinuate myself into de Gautier's grand plan. Understandably, Michel and Ambrose, along with the Camarilla Magica, the Temple, and most of the residents of the royal city, held something of a grudge.

Anne didn't like thinking about the choices I'd made during those years. I didn't, either, come to that. Once I'd met de Gautier and grasped the breadth and complexity and danger of his scheme, I'd dared not retreat from our plan to thwart him. The incisive brilliance of his mind—knowledge and insight that dwarfed even Portier's, and so far above my own haphazard education as to clamor that my proper place in the world was the coal mines I had escaped—told me he would pick up the least hint of duplicity. Thus I'd done what I deemed necessary to convince de Gautier I wanted to join him, acts reprehensible enough to convince my only friend, the stubborn, naive Portier, that I had deserted his cause. I'd buried myself so deep, I'd come near believing in my own infamy.

I refused to brood about it. That wouldn't change anything. The uncomfortable part was how easy it had been. The magic, both de Gautier's desired perversions of the Mondragon rites and the work I'd done to delay and subvert what I did for him, was elegant, intricate, and challenging, exactly the kind of sorcery I most relished. And to live as a man of heedless violence and moral indifference scarce took thought. I'd always manifested a perverse nature. For most of my first sixteen years, I had been convinced a daemon lived inside me. After four years of a double life, giving that perversity full rein, I'd scarce recalled any other way to live.

But there had come a night when I had driven myself ragged while raising the revenant of a dead king. I returned to my apartments, only to discover one of my erstwhile allies prying through my personal belongings. Rage had shredded what control remained in me. As I lashed out in mindless hate and fury, teetering on the verge of a murderous madness from which I might never have drawn back, a cry of pain tore through the aether straight into my skull. The shock of that cry—Anne's cry—had prevented me bludgeoning the queen's foster mother to death and thus losing the slim advantage I had gained on those who would upend the world. Anne had saved me that night and over the ensuing days offered me a companionship that became my refuge, a link to sanity and rightful purpose.

Ixtador Beyond the Veil was no divine realm installed by the Creator to teach us lessons about savage wars, but an unnatural result of magical experimentation by Anne's ancestors. Portier had a theory that its aberrant nature somehow corrupted true magic, requiring a practitioner to expend resources beyond nature's intent. He said it was going to kill me eventually or drive me back into that abyss of madness from which Anne had rescued me. I didn't believe him. There were plenty of good reasons to solve the mystery of Ixtador, but that wasn't one of them. Magic was everything of beauty and order and sanity in this world. I wanted Anne to see it.

But her family's disapproval weighed on Anne like an iron yoke. Only her terror that her raw, uncontrolled power might explode into violence had kept her from them for so long. Now that fear was gone, and so was she.

The clock struck tenth hour of the evening watch. As the next long hour passed, I found myself touching things—a chair, the bookshelf, the annoying clock—just to make sure the entire world hadn't vanished with her.

ELEVENTH HOUR. TIME TO BEGIN. Anticipation strumming my nerves, I removed my boots, picked up a blanket to ward off the night chill, and padded softly into the little chamber.

The room was filled with the grenadier's throaty breathing, the air rank with brandy and peppermint. He slept on his back, his face turned away from the door.

I'd instructed him not to move the chair, despite its cramped placement. He'd done as I asked. On hands and knees, I felt my way around the circumoccule, sealing the enclosure with intent and will. The barrier closed, I settled myself in the chair, grasped my staff between thumb and palm of my weak right hand, and laid my left on de Cuvier's forehead. I imposed my will on his mind, planting a simple humming inside him—a beacon of sorts, nothing like to disturb the natural course of his sleep. Then I opened myself to the aether.

Alien passions surged through my spirit—tenderness, fright, anger. . . . So remote as this house was, the relentless expressions of human feeling were subdued. Most folk within fifty kilometres were sleeping. But darker things drifted on the currents of night. . . .

The aether is a universe entirely apart from the one ordinary senses reveal, a place where human passions become tangible, alongside magical energies and threads of power, and keirna—the accumulated essence of every person and natural object. Strong remnants of hatred emanated from the darkness outside Pradoverde's walls. Bloodshed. Mystery. This land had seen more than one dispute. The wood to the west of the pasture was a remnant of an ancient forest that had once stretched hundreds of kilometres over the hills into Tallemant. Its keirna created a rich and mysterious presence in the deeps. Some things I could not identify, even after two years here. Eventually, I would. I never tired of exploring the aether.

Anyone with a scrap of talent for it could touch this other universe. Some worked true magic. Some glimpsed things other folk could not see. Some heard whispers or felt creeping certainties about what had happened in a particular place or what might happen there in the future, when they walked places rich with history. But as far as I knew, only Anne and I could interact with the energies of the aether—hear, feel, and speak.

But there was a great deal more Anne had only glimpsed. Since the days I'd come to understand the nature of the voices I heard, I had worked to understand the aether's structure and composition, its possibilities, its rules. Most important, I'd learned how to envision the structures of spellwork, and how to manipulate them.

Dreams were just another stream of energy feeding this ephemeral universe. My gift of hearing and a great deal of practice allowed me to trace, distinguish, and share the dreams of another. If the dream was spellwrought, there was a possibility I could alter or release the binding of the enchantment as I could with other magic.

Thus, with control and discipline, I sorted through the aether until I found the humming beacon I'd planted in de Cuvier . . .

. . . and a shattering of light, sensation, and urgency. *Horses, galloping like thunder. Windblown . . . racing across a great plain . . . past crofts and ruins . . . streaked orange and purple sky . . .* Ah, gods, all the unnamable colors of dream. *Hurry . . . hurry . . . there's battle to be joined. . . . To be late is to fail. . . .*

Blackness shrouded my sight in nauseating abruptness, as if my stomach had been yanked out through my nose. I waited in the dark.

Ear-splitting thunder . . . blood-splashed masonry crumbling, crashing, pelting, pummeling . . . shattered walls . . . Into the breach! For glory . . . for king . . . for brothers-in-arms . . . Hurry . . .

On through the night, I viewed these fragments, like snippets of conversation heard in a crowded room, many of them nonsense. Interspersed were fallow times, some brief, some hours long.

When my head lolled, I threw off the blanket and sat up straighter. Concentrate . . . focus. Sleep and you'll miss it.

Formless clouds and vapors . . . fleeting images of faces that evoked familiarity . . . Coming faster now. *A grin . . . a salute . . .*

I probed deeper. There! What was that?

Yellow sparks stretched into tendrils of shimmering light. Light without warmth. Even for one who lived in darkness, this was cold fire, as alien to the other dream stuff as stone discovered in the heart of a flower. More so, for stone and flower were both of nature, and this yellow infusion was of no relation at all to Masson de Cuvier and his dreaming.

The yellow tendrils grew more solid, interlacing, becoming stronger, like heated threads of glassy citrine cooling into the shape of a cyclone. This I had seen before—a structure of enchantment, a portal through which magic could flow.

Superimposed upon the structure was the dream, the woman wrapped in a fog of pearled white—she of the old soldier's story—dark skin, ebon eyes, pale hair, and wrenching grief. Beneath my hand de Cuvier groaned and tossed his head, and I almost lost contact with him. But I held on, for I could not bear to lose that vision. Such terrible beauty, prisoned by a milk white lake as deep as the Souleater's caverns.

"Noble warrior, please don't leave me here!" The great emerald rested on her outstretched palm. Huge, its facets glittered, transforming yellow-orange light into arrows of fiery emerald.

What sorcery could create so vivid a dream? The cavern's dampness chilled my skin. I felt as if I could reach out and touch her smooth skin and drifting hair. Such need filled me. Such desire . . .

De Cuvier resisted but, in the miraculous way of dreams, found himself standing beside her. Taking her hand, he led her into the shell boat and rowed her across the white lake. Once ashore, he accepted the gem and peered deep within it. So did I with him, unthinking, unwary . . .

Oh, gods, I could see! Not just phantasms and memories and dream stuff, but towering trees and hawks soaring from rocky heights. Soon I became the hawk and looked down on a boisterous river, rippling, frothing, burbling between rocks. . . .

And then I was back in Coverge, smothered by the raging heat of the smithy, while a frigid gale howled beyond the door. Blue-white flames thundered in the forge as a glowing shaft of iron glowed red and the hammer fell. . . .

My books . . . My fingers caressed the leather bindings on unfamiliar shelves. Ours here at Pradoverde, I knew, though I'd never seen them, each title familiar, each holding a treasure of knowledge open to me again. . . .

Green fire obscured the visions, and with de Cuvier, I reached greedily into the emerald's depths in search of more, only now the world was bathed in livid light, as if it suffered a massive bruise—a deep rot in the core of the Stone. New images coalesced in the dark center, and the woman convulsed in laughter. Young. Wicked.

Her laughter brought me to my senses. I'd entered the dream to help the man, not pursue my own desires.

I withdrew, pushing aside de Cuvier's lust and growing fear. Shoving aside my own curiosity and desire, I sought the pathways of enchantment . . . the structure, the hook, the point of linking where the keyword binds keirna.

I touched the apex of the citrine-hued portal. Enchantment thrummed with the energies of stars, threatening to incinerate me, but the spot darkened to a deep ocher, and one strand fell loose. Carefully, strand by strand, I unraveled the complex weaving, and the vision began to fade. . . .

The laughter ceased as I worked, but only at the end did I notice the woman staring at me. Her pale hair floated in the mist. Her black eyes, now flecked with silver, had narrowed in puzzlement.

"It's you at last!" she said, cocking her head. "My partner said you couldn't resist. But what is this you do?"

In an explosive rush of magic and a burst of yellow sparks, the dream evaporated, and profound darkness enshrouded me in sleep.

CHAPTER 3

PRADOVERDE

Birds squawked . . . argued . . . flapped angry wings. My neck felt like a corkscrew. When I shifted, trying to get comfortable, a hard bar dug into my side. What the devil?

I blinked. Blinked again, twisted my head, scrubbed at my face.

My stomach flopped over, chills shivering my skin. *Oh, gods, gods, gods . . .*

Wholly disoriented, I fumbled, flailing, for my staff. My feet thrust me upward . . . forward . . . and I crashed onto cushions, and the seat toppled out from under me, clattering to the floor. I'd been in a chair. The cushions . . . a bed.

I rolled to my back and felt the room settle into place around me. Ceiling above. Walls to the side. Warmth bathed my left cheek—so the window. My bare foot located my staff, fallen to the floor. Once my heart slowed, I slid down to sitting beside the bed to fetch it.

As on every morning, I pressed my head to the stick, near crushing the smooth, hard hornbeam. *Would I could slaughter you again, Gautier. And you, Jacard, you sniveling lackwit, do I ever find you, I'll set your bowels aflame. And you, Michel de Vernase, a pox on you for being so stupid as to botch a simple investigation, so that Portier inherited it and the ever-persuasive idiot librarian dragged me into that cursed conspiracy. . . .*

As I suppressed my trembling and the impulse to murder half the world's population, I recalled where I was and why. "Cuvier?"

I didn't expect an answer. My senses had already reached out—in better control than my mind—and discovered no one in the chamber. I rubbed my muzzy head, trying unsuccessfully to recall anything beyond the end of the spell-wrought dream.

What exactly had happened? Though I had unraveled the enchantment, I was under no illusion that I had destroyed it permanently. But I had also been a participant. The jewel showed me images entirely unrelated to Masson de Cuvier. And the woman *saw* me, recognized me as separate from the dreamer, spoke to me. How was that possible? Men of science, of religion, and of magic all dismissed true dreams as mystery. Those I had dealt with in my own practice were no natural dreams but pure enchantment, visions wrought by magic. And no one in any vision had ever interacted with me.

A tap at the door and a hesitant "Master?" announced Finn. He sounded none the worse for his raucous evening.

"Come."

"You look fairly well wretched," he blurted.

"A pig in *your* eye, too. Have you—?" The fragrant steam of black tea wreathed my face. "Ah, blessed . . ."

Finn had brought me that for which I'd forgive him any trespass. I inhaled until I was near bursting, feeling only mild guilt at the aristo luxury. I'd never tried the stuff till Anne teased me into it, promising a potion for clear thinking that rivaled any of magic. She delighted in pricking my weaknesses.

Only when the pungent beverage had swept the cobwebs from my head did I attempt another thought. "What's become of the grenadier?"

"He rose at sixth hour, tended his horse, ate half a loaf of bread and three boiled eggs. Asked about a farrier, as his horse has a cracked hoof. Said he'd be back."

"Good. That's good." I wanted to know what this dream meant, how it was done, and whether it would change now I'd been a part of it. Was the woman the enchantress or an illusion, masking the true practitioner? She looked younger than Anne, yet de Cuvier had seen her first some twenty years since. The tale was fascinating, the magic entirely new.

"Repairing the stable roof will have to wait," I said. "I've a need to prepare before Cuvier sleeps again."

"I can carry on alone," said Finn, already retreating. "Leave you to it."

"No. I need you in the study."

"But—"

"It's just to read," I snapped. "I'll not turn you into a slug. Not today." Anne insisted magic frightened Finn. Or I did. Likely both.

Reining in my devil temper, I described the books I wanted and where I thought they might be. While I fidgeted and bit my tongue, Finn searched the shelves and stacks. Anne's absence gaped, as if I'd opened a book cover to find no pages or spied a mountain removed from a familiar range.

"I think I have them," he said at last. "They look awfully difficult." Finn hated reading as much as I hated having him do it.

"Begin. The dream text first . . ."

The treatise on dreams was useless. Though we spent two hours slogging through its archaic language, it mentioned nothing of identical dreams shared between multiple dreamers or of dream images that reacted specifically to a dreamer's presence.

Neither my notes on Kadrian spellwork nor any other reference on the witchlords mentioned compulsive visions or dream sendings. Evidently Kadrian spelltraps came in only two kinds—short-lived things that slowed a victim's reactions till something extremely nasty dropped on his head, and some particularly virulent memory blocks.

Finn laboriously recited the chapter headings of the little text on gems.

"Stop! Try that one." "Gems of Legend" sounded worth a look.

Finn stammered through descriptions of a tiny Aesulpian emerald that could reshape the wearer's voice and of almond-sized stones embedded in Julithean god-masks, said to give the priest-wearers the gift of farseeing. Supposedly, the one who wielded a particular rough-cut emerald from the mountain kingdom of Sarkhazia could summon storms and mold stone if the person lived long enough, which seemed to be never, as the gem drained the life from anyone who used it. Sarkhazia had vanished in an avalanche a thousand years ago. Perhaps the diabolical gem explained why.

Sorting any real truth from the tales was impossible. Yet, one short passage sparked my interest enough, I had Finn read it three times over.

> Reputedly the most potent emeralds known are the Tyregian Emeralds, otherwise known as the Maldivean Seeing Stones. The earliest reference to the three occurs on a Cinnear tomb fresco,

> detailing the hand of their triune deity delivering to humankind a single jewel of extraordinary size in time of a great famine.
>
> The historian Podrenard claims that the Tyregian Emeralds, the single Stone split into three, enabled a petty mage-warrior named Altheus to bring down the savage First Empire of Aroth and create the hegemony of Maldivea. Unverified tales of Altheus, later known as the Holy Imperator, claimed him possessed of extraordinary magical prowess, as well as the gifts of augury, wise-judgment, and speaking in dreams. Temple records attribute the fall of Maldivea to the blasphemy of Altheus's successor, who, it was said, imprisoned the souls of his fallen enemies in torment.

Speaking in dreams attracted my notice. But the references to imprisoning the souls of the dead disturbed me more. Anne's description of the ravenous occupants of Ixtador Beyond the Veil—spectres, phantasms of living souls drained of individual humanity, reduced to gaping, walking starvation—was locked inside my head with my memories of sight. Unlike the memories, her image did not fade. Foreboding skittered across my skin.

"Are you sure there's nothing more about these Seeing Stones?"

"Naught I can see, Master."

Surely I was a fool to imagine any connection. Two years of investigation had convinced the king that Germond de Gautier had no other relatives lurking about, ready to plunge us into chaos with magical relics. I had destroyed de Gautier, and Anne had killed his partner, Kajetan, ending their grand conspiracy. Yet their journals, implements, and source books had vanished along with Kajetan's nephew on that same night. Jacard yet lived, but an untrained hedge witch could do more with those books and journals than my incompetent adept. Yet, it was most curious. She'd said, *at last* and *you couldn't resist* as if she knew who I was.

FINN SHOOK ME AWAKE IN late afternoon. Only the prospect of another long night would force me to sleep during the day; one bad waking in a sun's passage was usually enough. The abrupt ending scattered my dream fragments like shattered glass. As we shared Finn's offering of boiled leeks and overcooked fish, and the grenadier's interminable monologue on army food, I could not shake the sense that I had missed something of great importance.

I shoved my plate away untasted. When Finn asked if he could get me something other, I yelled that I would god-blasted eat when I was hungry. And then I had to ask pardon for the yelling, which only made the meal more awkward. The annoying youth did try. Finn and I could work for half a day with less than ten words between us. The grenadier's need to fill the air with words rubbed my spirit raw.

We retired to the study and de Cuvier asked for brandy. I kept to tea, as I needed nothing that would cloud my judgment or dull my perceptions. Only at that late hour did the old man ask what had happened during the previous night, and what was likely to happen during the coming one.

"I've questions of my own first," I said. "How did you find me?"

"As I told you, the folk in Bardeu—"

"But what led you *there*?"

"Ten years I've sought help to silence these dreams. The Camarilla said magic could not affect dreams, though some years later, a mage came to ask about the dream and the emerald. He couldn't help, but told me of a mage who had practiced mind healing in Bardeu, but then went off to court, caught up in royal politics." His voice slowed. Wary. "Indeed, your name was all over Merona. None denied your talents. But I decided you weren't one to be interested in me. Instead, I traveled up to Jarasco, where a Temple tetrarch named Beltan de Ferrau is said to cast out daemons. He claimed my visions daemon-wrought, but his incense and chanting did naught to help. He warned me to stay clear of you. But I've got desperate, and your name is ever rattling in my head as the only help I've not tried."

De Cuvier had heard no mention of the Tyregian Emeralds or Seeing Stones or Maldivea in his long search for answers. I didn't like hearing that some daemon-obsessed tetrarch knew of me.

"Last night I witnessed your dream," I said. "It's no daemon's doing. It's spell-wrought." I told him how I'd unraveled it before its climax. "Should it appear again, I can approach it with a bit more vigor. You should be quit of it tonight." I didn't mention the woman's interaction with me.

Tired from the day's activities, de Cuvier made his way to bed early. I stood and sat, paced and fidgeted. It wasn't de Cuvier's ultimatum caused my fretfulness; I believed I could preclude his self-murder. More like it was my own interrupted sleep.

When sufficient time had passed, I again settled myself at the grenadier's side. After what seemed but a moment, the yellow sparks flashed and stretched into snakes of citrine glass. The portal opened to pearly mist and moldering damp.

The woman beckoned and offered the Stone. Her eyes were deep gray, struck with silver, and she did not weep. "See," *she said.* "That which you most desire can be yours if you'll but rescue me. Please, take my gift."

Her brow was finely drawn. The form revealed by the rippling gown was womanly and ripe. But it was the gemstone drew me, as strong wine draws a drunkard. It seemed only natural that I was transported to her side and took her smooth hand. My shoulders strained as I rowed her across the milky water, my useless hand bound to the oar.

My hand? Was de Cuvier dreaming or was I?

Then we were ashore, and I looked deep into the Stone. Once again the veils of night and phantasm fell from my dead eyes, and the world lay before me . . . a library vaster than the collection at Castelle Escalon . . . the squalid alley where I had sought healing for my ruined hand and found my life instead . . . rolling waves of dewy grass . . .

From a distance, a woman sang a cheerful ditty, "The heart of a man charts a four-legged course. . . ." White-hot sunlight bathed my shoulders as I labored to build a fence to contain a horse that was naught but bones.

Three people stood outside the sunlit fence. I moved closer to see who they were. A short, balding man with shoulders like Coverge's mountains and forearms like cannons whirled round and halted my steps.

"Da?" How long had it been since I'd looked on Galdo de Raghinne? Seventeen years since my father had last laid a fist and a curse on me. Why was he here?

He vanished in the sun glare.

A slight, dark-haired man sat on the fence jotting notes in a leather-bound journal. A cane was propped on the fence beside him.

"Portier?" He peered at me over his spectacles, as if he'd heard me, then faded.

Left alone was a small woman, shading her eyes as she gazed into the sun. The wind tugged wisps and curls from her thick braid.

I opened my mouth to call her name. I needed to see her face, to read what lay there when she promised to come back—

Hold, fool. What's happening here? I was immersed in de Cuvier's dream, my sight restored. But no dream had this clarity. And the grenadier did not know these three.

Though my spirit hungered to look on her, I did not will the woman to turn. Rising dread forbade me even to speak her name. Names were rich with keirna and could be woven into spellwork.

The meadow and its occupants faded into a green haze, and I once again stared deep into the great emerald.

The world lay in shadow. Gloomed cities were crumbled to ruin. Towns and villages were barricaded in dread of what roamed in the deeper dark. People thronged the roadways through charred fields and vineyards, dragging scarecrow children—a tide of fear. Yet life had ever been so for many of the world's people. It was their eyes that shivered me. For some in the crowds, their eyes did not reflect their souls, but only empty hunger. And for some, hidden among the others so none could pick them out by shape or garb, the eyes were alien to the bodies that bore them—eyes of glass or ice. Not human. White frost curled from their mouths. They breathed malevolence as a dragon breathes fire.

A tall, comely young man with golden skin and hair that fell about his shoulders like strands of gold and gray silk walked among the crowd as graceful as a court dancer. He wore a long coat of a color I could not name, and it shifted with his stride as if in a goodly breeze, revealing a plain, well-used sword. He glanced over his shoulder at me, the hint of a smile on his radiant visage. For the duration of that glance, everything else faded into insignificance. Then he turned away and vanished into the crowd, leaving behind a faint scent of rosemary and ash. . . .

I'd no use for folk who allowed hopes of angels or fear of daemons to shape their lives. Nor did I heed the blather of philosophers who claimed they could expose the secrets of faith and reason in the truth of mathematics and planetary motion. But I knew what I saw in that dream, and I could only name it as de Cuvier did. *Unnatural. Evil.* Save, perhaps, for the enigmatic young man, who seemed no more a part of the scene than I was.

Revulsion spurred my magic. Goaded by the enchantress's wicked laughter, I wrenched my attention from the gem to the portal and its magical construction. I twined my own power in the structure like a grapple and tore the spell-wrought thing apart. With an explosion of yellow fire, the world was pitch once again.

Finn said later that he heard me cry out in the night. He likely did, but there was no help he could have given me.

WHEN DE CUVIER AWOKE IN the predawn stillness, I was not asleep. He yawned and sat up.

"How passed your night?" I asked.

"Ah, master sorcerer! 'Twas a miracle! No dream at all this night!"

His enthusiasm but affirmed my conclusions. The night's vision was not de Cuvier's, but my own.

"Good."

"So ye think I'm done with it?"

"Yes."

"Sonjeur, if this be true, I owe you my life. I'll not forget!"

He agreed to stay over one more night to test my theory.

"I do have a few more questions," I said.

"But if it's gone—"

"I collect such information in lieu of payment." That, he understood.

After eating, we adjourned to the study, snaring Finn to take notes. "Has the dream always been the same, identical in every detail?"

He puffed and blew. "Not precisely. Small things might have changed over the years."

"Give me examples."

"At the beginning, 'twas exactly as I remembered. Her so sweet and sad, beautiful as an angel, begging me and offering me the Stone. I'd look into the Stone and see . . . well . . . my desires. As I've told you. No wickedness. I would see women, *natural* women of my own sort. But it was mostly soldiering. Battles. Victory flags flying. Then it began to change; I'd still see fine things—houses or treasure that I'd earned. But the battlefields were littered with Sabrian dead, the flesh rotting right off their bones, or burnt villages. And in these two years past, it's got worse. I've not the words to describe it, save that it wasn't just battlefields anymore, but cities and streets and villages and desolation. Dead men everywhere and birds pecking out my boys' eyes, only . . ."

I leaned forward, as if to squeeze it from him. "Only what? What about the eyes?"

"The eyes weren't dead. Someone was still looking out of them, but it wasn't the men I knew. It was like the jewel would steal my boys' souls."

Knots uncurled inside me, and I settled back into the chair. I wasn't wholly mad. "Go on."

"The sights came more twisted and wicked, like the change when deviltry is done by a man, rather than a child. A boy would think that pulling wings off of flies or trapping a bird in a barn is a fair thing to do for nasty amusement, but when he comes a man, he might find the same fun gouging the eyes from a prisoner, or breaking the arms of an injured man on a battlefield so's he can't crawl out of the sun."

Exactly so. Two years. As always my mind reverted to Mont Voilline and the rending of the Veil. Connections. I who had lived half in the aether all my life dared not discount connections in the realms of magic and dream.

"When did the comely young man appear?" I described the fair young swordsman.

"Never saw any like that. Certainly not in the middle of the ruin. Only dead maybe . . ."

He wasn't dead. Nor did I believe him any more ephemeral than the woman in white.

Though we talked an hour more, I came to no additional conclusions. I'd witnessed an extraordinary enchantment that seemed singularly focused on eliciting an active response and that constantly adapted itself to the dreamer's life. Magic. Astonishing, incomprehensible magic.

Something else had occurred to me as I waited for the grenadier to wake, exploring the flimsy links of a soldier's obsession and the experiences of the past six years. "You said a mage had come asking you about the dream and told you about me. When was that? Did he give you his name?"

He considered that carefully. " 'Twas three or four year ago. He said his name, but I don't recall it. Wore a collar like yours and claimed he came from the Camarilla. A tall man. Gray-haired. Well spoken, talking of sorcery and how important it was to keep the world in balance. The kind of man soldiers would fight for, though he might have a plan to send 'em right off a cliff."

Great gods of the universe! He'd given me a perfect description of Kajetan, Portier's despicable mentor, who had been traveling to all sorts of places during the years of our partnership, who had raged when

Lianelle de Vernase's death and her sister Anne's interference had foiled some plan to bring "a new source of power" to our conspiracy. Of a sudden the connections I'd seen were no longer flimsy. Was de Cuvier's dream another loose end from Germond de Gautier's and Kajetan de Saldemerre's plotting? Or was the dream's sudden resurgence a trumpet heralding a new assault? There were not curses enough in the world to suffice for my dismay.

I did not sleep that afternoon. On this day, my preparation must be to empty myself of desire, of sympathy, of curiosity, stripping away everything in me that might influence the dream. Finn and I patched the stable roof, abandoning our guest to the company of his horse. Finn was so relieved at not being trapped in the study that he was practically babbling. All to the good. I didn't want to think. To the grenadier's surprise, after a supper of eggs and mushrooms, I suggested a game of stratagems.

"But how—?"

"I keep it in my head. Just tell me your moves."

My teacher, Salvator, had taught me the game in my first days with him, forcing me to play it blind long years before that would become a necessity. It required absolute focus. Ignorant and undisciplined, I'd come near running away because of it. But no training had stood me in better stead. De Cuvier was a good player—not very imaginative, but solid. After a few moves, he did not hold back. I worked at it harder, so I won.

When the game was over, de Cuvier bade me divine grace and headed to bed. Rain gusted against the windows. I pulled my chair close to Finn's hearth fire and forced my mind to remain fallow. I wanted to go naked into that night.

The clock struck tenth hour. Enough was enough. As on the previous nights I settled myself in the bedside chair. For some two hours I watched with the grenadier and saw naught but soldiers, horses, and women. I took my hand away, settled back in the chair, and let myself go to sleep. After a sun's turning without, sleep . . . and the dream . . . came quickly.

"Help me," she said in a whisper that could draw tears from stone. "I've been here so long. Please, you who hear me—come!" I saw no yellow sparks or portal, only the angelic vision and her wrenching grief and black eyes, weeping.

Across the milky pond the green gem sparkled, beckoning, resting on her pale hand. It promised to reverse the hateful future awaiting me, to repair the damage and rid me of the fire that lanced my nerves every time I strained to see. It promised me power: speaking in dreams, augury, wisdom, magic I had never imagined.

My preparation held. Because I had made myself empty, I could resist the compulsion to go to her. I refused to look into the Stone, or regain my sight, or in any way follow the path laid out for those who dreamt this dream.

In a shattering of yellow-orange light, the mournful weeping ceased and the fog vanished, as if blown away by the same wind that howled under the eaves at the remotest edges of my awareness. All that remained were chaotic patterns of light and shadow, as if I sat in the eye of a cyclone.

"So you're clever as well as powerful," she said from out of the chaos, her voice no longer soft and pleading, but edged with brass and wariness. "Long have I awaited a savior. When the dreary soldier stumbled into my prison, I believed Fortuna Regina had favored me at last. But the divina had her little jest, dispatching such a priggish fellow. So disappointing. But now . . . Tell me, are you wizard or godling? How did you confound the dream?"

Being in my own dream, I could not control what I did beyond the emptiness I had created of myself. Evidently that was enough, for I did not speak.

"Tell me!" Venom laced her rising temper.

But I had nothing in me with which to answer her.

"You hide yourself from me, cowardly. But it's too late, blind man. I know who and what you are. And understand this: I do not like teasing."

Blackness shuttered my dream sight.

I jerked awake. De Cuvier snored softly. A steady rain spattered the roof. I sensed it was still night but wasn't sure until the clock struck third hour. I laid a hand on his head and searched for enchantment. This time, the spellwork was truly gone, the structure shattered as cleanly as I had destroyed a thousand other spells.

Grabbing a cloak, I trudged across the soggy garden to the guesthouse. There was nothing more for me at de Cuvier's bedside. I slept the rest of the night in my own bed, neither dreams nor phantoms intruding.

As I KNEW HE WOULD BE, de Cuvier was up with the birds, claiming that he'd slept like a youth. "Ye be a saint's hand, Master! I've no way to repay you for this service."

"Have no more dreams."

I stood on the steps as he rode away, a chill dampness teasing my cheeks. Fog. The grenadier was scarce ten metres from the door when the sounds of hoof and bridle were absorbed as if he'd never been. I wished he'd never come. Surely the world could not face a new threat before we had healed the wounds of the last.

Ignoring his woeful sighs, I required Finn to write down all I could remember of what had occurred. It unnerved me that the woman had called me blind man and included faces I knew in her dream shaping. Yet, such complexity and power is unendingly fascinating, and I hungered to know more.

Unfortunately, every avenue to learn more seemed so wretchedly complex as to be impossible. I was forbidden to enter Merona. The mages of Collegia Seravain would scoff. At any Temple, major or minor, they'd likely hang me in the marketplace to rot, for to those who believed in soul journeys in the afterlife, necromancy was a mortal blasphemy. And even were I allowed to enter some scholarly library where I might learn more of dream sendings or extraordinary emeralds, I could hardly demand people read to me. They'd go voiceless in terror . . . or claim my condition righteous punishment . . . or preach at me of the Souleater and his daemons.

I'd have given much to talk of the experience with Anne. Her good sense and orderly mind would help me dissect it and decide if this was truly a trumpet blast foreshadowing a new battle. I felt her vibrant presence in the aether as if she were standing beside me. But she was two hundred kilometres distant, and beyond thirty or so our individual voices were lost in the maelstrom. I could do no more than touch her presence, like a beggar pawing the hem of a rich man's cloak.

All I could think to do was pass the inquiry to someone who might do what I could not. On a threat of withholding his pay, I conscripted Finn to make copies of all the notes he'd written and post them to Portier in distant Abidaijar. If the librarian could pull his head out of his saintly ass, he might be able to piece together something from it.

Not for the first time, I wished Portier had not chosen to seclude himself beyond the eastern borders of Sabria. Letters took a month or more to pass between. Yet, I could hardly blame him. Two years previous, de Gautier had crippled and drowned Portier, believing him a Saint Reborn who could not die until the holy purpose of his life was accomplished. Anne and I and

Portier's own resilient nature had kept him living. Though distance and secrecy likely kept him safe from any more madmen who wished to test his sainthood by killing him, I could use his good counsel.

Once the notes were dispatched to Portier, I forced the entire incident into my mind's refuse heap, where the rest of my life was rapidly piling up.

LIFE SOON FELL INTO A dull rhythm. Finn and I finished patching the stable roof and set about other such chores we wished to complete before winter. I had notions of a baking oven. I didn't dream of the woman or her emerald again, though I wasn't fool enough to imagine it had been only a dream after all. The incident nagged at me like street boys. Lacking recourse, I muted their goads and snickers with sweat by day and spellcasting by night.

Anne wrote. I came near tossing the letter before unsealing it. I knew what it would say. She had arrived safely. Her father was yet living half in dream and half in truth; her mother was completely absorbed in his care. Without Ambrose, only Anne was left to see to the grapes and the tenants' brats and the unending tasks of maintaining estates that diminished Pradoverde to the size of an anthill. She would have to stay longer than she planned. Perhaps until midwinter.

Finn's halting reading revealed exactly those things. Only she proposed no specific end to her stay, and she remained mired in self-deception.

I practice spell construction every day, though I lack the nerve to bind them where you cannot protect me from errors. Your instructive voice is quite clear in my recollections.

I've decided to use Lianelle's silver finger rings to create my own ancille. It will remind me that if my little sister could work with Mondragon magic, I can, too. Perhaps someday, I shall create a spell worth binding to them. Perhaps one to preserve her soul. (No, I am not content to wait until then.) Naturally, that will require my return to Pradoverde for further instruction.

Meanwhile, be merciful to Finn. Hire a reader from Laurentine. Maia Fuller's boy is fifteen now, and very quick. And very brave. Tell him it will be a temporary position until the damoselle returns.

It is good to be here, but I miss my home at Pradoverde almost as much as I miss my friend of the aether. If you hear from him, tell him I said so.

Anne

I burnt the letter and did my best to drive her out of mind with work.

Every spare moment I devoted to my seeing spell. After a tenday with almost no sleep, I came up with a variation I could maintain for three hours running. I could make out no more than gross shapes in a landscape of ink, tar, and charcoal. No colors. No details. I could neither read nor distinguish faces or textures. And as before, the binding demanded every spit of power I could scrape together; thus I could work no other magic while I used it—or for hours after—a price only desperation could make me pay. Nonetheless, on the day I walked the entire perimeter of Pradoverde without touching a cairn, getting lost in the wood, or falling in the stream, I felt as if I'd vanquished the witchlords of Kadr for myself.

ON A CHILLY MORNING LATE in Desen's month, more than a month after de Cuvier's departure, I received another letter, forwarded from Castelle Escalon, yet originating from the unlikeliest of sources. I'd not seen my elder brother Andero since I was fourteen. When I knew him he could neither read nor write, and I would have wagered a fortune he was long dead.

Dante,

I don't know how to address you, nor if your thoughts ever turn to us as knew you long ago. Like not, and none could blame you. A blowout at the forge has left Da hard broke and burnt. The old devil is not in his mind most days. But in or out, your name is ever in his mouth. This, after sixteen years without a whisper of it. He says an angel caused the fire to bring you back so he could pass you a message. I've no truck with dream angels, but I fear his shade will haunt us if he dies without you've come. Spare us that, little brother.

Andero

It was no sentiment for the man whose seed begat me that determined me instantly to go. Nor was it to soothe Andero's anxiety, though he was the only member of my family I would cross a room to acknowledge. What spurred me was a pent-up dread in my gut, released to flood limbs and soul and mind at the mention of an angel who passed messages in dreams.

CHAPTER 4

PRADOVERDE

I was not what my father wanted in his sons. He had no sympathy for a life of the mind, no belief in anything more ephemeral than the fire and iron from which he molded his life. He was the headman of our village and a smith, a man of skills among men who ground their short lives away hacking coal from the rocks of Coverge. Yet he prided himself that he, like the rest of them, could scarce count the coins of his pay or the heads of his children. Like them, he drowned pain and poverty in ignorance, ale, and brutality.

I had learned early on not to speak of the whispers in my head. When I asked other children what they heard inside their heads, they called me *ognapé*—crazed, like miners whose skulls had been crushed by rocks. So I asked my mother what was wrong with me. She locked me in the cellar without food until I swore that I was lying. Two days it took me to "confess." Naturally, my father beat me for the lies, and beat my mother for coddling them in me. My father was the most righteous of all those righteous villagers. I was five years old.

Books saved my life. Estebo Lemul, the mine steward's son, had gone to school in Fadrici, the principal town of Coverge. He came home to Raghinne to marry a local girl and open a school, bringing a treasury of five books with him. My father would not allow his children to participate in such frivolity as education. It was pointless for boys destined for the mines, he said, or for girls destined to bear miners' children or go whoring in the remotest mining camps. That meant no other miner's child went to school, either. As Estebo's wife would not leave her mother, Estebo was left to dig coal or starve. I spent every moment I could with him . . . until he died coughing up blood and coal dust. He was nineteen and left me his books.

As I neared fourteen, the voices in my head grew incessant. Half crazed with the noise, forever angry, my growing body entangled in hungers none bothered to explain, I discovered I could force my will upon younger children—to give me their bread or throw stones at each other instead of me. On the day an outburst of rage caused fire to blossom from my hand, I became convinced the Souleater had chosen me to join his legion of the Fallen. Desperate, I sought help from my father, hoping that because I spent long hours at the forge each day, working at his side, he would tell me the right prayers to save my soul.

His face had been red and sweating, as pitted and scarred as his leather apron. The heat from the forge throbbed in time with the pulsing of my blood, the fear inside me swollen near to bursting. But with fury that near split my skull, he called me daemon-spawn and promised to thrash the wickedness out of me so thoroughly I would never again speak my own name, much less such deviltry. He beat me with a knotted rope he kept for hobbling mules.

When I regained my senses, the smithy fires were banked and dim. The shabby bindings of my precious books lay empty beside the great furnace. Their pages were ash.

I could not run away that night. I could scarce crawl up to the loft I shared with Andero and two younger brothers. In truth, anywhere I knew to run, Da could find me and drag me home.

For a year I spoke not a word to anyone. I yet believed I was daemon-possessed, but I knew I was not as wicked as my own father, who was judged a respectable citizen. I worked hard and grew stronger and ever more skilled at smithing, determined to supplant my father and watch him wither in this life, even if I was destined to become the Souleater's smith and forge daemon chains in the next.

When I was almost sixteen, Da came by a few slips of silver from a dying bandit and schemed to coat some pewter slugs with silver and sell them as "magical charms" at Jarasco market. He set me to cast the slugs. As I poured the slugs, the molten pewter encountered moisture in the mold—

the mold I had checked three times to make sure it was dry. The pour erupted like a newly waked volcano, spewing scalding metal over my right hand.

My mother coated my hand with herbs and pig fat, and Da bound it tight. Out of my head with pain, I did not question that a smith and his woman knew how to treat a burn. On the day we finally unwrapped the bandages, my favored hand was a clawed ruin and my prospects as smith or miner or laborer were over. I left Raghinne that same day. I pierced my finger and dripped blood on the dirt as I walked past the last house, uttering a curse and a vow never to go back.

I COULD NOT PUT THE phrases of my brother's letter out of mind. The coincidence was like a cannon shot that crumbled my defenses and lodged iron in my bowels. Body and mind demanded I head north.

Which brought me to the dilemma of travel. Though I despised the idea of taking a minder to lead my horse, choose my bed, and point me where to piss, it seemed my only choice. The thought of hiring a *stranger* for the task left me ready to vomit. But Finn was the only person I knew roundabout, and even if the lad were willing to go, I needed him to finish the work at Pradoverde before winter settled in, to see to Anne's horses . . . and to be at the house when she realized she wanted her beasts and the rest of her things sent on to Montclaire.

A simple locator spell planted in the mind of a random traveler might keep me from riding off a cliff. But of course I'd be left alone and powerless should my guide decide to die of wound fever or alter his route or snatch my purse. Though I'd studied maps of Sabria, I'd traveled very little. In a practical sense I was as ignorant of the roads of Sabria as a bondsman who'd never left his master's land.

And whether I followed someone by magic, or buried pride and hired a nursemaid, the individual choice bore its own dangers. The law—the Concord that set the peace between king and Camarilla Magica—forbade me hide my mage collar. I was on rocky enough ground with the King of Sabria that I dared not be caught at so brazen a violation. That meant I needed a companion who wasn't going to stick a knife in me because his brats had died from inept healing charms or because her granny's fertility potion had gotten the crone whipped by the Camarilla.

More dangerous, if word dribbled out that Dante, the mad mage of Castelle Escalon, was away from his own demesne, unprotected, I could have a gaggle of Merona's outraged citizens in pursuit. Three times in the last year, the Temple had petitioned the king to hand me over to their discipline. Thus far, he had not allowed it, thank the fates. I'd seen what happened when a whip-flayed man was hung in a market square as rat fodder. I needed a minder who could handle a weapon.

Gods, what a mess! Half a day juggling vile alternatives set my hands shaking and heated spikes piercing my spine. I needed to be on my way.

"Get out of here," I snapped at Finn, shoving aside the tray of food he'd brought me. "Don't come back till sunset. If you see the house in ashes or my head smashed against the anvil, find another employer."

Needing no second hint, he ran. Anne somehow managed to channel my frustrations into work. She had a quiet, serious way of posing complicated little questions that sucked the vigor of my anger like a vacuum pump sucked air from a bell jar. But someday my daemonish temper was going to bring down the roof on our heads. No mystery why her family would send a son to war to keep her away from me.

I retreated to the small forge Finn and I had set up with clamps and guides and precise placement so that I could do small tasks on my own. I pumped the bellows as if to raise the fires of Vanyek, the Daemon Smith. With infinite care and focus, so as to preserve what parts of my body yet worked, I spent the afternoon pounding hot iron into useless shapes.

By evening, I had exhausted both muscles and mind. But when Finn came creeping back at sunset, I was ready to dictate a message. I had a plan.

"TO *COVERGE*? SAINTS AWAITING, MAGE, what amusements could one possibly find there? As everyone knows, I am devoted to adventurous travel, as long as there are no dreadful beasts to be found along the way. But I've heard there's not a decent hostelry in that entire demesne. Even the duc and his demesne lords refuse to live there. And at the very onset of winter? We'll frost our bones! Well, you've all your mysterious fires and smokes to keep yourself warm, but—"

"Hear me out, Chevalier," I said, straining my patience through gritted teeth. The peacock lord had arrived earlier that morning, scarce five days from Finn posting my letter, and I was already prepared to incinerate him. "You've told me repeatedly that you owe me a debt for preserving your sister's virtue. I never thought to claim it, as any sensible person would understand that pure necessity, not benevolence, determined my course. But I am without recourse. This is not a matter of pleasure travel, but of . . . family. A mortal illness. I cannot delay."

Ilario de Sylvae, the most ridiculous human being I had ever met, sagged into Anne's chair like a grain sack dropped from a loft. The rustle of satin and lace, the chink of jeweled chains and pendants, and the stink of perfume painted the spindly popinjay's portrait more vividly than any paint dauber. "Well, that's another matter entirely."

Without going into the unwholesome state of my family bonds, I recounted the message from my brother and detailed the unpleasant necessity for not only a nursemaid but a bodyguard. I did not mention angels who spoke in dreams or visions of the world's ruin.

"Naturally, there's no need for you to suffer the journey yourself, lord. Your Captain de Santo, should you allow him leave to go, comes highly recommended."

As always, the stalwart soldier had accompanied Ilario but remained outdoors, ever uncomfortable at visiting Anne's house. The Gautier conspirators had set up de Santo as a scapegoat for royal assassination. Anne's father had fallen for the ploy, stripping the captain of rank and cropping his ears—a disgrace that would follow the man to his grave. Yet after only a few words from Portier, the captain had allied himself with the king's party. *Honor,* Anne called it, a word that carried far more meaning to those grown up in privilege than to those who hadn't.

"But of course I must collaborate in such a venture!" chirped Ilario. "A Chevalier y Sabria cannot leave the unpleasant duties to his underlings, no matter how brave and loyal. And indeed where brigands are concerned, an extra pair of eyes—" He almost strangled himself trying to choke back the words.

"Exactly so," I said, as calmly as I could spew anything.

It was annoying that I could not get angry with the lackwit. He was Anne's great friend. At least once every month he arrived full of court gossip and took Anne out horse riding to share it. It always cheered her. His inanity had somehow endeared him to the king, as well, and to Portier, which made no sense at all. But that was why, six years past, I had used

Ilario to convince them of my alliance with de Gautier. I'd meant only to put on a great show by damaging the chevalier a little. But I had ever been convinced Ilario was himself a deceiver. As I worked the magic to contain him, such a rage had grown in me that in trying to knock the lies out of him, I had come very near killing him. The fool had never raised his hand to resist.

The episode left me squirming when I thought of it. I had to respect his choice to come here in Anne's absence. *Honor* again, perhaps, even in a moron.

So I swallowed my anxiety along with the excuses six years had made neither reasonable nor palatable. "Chevalier, I regret the severity—"

"Stop, stop, stop!" He pounded his walking stick on the floor. "You did what was needed to foil the dastardly conspirators. Though, truly, I've never understood even the most crass villains desiring a world where food flies off of tables, boats plummet into oceans' depths, and silkworms turn out kersey. And, by the holy saints, to think we might have seen crocodiles crawling about in houses . . ." A long gulping sound ensued. The wine cup Finn had brought him was surely dry.

"So when might Captain de Santo—and you, of course, as you wish—be able to go?"

"Unsure of your need and the length of my absence, I arranged with a gentle-mannered householder, the Baronet Montmorency de Froux, to attend my sister's ladies. And I've left my ever-reliable man, John Deune, in the village, as I know you prefer to keep private, but in the matter of an hour I can dispatch him to acquire the necessaries for travel to be delivered along our road. In short, mage, at your word we ride north."

"All right, then." I gathered my wits as if a whirlwind had scattered them across the landscape. "Half an hour. Dispatch your message, refresh yourself . . . and the captain, too. Then we'll go."

A QUARTER HOUR SUFFICED. Packing was simple. A spare shirt. Gloves. A wool jersey and my heaviest cloak. My staff and copper bracelet. My knife and a few small items from the laboratorium, useful for creating wards or directional charms or for treating injuries. A brass ring Portier had given me to demonstrate his newfound magical skills—useful if I needed to send him a message by some suspicious means. A heavy blanket, a skin of ale, a flask of clean water, and what portable provision we had in the larder. Once Ilario had scribbled a message for his valet and I'd left a few instructions with Finn, we were ready.

"All will be well here, Master. Never a worry," said Finn as he fixed a lead rope from my horse to Captain de Santo's saddle. The youth had been near giddy from the moment I'd said I was leaving without him. "I'll deliver the chevalier's message to his servant right away. Ought I post Damoselle Anne a message at the same time, telling her where you've gone?"

My fingers twined a small oval of silver on a slender chain. The pendant's magic, though created by Anne's dead sister, had been triggered by Anne herself. It pricked my fingers, as sharp and brilliant as the points of a queen's diamond. Anne claimed it was a nireal, a soul mirror, a simple variant of an enchantment I'd used to instill a dead man's soul into a living body. She had given it to me on the day she arrived at Pradoverde, some kind of sentimental token. I'd forever intended to study its magic but always found some excuse not to. I'd certainly never do so in front of Anne. No need to feed her foolishness. Or mine. I shoved it deeper in my pocket.

"No. If she inquires, tell her I've gone to Coverge to make sure my father's dead. I should be back before the turn of the year." Seven days to Jarasco. Another through the mountains to Raghinne. A day to hear the message and the mode of its delivery. Then back. "Seventeen days."

Portier had once said I sat a horse with all the grace of a fence post. And that was when I could see where I was going. Anne relished riding and had tried to get me comfortable with it by bringing more horses to Pradoverde. "Falco's smart and steady," she had told me. "Feel him. Move with him. Partner with him and you needn't depend so much on seeing. He believes you're in charge, so just act like it—as you do with everyone else."

Riding was a useful skill. Thus, I had tried. My attempts resulted in a twisted shoulder and a cracked rib. I had renamed the beast Devil.

As we set out north, I clung to Devil's mane and saddle like a leech to warm skin. Seventeen days stretched ahead like an eternity. Yet it could not pass fast enough to soothe my urgency. I had to reach Raghinne before my father died.

I would scarce have known Captain de Santo was on the other end of my tether, save for an occasional instruction growled over his shoulder:

Give him his head, mage. Or *You* must *hold him steady through the town.* Or *Friendly your animal, if you know aught of befriending.*

Ilario, on the other hand, prattled incessantly. Keeping some sense of the landscape around so I wouldn't get disoriented and fall off required so much concentration, I couldn't have said what the idiot talked of.

Northern Louvel comprised naught but rolling fields and vineyards, cows, and the occasional market town. The cows weren't a problem, but two years tucked away in isolated Pradoverde had left me unpracticed in dealing with human chaos. I needed no eyes to know when city gates appeared on the horizon. In the darkness behind my eyes, the aether surged with sharp-edged emotions and the layered residue of human striving. The noise and pressure trapped in my skull left me near breathless. To rebuild my mental discipline was rugged when I was so preoccupied with remaining upright.

In late afternoon, we rode into the crossroads town of Heville. Situated on the border between northern Louvel and southern Challyat, Heville likely hosted a customs station. The overpowering stink of manure, rotted grapes, and ripe cheese witnessed to a thriving market. Incense smoke and the clamor of bells bespoke a temple.

Ilario's reminder that it was First Day explained the incense and the crowds. But an unusual fervor gripped the town. Believers chanted prayers, holy verses, and songs. The Readers' and Sermonists' bells and clappers called them to the temple with the jangling, rattling clamor of a hailstorm in a bell maker's shop.

Off to my left, scratchy voices rose in a litany of the Saints Reborn—mendicants, no doubt, traveling brothers of the Cult of the Reborn, those who believed that saints were noble souls who had rejected Heaven, reborn to the land of the living time and again to aid humankind in our travails. Rowdies screamed "idolater" and "heretic" at them, though the Temple more commonly viewed Cultists as merely "excessively devout."

The crowd must not like mages, either. Whispered curses brushed my skin like spiderwebs: *Souleater's servant . . . Fallen.* A crier called the faithful to witness a tetrarch casting out a daemon.

My stomach lurched. I nudged Devil forward. "Chevalier, Captain, what's the name they're shouting—this tetrarch daemonist?"

"Sounds like Ferrow or some such," said de Santo.

Ferrau! Daemons! He was the tetrarch Masson de Cuvier had consulted about his dream. The Temple daemonist who knew of me. "Get us out of here. Now!"

"Hold on."

As I tightened my grip on reins and mane, they surged ahead, tightening Devil's tether. But the crowd kept our pace to a crawl.

A hand gripped my ankle. "What've you done, daemon-twister, you and your kind?" The gritty snarl dripped hate. "My dead wife comes in the night. Cold-eyed. Fierce. Verger says she's come to eat my boy's soul!"

A tale right out of the nightmare of the great emerald. "Wait! Captain, I need to hear—"

Devil sidestepped, pulling me away, and other bodies closed in. My companions pressed on.

The noise and shouting and the sense of so many bodies and unseen obstacles already had me sweating. Now haunted visions and phantom Temple bailiffs in their yellow robes and green badges pursued me through the dark inside my head. They'd know me. I doubted there were three blind mages in all of Sabria.

Our pace quickened as we headed north through verdant Challyat. Fewer hills. Fewer vineyards. More cows. Twice we had to detour around iron-wheeled coal wains. Passing riders called greetings of divine grace before leaving us choking in their dust.

Every alien hoofbeat made me flinch, which caused Devil to balk and skitter. I mumbled the friendliest words I could think of.

About the time Devil and I settled into some sort of truce, Ilario dropped back beside me. "We'd hoped to make it so far as Nanver, where there's a hostel with the most exquisite fish to be found this side of Tallemant, but the early sunset just won't allow it. Vino says the only sheltered spot for fifty kilometres is just ahead. Fortunately, I've a great fondness for sleeping out."

"No one's following us? None in Temple colors or mage collars? I've this nagging sense . . ." Surely at any moment a heavy hand would clamp onto my shoulder.

"Not as I know. I've a spyglass—much finer than the one I carried to Eltevire—and I've taken a look from time to time. Perhaps I should loan it to the captain, as he's expert . . ."

"Good. Yes." No assurances were going to calm this fever. Not until I got to Raghinne and heard what the *angel* wanted of me. Practical sense must rein my impatience.

Not long after, de Santo issued a clipped, "Leftward just ahead."

Devil slowed and turned in response to his lead, and we soon passed into a narrow pocket of cold dry air and old vegetation. And something else . . .

"Wait," I said softly, raising my hand.

We halted, blessedly without argument, and I patted the side of my saddle until I touched my staff. Ruing the power I'd wasted on the seeing spell throughout the day, I slid my forefinger to a grooved pattern of a half circle and infused the waiting enchantment with power and will.

My ears tingled, and the ravine came alive with sound. Burrowing voles. Scuttering shrews. Sparrows or pipits crunching seeds or yanking overlooked berries from dry stalks. Moth wings fluttering, spiders weaving, beetles clicking, and something larger . . . breathing . . . waiting . . .

Leathers creaked, and I waggled my hand for continued stillness. Aided by the enchantment, I stretched my hearing farther. A soft thud. Movement . . .

I shouted a warning, and a body came crashing through the dry weeds.

De Santo grunted. A thrum . . . and an arrow whined past my ear, resulting in a solid thud just behind me. Devil snorted and sidestepped, and I flattened myself forward and flung my arms round his neck as the world spun and sloshed in the cursed blackness.

"Chevalier?" I yelled. "Captain? Who's there?" I dared not loose my hold on Devil to pull out my staff.

"Only a roe deer," called Ilario, entirely where I didn't expect him to be. "Soothe your mount, mage! Reassure him!"

"Easy, easy, you black-hearted villain," I mumbled, heart crashing against my ribs. Someone else could judge whether I addressed the beast or myself.

Once I'd got Devil calm enough I could dismount and take out my staff, I poured more power into the hearing enchantment, listening until my head near turned inside out. But I heard nothing untoward. Ilario and the captain were murmuring briskly about wood and fire.

"Are you all right, mage?" Ilario unwound Devil's reins from my dead fingers. "Angels defend, I was sure my heart would leap from my breast!

But we shall reap the benefits of your warning and Vino's skilled bow. My stomach—always tender, if you recall—was rebelling at the thought of jerky and cheese."

Again lies, I thought, lifting my head as if I might view the chevalier's mind. Ilario's mount had not startled. Perhaps the beast was just extraordinarily calm. But Anne's teaching and my own limited experience testified that the mount most often reflected the rider's nerves. Ilario was not, and had not been, at all anxious.

That needed to change. It was not my companions' leathers I'd heard.

"Someone wearing plated leather and a sword was lurking down the ravine," I said. "Likely he startled the roebuck apurpose with a rock or a dirt clod."

"How could you possibly know that?" barked de Santo from just behind me.

I spun so fast I near lost my balance. Defensive fire spurted through my staff, scorching my cheek. "Haven't you heard?" I snapped, furious at my lack of discipline. "Blind mages develop a god's skills."

I recognized men's fear of magic in de Santo's gruff question. Indeed, he had reason enough. But I could have killed us both. "Don't sneak up behind me."

While the captain butchered the deer, Ilario tethered the horses. He stuffed a rag in my hand. "Your horse will treat you princely if you rub him down."

Work always helped me think more clearly. I took on all three of the beasts. Later, when Ilario started dithering with flint and steel, I provided fire.

"Chevalier," I said, as the fragrance of roasting meat warmed the chilly ravine, "if you would guide me around a reasonable perimeter, I'll set wards to warn us of intruders. We'd best keep watch through the night, as well." Someone had been waiting here along the Coverge road at the "only sheltered spot within fifty kilometres" and didn't want to be seen. I didn't like it.

"A most excellent plan! Here we have a most delightful, prickly stand of hawthorn. . . ." Ilario's descriptions of trees, vegetation, soil, and rocks suffered from his usual excess of good cheer and verbiage, but I was able to sort out useful details. Using my knife, samples of earth and vegetation, charred sticks from the fire, and the deer's bloody bones, I worked a tightly warded enclosure. An hour's concentration left me feeling a bit less scattered and a bit less naked.

Twice in the night my right hand burst into flame—sensory flame—as something sizable tripped my wards. Another deer? A boar? Human? Each time I leapt to my feet, and my staff blasted fire into the sky, waking my companions and terrifying the horses. Each time, the intruder retreated before I could learn more of its nature. After that, Ilario and de Santo made sure to sleep or watch well away from me.

Daemon. Servant . . . In the deeps of the night, whispers bathed face and limbs, tickling, rousing me to wakefulness. Cold fingers pressed firmly between my eyes. . . .

"Get off me!" The touch vanished. "Do you crave death?"

My flailing staff encountered naught but scrubby plants.

De Santo mumbled curses from a goodly distance. I was left feeling foolish, save when I returned to my blanket; it smelled of fresh herbs and cold ash, much like . . . Soggy with sleep, I couldn't recall. Someone had been here. Either my wards had failed or I had been dreaming. Indeed, the fingers might have been pressing from inside my head. Gods, I was a madman.

Before we rode out the next morning, the three of us walked my perimeter. Ilario reported disturbed brush but no tracks, save those of roe deer and lesser creatures. De Santo concurred. Yet, just outside the circle deep in the ravine, a scent lured me to my knees. No magical residue lingered nearby save my own, and I detected no remnant of the herbs I'd smelled in the night. But beneath the forever green leaves of a laurel lingered a scent of incense.

Likely no milkmaid had come here to honor her dead or dabble in ineffective conjury. Incense was very expensive. Nobles had access to it. As did sorcerers of the Camarilla. As did Readers, bailiffs, and other servants of the Temple. No one I cared to meet.

DEMESNE OF CHALLYAT

Ilario's manservant, John Deune, caught up with us late on our second day out. I'd seen him occasionally about Castelle Escalon, a bony, pinch-mouthed man who scuttled about the edges of rooms and passageways like a well-dressed mouse. More than once I'd spied him filching coins from the palace servants' pettibox, a tawdry little cheat by one in private service.

I'd surmised the chevalier retained such an awkward, ill-spoken servant to better exhibit his own flamboyant graces.

"'Twasn't easy finding fit netherstocks or gloves roundabout Laurentine," said the manservant as the four of us crowded into a cramped well yard in the town of Grousse. "Nor would the scurrilous apothecary stop complaining about the brewing of your stomach medicament. Said it stank up his shop, as if a lord's will could ever be an inconvenience. *Not* that I spilt the supreme elevation of your position to the tradesmen, lord, though it would have resulted in much better service, I'm sure, and I've never grasped what possible business forces you to lower yourself"—his tinny whine scarce dropped, as if a blind man standing three paces away might not hear—"to associate with the present company. A good thing I can help watch for his unholy perversions—"

"Bridle your tongue, sirrah!" Tremors shivered Ilario's command. "The mage is a hero of Sabria and my sister's loyal servant. I am forever in his debt and offer my service freely to accompany him on this journey of tragic family circumstance."

"Uh . . . naturally, my lord. Inexcusable rudeness . . ." The servant swallowed each word as if it were a porcupine.

At one time in my life I would have delighted in conjuring wolf fangs or claws to flash from beneath my cloak. A bit of fire and a view of my burn-scarred hand had often sufficed to fright alley thugs. But somehow as the decreasing number of my days as a sorcerer weighed so heavy, using magic for low personal satisfactions seemed somehow . . . unrighteous.

"I'll not gnaw your bones this month, John Deune," I said, leaving them to check on Devil.

". . . silk of wretchedly poor quality . . . only the crudest tooth cleaners to be had . . ." The manservant reeked of anise. I detested anise.

Ilario held indignation no longer than he held mathematical formulas. "Ah, my faithful John Deune, you've brought me everything required for this journey. You must now fly to my royal sister to inform her of my journeying and expected return at the year's turning, and then plunge into the bosom of your family for a holiday."

"But, lord, I should—"

"Nay! I am in good company. Your sons must be quite colossal now. . . . So astonishing how children's bones and flesh just keep growing all of themselves . . ."

A quarter of an hour and we'd left the sniveling servant behind. Our mutual distaste was well served by separation.

THE WEATHER HELD COLD AND SUNNY. We rode hard. We slept out. De Santo bought or scrounged supplies from freeholders or village markets along the way and supplemented with rabbits and other small game. I patted Devil and mumbled sweetnesses to him. He remained skittish and I felt a proper dunce. When Ilario bought us apples, I kept mine back for the horse, and he liked that better. Neither man nor beast tripped my wards at night.

Yet after that first disturbing night, every kilometre closer to Raghinne tightened some screw in my head. Spikes of flame pierced my eyes, just as in the first months after they were ruined. Sleep was impossible. I couldn't eat without nausea. As we neared the city of Jarasco and its well-traveled crossroads, the aether boiled and my spirit was chaos.

My companions suffered for my madness. I swore at them to cease coddling my blindness and whispering between themselves or I'd rip their own eyes out. Twice I almost strangled de Santo when he nudged me, ready to give me a hand up into the saddle. He took to poking me with his sword tip instead.

Too late, blind man . . . The enchantress in white had promised vengeance. Sometimes, in the dark, I heard her laughing.

CHAPTER 5

JARASCO

On our sixth day out, we rode into thick-walled Jarasco, the bustling city that straddled the borders of Challyat, Delourre, and Coverge. Ilario, claiming he was *wholly dilapidated*, insisted we take accommodation at a local inn. "It's already dusk, Dante, and it's threatening rain, and the gate guards told us the entire town will be locked down less than an hour hence, so we can't change our minds later."

"But surely we can squeeze in a few more kilometres before nightfall." Though it was true the day's overcast had my hours wholly confused.

"You'll be there tomorrow no matter—and likely sooner if you sleep in a bed. Beds are one of humankind's finest inventions. . . ."

"You must understand, Chevalier. I need to be there. If I could push on alone, I would. You can ask whatever you wish of me once I've seen to my business: charms, protections, or potions, far more effective than those you buy in the markets. Something's terribly wrong. . . ."

Everywhere. Inside me. In the aether, the realm of souls and dreams. In the land of the living and the land of the dead. Not even at Mont Voilline had I felt it so strongly. If someone had said my body was stripped of flesh and muscle and the winds of the netherworld were howling through my bones, I would have believed it so.

"We need to save the horses for the mountains." The chevalier rode close beside me. "Saints' mercy, you didn't tell me we'd be climbing a rampart! Besides"—he dropped his voice—"Vino says three fellows have kept us in sight since we entered the gates."

"That's hardly surprising when a fine lord rides in with such a small party." Every cutter and snatch in three demesnes would be after Ilario. Especially as one of his companions had to be led by a leash. "Another reason to keep moving."

"Honestly, mage, I've a tad of sense. I've . . . subdued . . . my wardrobe for our journey. Only kersey and leather. No lace, no jewels, not even an earring. I feel quite frumpish. Even you would think me a right common fellow. Besides, I've spied a dust cloud behind us for two days running. Stopping when we stopped. Rising again when we rode out."

"You never thought to *mention* this dust cloud?"

"What would we have done differently? You've hardly welcomed any insight of ours."

Indeed. Officious twit. I should congratulate him on being bold enough to address me at all. I summoned patience. "So are these on our trail thieves? Or mages? Temple bailiffs?"

"Not mages, unless they're hiding it. The captain spied no mage collars. But it's why we've taken so many turnings. None will threaten us in a public house, and we'll be better fit to face them after a decent night."

His logic was worthy of Portier himself. Perhaps the events at Mont Voilline had sobered the fool a bit. I'd never understood how Anne could bear his company.

"All right, then. But make sure we've more than one exit, even if it means we sleep in the washhouse." I'd rather run than be delayed. "Of course, I'll set wards as before. . . ." If I could make the damnable spells work. My working senses were dulled with lack of sleep.

All but one of the city's five public houses were already bolted up tight for the night. The fifth had no accommodation save the common bunkroom. When de Santo informed the hostler at the Bell Shaft that his traveling companion was a veteran of the Kadr war who oft screamed in his sleep, we were offered the stable loft.

The captain offered to fetch our supper. I swallowed pride yet again and entreated him to bring something more palatable than the pig whose scorched fat filled the yard with rancid smoke. As Ilario supervised—and distracted—the hostler's lad, I climbed up to the loft alone. The fewer people who noted the blind mage, the better.

Before anything else, I crept about the small loft, using smell and touch to learn of its size, shape, and materials. More familiar with haylofts than public hostelries, I constructed wards across the trapdoor and the hay doors at either end.

The effort wrecked me. As Ilario and the stable boy chattered and rattled about down below one of the hay doors, I fumbled through my pack and found the skin of Pradoverde ale I'd saved back for an emergency. Yearning for sleep, I crawled into a corner, savored a long pull, and begged the pain in my eyes and the noise of the aetherstorm to go away.

They didn't. Instead, the brush of spiderwebs, the smell of hay, tar, and mouse droppings, and the cramped joining of wall, floor, and roof beams roused memories of the sleeping loft I'd shared with my three brothers. Andero, as the eldest, had a mattress to himself. Though Andero and I had played together when we were small, he'd kept away from me once I spoke of voices in my head. Yet on the night my father beat me half to death, it was he who'd come to me once all were asleep, bringing a wet cloth and what clumsy comfort he could manage. Big and sturdy as a man grown, he was but sixteen himself and could not read. But he knew I'd done naught to justify such punishment. He offered to carry me to a cave we knew and tend me till I could run. I refused. Da would have killed him. Not a tenday after, Andero himself ran away to serve in our duc's legion. Da was livid. That's when I decided to wrest the forge from him, never imagining he would mutilate me to prevent it.

All these years I had assumed Andero dead. To think that I would be with him in one more day, back in that hateful place . . .

I took another pull at the ale skin. And another.

Cheery farewells echoed from below. The rusty, misaligned hinges of the stable doors screeched. The footsteps on the ladder triggered the scalding signal in my hand.

I stayed where I was. Ilario's smell was unmistakable. Somehow he always managed to be clean. And no matter the crudeness of his garments, they carried a trace of his favored perfumes.

"You look a fright, mage. Are you ill?"

"Would you mind moving through the ward a bit faster?" I said, pressing my hand under my left arm. "The sensation of burning flesh is an effective alarm, but not at all nice."

He dropped a heavy bundle off to one side, tramped across the creaking boards, and crouched in front of me. "Ye graceful gods, Dante, have you ever considered using some warning signal that is not *pain*?"

His question must have tweaked a long-dead nerve, or perhaps it was the half skin of ale I'd drunk, but laughter burbled up from my gut. I sagged into my corner cackling like a goose. It was true. What kind of perverse creature couldn't trust anything but agony to rouse him to attention?

Ilario's boots shuffled backward. "Perhaps I should leave you alone for a while."

"Not—having—a fit," I croaked, gasping for air. "Not mad." Though I was and ever had been. "Tired. Drunk."

"Is that wise?"

Another spew of hilarity flooded through me, uncontrollable as a flux from bad meat. Unfortunately it spurred the lightning in my eyes to new vigor and sapped my control of the babbling torrent pouring through the aether. I pressed balled fists to my face, all humor fled.

"Not at all. I never—" I clamped my mouth shut so as not to heave and curled up in a knot. "Just need to be still . . . sleep."

"DANTE." THE EARTH RUMBLED IN WARNING. "Dante, wake up. Saints, Dante . . ."

My teeth rattled in my skull, setting off spikes of agony behind my eyelids. I blinked. Blinked again. Scrambled to sitting and whacked my head on something painfully solid. The bottom dropped out of the world. Growling, I lashed out at the prodding hands and the body attached to them, groping through the blackness to find boundaries . . . limits . . . solidity.

"Glory, Dante, it's just Ilario." An iron grip on my wrists stopped my flailing, while the sharp whisper penetrated my thick head. "We're at the Bell Shaft in Jarasco and there's trouble afoot."

A taint of sour ale coated my mouth. *Ilario. The Bell Shaft*—a hostelry, not the pit shaft of a coal mine. My head scraped the rafters of a loft. As the image settled around me, I dismissed my waking panic. "What trouble?"

He released my hands. "De Santo hasn't come back. It's been two hours, and the common room's dark. You need to be awake and . . . sober."

Had I not recognized his scent, I mightn't have believed the man crouched in front of me to be Ilario de Sylvae. His voice had dropped a full register and taken on a gravity entirely alien to him.

"It's full night, and someone's crossing the yard without a lamp. We need to be ready."

"We can't afford confrontation," I snapped. "I can't be delayed."

"We're not leaving here without Vino." Impregnable, unwavering in his resolution. "The loft door is two metres to your right. Below the door is a hay wagon. Distract and delay them as long as you can, and then get out. I'm going after him. Do you understand? You can . . . work?"

"Yes. Yes, certainly." Discipline reasserted itself. I shoved aside the aetherstorm and my astonishment and the fire in my eyes. Only . . . "Chevalier, how big is this hay wagon?"

"Jump from the center of the doorway. You'll not miss it. I'll fetch you after."

He evaporated into the dark. Gods . . . Ilario?

Taking up my staff, I groped for the edge of the loft door. The opening was some two metres wide, the latch simple. The prospect of jumping into blackness did not bear thinking of.

I slid deep into the corner. My foot encountered the ale skin, and I kept it beside me. Then I closed down all fear and distraction and listened for movements below.

My fingers slid down the smooth hornbeam of my ancille and touched a raised pattern of points here, a carved crescent there, shaping the waiting enchantments into a pattern on my mind's canvas. As I hammered and molded the stuff of magic into the pattern of my desire, a draft wafted through the trap. It carried the savory aroma of broth and a faint metallic noise—screeching hinges, muffled as if someone had laid sacking over them. Had Ilario not alerted me, I'd never have noticed how long the door stayed open. Enough to admit several men.

I sat on my haunches, staff laid across my lap. Still. Focused. Waiting. Sorely tempted to touch my copper bracelet and see what shadows I could. But I dared not waste power.

My right hand spasmed with phantom pain, then quieted. Someone had crossed the stair ward and moved slightly left. "Who's there?"

A second body paused at the top of the ladder, exactly in the middle of the ward field as Ilario had done earlier. He emitted a small grunt.

"Just me. Brought your supper, Master." De Santo was under duress. He never called me *master.*

"Man could starve, waiting," I snapped, listening.

The burning in my hand relented as de Santo shuffled forward, and then pulsed again right away. A second intruder had masked his movements with the captain's. And yet another passage. Three of them besides de Santo.

"Bring it over here, Vino," I said. "My leg's cramped from the damnable horse and I'm like to fall flat on my face if I try to get up." I never called him *Vino.*

"Aye, Master."

I felt—or imagined—two men slipping toward my flanks as de Santo and his shadow moved across the creaking boards. It was ten steps straight across from the ladder. At the ninth I detected the flankers' breath closing in. At the tenth I whipped my right arm across the air in front of me, knocked the soup bowl away, and caught hold of Captain de Santo's leather jerkin. Hauling down on it, I spat a whisper, "Eyes closed!"

Hot soup splattered. The captain's massive body crashed to the floor. Meanwhile, I tossed the ale skin into the air and snatched up my staff. *"Luminaire!"*

Heat burst in front of my face. The air hissed and steamed. Hot droplets kissed my skin, a satisfying discomfort as three voices rose in pained surprise. I bound the second part of the spell—streaks of eye-searing light should be bouncing about the walls and roof. Harmless, but they didn't know that. They were already screaming.

"Clear," I whispered, nudging de Santo.

He leapt up with a savage yell. Bodies crashed against the floor and walls.

The long-dead nerves in my hand flared again. Someone else had crossed the ward.

I edged backward crabwise and gripped the edge of the hay door, only to have someone plant a boot in my chest and shove, crushing my back to the door frame. His fingers clamped my jawbone, and his enveloping stink reeked of incense, burnt skin, and righteous anger.

"Dante, daemon mage of the Camarilla Magica," he said through clenched teeth, "by the authority of Tetrarch Beltan de Ferrau, you are under arrest for the blasphemous evil of necromancy."

Snarling, I brought up my right arm to break his hold, but before I could raise magic, someone ripped him off me. A heavy impact shook the floor. The wall at my back rattled. I planted my staff and leapt to my feet. The hay door latch dug into my hip.

"Go now!" A solid blow punctuated Ilario's breathless command. Scrabbling feet, a ferocious growl, a cracking noise, and a roar, and he was back beside me. "More coming from below."

Though far from helpless, I dared not spray true havoc about the loft, lest I injure my allies. So I ripped open the latch, swung the door outward, and positioned myself in the approximate middle of the opening. Cold, damp air bathed my face. *Gods, gods, gods . . .*

"Fly, mage!"

A solid thud behind me elicited someone's stifled cry. Hinges screeched and more boots thudded below the trap.

I jumped.

An eternity of stomach-hollowing nothing, then my boots hit and slid out from under me. My elbow whacked a wooden edge, and my staff struck the bridge of my nose. Sprawled twisted and sidewise, I embraced the hay that was scratching, prickling, and poking into ears, eyes, nostrils, and mouth. I wasn't broken, but my heart was going to require a goodly while to settle.

"Move!" The heated whisper from above set me scrambling, envisioning bodies dropping on top of me. I dove over the side, reaching back to grab my staff just as a solid rush and a quiet, two-footed thump signaled that someone had landed much more gracefully than I. A hand yanked me aside just as a third body caromed into the wagon. De Santo's curse roused my better humor. The captain was accustomed to doing everything right.

I limped across the yard, my hand on Ilario's shoulder. The chevalier's clean smell now bore the distinctive taint of blood.

Someone—the chevalier again?—had cleverly stashed our saddled horses behind the washhouse. Four hands shoved me onto Devil's back and we were off. The bells of Jarasco's Temple Minor struck middle-night.

My satisfaction was short-lived, the race through Jarasco unnerving me entire. Not even at the dead hours would I expect we could thread the streets of Jarasco at a gallop.

"Where is everyone?"

My yell slowed Ilario enough to drop back. "Mayhap they warned—Creator's fire, what is *that*?"

"Tell me," I said.

"Just hold on!"

As I cursed, he slapped Devil's hind end and we sped faster, turning, scarce slowing, until walls closed in around us, trapping the stink of offal and soot. I had to trust them, Ilario, de Santo, and Devil. I couldn't spare time or thought for second-guessing, for the aetherstorm surged into pandemonium. Howling, raging, hungry . . . threatening to scour me dry.

Winding Devil's reins tight about my hands, I summoned discipline. As a scribe prepares a new page, I erased thought and fear. Next vanished memory and prescience, past and future fading into transparency. Pain and desire followed—a task far more difficult when one could not use eyes to focus outside the body. Once reduced to naked bones, I reopened my inner ears and promptly shut them down again. This wasn't just the mindstorm, but a desolation so pervasive it could sap the will, a tempest of anger, of terror, of howling hopelessness and starvation. I'd felt this only once before. Better to remain empty. . . .

"Dante! Are you wounded?"

I lifted my head, only to realize we'd halted. The air was foul. Damp. Walls on three sides.

"The sky was pulsing, wasn't it? That's what you saw," I said, my throat as raw as on the day my hand was burnt. "Like a pregnant woman's belly."

Anne had seen such a display at Mont Voilline on the night I had ripped a hole in the Veil between life and death, the night I'd heard the howling of starving spirits, the night I'd come to believe something was devouring the souls of the dead.

"Saints, yes, but we've no time. We're just off the ring road inside the postern. The gate's deserted, but we've a horde of Temple servitors in pursuit. Unfortunately, the portcullis is down and the mechanisms appear to be rusted shut. Doesn't look as if anyone's opened the thing since the Blood Wars. If you can't get it open, we'll have to backtrack—which will get very ugly—or climb the wall and escape afoot."

I dredged up memory. Jarasco was the only town I'd ever seen until I escaped Raghinne. "They've not replaced the portcullis? It's a wooden lattice, only the barbs tipped with iron?"

"It's dark as a pit down there, Dante."

Iron was the bane of sorcery. In the presence of iron, enchantments could fail or rebound in dangerous ways. But if the crosspieces themselves were wood, no matter if they were old as the mountains and thick as trees, I could likely account for smaller amounts of iron.

"Take me there," I said, dropping to the ground and clutching Devil's neck until the world stopped spinning. "You'll want to keep the horses well away."

Ilario marched me down a cobbled road. The flanking walls were close.

"Wait here," he said, pressing my back to the cold stone. Spits of sleet pelted my face as his light footsteps covered the few metres to the portcullis and back. "Wood lattice, spikes tipped with iron, just as you said. It's seven metres, more or less, straight ahead of you. What should I do?"

Astonishing how terse Ilario had become. And how competent. A preening aristo with the intelligence of a sparrow. Yet Portier hadn't spoken a slighting word about him since our adventure at Eltevire six years ago. And Anne, who had no use for courtly games, laughed with him, confided in him. . . . Secrets and lies. A heated wire tightened in my belly.

I shook my head to clear it. This wasn't the time to challenge him. "Be ready to grab me and run," I said. "Every man searching is going to see this."

He retreated. I fingered my staff, locating the carved triangle with a smooth depression in the center. That was fire. And then the recessed nub, the carving of an eagle's eye. That was death. I hoped no innocent came knocking at the postern.

Summoning the power that threaded my veins and sinews, I poured it into the melded pattern of the two waiting spells. Bracing the heel of the staff waist-high on the wall at my back, I let the enchantment build. The ancient postern was likely steeped in spellwork. As Salvator had hammered into me and I had hammered into Anne, a wise practitioner would study its making before attempting any such working as this. But we had no time, so the sheer magnitude of my enchantment must overpower whatever lingered there. When body and spirit felt swollen to bursting, a simple infusion of my will bound the spell.

Flaying heat burst from the head of the staff. The eruption raised a clamor worthy of a typhoon slinging hailstones the size of pigs. Its light would be red and orange and a thousand colors that had no name—a lethal beauty that would carve a hole in the night.

Power drained out of me in a flood. When my knees began to quiver, I declared it enough and released the binding.

Frozen raindrops whispered across the world. Though the stench of burnt oil and charred timber set me coughing, it was the silence worried me.

Hooves clattered on the cobbles, and four hands boosted me into the saddle. "By the Creator's mighty hand, Dante," said Ilario.

"Was it enough?" I said between coughs, as we passed through a wall of heat. "I can't hear flames."

"There's naught left to burn. Gate, portcullis . . . you brought down the gate tower and half the wall!"

"Sure they'll know which way we've gone," said the captain. "Give us a bit of light and we can go faster on the straight. Once we're in the rocks, you can let it go. I'll dismount and lead."

I bit off my earnest desire that the bullnecked soldier stick his head up his ass and triggered the spell. Fortunately, to cast a faint light on the road ahead required little effort.

In general I recovered quickly from an intense working, but it required food and sleep, not jouncing in a saddle in the dead hours, raddled by the virulent aetherstorm and burgeoning dread. But I had to make use of what peace I had. I attached myself firmly to Devil, promised him apples at our next stop, and closed off the world, setting myself adrift in the gulf between sleep and waking. I had to trust my companions.

From time to time my finger touched the grooved arc on my staff and I stretched my hearing backward. Slow, measured hoofbeats followed. Perhaps the Temple riders were less expert than the two who led me. Perhaps they had no way to make themselves a light. But they were coming.

CHAPTER 6

DEMESNE OF COVERGE

"Let go the light now, mage," said de Santo, softly, drawing me back to full wakefulness.

We'd come to a halt. The sleet had turned to snow. I licked my lips, perishingly thirsty, and the captain pressed a cup into my hand, and my hand into a trickle of water dribbling down a cliff.

"We're into the mountains, and the horses need a rest," he said. "Chevalier is scouting ahead to make sure the pursuit hasn't sneaked ahead. We've yet to spot them."

"Behind," I said, my voice crusted with the hours of silence. "Heard them all night. The three Temple bailiffs in the loft—did you leave them dead?"

"One was sorely broken, the others just out of sense. Chevalier said we'd best not finish them, as they knew your name."

I doubted a few dead Temple servitors could damage my reputation, but these two . . . "They didn't recognize Lord Ilario or you? Hanging about with a blasphemer is dangerous."

He hesitated. I could almost feel a shrug. "Nay. They wouldn't. We've a way about it."

Disguise? Charms? Ilario was a devoted magic user. "An efficient way, it seems."

He gave no answer to that. Cup by cup, I swallowed half a litre of water and gratefully sloshed a little over my face. I rummaged deep in my cloak and found one apple. Devil snuffled it out of my hand and nosed my pockets for more.

"There's a notch up ahead with a bit of grass," said the captain, taking Devil's reins. "I'll take him. Wait here."

Staying in contact with the cliff wall, I paced and stretched, trying to loosen my stiff joints. My nap in the loft and my hours adrift had left my mind better refreshed than any time in five days, but the body felt battered. Beltan de Ferrau, the Temple tetrarch who claimed to cast out daemons. Of all the ill luck . . .

Captain de Santo's footsteps were quite distinctive. Forever brisk, but much heavier than Ilario's. As he rejoined me, a quiet drop onto the dirt brought Ilario as well.

"It's still black night, so I couldn't see much of anything, and yet . . ." It was the first uncertainty I'd heard from the chevalier since he'd waked me in the loft. "I should have taken you with me, Dante. The sky isn't squirming anymore, but I've a sense we're walking into trouble."

"I've a notion your *sense* is better than I've been led to believe all these years. Tell me where we are."

The two men described a narrow defile threading a fortress of granite walls and man-high boulders. I knew the place exactly. We'd come some five kilometres beyond the point where the foot track into Coverge's interior diverged from the wagon road. I had hoped the foot track, rougher, shorter, less traveled, would shield us from attention. Evidently not.

"An hour's walk ahead, the defile opens up to a meadow—much of it a bog," I said. "Quarter of an hour across if we pick our path right; eternity if we don't. Then we climb again through a forest patch." The details of this route had been etched into my mind the first time I'd ever left Raghinne. "The track comes out of the wood onto a shelf path. Cliff on one side, chasm on the other. Wide enough for a horse, though I've never *ridden* it." The imagining drew a cold sweat to my back. "If someone's circled ahead of us, they'd have had to come around from the wagon road and through the bog. I don't see how they could have done. It's a much longer way, and they've lagged behind us since Jarasco. Perhaps . . . it's just a very bad night."

I wished I could explain this night's mysteries. Anne and I had destroyed the enchantment that allowed movement between the realms of living and dead. I had assumed our act had closed the physical portal—the "rent in the eternal Veil"—as well. We had pulled Portier from the pool where de Gautier had chained him, believing that Portier's supposed inability to die would make the gap in the Veil permanent. Yet this night felt so like that one . . . ragged, unnatural, hollow, as if the flesh of the universe had dissolved and wind scoured its bones. Someone, somewhere, was working powerful, dangerous magic.

A low thud shuddered the ground, as if a cannon had fired deep in the earth beneath our feet.

"Crei diavol!" shouted de Santo. "Where's it coming from? Get over here."

"Saints' mercy!" Ilario wrenched me aside as an arrow whined past my arm. As the arrowhead clattered on the rocks, the chevalier crushed me to a slab of granite. "They've lit up the sky like a midsummer firework. Cascading green light, but slow. There's six . . . eight . . . of them . . . just ahead of us. An archer to either side, and half a dozen swordsmen at the ready." His sword slipped out of its sheath. "Stay here. Stay flat. There's a bit of an overhang will keep you in shadow."

"But what—?" They ran off. Shouts, grunts, and the clash of swords filled the narrow space, bouncing from wall to wall, preventing me from locating any of them.

Great gods of men and beasts! I could kill a man with my bare hands. I'd done it more than once. But I could no longer aim a blow on my own any more than I could aim a bolt of magical fire.

Yet, if the enemy's advantage was enchantment, perhaps I could do something. . . .

I tasted the air, pulled up my sleeves, and let the swirling snow tease at my arms. Inhaling, I probed the roiling aether, ran through the steps of subtle detection, did everything that might reveal spellwork that I could dissect and wrench apart. But whatever had created the light that exposed us was entirely mundane. Incendiaries, I supposed, like the royal legions used. Without a device to examine or someone to describe its effects more thoroughly, I could do nothing.

Frustration smoldered into rage. Why was I born to such skills and left no way to use them? Every night these two years past I had screamed that question into my blankets, where none could hear my shameful display. So many in the world had nothing. As a boy in Coverge, I had been destined to stand ankle deep in muck, hacking at the ground until I coughed up blood up like Estebo. And then Salvator had shown me glory, guiding me down paths of illumination and power he himself was too unskilled to travel. I was born to wield magic. And now . . . Had I believed in Heaven or the netherworld or fate or destiny or gods who took pleasure in tormenting the objects of their creation, it might have been easier to cower in the shadows and leave the fight to others.

"Captain, behind you!" Ilario's shouts were punctuated with grunts and blows. Arrows whizzed through the air like murderous insects. "Mage! Any help you could offer! Soon, please!"

Stupid, self-pitying fool, Dante. Of course there was another way. "Need time!"

Shutting out the noise, the cold, and my anger at the empty cosmos, I dragged my staff in a half circle in front of me, beginning and ending at the granite cliff wall. Then I summoned my ready spells for light, for fire, for warmth and color. Their patterns were as much a part of me as the articulations of thighbone and knee, ankle and foot. I linked their sundry aspects on the canvas of my mind in scalding blues and yellows, reds and greens. And then I gathered in the spell of my copper bracelet and wove its white threads throughout my work.

Two souls I drew into my scheme: a dour man of war, grievously wronged yet offering good and loyal service in the cause of right, and a man wholly different from the one I would have included before this day—a man of deep-buried secrets, of intelligent command, a swordsman of skills, a serious playactor wrapped in foolery and lies. Anne's friend. Portier's friend.

Though time was critical, I dared not rush. Mistakes could have consequences far beyond this battle. I examined the pattern yet again and tested the logic of its working. The spell should create a surge of power far beyond what I had used to bring down the Jarasco postern, though without the same destructive force. I hoped.

Satisfied, I raised my staff and summoned power to create a circle of brilliance perhaps twenty metres in diameter with my everlasting darkness as its hub. But with a twist of mind and will, I inverted the pattern, reversing light and dark. I would be suffused with light, while every breathing creature within my circle, save my two protectors, would be left blind.

"Take them," I yelled. "Hurry."

I could not attend the sounds of dismay and death that ensued. Nor could I fret about the raging heat trapped inside the enclosure with me or the light that would announce my location to any human predator not trapped within my working. Determined to give Ilario and de Santo the time they needed to take out both swordsmen and archers, I emptied myself into the enchantment. If the captain and the chevalier failed to win this battle, what strength I did or didn't have left would not matter in the least.

Time lost its shape. But when I felt snow melting on my eyelashes and the cold from the stone at my back seeping through my thick cloak, I knew I was approaching the limits of my endurance.

I drew in the ragged threads of conscious thought. Heavy breathing and steel-clad leather at my side. De Santo. Naught else broke the uncanny silence. . . .

"They're all dead!" The anguished cry shattered the quiet. "Go back, Robierre! Run! Tell the tetrarch that the mage is Fallen!"

So confusing in the dark. Footsteps pelted back the way we'd come. Two survivors, clearly Temple bailiffs. Not so worrisome as long as they were leaving. It certainly wasn't the first time I'd been mistaken for one of Dimios the Souleater's rebellious brethren. Yet I still didn't understand how they'd come to be ahead of us. Waiting.

Their steps faded, yet de Santo did not move. His breathing slowed.

"Tell me—"

De Santo's hand clapped over my mouth. The taste of blood near gagged me.

He whistled two short bursts. More enemies nearby? Gods, how many had there been? Where was Ilario?

De Santo pressed one finger across my lips hard enough to reinforce the importance of continued silence. Gripping my shoulder and pressing my back to the wall, he guided me to the left. Up the steep track.

Fa-de-la, and hey and ho. To the deadhouse we shall go.
Seest thou, my ladies fair? This bold lad shall certain dare.
To venture realms none live should know.

The tavern ditty was rendered in Ilario's clear and unmistakable tenor. For all anyone would tell, the man was drunk as a rat in an ale cask.

Fa-de-la, and hey and ho. My favored lady does not know. . . .

I tried to slow de Santo, but he drove me away from Ilario as quickly as was possible without noise. We crept onward. Upward.

"Who are you who declares himself Pantokrator?" The chevalier's thick-tongued challenge was the kind one would hear in any tavern or fencing yard in Sabria. "You make the sun to rise in the dead hours and change snow to a rain of arrows! You slay a herd of Temple servitors like cattle. Your minions attack one of Dimios's favored Fallen! Have I, a poor chevalier-for-hire, stumbled into the War for Heaven renewed?"

A rain of arrows? A *herd* of Temple servitors *slain*?

"I am merely a broker in this enterprise, Chevalier. Not heavenly, though your master shall certainly forever be known as the enemy of Heaven." The voice emanated not from the heavens, but certainly from a position well above our heads and beyond my twenty-metre circle. He might have been discussing the price of a goose at the market. "No, someone wants him. Alive. Give him up, and you shall be on your way, skin intact. Understanding something of magical expenditures, I surmise his power is at a low ebb just now—unless he is Dimios himself after all. We've proper chains to bind him, so he'll not wreak his formidable wrath on you."

Boots shuffled on the road between us and Ilario. Gods, more of them. And still we stole away.

"Oh, so tempting," said Ilario. "But he's paid me well, you see, and what worth has a chevalier's honor if he fails to defend his employer? *You* may wish to hire me next."

"Sadly for you, hireling, we've no interest in your skills. We were paid to fetch your employer, not kill him, so your honor is intact. And we can take him at our leisure."

"Do you hear that, Master?" called Ilario. "I'd advise you hotfoot it after those pious Temple dogs. Offer yourself up to them *if* you can persuade them to slow down before they get to Jarasco and their tetrarch. I'll fend off these unholy persons until you're away, and if you're speedy enough I'll not trample you! Then I'll expect a bonus, sonjeur, as there's three of them to one of me. Four if we count this false Pantokrator. Yet the Creator has ever taken my part in quarrels."

So the speaker and his three were *not* Temple dogs. I was more confused than ever.

"Take this fool down," said the broker, or whatever he was. "Then we'll see who's cowering in the cleft he's guarding."

At the first scrape of swords, de Santo dragged me faster, no longer concerned with noise.

I pulled back. "We cannot leave him—"

The captain crushed me to the wall. "Arrows from atop the cliffs felled a dozen Temple bailiffs. These swordsmen mocked the Saints Awaiting and called upon them to show themselves or betake themselves to their true master in the netherworld. Must I spell out Lord Ilario's feelings about such words?"

"No. Gods, no."

Ilario was a devout member of the Cult of the Reborn. I'd always thought it odd for such a flea-wit. Only he wasn't such a flea-wit. Did he, like de Gautier and Kajetan, believe Portier a hero saint, reborn to serve humankind? Was he willing to sacrifice himself for superstition? Or for *me*?

"Move," spat de Santo.

As many times as I'd wished Ilario muted or dead, abandoning him split my craw. But if we went back, both de Santo and Ilario would die, and these villains would have me, too, and I'd never learn what was to be learned from my father's dream. If such was their intent, I damned well could not allow them to succeed.

We pelted up the track as fast as my jellied knees could carry me. Behind us, Ilario's fight involved far too many swords at much too fast a pace. Around a bend and we could no long hear it. A few steps farther and soft whinnies welcomed us to the notch where our horses cropped the tough grass.

De Santo's gut was as pained as mine. He near broke my wrist when I would not allow him to send Ilario's mount back to the chevalier.

"If we send the beast down now, the others will know we've gone this way," I said. "We'll have wasted this time he's gifted us. If he survives, he knows where to find the beast. He'll need it, yes? And if the chevalier doesn't fetch his mount, we can collect it on the way back."

"Angels' wretched, cursed, shite-eating mercy," he said and hefted me onto Devil's back.

We rode until we emerged from the defile. Then de Santo led us afoot. Reaching deep into bone and fiber, I summoned him a light. Though he damned it as no better than a firefly's, we crept safely across the stinking bog and into the wood. As we emerged from the patch of dry pine onto the cliffs of Tark's Spine, the last of my power drained away. My light failed, and snow-laden gusts left de Santo as blind as me. On the point of collapse, we tethered the horses to a protruding branch and huddled in our cloaks to wait for day.

Neither the captain nor I slept more than fitful minutes at a time. It was too cold. Too dangerous. I could not stop shivering, no matter that I stuffed every morsel of food from my pack down my gullet. Fire could bring our pursuers down on us, and neither of us was fit to piss, much less fight. The cold froze out all thought save endless repetition of the night's strange happenings, rearranging themselves into random patterns.

"Shelf path's visible," announced the captain, on his feet and untangling our cloaks. "Snow's mostly blown off it and sun's peeking through. It'll be naught but wet before long. I'll look ahead."

While he was gone, the scenes I'd conjured in the restless hours snapped together like one of Queen Eugenie's puzzle pictures.

"So a dozen Temple servitors arrived while you were taking care of the eight attackers in the rift," I said, when he returned. "And they could *see*?"

He hawked and spat. "We thought you'd gave us the victory. Took down all eight. Then, aye, this same Temple rabble had chased us through Jarasco came running up the road. Some were blinded like the ones we'd fought. Some could see and demanded we turn you over."

"And then *arrows rained from the sky* and killed all but two of them. So there were three separate groups. The Temple servitors behind us, the eight fighters in the rift, and this 'broker' and his archers on the cliff tops." The latter had watched and waited outside the range of my enchantment. "Who were they? Did you get a look at the leader?"

"Don't know who they were—the ones in the rift or the ones up top. The leader was sturdy as a boar, skin blacker than my own. But neither the ones we killed nor the ones up top wore badges of any kind. One archer fell to his death, but four remained at the end, as my lord told you. The only Temple men left alive were the pair of laggards that ran off. The laggards thought the slaughter was your doing. I did, too, at first."

So those who had ambushed us weren't from the Temple. And common bandits would never bother travelers on the foot track into Coverge or possess incendiary devices to confuse us. But an entrapped enchantress who preyed on dreams might. One who could learn enough from those dreams to insert my own experiences and the faces of people I knew could surely send hirelings to fetch me when I didn't come to her by choice. . . .

"So we go on," said the captain, as I remained silent. "I am bound to you by Chevalier de Sylvae's orders."

The urgency that drove me toward Raghinne had the force of a cavalry charge. Yet a swelling certainty raised such a fear in me I hated to speak it, lest speech affirm it as truth. I squeezed Anne's nireal nestled in my pocket, its telltales of enchantment like warm feathers on my skin.

"No. I believe this attack part of a larger scheme—the same that brought me here. To understand it, I must go on to Raghinne. But you . . . you have to go back."

"The chevalier said I wasn't to leave you. Six year ago, he gave me a life. He and Duplais." The captain's graveled voice grated rougher than usual. His resentment could have lanced a boil. "And how will you piss on your own?"

No use to mince words. "The chevalier is dead or as good as. And yes, I do regret his sacrifice . . . and that it was made on my behalf. But hear this, Captain. Two months ago, three people I knew appeared in a spell-wrought dream. One lies dying in Raghinne. One was Duplais, who hides in Abidaijar, yet whom I've not heard from since that day. The third was Anne de Vernase. The damoselle is a woman of . . . extraordinary . . . gifts. I believe her to be in mortal danger, and I suspect Chevalier de Sylvae would agree that your most important duty this day is to protect her, no matter your rightful grudge against her father. You must ride for Montclaire, Captain. Tell her everything that's happened tonight. About the sky and the magic and the chevalier's deeds. Have her send to Pradoverde for my notes about the dream sending. They'll explain all I know. But she"—fear broke a cold sweat—"she must *not* go there herself. She must *not* try to find me. Take her to Merona, where the king's men can guard her. Tell her I said—" So many things I needed to tell her. "Tell her she must *focus*. I'll come to her when I can."

His silence near had me bellowing. But I waited.

Abruptly, he stuffed Devil's reins into my hand, then swung into his saddle. "No harm will come to the lady if I can do aught. The chevalier would die for her. And she's not to blame for her parentage."

"Exactly so. Ride, Captain. As if your honor depends on it. As if the world's survival depends on it." For no explainable reason, I believed it did. "The turning to the wagon road is exactly south of the larger pool in the bog meadow, between the hillocks. Watch your back always."

"Aye. And *God*speed yourself, mage."

CHAPTER 7

DEMESNE OF COVERGE

The hooves faded quickly from hearing. I hung Anne's pendant around my neck. First business, wall off my fears for her and Portier. I could do nothing more for them from here save learn what was to be learned. I promised Devil decent grazing soon, and let his warm and sturdy bulk calm me in return. Then, I drew my knife and carefully cut a few strands from his mane.

"You'll wait here for me, I trust," I said. Using my staff to make sure the shelf path was clear—and solid—I climbed a few metres farther along the track, around a bend where I could no longer hear the horse's movements. I was alone with a soughing wind, a squawking crow, and blackness. It was all I could do to keep my hand from the copper bracelet.

Crouching low to the ground, I felt about for a fist-sized rock and set it at arm's length. Arm outstretched, I spun slowly in place, using my finger to scribe a circle, complete when I found the rock again. A word of binding, and the enclosure settled about me like a blanket.

I grasped a fistful of dirt and drew in the keirna of my birthplace. No fear that it had changed since I'd lived there. I doubted it had changed in a thousand years. Coal, sweat, ignorance. Harsh winter, wet summer, cabbage soup. The annual visit from the mine stewards, dressed in finery Raghinne's women could only dream of—those who had any dreams remaining.

Using the horse's hair to incorporate Devil and his patience with a spooked novice, the dirt from the familiar ground, and the terror that had become a fixed part of me the night I knew de Gautier and Jacard had stolen the light forever, I wove a guide spell I hoped would get us to Raghinne. I'd be warned should the horse go astray. It helped that the road led nowhere else.

I retreated down the path and patted Devil's neck again. Then I felt around for a steady rock and stepped up to give myself a boost into the saddle. Awkward but sufficient.

"So it's just the two of us, beast." My voice quavered like that of a grave digger on Feste Morde. "On we go."

Devil moved forward at a slow walk. I tried to be firm and withhold the curses that stung my throat, all the while questioning the conviction that had caused me to travel this vile road, endangering two good men. As every hour passed, the fearful dream of death and ruin took on the shape of truth. Just to think what the Temple servitors had seen: their fellows blinded, two blood-soaked warriors, a half-mad sorcerer enveloped in a column of light, and a rain of arrows from the cliff tops. They would believe every rumor they'd ever heard about the daemon mage.

26 DESEN, EVENING

The road wound steeply for some twenty kilometres—an eternity—to the rocky summit of Tark's Spine before descending into the U-shaped valley where Raghinne lay. The horse's gait and the feel of the earth told me when we reached the valley floor—as did the burgeoning whispers in my head. People were scattered throughout this region.

With a great release, I leaned forward onto the horse's neck. "We've done it, Devil. Gods' holy hammer, you've brought me safe. I'll tell your mistress she picked a fine beast. Apples and oats all winter, I swear to you."

So much to tell Anne when I rejoined her. I'd refused to fall into casual conversation with her these two years. I could not be her friend. She was never going to acquire the discipline she needed or to see the world in any true perspective if she held on to her womanish imaginings about her *friend of the mind*, as she had called me. But gods, those night hours we had talked had been so very fine. *Swift roads, Calvino de Santo. And you, too, popinjay.* Then I summoned discipline to bind my fear and focused my attention outward. I had no idea what to expect in Raghinne. A second trap, perhaps . . .

A LEFT TURN. A PINE-SCENTED breeze that replaced the unremitting wind of the heights. Weak sunlight played on my left flank. Even without eyes, I knew exactly where I was.

The outcropping boulders to my right had been a wonderful place for a child to play—rocks and caves that became fortifications or ships or palaces. Andero and I had called it "the fortress." Laughable, our notion of a palace in those days: a house with two rooms or three, a whole bed for each person, a chimney, a privy inside.

"Dante the necromancer raising ghosts again," I murmured to Devil. Prideful to think my coming might have meaning for Andero. He was most likely an image of my father by now.

"Dante?" As if the earth had heard my whispered word, my name echoed from the outcrop in a timbre wholly appropriate to a slab of granite. Sure-footed steps and skittering pebbles testified to a human person's presence.

I reined in, released the guide spell, and poured magic into the copper bracelet, squinting up at the boulders. Of all times, I needed to see.

The rocks were not so high as I remembered. Atop them a bulky silhouette, more than two metres high, moved against the charcoal-hued world. A man, not a rock.

"Andero?"

"It *is* you, then!" He leapt across several great rocks until he was almost on a level with me.

"What are you doing here?" I said, averting my eyes. "Playing in the fortress?"

"Waiting for you. Gave you a sevenday, then started watching. I can spy Harrow's Drop from the forge. Knew you'd come."

"Then you know me better than I know myself. A half hour since, I wasn't sure I'd keep on."

A solid thud. My brother's boots crunched on the gravel as he came round Devil's head. "Spirits and demons, Dante. You look like the Souleater's cousin. What's happened to you?"

Though Anne had told me the yellow-orange streaks in my eyes were no longer visible, I kept my face turned away. "More than a moment's telling."

"I'll make sure we've more than a moment, then. And the mage collar . . . I heard about it when I was hunting word of you, but to see it on you . . . so big . . . sealed forever."

"Proper like a beast's," I snapped.

"Don't mean to stare." He didn't quail. "Glimpsed 'em when I was in the legion, of course. But never so close. Never on someone I knew."

Of course he'd wonder. Everyone did. "It's light. Doesn't hurt. Itches sometimes, as if the masters who fixed it on me left a burr in it apurpose, you know. They didn't like me. No surprise that, eh?"

His laughter rumbled the earth. "Not a smat, little brother! Not a smat! Come, let's share a stoup. No rush to face the lion."

"He's not dead yet? He can talk?" I'd explode a mountain if I'd come all this way only to find Da unable to answer my questions.

"Aye. He lives. Just asleep."

Sagging in relief, I thanked Devil with a pat and bade Ilario and de Santo Godspeed yet again.

My brother grabbed Devil's bridle and, without further discussion, led us down the track into the village.

An advantage of my state: I didn't have to look on the black-dusted blight of a valley that must once have been fair and green. I'd spent a number of days in my youth imagining Raghinne scoured of rock dumps and ash heaps, iron carts, timber slabs, jacks, frames, and the pocked ugliness of abandoned pits, shafts, and spoil heaps. It shivered me a little to think I now had the power to cleanse it. But the place would remain a blackened scar. No sorcerer had power enough to restore what had been destroyed.

"We've a real hostel now," said Andero, as he led Devil into a hay-scented shelter. "Only one room over Grev's house and the common room in the front, but he has this horse shed, a bit of grass out the back, and the best cider in Raghinne. His wife makes a fine douple and a decent pie if you're hungry, but her fish tastes like old boots. Do you remember Grev Tey? It's his place."

"Never knew him."

"Let me fetch his boy to see to this fine fellow." He smoothed Devil's shoulder.

Dismounted, I yet held tight to the saddle. My legs were porridge.

Partly from the long, terrifying ride. But also because I was pouring every smat of my power into the copper bracelet. To walk this road a cripple would be unbearable.

Andero returned with a boy who grunted with a sullen air and took charge of Devil. "Come on, then," said my brother. "Ale or cider?"

"Cider." Gritting my teeth, I clutched my staff and followed his bulky shadow across a yard that slurped at my boots. Up two steps and through a gaping doorway. So far, so good.

The place smelled as any common room—of cider, ale, smoke, and charred fat, laced with mud and sweat. But this was Raghinne, so the smoke stank of sulfur and every surface was gritty with cinders.

Andero left me at a plank table and returned a short time later, thumping a heavy cup in front of me. "Grev will bring you supper. You look all in."

As my brother took the stool across from me, I tried with all I had to see what manhood had written on his face. His youthful mien had been broad, fair, and open. My time here might depend on the change. But it was no good. I thanked him for the stoup, drank deep of the thin, biting cider, and fixed my gaze on the slab of night that was the table. With a touch of the copper bracelet and a whispered word, I was blind again.

"Are you all right, little brother?"

"It's a harder trek than I remembered," I said. "So tell me, how is it with all of you?"

"Da's for the Souleater at any hour. Burnt awful. Lungs ruint. Healer says there's not enough left to mend. Sheer meanness keeps him this side the Veil." He sighed. "It'll be a relief for Mam when he's done. He's not mellowed these past years and was a raving loony in the days before the blowout."

I held off questions about the dreams. Better to learn what I faced between here and Da's bedside. "What of the others?"

"Marta and Naina stayed. Marta feeds herself by sewing. Does my laundry and such. Looks to stay a spinster. Too hard to get along with anymore is my thinking. Naina married Lecue's boy Frigo, and they've six brats already. Not a smat of wit in the lot. Jalene married a turnip digger down Jarasco side when she turned fifteen and's never come back. I sent to her, but she doesn't read and won't ask. Wouldn't come anyway. Da gave her a rumpus about the marriage, and she's no more forgiving than him."

No surprises there. "And our brothers?"

"Renit boodled for a while, too lazy to lay hands or mind to aught but a shovel. Ran off in a bother a year or so after I came home. Couple of men said he was dead did he come back but wouldn't say why. Bandits. Gambling. Something like. Benno grew up bigger than me. He smiths at Corflet pits. Married into it but got a bad bargain, I say—Letitia makes Marta look like a sweet cake. Some happy family, eh?"

"And what of Andero?"

"Andero is as he always was," he said after a long pull at his stoup. "Works the forge. Plods along day to day, never quite figuring out where he wants to be or what he wants to do, so he lags till summat better comes along."

Everyone in Raghinne had been astonished when Andero ran away to war. He was big and quiet and moved slowly for the most part. But I had wrestled him enough to know the danger of assuming him either gentle or lazy.

Quick footsteps brought a steaming dish to the table in front of me. It smelled of fennel and bay. A ladle slopped the contents into a smaller bowl and plopped a fat chunk of bread atop it. I knew how things were done here.

"Douple, lord . . . great master. Though for a refined palate mutton pie might suit better, or a nice dock salat before winter sets in?" His whining set my teeth grinding.

"Naught else, Grev," said Andero, quickly. "If you'll excuse us, we've business."

"Certain, Andero. Certain." The hostler withdrew.

This time of year, douple would include beans, turnips, carrots, barley, onions, and mutton fat, and if times were good, scraps of meat. By spring it would be turnips and grass. I scooped a healthy dollop on the bread and forced it down.

Decent for what it was. Filling at the least. Though even Queen Eugenie's rarest fruits would be unappealing at present, I needed the sustenance.

Honoring custom, Andero let me eat undisturbed, sipping at his cider and refilling mine as I emptied it. Other people drifted in and out, naught but shuffles and whispers. No one would dare interrupt us. No Covergan liked strangers. We ignored them, as if refusing to acknowledge such untrusty folk might make them go away. But for sure from this day forward Andero would be besieged with insults, prods, and challenges, all aimed at discovering the identity of his visitor with the silver collar. I doubted a mage had ever visited Raghinne.

"So you boss the smithy now?" I said, when I'd eaten all I could stomach.

"So it is. Da thinks he does, of course, but even before the accident his hands weren't steady enough to finish things proper."

"You didn't find soldiering better than being here?"

"I stayed out near ten years. But enough was enough. Didn't mind the fighting or living rough. It was the bossing around I couldn't abide. Too much like a barrelful of Das, always telling me to sleep here, oil that armor, stick that fellow, run away from that one. I figured I'd come home and put up with just the one bully."

His tale couldn't but revive thoughts of Masson de Cuvier and his "boys," who never loved him, but stayed alive, save in his dreams. I was glad Andero had stayed alive.

"And is there a Sonjeura Andero?"

"Not for want of looking." He shoved the douple bowl out from between us. "Now, what of you, little brother? A few years ago I took some knives down to Jarasco market. A couple of traders told me outlandish tales of upheaval in Merona. And in the same breath as *the King of Sabria*, *haunts*, and *villainy*, here comes the name *Dante*—a master mage hobnobbing with royals or the Souleater, depending on who was tale spinning. God's truth, I knew it was you."

He paused for a moment, his curiosity dangling. I didn't bite.

"When I decided to send to you about Da, I hiked down there again. Some Jarasco folk said the daemon mage was exiled. Some said in Ixtador. Others said in the ice caves of Gedevron, joined up with Dimios himself. I suppose the tales were wrong, as my writing got to you after all."

"I don't live at Castelle Escalon anymore. They forwarded your letter on to me."

"Out of favor, are you? In disgrace or something? It's nowt by me, you know. I figured I knew you better than those telling the stories." He was almost apologetic—but I detected no fear. Considering what *outlandish tales* he'd likely heard, that was amazing.

"I was never *in favor* so much as *useful* to people of importance. And now that use is done and they prefer me elsewhere. But I reside neither in the netherworld nor in Ixtador. Not yet at least." I swallowed the last of the cider, and he refilled the stoup yet again. "Not many know me well."

He laughed—a full, honest laugh from his gut. "Now, that's summat I can believe."

It was much easier to talk to him than I'd expected.

He leaned so far across the table, I could smell the iron and coal soot on him. "Marta told me about the spill at the forge," he said, his voice fallen almost to a whisper. "Was it as bad as they say? Where did you go after?"

I yanked off my right glove and laid my claw on the table.

"Glory, Dante!"

"I'm used to it now. But I wasn't then. I went off looking for a healer."

"But it was too late."

"Aye, for my hand. Instead, I found a teacher. . . ."

I told him all of it. About the voices and the aether. About fat, illiterate Salvator with rotted teeth and a gift for teaching, and my odd schooling in the ways of sorcery. And while whispering patrons came and went, I told my brother of my bargain with Portier and the King of Sabria, and the long years of deception, and the voice in the aether that had given me a lifeline to sanity. I even relived for him the terrible climax of the Gautier conspiracy and the years since. Not even Anne or Portier knew the whole story. Stupid to be so free. This man was a stranger to me.

"Bones of the earth, if anyone else in the world had told me such a tale, I would have thrown him down a void shaft as a raver."

"Didn't mean to wear out your ears." My own likely glowed like a forge bed. "It's not like me."

"We all have to shovel out the ashes sometime, but some things don't bear talking about with people you're with every day. And we were all right once, you and me. A time or two these past years, I'd have given a trunkload of silver for *your* ear to fill. You could always figure things out, explain things in a way a person could grasp. But god's truth, tonight you've flummoxed me entire. To know you're blinded, and in such a way, I can scarce believe it."

"Comes the time for me to piss away all this cider, you'll know it."

"Aye, that would be a difficulty," he said. "So will you come home with me, little brother? I'll stand for Grev's room upstairs if you'd rather; he owes me for fixing a broken axle."

"I'll not sleep under Da's roof."

"Nor will I," he said. "I've my own place out past the bog. No palace, but two whole rooms all to myself. It's fortunate the way you are; you'll not be able to criticize my housekeeping nor tell if my bedding's not so clean."

I ought to sleep out, on the chance the broker's remaining swordsmen or the daemon-crushing tetrarch came after me. Yet I'd neither felt nor heard any hint of pursuit through the day. Perhaps Ilario had taken them all out. De Santo had implied that the chevalier was a master swordsman. I shook my head and again wished the two of them safe. Truly, the prospect of a bed ranked near the prospect of Heaven. Nearer, as I'd a hope of the bed.

"I'll share your house, brother," I said, "but not your pallet." Which caused Andero to explode in laughter yet again. Years ago he'd managed to get himself a pallet of his own by squashing younger brothers and sleeping through our pinches and whining.

Grev Tey snored loudly in the corner. The whisperers had given up hours before. Still chuckling, Andero jingled a few coins, bringing the snoring to an abrupt end.

"On the morrow, Andero," said the hostler thickly. "On the morrow, lord mage, may the Creator's light shine upon your path."

I snorted at that most unlikely of all prospects.

ANDERO HAD BUILT HIS COTTAGE tucked into a hillside at the near end of the village, about as far from the coal pits and the forge as one could be. Leaving Devil at the stable, we walked companionably down the cinder path. Our frosty breath dampened my skin. No one else was about so late. My brother was easy to follow. Our gaits were similar and he was a very large presence. I asked him just to walk a little ahead on my right and yell if I strayed toward the stinking bog. He laughed more easily than anyone I'd ever met.

"You know what's the most astounding, Dante?" he said, as we left the bog behind. "To think of you, as good as married to the daughter of a conte—"

"Married? Gods, you can swallow that one entire. She's the King of Sabria's gooddaughter. She's read more books than I've seen in my life, has traveled all of the Middle Kingdoms, and speaks something like nine foreign tongues. She dances, curtsies, and dresses in silk. They cleaned me up for my playacting, taught me about forks and how to use an indoor privy. But I am and will ever be a blind, half-mad, vile-tempered son of Coverge, who happens to have a decent talent for spellwork and will likely die in a cage. Now she's away from me, she'll realize what nonsense she's spewed."

Reflections, she'd said. Our souls were mirrors. What did that even mean?

"Anne killed two men to defend her family, her king, and the safety of the world, yet she will never in this life forgive herself for it. I once broke a man's neck because I was hungry, and drove two more to kill themselves because they wronged my teacher. I've cracked minds, Andero, and battered a man half to death to convince my only friend I had turned against him. Never once did I feel guilty. Every hour, every day of my life, I have to hold back this daemonish temper before I murder someone else for crossing me." Anne de Vernase and I were not *mirrored souls*. "Anne sleeps in the main house. I sleep in the guesthouse. She raises grapes. I raise the dead."

"Hmmph," he said, pondering. "I suppose I'd have to meet the lady to understand, which meeting would likely do your prospects no good at all. But truly, Dante, an indoor privy? Sacred spirits, you *did* live in a palace!"

He burst out laughing—and I laughed with him, though it came out creaking like a rusty gate. Not at all what I expected from my journey home.

CHAPTER 8

RAGHINNE

The unexpected harmony of the evening changed nothing about a morning's waking. As I had chosen a pallet next Andero's delicious hearth, rather than his bed in the cold second room, he witnessed my daily panic as he drank his morning ale. I hated that.

"Hadn't thought it would be so bad for you," he said, from his kitchen table, "with your magic and all. You seemed so matter-of-fact about it."

"I'm fine," I snapped.

"So you are. There's hot water on the hob, cups and Marta's best herbs on the shelf to the left of it. New bread's under a towel on the table and butter beside. I've got to feed my dogs, so I'll leave you to it. When you've done, we'll head for the forge."

My brother was a far more graceful man than I. . . .

"Oh, and you can piss in the yard, if you'll aim to the right, or there's a jar just round the corner in my sleeping room. Anything more, the privy's out the back door; head directly right for about fifty paces. I showed you last night, but I've a mind you were too nogged to recall it."

And direct.

After many false starts I did what was needed. Andero returned about the time I finished my tea. "Didn't like my bread, eh?"

"Not hungry." Indeed I was like to burst my skin with the need to get this done.

I had dabbled in mental compulsion through the years, using the sheer weight of power to impose my will upon other minds. But I had found success only when the person was already open to my desire—a child or a slobbering drunkard. I had nudged Portier once or twice early on, but he had detected it and resisted. That's when I knew he had more substance than I'd suspected.

That this enchantress had planted answers with the last person I could ever wish to confront, here in the last place I could ever wish to go, spoke of tremendous power for magic, heating my natural fever to understand. Intellect told me that the trap in the defile was her true objective. For whatever reason, she wanted me. Yet my every sinew was wound tight with certainty that my father's words would reveal some evidence of immense importance. I could no more have left Raghinne without hearing him than I could have slit my own throat.

It was mostly women's voices that greeted Andero as we tramped through the village. One asked if he'd thought to bring in a healer to look after our father. Another speculated that Andero might be planning to send the old devil to his grave cursed. Only one inquired if he'd sent for the rest of his brothers and sisters. None of them acknowledged me directly. That suited me very well.

"Da's a mind of his own how and when to die," Andero told them. "And he's settling his own accounts with the divinities; neither prayers nor cursing from me will change it."

No clank of hammer, no roaring fire or heaving bellows marred the quiet at the far end of the village road. The mingled odors of hot iron, coal, mules, and boiling cabbage that had forever bespoke my birthplace had been lost in an overpowering, throat-clogging stench of charred timber. A touch of my copper bracelet revealed the shadowed rooflines of ramshackle sheds and buildings, clustered against a swale of earth, rock, and mine spoil.

"So the forge yet stands?" I said.

"Not that a strong wind or a hard kick would heed. We lost the roof and three walls in the fire, as well as the stock sheds. I've got flimsy walls up and a few roof timbers set. If the weather holds a bit longer, I might get it closed up before the snow piles. But I couldn't let the paying work lag. If I thought I could bribe you to bide a while, I'd do it. Likely your one hand is better than most around here."

"I'm far more trouble than worth." And I'd rather be prisoned in a sorcerer's hole than trapped in Raghinne again.

My father's house stood some twenty metres from the smithy. The oak that separated them yet grew there, the only living thing in a close of gravel and iron.

"Hey, Mam!" yelled Andero, as our boots crunched across the rutted yard. He halted by the tree. Village manners forbade a closer approach without invitation, even for family. "Come see who's here to watch with us."

"I'm out the back, washing." Her voice was frail and querulous. "Can't keep the quilts clean."

I could envision my mother old no more than I could envision her young, though in my years at home she'd been scarce past thirty—my own age. I recalled her as forever gray and bony, forever tired, and forever of one mind with my father. Truly, I'd never really considered her a separate being.

"Is't Jalene come?" Hope livened her question as her dragging steps rounded the corner of the house. The stink of bitter soap identified her, accompanied as ever with the spiked scent of the angelica root she used for every conceivable purpose.

"No," I answered, before Andero could.

"Who then? Benno's never—?" Her steps halted. "By the Souleater's true name, why are *you* here?" I'd not expected welcome, yet neither did I expect hatred that dripped from her like etching acid.

Andero stepped forward. "I summoned him. It's time all's made up among us."

"'Twas too late for this one long ago. Dasn't you know what he's become and what he always were? Just look at him! Even the daemons are feared of him."

"I know what's said in Jarasco, but I also know what's true and what's not."

"I'll not have him here!" she spat. "This witching is his filthy doings."

"Well, well, has our runaway lamb come home? Did you think there would be an inheritance to share?" The flat, hard voice was unmistakably my sister Marta's. Somehow the third of our seven had sneaked up behind me.

I refused to startle. One show of weakness and Marta's jibes would draw blood.

"So you've found naught to do with your mind but hone your tongue?"

I said. "Or did they finally convince you that intelligence was the Souleater's mark?" I'd once found Marta peering curiously into my books, but my offer to teach her to read them had been rebuffed with curses.

"I live humbly in the ways of my forefathers," she said, not at all humbly. "I serve and I labor and need naught of a daemon's allurements. All know the Souleater's mark is pride. When the angels flay you on the last day, it will make the sight all the more pleasurable to watch."

The sentiments didn't sound like Marta, who had forever chafed at Coverge's strict and gloomy interpretations of Temple teaching. Did her face reveal a rebellion her words denied?

"Trouble not, sister mine and loving mother," I said. "I'll speak to my father before he dies. Then I'll depart, and threaten your souls no more."

"Never," said my mother. "You'll not set foot—"

"'Tis not yours to say, neither of you," said Andero. "Da's asked for him, and he's not come all this way just to leave again. He lies in their bed, Dante, where it always was. On your way in, you can admire my fine new latch."

Warned by his hint, I fingered the bar-and-hoop latch rather than reaching for the old handle. It was surely the height of vanity to hide my incapacity from these people. My belly churning—an entirely nonsensical relic of childhood—I shut the door firmly behind me.

The stench near drove me straight out again. Charred, putrid flesh. Billowing smoke from the firepit. The bitter soap, ash water, and boiled herbs my mother swore by for healing, purification, and every other practice of ignorance and superstition—odors that would forever reignite the agony of my ruined hand.

But I had come here to learn. I had gambled lives and safety because I believed this was not merely a personal journey, but something larger.

Ten steps to the loft ladder. Five more to the curtained niche where the seven of us were begotten in wordless rutting. The curtain was open. My father's breathing ground like a slurry of crushed rock.

I kicked aside the stool I knew would be next the bed. Nothing would have changed. "Da."

The labored heaving stilled. "Benno?" His croaking whisper bubbled and wheezed. "Renit?"

"Neither." Returned to the demesne of my long silence, I could scarce force words from my mouth.

He cleared his throat painfully. "If they'd open the shutters, I could see ye."

"You've another son."

"Dante?" Though his fingers could yet pinch to the bone, I no longer flinched from his grasp. "Come to gloat, have ye? Come to taunt?"

"Why would I?"

"Ye've no care for your kin."

"And so I do not. I'll not lie and say elsewise."

"Aagh, prideful still. 'Tis thy daemon nature. Tha'rt Fallen, Dante. Darkborn in frost-cold blood. Suckled on pain. Thy repentance was ever a lie."

"My *repentance*? On the day you half killed me? I was fourteen!"

"Had to beat the evil out of ye. As I tried when ye were a nub."

"So you knew all along my claims were true."

"Expected it. Spawn of sin and devilry. Come the last day of the world, the Souleater will flay thee naked and prison thee in ice. But here—" He coughed, struggling for breath, his bruising grip drawing me close. His breath stank of putrefaction and his fever near scorched me. "Tha'rt shifty, Dante . . . cruel. I shaped the chain as I was told: the setting of silver wire drawn fine as hair, each night a new link from pure silver, each night the sigil graved on it, fine and perfect—"

"A chain? I've come to hear of your dream and the angel who had a message for me."

"Aye." His voice was naught but a throaty whisper. "She said ye'd come did I send to thee. Who could deny her? Never saw such a creature. She said forging the chain to prison thee would ensure my soul's passage through Ixtador. And in each dream another sigil appeared, writ in green fire, that I must grave on the links. But the dreams stopped before she told *how* to bind thee, before even the full length of the chain was done. I feared I had angered her. Drabbing fool. Couldn't think straight. Couldn't sleep. At the end, I decided to melt down the last link and rework it, lest I'd fashioned it wrong, but that's when the silver grew like a fungus and boiled and spewed fire. And then, lying here in death's maw, I weened what had transpired."

I scrambled to make sense of what he told. Spawn of sin? A chain to bind me? Iron links could mangle any spellwork, inhibiting a sorcerer. But silver wouldn't, unless the sigils . . . Could the enchantress send *spells* through dreams, too? That fit with nothing I understood of magic.

Da yanked me closer, as if every smat of bile he had left gave strength to his arm. "Ye vanquished her, didn't ye? The madness . . . the boiling silver . . . the fire . . . this be *thy* vengeance, because I wet the mold and maimed thee with the mark of the Fallen. But hear this, daemon: thy hate has undone thee anyways. She said I'd given her time to fetch your false saint from his hiding place and bury him where you'll never find him. The chain may not be finished, but the dream showed me what is to be."

Coughing scoured his lungs, leaving him gasping. His hand fell away.

"What?" I shook him hard enough to rattle his teeth. "What did you see?"

"I looked into the great emerald and saw him—the Righteous Defender, the fairest of all beings immortal or mortal. He will take you down, Daemon. You are bound to him, Fallen to angel, as was ever the Creator's plan. So say the prophets: *And so will come the last battle of the War for Heaven and guardianship of the Living Realm, when the Righteous Defender will rise from the ashes and battle the Daemon.* He waits for you."

My father's chortling dissolved into wet gurgling, hawking, choking. A warm flood spewed from his mouth over my hand. Blood. And so was the frenzy triggered by my brother's letter, the mania that had resulted in twenty dead, answered, only to be replaced by horror.

I backed away from my father's bed. It was not Temple myths of heavenly wars that wrenched my gut, and certainly not my father's appraisal of my soul's allegiance. I'd heard such tales and accusations since infancy. But the "false saint" could be none but Portier.

De Gautier had believed the incessant dying and return of a reborn saint—Portier—could preserve the opening in the Eternal Veil so that the living and dead could be exchanged at our pleasure. Anne and I had kept Portier from drowning at Mont Voilline, her power enabling me to draw him back to life whenever I lost him. But now this enchantress planned to bury him living . . . and we weren't there to preserve him . . . because I had let Anne go . . . because I had allowed myself to be lured to this vile man's bedside with the one thing I could not resist—a mystery bound in magic. She had driven me four hundred kilometres in the wrong direction so I could not save Portier.

"Begone, daemon!" My mother and sister crowded between me and the bed.

Nausea overwhelmed me. I stumbled backward. *Find the door; find the latch; breathe.*

I burst through the door and across the frigid yard until I could embrace the scratchy bulk of the great oak.

Stupid, arrogant, weak-minded fool of a sorcerer. A diversion. A trap. Portier, my only friend in this blighted world . . . buried alive. Those two words told me that this was not about some Kadr spelltrap in the desert, but my worst fears realized. This was all about rending the Veil. About Ixtador. About leaching the souls of the dead. This was about the remnants of conspiracy—and very likely about Jacard de Viole. Jacard was the surviving member of the de Gautier inner circle, those who knew of Kajetan's contention that Portier could not die and how that might be used in rites that could violate the order of nature. Kajetan had known of Masson de Cuvier's dream, and Jacard had Kajetan's books and papers. And no matter his magical incompetence, Jacard knew that I would never allow Portier to be taken so he could start up the wickedness again. Then came the next question. . . . Jacard knew Anne had killed his uncle, but did he have any idea of her magic?

"No!" Thunder exploded from my ancille.

I dropped the staff lest I slaughter the next person to draw close. Roaring, I grasped the nearest branch of the oak, wrenching and twisting as if I could tear it from the bole and stuff it down the devil woman's throat. When it failed to loosen, I sagged against the tree, my forehead pressed to the rough bark. "Wretched, god-blasted, everlasting night . . ."

A great hand clamped my aching shoulder. "I'm glad to find you still here. Thought for a moment we might lose you and Da both."

"Don't touch me!"

Even as I yelled and whirled on him, I trapped my hands under my arms. Madmen . . . both of us. I could easily have broken his arm. And yet . . .

"I must leave here," I said, scarce able to control my frenzy. "This was all a mistake, a fool's errand to take me away from my responsibilities. Portier, the friend I told you of, the librarian, is in dreadful danger, and I need to get to him. Find him. Save him . . ."

Every nightmare of my life rose to haunt me. Long before de Gautier and Jacard's vengeance, long before I understood what happened to unlucky miners, the dark had terrified me. In our crowded loft, I had pinched and bullied my younger brothers for the space nearest the wall, so I could breathe the air through the seams in the logs and glimpse the light of moon or stars. My first visit to the coal pits had left me screaming, earning my first beating and my father's everlasting scorn. Darkness. Suffocation.

". . . and Anne. These people who tried to capture me might aim for her, too. Please, brother, you've got to help me." Pride, the glue I had created to hold myself together since leaving this place, lay in shreds.

The Temple pursuit was only a nuisance. It was these others I had to fear. If Ilario had left any of the last four attackers standing, they'd be waiting along the foot track. Perhaps they had fellows on the wagon road, too. They could be lurking in the village already. No one in Raghinne mentioned strangers.

I summoned reason, reexamining theories formed in panic. "They know I'll go after Portier. I've power enough to defeat them, but . . ." Not without aid. Not anymore. If I was isolated . . . helpless . . . they could take me. "I don't think they want me dead. They want me alone."

"Here, pick up your stick—I'm not fool enough to touch it—and let's walk," said Andero, taking a firm hold on my arm and shoulder. Though his voice exuded a calm wholly at odds with my ragged wildness, his touch demonstrated a fierce urgency. "While you were inside, I spied riders descending Harrow's Drop. We've perhaps two hours till they're here. And by now, none from Raghinne is going to mistake who you are or where to find you."

My sweat congealed. "Then I need—"

"I've ears and a mind, Dante. You need to get away fast and secret, and it sorely wears on you to manage it all yourself. So I'll take you through the Sweats; I've always had a fondness for them. None here will imagine we'd go that way. But I've a task or two to do before I can— Now, hold your fidgeting. 'Twould be a fool that set out from Raghinne in Desen's month without provision, and I'll not leave my dogs to starve."

"But no one—"

"None will know but that we've gone to choose which pit to throw Da in when he crosses. So we're taking a stroll out the spoils, and I'm going to leave you stewing for a bit. We've time. A stranger's got to learn our ways ere he'll get much of an answer, even about such a fright as you."

He forced me to a reasonable pace. A bitter wind nipped my cheeks and cut through my jerkin and shirt like honed steel through paper. I'd left my heavy cloak and gloves next Andero's hearth. One night in the mountains without and I'd be frozen sure, ready for the Souleater's flaying.

HALF AN HOUR . . . AN HOUR . . . half a day . . . I'd no means to judge how long I sat amid Raghinne's spoil heaps, trapped in a wasteland pocked with dangers. How stupid I was to trust a man I'd not seen since childhood. He could be leaving me out here to stew while charging my pursuers a pretty price to bring them down on my head. Or was it merely a reflection of my own villainy that I could not believe Andero the genial, stalwart man he seemed? Maddening to know that my odds of survival were no worse to wait for his treachery than to take out on my own.

Muffled hoofbeats and a single pair of boots, too light for Andero, drew me to my feet, my finger on my staff's crescent sigil.

"This is no simple *poulon*," I said, softly, lest someone mistake my ancille for a fighting staff. I angled its head toward the newcomer and fed power into the waiting spell. "Identify yourself."

"I've heard the Souleater devours the flesh in exchange for his favored gifts. First the hand, then the eyes. It looks as if he gnaws the very flesh from your bones." Marta's voice snapped like a hot chestnut in the cold air, not at all humble. "He must have gifted you fairly."

"What do you want?"

A few more steps, hers and a horse's. A bony hand, as rough and cold as the ice crowns on Tark's Spine, thrust reins into my hand. With a gentle whuffle, Devil nosed my neck and pockets, his warm breath enveloping me.

"I've provisioned your steed and brought him as I was asked. None heeds the smith's spinster daughter. Now, get thee gone, and leave Andero out of your schemes. He's kind, and—" Her steel-edged voice near cracked.

With six of us run off or married, Marta would have borne the brunt of my parents' abusive attention all these years. Until Andero's return.

"Perhaps you should run, too," I said.

"I wouldn't whore for Da," she said, emotions tucked away behind her bitter wall. "Why would I whore in unfamiliar streets?"

Bile stung my throat. Of course Da would have tried to rent her. With only two of seven respectably married, he would have craved better surety for his failing years. Whoring a daughter paid almost as well as a son's labor or a husband's tithe. If she had defied him, he would have whipped her publicly, ensuring no man would ever take her to wife. She'd whore or starve. But Andero had come home and given her a choice.

"You might find something other to do with yourself in the world." But likely not, unless . . . "Do you—? Does Mam—? Da said something about beating the evil out of her. Have either of you some talent for magic?"

She hissed scorn. "Once when she was drunk, Mam told me she'd heard that the daemon Panthia would trade magic for a child born in the dark. So Mam birthed each of us in Grymouth Caves. Her firstborn she left down in the cave, believing Panthia would take her. The babe starved, of course. The second, Mam cut and held until he died. Still Panthia did not come with her gift. When Andero was born, Mam offered his blood and her milk to summon the daemon. But Panthia still did not come, and she took Andero home, and so on with each of us seven. When you showed daemon signs as a babe—talking to people who weren't there, altering small things when you screamed—the hope rose in her. She would leave you in the caves alone for days, telling Da her milk was slow and you needed wet-nursing. But the daemon never took you. Mam hated you for that. When you were older and held yourself above the rest of us, I watched Mam try charm setting till Da beat her will away entire. I tried, too. Every day. Every night. But there's naught of magic in our family's blood save what the Souleater has gifted you. Send Andero back whole or I'll sell my own soul to lay a death curse on thee."

"Marta—" As so often, words failed. I could neither remedy such ignorance nor reconcile such sorrow, save by leaving. But I shifted my fingers on the ancille and called up a small spell I'd worked in the long years of my double life, little more than an illusion of a lighthouse on a stormy coast. I could no longer see the gray-green sea or the lighthouse with its fiery beacon, but even here surrounded by Raghinne's misery, I could smell the salt air I conjured and hear the faint cries of gulls and the crash of waves. In the days before I'd heard Anne's voice in the aether, the illusion had reminded me of a world that was not solely death and turmoil.

My sister's quick inhalation . . . a held breath . . . told me she experienced the illusion.

"Get out of this place," I said as I let it fade. "There is life beyond what we were born to."

"Daemon . . ."

"I am just a man with skills. Daemons cannot create beauty." Of all things, I knew the vision beautiful.

She spat at my feet. "Whyever not? Dimios himself is said to be the fairest of the Creator's works, and he knows exactly the cruelest torments, the vilest temptations to lay before a human soul. By the name of the Creator Spirit I bid thee go from here, Fallen. Take no one and nothing, and never darken this vale again."

Born in a cave. I might have known.

CHAPTER 9

RAGHINNE

"Spirits' blood, Dante, I told you to wait for me." Andero forced Devil and me to halt, as I crept through the interminable spoil heaps toward the narrow end of the valley. "Are you loony?"

With Devil's lead wrapped about my dead hand, I had used my staff to feel out each step and my seeing spell to judge the shape of the landscape. I knew I needed to go *up*. Meanwhile I'd racked my mind to recall everything I could about the Sweats, a rugged, stepped plateau of scalding mud pits that lay beyond.

"You sent the horse and provisions. It was idiocy for me to wait longer." So I had convinced myself after Marta's dismissal. "Magic will take me through."

I doubted a voice that shook as much as mine could convince a rabbit to hop. Twice, I'd come a step from falling into an open pit shaft—only instinct warning me of the waiting void. Whether it would be worse to starve in an abandoned bell pit or be instantly consumed in a sink of boiling mud, I'd not yet decided. After hearing details of my infancy, either end seemed fitting.

"Told you I had to pawn off my dogs. And I heeded Marta's suggesting to down a stoup at Grev Tey's before I left. I grumbled at considerable length about a man too iron-headed to die when he ought, and terrifying brothers come back from the dead to fright the old buzzard. I warned those who listened not to repeat my story of your abrupt departure, flying on batwings to the north, lest a chase of daemons come ravaging in the night and boodle Raghinne into its own pits. A good story, I must say. I doubt a tongue will flap or a door will open for a tennight."

He took Devil's lead rope, curled my dead fingers about a stirrup, and led us forward at a brisker pace. "You've only wandered half a kilometre out of the way. We'll make it through the Sweats by dusk. I doubt the fellows coming down the Spine will figure it out."

Resolution crumbled. I didn't tell him to go back. I didn't tell him he had matters in Raghinne to deal with. My urgent fears for Portier and Anne were undeniable, but, in raw and humiliating truth, I simply had never been so grateful for a companion.

Even so, I dared not leave one matter unaddressed. "Da said he was working on a silver chain before the accident. Did you see it? Did it survive the fire?"

"Fire was hot as Dimios's forge, little brother. Naught was left inside but ash and a mound of debt to pay for it. He said he'd got a proposition that would make him rich beyond imagining. He used every kivre he had, sold half his tools, and pledged our work to the steward for a year to buy forty slugs of silver. I'd seen no customer, nor could I find anyone who knew what he was up to. And though I nagged him about it, he kept his work hid, doing it all in the night after I'd gone home. So what did the devil say that set you off in such a pother?"

I recounted Da's rant as near word for word as I could recall it, as much to imprint it on my memory as anything. When I got to my father's presumption that I had confounded his dreams to spite him, my brother halted so suddenly as to startle Devil, whose buck near yanked my right arm from its socket.

"He wet the mold? Burnt his own boy apurpose?" Andero hawked and spat. "Saints blight his soul forever! I'd have broke his neck had I known it. You never hurt none with your oddment. Always carried your share of the work."

He couldn't understand, of course. I couldn't loathe my father any more than I did already.

"What's done is done." I kept my voice level and stroked Devil's neck. "It's the rest of it that's important. These people are going to bury a man alive because they think he's a being who cannot die. They believe it will give them power over life and death."

"Night's balls. Is that possible?"

"Possibility doesn't matter as long as they believe it. The conspiracy we believed thwarted two years ago could be raising its head again, but this time it's all bound up with this angel woman and the dream." Which I desperately needed to understand better.

With Devil settled, we took out again. Though the ground was increasingly steep and rough, we quickly established a comfortable rhythm. Andero assured me we were not followed. Walking in the cold air was good. I needed to think clearly.

"I'm doubting she was an angel," Andero offered.

"No," I said. "No angel. I'm not sure what she is. But somehow she's involved with a devious little cretin with all the magical talent of an earthworm. When Gautier decided to punish me for double-dealing, it was Jacard who told him to blind me. . . ."

Kajetan's nephew Jacard, an adept of the Camarilla, had been set in place as my assistant at Castelle Escalon to spy on my works. He'd been too thick to see what I was doing . . . until the end, when my arrogance and de Gautier's clever scheming left him an opening. By then he knew me well enough to know what punishment would unhinge me. He just didn't understand about Anne and how our shared curse allowed us to work together. Fate grant that he had never figured it out.

"If he's not so good with magic, and the enchantress is a prisoner, then how's he mucking about in dreams and burning smithies?"

"He's got Gautier's and Kajetan's books and journals that detail a great deal of magic," I said, "and now . . . if he's found this woman and her emeralds . . . Last time, thanks to Portier, we knew where the conspirators were and had a hint of what they planned. This time I've no idea of either—Merona or Abidaijar or Jarasco, glory, chaos, or rending Heaven itself? If they've power enough to compel us through dreams, and to learn our fears and desires from them, I just— I just don't know what the limits are. I've got to find Portier."

Sulfurous smokes and blurping bubbles of mud greeted us as we topped the rise at the end of the valley. The Sweats. We had no leisure for conversation for many hours after.

DEMESNE OF DELOURRE

"We can't afford the delay," I told my brother as we broke camp. Exhaustion, and the bitter wind battering the rocky hilltop beyond our sheltered niche, had kept us in our blankets late. The patchy sunbeams were angled halfway to midday. "We need to head straight for Mattefriese and the roads east." Though to bypass Merona, forgoing the chance to confirm Anne's safety, left acid in my mouth.

Four days after leaving Raghinne, Andero and I had emerged from the mountains into the rolling border country between Coverge and Delourre. Ferocious blizzards that seemed aimed directly at the two of us had forced us relentlessly eastward. Now, the fastest route to Merona would require days of backtracking to Jarasco, where Tetrarch de Ferrau's bailiffs would surely be on watch, and then ten days straight south, leaving us far west of Mattefriese, the gateway to the pilgrim road and Abidaijar. Yet Anne might not yet be in the royal city or anywhere within range of our mind speaking. If Jacard and the enchantress had discovered a way to revive de Gautier's plan, I would need Anne and her power. But for now, it only made sense to head directly east to Portier.

I shook the dusting of snow off my blanket and rolled it tight. "Everyone's always after me to trust people. So I'm trusting de Santo to see Anne safe. He's blighted stubborn. Sacrificing himself for the daughter of his hated enemy will suit his nature. Anne has friends and family to protect her, too, while Portier's got no one around him but scholars and Cultists. If these people abduct him . . . try to bury him somewhere hidden . . ."

I could not accept that some immortal nature prevented Portier from dying. True, he had shown an extraordinary ability to survive events that would kill other men, but scientific people could likely explain such a result. And even if such a thing were true, how could it improve his fate? To be a mortal soul buried alive, clawing at the dirt as your air ran out once and for all, was the stuff of nightmare. But how much worse to be a Saint Reborn, repeatedly dying and waking in the dark, knowing you would never again, in all eternity, breathe the air of the world. The imagining shivered me to the marrow.

If we maintained a southeasterly course and the weather did not worsen, we could be in Mattefriese in the same twelve days that would take us to Merona. And only six or seven more would get us to Abidaijar.

Keep yourself hidden, student. I could not bear the thought that they had him already. And yet, the woman's words to my father . . .

"Perhaps you're right," I said, attempting to rub the sticky residue of sleep from my face. "If they've taken him from Abidaijar, we'll waste precious time going. Gods, I'd sell my soul to speak in dreams like this daemon woman, to interpret and learn. . . ."

Andero took my rolled blanket and worked with straps and buckles. Devil whuffled and blew. "You found your way to Raghinne by magic. Seems to me you could do the same to find where your friend's hid."

"It's not at all the same. To work a guide spell to a particular location you've got to know details: geography, history, stories, everything your senses can tell you about it. I know every rock in Raghinne, every path, the smell of the food, the feel of the air, the noises. I can still *see* enough of the blighted place in my mind to work a spell like that. But they could have taken Portier anywhere." Was ever a mage so ignorant of the world? "I wouldn't even know where to start."

"But it's not the *place* you want to find. It's the man, yes?"

"It's not that simple—"

"He's your friend, by god, which is more than Raghinne ever was to ye, and from what you've told me, you've few enough. Angels' mercy, your magic kept him living when he was drownded."

I'd never successfully worked a locator spell entirely focused on a person. To do so without that person's physical presence or some physical bit of him—hair, fingernails, skin, tooth—was likely impossible. Yet trying it would take far less time than traveling a thousand kilometres out of the way. . . .

"I'd need your compass," I said, "and do you have any kind of map?"

"Aye, as it happens. But it's a poor sort and not so accurate." He sounded embarrassed. "I scratched up one as I traveled with the legion, so's I could find my way home again. Been keeping it up as we've come away from the Sweats."

I muzzled a smile. "Only sensible. Good. Lay it down someplace dry and show me where."

Forgoing the usual reminder that a *blind man can't do squat with a map*, he guided my hand to a well-softened fold of paper spread on a scrap of leather. A search of my own pockets brought out Anne's silver pendant. I dropped it beside the map.

"It's a trinket of Anne's," I said. "She values Portier. Any physical artifact that might connect me to him will lend power to the spellwork." Which reminded me of the prize I'd brought—Portier's own ring, made to tell me of the power I'd released in him, a connection of true significance. Perhaps I could make this work after all.

I found my way to Devil and rummaged through my pack, coming up not only with the ring, but with a wadded cloth that smelled distinctly of horse. "Ilario gave me this to rub down Devil. He and Portier were better friends than I knew. They had secrets. . . ."

The three of them, Anne, Portier, and the chevalier. The three aristocrats. They'd kept secrets even these two years since they learned I'd worked for their same ends.

With a fierce shove, I banished the annoyance the idea raised, along with the cold, the wind, my empty belly, my brother, and the horses. Spellwork needed surety and focus, especially when the physical elements were so lean. Kneeling beside the map, I set a marker stone and scribed a circle in the dirt, enclosing myself and my paltry collection of artifacts. Then I retreated from the world.

With my own peculiar hieroglyphs, I sketched a portrait of Portier—slight of build, dark hair, prominent chin, dark eyes crisp with intelligence, yet filled with unabashed wonder and visible yearning whenever I demonstrated the truth of magic. Eyesight weak enough to need spectacles for reading. His usual garb of dull gray and black. The cane that supported his limp; the bloody wreckage of his leg when de Gautier dragged him onto the ledge at Mont Voilline. The profound peace, the trust, I'd felt from him through Anne's mind as the water closed over his face . . . as he relied on me to save his life. It humbled me to recall it, shamed me as I understood the arrogant stupidity of my actions this month past. Fear and pride had kept me at Pradoverde. I should have gone to Portier the moment de Cuvier left.

Deliberately I opened the wound I had just discovered, the intimacy of Portier's friendship with Anne and Ilario. Only now did I understand the full magnitude of the chasm between the three and me. Portier's scorn for Ilario had diminished after our journey to Eltevire—six years. And I'd ever believed that Anne and I—and perhaps the King of Sabria—were the only ones to glimpse the depths of the librarian. But Ilario, no fool, but a serious man, believed him a Saint Reborn.

I sketched that into my working, too. Even the possibility was an aspect of Portier's keirna, affecting his view of himself and his relationships with others. I needed everything to make this work—his scholarship, his father's resentment at his family's impoverished aristocracy, the physical and spiritual scars left by Portier's relationship with his father, the trust of his royal cousin, Portier's devastation at the fates of the children murdered by de Gautier's conspiracy. . . .

Once his image was as complete as I could devise, I touched Andero's map and drew our need into my working—the malevolent voice of the enchantress in white, the dread visions lurking inside her emerald, her threat spoken through my father's dying breaths—and I sketched a wider map of Sabria and the bordering lands of Aroth and Norgand, deserts and mountains and far Syanar. Feeding power into my structure, I bound it with will and intent. Magic erupted from the brass ring . . .

. . . and I felt him there with me . . . my friend Portier, breathing rapidly . . . frightened . . . lost.

Eager, I poured in every scrap of power I could muster. *Where are you, student?*

The map I'd sketched with magic floated in my inner darkness like a stratagems game board, mountains, cities, rivers, and roads where I knew of them. My ignorance left vast stretches blurred. But with every scrap of skill I could muster, I focused my inner sight on the place I believed the ancient city of Abidaijar stood.

The sense of Portier, though still faint, solidified. My attention traveled east and then west along the Great East Road, but naught changed in my perceptions. North from Abidaijar, and I came near losing him. Southerly . . . *Gods, yes.*

My power began to ebb, the map's strength wavering as I drew on my reserves. Southeast, no. But southwesterly from Abidaijar, the sense intensified. *Where are you?*

I traversed the shimmering map west and south, caught glints of green . . . and then shafts of light, deep green rays as if the sun poured through window glass made of . . . emerald. . . .

Blackness erased my inner vision, but I clung to the waning enchantment a moment longer. "I'm coming, student," I whispered, as if he could possibly hear if I only willed it enough. "You shall not die in that place."

"What place? Did it work?"

Andero's sharp questions yanked me back into my skin. My lips and cheeks were numb; hair and garments crackled, stiff with frost. My frozen joints cracked as I dug in with my staff and pushed up to my feet. Somewhere in the bluster, Devil cropped dry grass.

"Better than I'd ever have thought," I said, commanding my knees to hold me up. "He's wherever the emerald is."

"Abidaijar?"

"South and west of there. Gods, how long was I working?" The day had most definitely changed, and my stomach felt like to devour my bones.

"Most of the day. We'd best twitch our tails if we're to get inside this next town before they close the gates."

No wonder I felt as if my age was nearer two-and-eighty than two-and-thirty. But discomfort could not damp my elation. I'd worked something new and complex from little more than memories, and located a certain sense of Portier. Yes, he was captive, but alive. And I'd saved us half a month's wandering. Perhaps I could try the spell again as we got closer and conjure a better sense of him. Was the emerald light some aspect of truth or was it only the proximity of the gem?

And then, as if my map had taken shape in the real world, truth spread itself before me, the echo of an old soldier's desperation. The place de Cuvier had told me of, the place where this journey had begun . . .

Gods, how I loved magic! "You'll need a horse, elder brother, and a good look at a map of Arabasca and Aroth. We'll find Portier south of the pilgrim road, halfway between Mattefriese and Abidaijar. It should definitely be warmer there. We start our hunt in Carabangor."

"So that's the plan, is it?" he said as he brought Devil up. "We find me a decent horse and I ride beside you off the edge of the world."

My belly tightened as if he'd slammed his fist into it. Caught in between our difficult journey these past days and my deep-rooted fears, I'd never questioned Andero's intent. In truth he had agreed only to get me away from Raghinne.

"Naturally, you've a choice." This came out stiff as a dry plank. "It's a very long way. The danger won't be small, and I've a notion we've not seen the last of pursuit. But my power, my magic— The blindness takes its toll, but I can still protect you. And if we survive it"—gods, there was just no acceptable alternative—"I'll see you're well paid for your time."

The noises of preparation ceased. The silence seemed eternal.

"You've no bat wings to carry us?"

The question blurted out of the eternal dark so abruptly and in so grave a tenor, I spat the answer before thinking. "I work magic, not miracles. What kind of idiot—?"

Hands clapped my shoulders, thick fingers gouging dents in my bones, affirming that a wrestling match with Andero would end worse now than when we were boys of seven and eight. "I'll take you as far as you need, little brother." He squeezed the words through his teeth. "But if you ever mention paying me for it, like I'm some pissing manservant or a whore to be thrown aside when you've better company, I'll break your limbs into such small pieces, you'll need to lap your food from a dish on the floor."

"I didn't—" My intents made no difference. I *had* insulted him. *Stupid, Dante. Bridle your temper.*

He tapped my ankle in warning, as was his practice, and in one huge thrust shoved me onto Devil's back. "No bat wings. That's a disappointment."

Tutting like a disapproving granny, he led me down the hill and toward a town a signpost had announced as Castelivre.

CASTELIVRE

"I've never seen so many Temple folk in one place. Yellow badges. Yellow robes. They're stopping everyone who wants inside." Andero's anxious ambivalence mirrored my own.

"Then we turn around," I said, attempting to be halfway intelligent, rather than following my most urgent desire to be under a roof before another storm came down on us.

"No . . ." Andero drawled his contradiction out long and thoughtfully. "If we're to get me a horse when we've not twenty kivrae between us, then you've a bit of confusticating on order. It's too late, anyhow. We retreat and they'll notice. Follow my lead. We'll go a steady pace, but always stop when I get to three. Now, dismount . . ."

These commands made no sense whatsoever until the next few moments resolved themselves with Andero on Devil's back and the lead rope wrapped around my wrists.

"You blasted, bloody-minded foo—"

"The road's smooth, little brother. Trust me."

The rope grew taut and I had no choice but to stumble forward. I had just shaped a spell to burn through the cursed leash, when someone not ten paces away yelled, "Halt."

"Eyes down," snapped Andero quietly. "One, two, *three.*"

I halted.

"What have we here?" The man's garments reeked of incense and jasmine. Temple. His nasal tones smacked of excitement.

I ducked my head and hunched my shoulders, tugging at my cloak with my bound hands, unsure whether I should try to expose my collar or muffle it. *Damn, damn, damn you to the netherworld, Andero.*

"I am Manet de Shreu," announced Andero, "sergeant major, First Legion of Coverge, fetching my lord duc's third mage to Castelivre as ordered."

"The Duc de Coverge's third mage? I sincerely doubt that." The Temple man sounded as if he already envisioned himself draped in a High Tetrarch's furs.

Not since the first vile nights after my blinding had I felt so helpless. Though anger boiled in my veins, it was heat without flame, a knife without an edge. I had naught but the dregs of power left after my day's spending.

"Even a Temple bailiff must recognize His Grace's badge on my cloak. And anyone who's visited an alehouse since summer must have heard how my lord duc trusted his third mage, Talon, to beat back a raid from the Igoni *banditieri* by bringing a rockfall down on top of them. But this slimy crumpet of a spell-twister couldn't budge the boulders, despite all his grand assurances."

Andero bellowed this nonsense with the bombast of an alehouse tale spinner, and accompanied it with a sharp haul on the leash that caused me to stumble forward. I would have fallen flat had I not bumped into Devil's flank.

"Caused my good lord to take a loss of both men and coin. Between you and me"—he dropped his voice—"a *considerable* loss. And now we're sent here to be met by a mage from the Camarilla Magica who's charged to reive this cursed sorcerer's mind to discover if he's suborned or just incompetent."

I could have given lie to his prating by triggering a firespout. My staff was tucked away in its saddle straps right between my nose and Devil's hind end. But I didn't wish to harm the faithful Devil, and reason whispered that my brother had spun us a decent opportunity.

Thus, instead, I stepped away, raised my hands, growled a few menacing nonsense words, and conjured a minimal illusion of a copper-ringed whipsnake. With a worthy display of grumbling and curses, I dispatched the slithering snake in the approximate direction of the Temple servitor and had it rise up in its attack posture, only to fall limp as a wet ragmop and dissolve. Two even more ridiculous failures, accompanied by puffs of smoke from the leash rope as if I were trying to burn it through, drew a crowd round us. They all stank of incense. My knees were jelly, not entirely from magical depletion.

Andero bawled curses at me, and I shook my leash and mumbled over it, setting off cold sparks that would accomplish nothing. The onlookers taunted and guffawed. Warm spittle splattered my nose and cheek, just as a hard boot to my shoulder sent me reeling. Keeping my telltale claw of a hand hidden inside my cloak left me unable to catch myself. Thus I sprawled ignominiously, face down in a sea of half-frozen muck.

"None fails my liege in his need, Talon," Andero bawled. "May the Camarilla leave your skull a burnt hollow. Now, stay there until I tell you."

Trust him. Trust him. Devil's hooves splashed terrifyingly near my head. I held absolutely still. The frigid wetness seeped through my cloak and into my boots, as my brother fell into conversation with the Temple guards, jabbering like a gossip at the village well.

"So, tell me, honorable bailiff, why is a Temple servant questioning visitors? Don't know as I've seen that in all my years."

"Our Tetrarch de Ferrau is hunting a devil mage, accused of necromancy and murder," said the nasal-voiced Temple man. "But your buffoon doesn't look as if he could heat a stoup of cider, much less draw fire from the sky or flay a company of swordsmen with his eyes. You've till tomorrow, middle-night, to do your business and be on your way back to your lord."

The cursed de Ferrau again.

"Well, then." Andero yanked the tether and hauled me up. "Perhaps you could give me a hint as to where a Camarilla visitor is like to shelter in Castelivre. Their kind ever cluster together. Perhaps with your town mage?"

"Castelivre's got no town mage or any magic practitioner for hire. Not since the Blood Wars. The land doesn't forget. People don't forget, though most who lived here died. The Concord prevents us from barring them altogether, so we let Adept Denys keep the house up top of the hill, next the ruins. But he's required to house any others come to town and give them fair warning of our laws. I'll advise you get your prisoner up there and out of sight or he'll have no skull to reive."

"Aye, I'll do that. Get up, you bumbling fool, or I'll drag you."

A firm tug on the rope and I staggered to my feet, frantically estimating the position of Devil's hooves. My awkwardness set the onlookers guffawing again. Yet even humiliation could not thaw my skin. I was near paralyzed with the cold.

Creaks and clanks and a wafting exhalation of smoke and sewage signaled the gate's opening. Once through and slogging through muddy streets, we were surrounded by the noise and bustle of commerce. I'd forgotten it was afternoon.

Focused on keeping my footing behind Devil, I had little attention to spare for the angry mutterings that followed us through the hawking of jams, olives, and chickens, the barking of prices, and strident calls summoning children. Like fog from a river rose the market-day odors of raw fish, stewing turnips, frying meat pies. But something fouler rode on the chill air—worse than the street or the middens, worse than my muck-soaked self, who stank like a dung heap.

Andero's three sharp tugs on the rope signaled something. Hurry? Impossible.

"Keep close, bumbler."

He was drawing me in. The chinks and creaks of Devil's tack were in my ear. I hooked my bound hands to his stirrup.

"Indeed they've no love for your kind here. See those cages hung up just ahead of us? Fool or betrayer, that's where you'll be once you're judged, mewling like those fellows, splatted with spit and dung. Get out my way, citizen! I'm taking this scum to his trial." He jerked the rope again and fixed it so I was tethered close on his right. "Eight, ten of your kind are lining that road up the hill. You'll look fine in yellow rags, the mark of the Souleater seared onto your brow. . . ."

As we climbed the steepening road, Andero's preachments painted a vivid picture. Cages hung on posts. Prisoners, branded on the face—a degradation reserved for practitioners of illicit sorcery—in various stages of humiliation, disease, and starvation. But wearing *yellow* rags, not crimson. These were Temple prisoners, not the Camarilla's.

The Camarilla diligently prosecuted hedge witches and charm sellers, folk who might carry enough talent for magic to make their granny's healing potion work or their family curse have some effect, but deigned to practice without sanction of the prefects. My teacher Salvator had died in a Camarilla cage. But the Temple usually confined its cruelties for those like me who dabbled in the mysteries of the Veil between the mortal world and Ixtador, threatening the orderly progress of the dead on their final journey. The Pantokrator had given us one road to Heaven, so they taught, and it was a mortal crime to interfere with it.

What gave the Temple such sway here? And what had these poor bastards been up to? Was this the damnable de Ferrau's work, too?

We left the market crowd behind us as we climbed the hill road. But not the bitter wind that flapped my sodden garments. And not the stench.

"Brother mage, have mercy. . . ." The whisper came from my right, where the stink of excrement and mortified flesh placed a captive whose life numbered days, not months. But the plea was soon echoed from before and behind us.

"Mercy. Mercy, mage. Master . . . please, kill me."

The quiet desperation was more terrifying than the spite below. These captives were as good as dead, no matter the term of their sentences. Without knowing them, without sight to learn their faces and hone a spell, I could deal them no kinder mercy than the blizzards following us out of the mountains. Bending my head lower, I growled through chattering teeth. "C-cannot. Imp-possible. Sorry . . ."

"Have a care. Turning right." It was Andero whispering, not one of the captives. The wind spat spicules of ice in my face. The ground leveled from the rutted hill track to rough grass and rocks. "One, two, three."

My feet stopped. My shivering did not. My blood was slush. My heart ice.

Andero dismounted and unbound my wrists. As I shook out my cramped shoulders, a soft, encompassing weight dropped over my shoulders, was gathered in the front of me, and stuffed into my numb fingers. The wool blanket smelled of horse and felt like Heaven's own bliss.

"B-b-bless—" Before I could thank him, something more than woolly warmth crept through me, toes, legs, groin, torso. . . .

"Didn't think you'd wish to actually visit whoever this Adept Denys is like to be, though it seems accommodation's sorely limited and the weather's failing. There's ruins enough here we could likely— Dante? What is it?"

But my attention had turned inward, where a chaos of light and indefinable shapes and colors lay . . . crystal towers . . . bridges . . . arcs and whorls, a landscape as broken as any physical ruin that lay around us, yet as vivid as knife blades plunged into my gut. Magic . . . everywhere.

My teeth ripped off my left glove, and I brushed my bare hand over thin soil, rocks, crumbled masonry, tufts of hard grass. My knuckles grazed dressed stones . . . a wall that ended thirty centimetres above the earth. Every pebble, every blade, and most especially the broken wall reeked of enchantment. Complex. Luminous.

"Where in the name of all g-gods are we?"

"Ruins. Spread all over the hillside. No single piece big enough to identify. The outer walls have been repaired to connect down to the town walls, but there's naught else new been built up here since these were knocked down. A deal of years, I'd say, from the overgrowth. Nobody even took what stones were left to use elsewise. Gives me the crawlies, like a graveyard."

Why hadn't I heard of such a place at the boundaries of Delourre and Coverge? Perhaps Castelivre was a modern name. . . . I inhaled sharply. *Castel. Livre.* In Aljyssian, the most ancient language of Sabria, it meant *palace of books.* And it explained exactly why the locals detested sorcery.

"Yes, we must most definitely visit Adept Denys. Gods, Andero, this is the ruin of Collegia Magica de Gautier. The Gautieri Library. The place where the Blood Wars began."

CHAPTER 10

CASTELIVRE

"Don't seem as if anyone's here." Andero had already yanked the bell cord three times. A squat stone house, he'd said, one many times repaired and tucked into the bend of the outer wall.

"He's here. Just preoccupied." Active spellworking tickled my mind through the aether, weak and awkward as a hedge witch's charms. It was an inharmonious contrast to the layered enchantments of the ruins around us. And yet . . .

"Ring again." I reached again. A pinpoint of purest magic darted through the aether like a sun glint on silver. "Once we're settled, leave me alone with him. Camarilla sorcerers keep their secrets close. He'll never say anything in front of an outsider."

The gusty wind swirled up from behind me, flapping the blanket around my shoulders and my sodden clothes underneath. I was glad of the scarf Andero had tied about my eyes, just for the sheer warmth of it. Shelter would be welcome.

Gripping my staff, I stretched my hearing again. Faint footsteps, quick and light. A solid door slammed, metal, from the muffled clang of it.

"You said this house is small? Someone's coming from a long way inside." After four days together, Andero no longer questioned such observations.

"The place is no bigger than my own, and we'll both need to duck to go through the door. Mayhap he's dug a deep cellar."

Even a man so dismissive of fate and destiny as I was could not ignore our happening upon this place. The Blood Wars—a century of savage strife among magical dynasties—had come near destroying Sabria two centuries ago. Our ordeal at Mont Voilline had proved its embers held fire enough to flare again. And here we were at the very hearth where those flames had first been lit. The voices in the aether had surged into scarce-controllable chaos, the echoes of ancient triumphs, cruelties, and magic merged with the hectic mindstorm of the town.

Why would a Camarilla adept take up residence in a town that had witnessed the ugliest and most destructive events in the history of magic, a town that remembered that history, rightly despising any who wielded enchantment? Our best chance to obtain a horse by "confustication" would be late night, when the chance of scrutiny was lowest. Surely spending a few hours to salve my curiosity would be well spent.

The scrape of unoiled hinges interrupted Andero's fifth ring. "Greetings, sir! You're Adept Denys, I would assume. And very grateful am I to find you at home this foul day."

"Who are you?" The snappish query came from a man of height similar to mine, whose voice exhibited no rust of age.

"I am Manet de Shreu, sergeant major, First Legion of Coverge, and this mage is my prisoner. . . ." With all proper indignation, Andero repeated his story of my imminent interrogation by a Camarilla Inquisitor. "Though I must say, I'm thinking my lord's messenger bespoke our destination entirely wrong. These locals bear a fearsome hate for the magical arts. Why would your noble prefects choose such a town for this interrogation?"

"They wouldn't. Go away."

My brother's quick forward movement resulted in a solid thump. The door remained open. "Now, now, my good fellow, let's not be hasty. I've no wish to put you out. But them at the gates told me in no uncertain manner that a mage admitted into Castelivre must take lodging here. That, in fact, you are *required* to shelter my prisoner and me. We've provision for ourselves, of course, and would be pleased to share with you . . ." That was a stretch of the imagination worthy of the story writers Anne favored. ". . . but I must insist you let us in. My weakling charge is about to shiver himself to splinters, which my lord duc would sorely disapprove, as he'd rather chop the vermin's hands off for himself. Tomorrow I'll send messages to my captain in Jarasco and confirm the location of the interrogation. Mayhap we'll only be with you three or four days, instead of a month!"

"A month?"

The fellow's screech evidenced such dismay, it was no wonder Andero was able to shove my head down, drag me under the lintel, and slam the door behind us. The small house—indeed I could feel the door closing's echo bounce off thick walls not three metres apart—was stifling. Somewhere to my left a hearth sent out a blast of smoky heat worthy of Da's forge.

"You are not welcome here, Sergeant Major. Neither of you. What are you—?"

"We'll have a jolly visit," said Andero, cheerfully, as he sat me on the floor and briskly wrapped his end of my leash about my ankles. "I like nothing better than meeting new folk. It's one reason I joined the legion. This mage is sour company, I can tell you. Perhaps you could send him up your chimney to unclog it."

"I've no time for you. I've important work—"

He might have been a dog yapping for all the note Andero took of his protests. "I've left my horse in the lee of your south wall. Lest you've a supply of hay, I'll be off to fetch some from the town, soon as we've settled in."

My brother was an artist. He rattled on about my crimes and his noble liege in a verbal shower worthy of Ilario de Sylvae, leaving no opening for this Denys to speak, much less object. By the time he took a breath, our packs, Devil's saddle, and I were ensconced in a corner next the adept's grain casks. I was already sweating beneath my damp, heavy garments and had no way in the universe to get them off.

"Good riddance to you, clodwit," I murmured. "Just like you to dump your responsibilities on this good fellow. Be warned, adept, he'll likely *take his time* in town. Drinking and whoring. Best make him swear he won't run away altogether."

"Need to get a lay of the land, now, don't I, and send my question to my captain?" Andero poked at me with his boot. "Prepare what you have for supper, adept, and I'll see to the morrow's provision. You must control this mage carefully. Being unmagical myself, I've found brute force effective. He's a craven sort. And sly. Leave the blindfold; it keeps him off balance, so he can't try any diddling. Lose him and I'll report you negligent to these Temple folk."

My brother's bulk bent over me. He tugged at my blindfold, belt, and bindings, though, indeed, my wrist bindings fell looser than before. When he moved away, my knife was tucked neatly up my right sleeve where I could reach it. "Now, behave, groveler, or I'll beat you till your bones crack."

"You'll wha—? Oh." The adept must have grasped that Andero had addressed this last to me. "I don't know, Sergeant. He has a brutish look. You *will* come back?"

"Might have a stoup or two so's I don't presume on your ale barrel," said my brother. "But sure and I'll be back to see to the daemon. Good comrades died in that rift. He's no better than a murderer, and I *will* see him punished."

A blast of cold wind—welcome in the stuffy room—ended the conversation. Andero had promised to stay close.

I decided to let the adept take the lead. After a short stillness he began messing about with his hearth fire and his pots.

"I suppose you expect something to drink." He was as sullen as a lazy child.

"Yes." I was indeed parched from the climb and the wind. "And food. The brute refuses to feed me."

More clattering and banging brought him close, and he pushed a cup into my gloved hands. I swallowed the lukewarm ale in a single pull and held out the cup. He snatched it and scuttled backward. "So, what's your name?"

"Talon," I said. "*Mage* Talon. Come get these off me." I extended my bound hands.

"I won't." His bravado sounded thin. "If you've not skill enough to get loose of a layman, it's not my warrant to help."

"So says the white-livered milksop skulking about on *Temple* sufferance." Cursing and mumbling, I wrestled with the length of rope between wrists and ankles. Andero had left them so I could slip out if needed. But I didn't. Not yet.

"What do you pay the holy drudges to keep you out of a cage, adept? Or is it your mentor's coin holds them off?" I lifted my head sharply. "You *do* have a master mage supervising you, as the Camarilla requires, yes?"

"Certainly. I've permission to stay here . . . and pursue my important work . . . and deal with the Temple as necessary." His quivering hesitation revealed the lies better than any truth charm ever made.

I didn't call him out but decided to gouge a little deeper. "So you're a housekeeper."

"I provide shelter for our brothers and sisters who come to study the ruins. What pompous, know-everything *mage* would be willing to be forever derided and spat upon in this vile town?" The adept was aggrieved. Petulant. Rebellious enough to do as he pleased, but frightened of his own boldness. "Few come here. That's not my fault."

So he was in Castelivre unsupervised—either a rogue or considered not worth the effort to supervise. Or perhaps merely forgotten.

Liquid sloshed into a pot. A series of sharp raps on wood charged the air with onion and garlic. Two blasts of cold air resulted in the clatter of firewood dumped on the floor. Another foray resulted in something solid dropped into his pot. And then he left a third time, only this time with no blast of winter. My enspelled hearing followed him down and down and down. . . . Gods, how deep was his cellar?

When he returned, he settled. And worked magic, little more than a weak and muddled summoning of power. I'd not a clue as to his activity, until I heard the soft flutter of a page being turned. A soft click was followed by a dart of magic, bright as quicksilver as it pierced the aether, wholly different from what had come before.

"I know what this place is," I said, as if the dart had pricked me awake. "To hear your pages turning . . . It conjures images from history. I didn't know anyone occupied the Gautier ruins."

"Be quiet. I don't like company. I'll speak to the Temple about a sorcerer's hole for you. I oughtn't have to mind a prisoner like an infant."

I settled back in my corner as much as my bindings would allow.

"Excuse me for enjoying the prospect of company of my own kind after tramping about with soldiers for a year," I said. "And this dullard sergeant . . . gah! I never claimed to be a war mage. The duc hired me because I was stupid enough to learn the Covergan dialect in my youth. I thought hiring out to a noble would give me living enough I could get back to my real work. A *mage's* rightful work."

Denys harrumphed. "You're a fool to cast your lot with Covergans. A more ignorant, superstitious lot was never born."

"Aye. I doubt one in ten thousand can even read."

Another page turned. Another click. Another dart of true magic. De Gautier spellwork without doubt, though I'd no idea to what end. The hunger rose in me, as if I were a beggar glimpsing a royal feast through a crack in a door. A good thing my hands were bound, else I might choke answers from Adept Denys.

"So you must be here to study the Gautier magic," I said, "what's left buried in the rocks and dirt, eh? Disentangle it?"

"It's none of your concern what I do here."

"No need to be snippy, adept. It's just there are a thousand places to study and be left alone that are more hospitable than this town. So it must be some special work that draws you here. And there's naught else but magic and spilt blood, is there? Every time I find a book to study about gemstones, it tells me that the true information was only to be found in the Gautier Library. That's my own work—studying formulas that use spelled gemstones. The librarian at Collegia Seravain—a priggish sort of fellow who couldn't even work a candle spell—he swore naught survived the destruction of the Gautier Library."

Soft, solid shuffling from the direction of the adept. Was it only desire and imagining that told me he was stacking books?

"That would have been Librarian Duplais, no doubt. I heard he was intelligent." The adept was insufferably deprecating. "Even he didn't know all. Didn't you hear anything about the doings at Mont Voilline two years ago? Seems a few books did survive the destruction here. Books of *serious* magic."

Adept Denys was as smug as a fat courtier. There's naught like secret knowledge to make a fool prideful . . . and stupid. He was bursting to tell someone his secrets.

"I heard rumors of fell magic." *Careful, Dante. Not too eager.* "But Gautier books? I don't believe it. The Camarilla's rife with empty-headed gossips."

"Then you don't know all, either, mage. Not by a long ways."

"Even if any books survived in this wasteland, they'd be no use. The Gautier encrypted every word in their library so that none but their blood kin could read them. Anyone who says different is a moron or a liar." I squirmed in my restraints. "Excuse me while I sleep and dream of spells that turn lead to gold and rope bindings into spiderwebs."

The silence drew out so long, I feared I had nudged Denys too hard. Pages turned with the same accompaniment. Unfortunately, the spikes of enchantment were too brief for me to disentangle, even if I'd known where to begin.

"So listen to this, mage-who-knows-all." Denys cleared his throat. " 'For afflictions of the blood, the most effis-efficacious remedies require amplify . . . no . . . *applications* of the basic periapt centered by a twelve-facet ruby of deep color. The pro-provid-provis-provenance of the gem, as well as the gem itself, must incorporate clarity, virtue, cleanliness, and immediacy, as afflictions of the blood spread quickly throughout the body.' "

Denys's uneven spurts of verbiage caught me off guard. But I recognized instantly what he was doing. "You're *translating* from your book."

Did he have a Gautier device of some kind? That would explain the disparity between the weak expenditures of power—his own—and bits of glory such paltry skills could never produce.

"Too bad you're blindfolded. Too bad you're an arrogant shitheel just like everyone from Collegia Seravain."

Provenance . . . the nature and history of the gem . . . its source, its cutting and the one who did it . . . *Clarity and virtue*. The passage implied that to produce healing magic, the gem cutter must have imbued his work with his own virtue. This was not the formulaic magic taught by the Camarilla Magica. Nor was it anything a dull-witted adept could contrive. This was magical heresy of a kind that could get a sorcerer's tongue ripped out and his body burnt to cinders. Did this fool Denys understand? His book spoke truth that had been buried for two hundred years—truth a one-handed, rebellious son of Coverge had happened upon by purest chance fifteen years before. But never had I *read* anything to affirm what my bones had known and my hands had worked all these years, that true magic stemmed from the essence—the keirna—of objects in the natural world. No one save Portier and Anne had ever believed me, not even Salvator, whose motley collection of practitioner friends had provided me the evidence.

I could scarce contain my rising fever. "It's only in the past few years that the Collegia Medica has proposed that human blood actually moves through our veins carrying disease or health. To associate that with magical healing two centuries ago . . . what a leap of insight!"

I dared not fright Denys with talk of heresy and flaying. Let him think me enthralled with the natural science. Indeed the short passage was a profound example of the immensity of nonmagical knowledge lost in the Blood Wars. But unlike alternative magical theories, new scientific ideas bloomed throughout Sabria in these days like the flowering of the maquis after a rain, welcomed and discussed and called *a marvel of our generation.*

"Not so much a moron, am I?" he said, preening.

"No! Certainly not. Forgive me. . . . How could I imagine?"

"And there's naught you can report to anyone, as you're blindfolded. And none's going to believe a conniving spy, anyway, and none's going to find what I've got hid. I could as easily tell them you confessed your treason to me, couldn't I? If I tell the Temple tetrarch you've blasphemed, they'll muzzle you with an iron tongue and hang you up in a cage before they kill you."

"Indeed so. Tell me, adept, do you have more about gemstones? I could pay. If I could get an advantage on my rivals . . . especially in the matter of healing diseases of the mind, ill dreams . . . I've coin banked in Fadrici."

"I've learned a deal about gemstones that I could share." Despite a vivid lust, he blew an unhappy note. "But then, you might not live long enough to fetch my pay."

"A spell, then. What would you like—a grand illusion to confound these Temple folk? A charm to keep your water clean? Something better than a bell to warn you when someone's coming?"

"The soldier claims you're inept at magic."

"Ordinary folk have no idea what we can do, eh? I'm just biding my time."

Hesitating, he tongued his mouth as noisily as a dog. "I want to kill someone undetected."

"No, I won't—" Surprise made me blurt the denial harsher than I would have liked. "That is, I *can't* do that. I wouldn't be in this much trouble if I could, now, would I?"

"That makes sense, I suppose."

His disappointment nauseated me. Nasty little weasel.

"The warning, then. I don't want anyone sneaking up on me. Gautier books are forbidden, you know. And I've more secrets than that. . . ."

My mind raced, fully committed to the chase. "Did the soldier bring in a white walking stick?"

"Aye. Stood it by the door."

"It's my ancille. Touch the anthera sigil. One finger only and quickly." That's where I'd linked the warning key to my warding—a spell bound to my own keirna, not any formula.

His scream bounced off the walls. The clattering of the dropped ancille, the solid thump of a hind end on the floor, and some very hard breathing, as he discovered his hand was not immersed in molten silver, brought a smile to my face. I knew he'd hold it too long.

"Night's daemons!"

"I told you to use only one finger. Now, read me what your books tell you about gems—emeralds in particular—before the damnable soldier comes back, and I'll teach you to make such a ward for your front door."

"Teach me the spell formula first."

"And let you choose not to read? Indeed not! You've got all the advantage here. I'm trussed like a goose. Leave the blindfold in place, so I'll have no way to know what books you have or where you keep them. . . ."

Lies had come easy during my years as king's *agente confide*, and I'd not lost the knack. It was a measure of Denys's dullness that he could read passages like the one he'd just recited and still believe magic was worked with rote formulas.

"All right, then. I've got two here with mention of gemstones."

And he read. Slow, halting. Using his clicking device. Marvelous, detailed explorations of spellwork that could be worked with emeralds. I could have spent years and not learned so much as in that half an hour. But none of the passages referred to speaking in dreams or trapping the souls of the dead, or any of the other properties referred to by the history Finn had read to me. My mundane text could be entirely wrong, of course. Denys's information was more substantial. And yet . . .

"Have you seen any mention of the Maldivean Hegemony? My rival is obsessed with some emerald mentioned alongside Maldivean healing."

"Maldivea? Mother of mayhem, you're after the Seeing Stones!"

His laughter spewed in chortles and snorts, as grating and cheerless as a donkey's bray. More unsettling, he swallowed it whole as suddenly as it began. "Aye, I can tell you what was known about those," he said, more smug than ever. "Don't even have to fetch the books. A master mage came here a few years back. Thought the Stones might be hidden among the ruins. But, of course, I told him there was naught left here to search. Lucky for you, I looked them up once he was gone. Searched for 'em, too, but they weren't in my vault. So we'll trade, as I agreed, but for this you might have to pay more than just the one spell."

"Let me judge if you've aught worth the barter." It could easily have been Kajetan or de Gautier himself hunting the information. Neither had power enough to work the rites at Mont Voilline—which was why they had needed me. But for the moment, knowledge of the Stones was far more compelling than the identity of the seeker. "We'd best get on with it before the soldier comes back."

Denys didn't rush. He rose from his seat and clattered about his pots at the hearth. He was enjoying this very much. I reined my temper and rubbed my throbbing forehead.

"First off," he said at last, as he poked at his fire, sending new billows of heat and smoke my way. "The Seeing Stones weren't emeralds at all. They began as a single crystal, not quite so hard or so clear as a gem. More like to glass. But it was possessed of such strangeness that the ancients called it a godstone and said it was gifted to us by the gods, who would take it back one day. When you looked through the crystal, you saw things that were *other.* Double images or skewed images or things that were round the corner or not there at all. Don't know what the ancients used it for. Soothsaying, maybe. But at some time, their god deserted them. The Arothi Empire swallowed up half the world and no one knows what became of the stone for a thousand years."

The adept passed by me again, and wood creaked, as if he settled into a chair.

"But then a man named Altheus of Sirpuhi followed the legends into the desert and found the crystal in a ruined Cinnear temple. He commanded his favored wizard to cut it into three and polish the crystal faces, so as to *allow the Creator's light to pass through.* Seems this Altheus, too, believed them holy."

The description could not but recall the quartz prisms I'd seen at Ilario's Grand Exposition of Science and Magic so long ago. Men of science had shone sunbeams through them, showing how the angled faces bent the light and split it into the colors of the rainbow, exposing mystery and glory hidden in common sunlight.

"It was Altheus himself who named them Seeing Stones," said Denys. "Do you know their names, high and mighty mage?"

I shook my head, bridling my tongue lest my barrage of questions fright him to silence. Double images . . . skewed . . . I'd heard mention of such things when investigating lens making. Such provenance would make a fine element for spellwork.

He continued. "The history I found says: 'The Maldivean Stones, gift of the Creator to his favored son, Altheus, are three: Rhymus the Red-Hearted, the Stone of Passion; Tychemus the White-Hearted, the Stone of Reason; and Orythmus the Black-Hearted, the Stone of Command. From the Three shall rise the Righteous Defender, who shall battle the Daemon of the Dead on the doorstep of Heaven.' And sure enough, in the matter of a year, Altheus brought down the Arothi, who outnumbered him *fifty to one*, conquering everything from the borders of Syanar west to the sea. Always he carried the Stones with him."

"History calls Altheus the Holy Imperator," I said. "Not the Righteous Defender." I was near drunk with excitement. My father had mentioned the Righteous Defender, the Temple's mythic warrior who would crush the Souleater's Chosen—the champion of the Fallen who would battle him before Heaven's gates. Surely the enchantress in the dream possessed one of these very Stones.

"Aye. Altheus himself insisted he was not the Defender. But many believed it and named his birthplace holy ground . . ."

Sirpuhi meant *holy*. The place had likely been some burial ground for centuries before Altheus.

". . . and Altheus was quite the opposite of the Arothi, who ruled by sword, whip, and chain. Opposite most conquerors, as he was generous in his victories. He gave each of his men a bit of the lands he conquered and forbade slaughter or savagery among them. He let conquered peoples worship what gods they wished and sent out teachers that all might learn to read and write. Two-and-fifty years he ruled his empire."

"So what happened?" I asked. The history, part of the Stones' keirna, was important, too.

"Well, he just lay down and died. He was old by then. Said his work was done. He had three sons, and he gave each of them a third of his empire and one of the Stones. He warned them that they must use the Stones together, as elsewise their magic was out of balance. Altheus had his magus bind a geas about the three, preventing the owner of one stone from harming the owners of the others. His heirs would have to cooperate to keep Maldivea intact and at peace."

But I could see it clearly. No matter the intentions of the benevolent father, human greed would ever win out. "One of them figured out how to circumvent the geas."

"You're quick, mage," said Denys, leaning close enough I could smell the onion and garlic on him. "For years the brothers scrambled for influence among their subject states. The youngest brother, Maldeon, the holder of Orythmus, began to hunt down sorcerers and force them to work for him."

"The Stone of Command."

"Some of the sorcerers disappeared. Some were released but were forever altered, unable to speak of their experiences. Eventually, Maldeon assassinated one of his brothers and seized Rhymus. Not long afterward, an earthshaking devastated the kingdom of the third brother. If Maldeon caused it, the attempt didn't go to his plan, as Tychemus was lost in the rubble. By this time, barbarians were attacking from the east, weakening the hegemony, and the Arothi took advantage. It's said the Arothi reduced Maldivea to dust and poisoned the land so that Altheus could not rise from it again. No one knows what became of the Seeing Stones after that."

My heart rattled in my breast. "The book said that: 'so that Altheus could not rise from it again'?"

"Aye. Evidently he was very difficult to kill. So, is that what you wanted to know?"

"Some, yes." Not nearly enough. And it raised even more questions. Portier . . . Saints Reborn . . . I didn't believe in daemons and angels and reborn saints and holy imperators. Where was the truth behind the gibberish of superstitions?

Sweat beneath the wool blindfold dribbled into my eyes, the salt drops causing them to burn. Orange streaks split the darkness, as in the first days, causing spikes of pain through my pounding skull. The aetherstorm boiled behind my barricades. But I had to go on.

"Did your books tell how the Stones were used? I've heard of speaking through dreams, of imprisoning the dead . . . or keeping men alive when they ought to be dead."

"Aye, it was said that Altheus frightened his enemies through their dreams on the night before battle. Some said he enslaved his people through dreams, but other writers disputed it."

"Go on . . ."

"It's time you teach me the formula for your ward. Then I'll tell more."

I pressed the heels of my hands to the blindfold and gritted my teeth. My head was swimming with smoke and pain and this hunger to know. "It's not enough yet. Men pay me a thousand kivrae for such a ward. I need to know more of this Altheus and where Maldivea was." How ignorant I was, not to know common history.

"A thousand kivrae . . . to the prisoner of a low Covergan? Though you're asking questions as if you'd come here apurpose to steal my secrets."

"That's ridic—"

He pounced, all knees and elbows, stinking breath, harsh panting and fumbling at the clasp of my cloak.

"What the devil?" I wrenched away and rolled to one side, fending him off with flailing elbows and my bound hands and feet. "Get your hands off me!"

But like an angry cat, he pressed me to the floor, clawing at my cloak and shirt. Only when my neck . . . my collar . . . was exposed, did he back off. "A *master* mage!" he said. "What master serves as third mage to any mundane noble?"

Before I could answer, his breath caught and he brayed his donkey laugh. "God's teeth! You're the daemon murderer!"

Wood . . . iron . . . whatever it was . . . the heavy object that hit my head set off such a firestorm within my skull, I could do naught but moan.

CHAPTER 11

CASTELIVRE

Adept Denys grasped the tether between my wrists and ankles and dragged me across the room and down a very, very long staircase. To my sorrow, I never fell insensible. With hands and feet unavailable to brace, my body bumped and ground against every centimetre of stone. I strained to prevent my head repeatedly whacking itself on the stone steps. Surely red-hot irons were holding skull to shoulders. As the stair ended, and we traversed a stretch of more level terrain, I attempted to summon a defense. But I couldn't hold on to any spell long enough to bind it. When he dropped me on cold, smooth stone, I was sure my brain had leaked out my ears.

"Now, what to do with you? Tetrarch de Ferrau's offered a hundred kivrae bounty on your head for murder and blasphemy, but he wants you alive. Too bad, as it would be easier to kill than keep you. But first we must convince the sergeant you've run away."

Denys hurried off, back again before I could move without blubbering. The pressure of ceiling and walls had already begun to crush me.

"Don't leave me down here," I mumbled through bruised lips.

He didn't bother to answer. With a miraculous efficiency, he cut Andero's bonds from one limb at a time, replacing them with thick ropes that snugged ankles and wrists together behind me, bending my back into a painful arch. He ripped away my gloves and half my sleeve, cackling when he exposed my mutilated hand.

"Please . . ."

Footsteps moved away. Then a heavy metal door slammed, sending a shock through my head. I vomited.

Swelling bruises and airless silence pressed inward on my skull, while inside that sorry bone, the aether raged in uncontrolled chaos. Experiencing both at once near unhinged me. Groaning, I ground my temple into the floor and strained my limbs as if sheer will might burst the ropes. Wrists and ankles soon bled fire.

Andero would know I hadn't run. But could he find me? Gods, I had power enough to raise the dead. Surely I could get out of a cellar.

Focus on the ropes. All it would take was a bit of flame. Fire and I were old acquaintances. Though I knew little of the ropes' provenance, their purpose was clear. More than simple control. Pain. Punishment. Vengeance. Malice. Adept Denys detested mages. Pain and mind's chaos tore at my reason as I bound the spell.

Nothing. Gods, was I entirely depleted? The chamber itself did not inhibit magic, else the aetherstorm would have fallen silent.

Patience, fool. Again, I wove. More of Denys . . . isolated here . . . despised by the Temple officials . . . sitting on remnants of the greatest library of magic the world had known, yet unwilling to let anyone know. Greedy, then. Hoping, perhaps, to learn enough to trump those who scorned his weak practice. I twisted my hands to feel his scratchy ropes. A centimetre thick. Not enchanted. I bound my reworked spell. Nothing.

"Aagh!" Again I squirmed and strained on the dusty floor, cursing de Gautier and Jacard and the nonexistent gods and my own stupidity, accomplishing nothing but heaving up the last of the ale.

Fear seeped into my aching bones. So deep belowground . . . I'd go mad down here. I had known for all these months what blindness would cost me, but this was simple magic. Rope was rope. What was I missing?

Born in a cave . . . left alone in the dark to be devoured by daemons. Starving. Frightened. Reason denied that I could remember my infancy. Yet even now I heard them whispering, *Daemon.* And another voice soothing, promising to protect me. Gods, this was madness. . . .

Madness—perhaps that was it. Perhaps Portier was right about the corruption beyond the Veil—that the existence of Ixtador and the starving souls who abided there had corrupted the energies of true magic. And perhaps the corruption infected those like Denys who *used* such devices, as well as those few heretics like me who worked with true magic.

I wove the spell again. My useless writhing had dislodged the knife Andero had tucked up my sleeve. Its tip was now slowly digging its way into my elbow. Instead of amorphous fire, I incorporated the keirna of the familiar blade, nicked with abuse from using it for other tools I could not locate. The blade was out of proportion to the hilt. I'd had to file the broken tip short when I used it once too often to pry up a nail. I kept it very sharp. This time I added incipient madness to the working, as well. With will and power I bound the spell and triggered it.

The ropes snapped.

For one blessed moment, I lay gulping the musty air, begging the agony in my head and neck to ease. But as the bright residue of the spellwork faded, the suffocating darkness settled deeper. Even were I willing to waste power on triggering my copper bracelet, I dared not try it. To use it and see naught but unrelieved dark would set me wailing like an infant. Ridiculous that the absence of light should unman a blind man so.

Mustering my limbs, I crawled forward, kneeling up every few centimetres to wave my arms like an idiot. Better to discover obstacles with hands than with head.

Splinters raked my knuckles, the culprit a heavy wooden crate. Denys's path from the door had been unobstructed.

Altering my course slightly led me into more crates and a wall of stools and broken chairs. An exposed nail pierced my palm. Growling, I shoved the offending crate aside. But it rammed into something else, and in an explosive cacophony of rattling wood, a collapsing mountain of crates, slats, and heavier objects with solid corners battered me to the floor.

I scrambled back to all fours and altered course yet again. Cursing, terrified that my clumsiness had blocked the clear path to the door, I fumbled through the debris, trying to judge what might have been there before and what I had scattered.

Books. Saints have mercy, books lay everywhere. Scattered across the floor. Stacked. Crammed into the crates, spilling from cupboards, stuffed into shelves that seemed to block my path in every direction. Large and small, bound, stitched, or rolled, they smelled of dust, old linen, and musty leather. The magic that encrypted them tickled my skin like threads of spidersilk.

Books had ever been the measure of wealth to me, the only possession I coveted, the door to knowledge and understanding and a place in the world. Now I was surrounded by more books than one could read in a decade, and they did naught but whisper and tease, taunting of magic lying just beyond my reach . . . forever.

A cold, glutinous liquor of rage and hate welled from toes through bone and sinew, straight into the frenzy behind my brow. Power burgeoned in its wake, a new sort of power that numbed the aches of the body and slowed the heart, cooling fear and frenzy, shadowing thought and reason. My hair crackled with the *virtu elektrik*; my hands steadied, capable of grasping the world and twisting it in knots.

I bellowed in triumph, mustered a mighty will, and with a thought raised a whirlwind. Books, crates, casks, rope, and whatever else occupied that cellar room went flying. Objects crashed into each other in a roaring, rattling circle around me. Heedless, I raised my arms to the ceiling, summoning the storm of fire and destruction I had created back in Jarasco.

Heavy metal scraped stone. I spun in place. From far beyond the pandemonium, bright reason cried warning—a faint, steady gleam, a beacon of light and heat centered on my heart that penetrated the eye of the hurricane. A ridiculous notion: that there existed some cause *not* to unleash chaos. Yet, reason insisted I would destroy something valuable . . . something irreplaceable.

So I hauled back on the swollen enchantment and wrestled it into submission. Only a single burst escaped me.

"What in the Souleater's demesne—?" A man's guttural scream choked off his words, only to be itself engulfed by the din of flame.

Rage, hate, and power emptied out of me like a torrent of filth, and I threw my arms over my head as the contents of the room crashed to the floor all around. Thundering flames were quenched in a billowing stench of burnt flesh.

Burying mouth and nose in my arm, I sagged to my knees. In all desperation, I tried to recall the voice I had just silenced, for as sure as my name, the person who had opened the metal door lay dead. Gods of all the universe . . . my brother . . .

Heedless of cuts and splinters, I scrambled through the wreckage in the direction of the heat and stink, shoving obstacles aside as if they were feathers.

"Spirits and daemons, Dante!" A whoosh of cold wind cleared the smoke and stink.

"Andero?" My strangled question fell dead in the close space. "You found me."

"Waited outside the house, as I thought that's what you wanted. But then I heard— It sounded like the end of the world down here. I just followed the noise." He paused to take a breath. "This . . . mess . . . this is the sorcerer? You've killed him."

I threw my arm across my face to block the stench and nodded. Relieved. Disgusted. Horrified.

"I didn't think him the kind to fight—such a scrawny, cringing thing—else I'd never have left you. But here you've had to kill him . . . with magic."

His childish awe sickened me so thoroughly, I could scarce speak. I reached out my hand. "Get me out of here."

"Aye."

He guided me past Denys's remains, still pulsing with heat. Only when the metal door slammed behind us and we headed up the stair did the tightness in my chest ease enough to allow a full breath. My head felt as hollow as a fire-scoured bowl.

"Mercy, Dante, half your face is pulp. What did he—?"

"It's none of your concern."

"You know"—he hesitated, then plunged ahead—"one thing I learned in the legion. You're never quit of a battle without you've talked it out."

"Not this one."

To talk about what had happened was to think about it. To think about it was to relive it. And I wanted never, never, never to do that. A few times I had experienced true rage, but never had I felt . . . transformed . . . into something else altogether. Uncontrolled. *Triumphant* in my madness. What did that mean?

"Later, then. We oughtn't stay. What if someone comes looking for him? What if one of these Temple folk comes to question you? There's a stable next the southeast gate with only a boy guarding the horses. If you could distract him . . ."

Impossible. "We've got to sleep. A couple of hours each. We'll snatch the beast before dawn and leave with the early caravans."

He nudged me to a stop before we'd reached the top of the stair.

"We've another problem," he said, low and quiet, as if what was left of Denys might overhear. "I found someone lurking in the ruins. Near Da's age, skinny, small, dressed gentlemanlike, though he looked as if he'd been living hard, and his speech weren't so fine as his clothes. For certain not a Temple servitor. Said he followed us up the hill and needs to speak with you, as he has knowledge of a friend of yours. He knows your name, Dante, and doesn't like you much, but he hadn't run off and babbled, neither."

With a ray of hope my thoughts flew to Ilario, who was skinny as a sapling. But even Andero could not call the chevalier *small*, and, no matter his adventures, Ilario would never be dirty or crude-spoken. "What friend?"

"Wouldn't say. Said I might as well kill him if I wouldn't let him speak to you. The upshot is, he's outside waiting."

Though speaking to anyone was the last thing I wanted, we had no choice. "Bring him in, if he's still out there. And I need my staff."

Andero left me at the head of the stair, cloak around my shoulders, its hood raised to shadow my battered face. My hand gripped the welcome solidity of my staff, though my fingers stayed well clear of its trigger points. A gust of bitter wind and the kiss of snow brought my brother back with the newcomer.

"It *is* you, noble mage. I was r-right. Seeing you on the t-tether with this b-brute gave me doubts, and I've never seen you with any growth of b-beard. But I've been watching all these days, as I thought surely someone must come after my master. Assumed it would be Captain de Santo. Your concerns were always for greater things."

Despite his chattering teeth, I knew him. Hostile superiority masked by servility; he had ever grated on my patience. "John Deune?"

"'Tis I, Master Mage, though sorely filthy and unkempt, which must provide a fit disguise though it d-dishonor my lord's memory."

"His memory . . ."

"To the world's sorrow, my master lies dead, pierced through on that t-terrible night when you— When he saved you. I saw him fall, a sword pierced through his belly and out the other side."

The emptiness inside me rattled with echoes of Ilario's foolery . . . and the deeper truth of him I'd only guessed at the end. "How were you there? How can you be sure he's dead?"

"*I* would never desert him! I followed the three of you all the w-way, even through Jarasco. Thought my lord might need me, as he rarely traveled without a gentleman c-companion. So I saw the battle. Soon as all seemed quiet, I ran to him. I tried to bandage his wound with oddments I carry in my bag. But there was so much blood, and he'd no patience to be quiet. Though his breath was short, he swore me to find you and serve however you commanded. Said the Saints Reborn *valued* you. And then his hand dropped away, and I thought he was passed. Before I could decide how to load him on my beast, a troop of Temple bailiffs came to fetch their dead. I hid, but as they threw my lord on their dead cart, he moaned . . . and so I followed. . . ."

"You disobeyed his last order?" I said. The story was too smooth for me to swallow.

"My loyalties lay with my lord as long as he breathed," he said, indignant. "The bailiffs brought their wounded straight here to Castelivre. A scrubwoman confided they'd a hospice and better healers here than in Jarasco. But, alas, she reported that the 'tall, skinny prisoner with hair like sunlight' crossed the Veil before they arrived. I didn't know what to do . . . till I saw you arrive with this . . . bulldog."

"You be watching your tongue," said Andero with a menacing growl that set my own blood cold. "I serve the mage."

I ground the heel of my hand against my pounding forehead. I didn't believe half what the squirrelly manservant said and could happily have thrown him from a cliff. Yet, truly, I was no judge of men, not when it came to honor and loyalty among servants and masters, the kind of things Anne and Portier took for granted. Anne's own adored father, whom she held up as a model of chivalry, had mutilated de Santo just because the loyal captain had failed to anticipate a plot no one in the world could have predicted.

Honorable or not, we dared not dismiss John Deune before we were safely away from Castelivre. The temptation of Temple rewards might sap his loyalty to a dead man.

"We'll take you out of the city, but I've no need of your service after that."

"But—"

"We're going to sleep for a while, then steal a horse for my bro—bulldog, as we've not coin enough to buy one. After that we'll be traveling hard for many days. You'll be safer to keep well away from us." I wasn't about to tell John Deune that Andero was my brother. Blood kinship was a powerful weapon in the hands of an enemy, too risky to share with the untrustworthy.

"I'll d-do as my noble chevalier would wish," said the manservant, his voice not half so bold as his words. "I've my own horse. And, as it happens, I have my lord's purse. Yes, I took it, as I thought to return it to his royal sister. But I know he would buy a mount for you, mage. If you command me, I'll buy a mount for your man instead."

My lip curled. A dead-robber. Another reason not to trust him. But whether or not divine intervention had brought either of us here, I'd not turn down his offer. Ilario would, indeed, buy my brother a horse, or whatever else I needed if he were here. I only wished I'd understood that sooner.

"The horse would be a boon."

"And I'm sure I could be of more use than that." He pounced, eager as a cat on a bird. "You lived as a gentleman in Castelle Escalon and currently reside in the house of a noble lady at Pradoverde. I cannot imagine your rough companion taking care of your nether linens or shaving you as your man Finn does or providing other such intimate services."

Not hard to detect that the prunish servant would rather take up residence in a midden than care for my *nether linens*. Which made his annoying determination more incomprehensible. "I don't need intimate—"

"Do you cook?" Andero shoved his way into the exchange with an exasperated abruptness.

"I'm a fine cook. My lord hired me from an inn in Nanver precisely because he enjoyed my fish and my dedication to cleanliness. And be sure I'm accustomed to cooking in the rough, as Lord Ilario—divine grace accompany him on his Veil journey. . . ."

Even as John Deune exuded servility, Andero pulled me aside. "We might have need of someone who could cook, Dante," he murmured. "From your stringy aspect, I would guess it's not you, and to tell the truth, Marta's done for me since I came back from the legion. So if you can't conjure us up a brace of roasted rabbits now and then, and you've no other objection, I'd say bring the little hoptoad along."

"I don't trust him."

"Then best keep him close, eh? And I'm not going to be shaving you nor washing your drawers, that's certain."

I was too wrung out to argue with both of them. "We'll take it day by day. Andero, give John Deune a torch and find him a closet—a *secure* closet—to sleep in."

"I know just the place. No wickedness will find him in the coal house."

While Andero was gone, I sank to the floor where he'd left me and suffered a proper fit of the shakes. Before I knew it, he was back again, slamming the door against the howling wind.

"Locked up tight, cozy as a ewe in a lambing shed. Won't be carrying tales anywhere tonight. He's an odd sort. Don't seem to be the kind for a great lord's serving man."

"I never understood it, either. But now . . . If Ilario was the man I suspect he was, he wouldn't have wanted a friendly manservant who might tempt him into confidences. He'd want someone awkward, not too clever. I wouldn't trust John Deune farther than you can spit."

"I won't." Andero grasped my elbow and hauled me up. "You look done in, little brother. I've thrown your blanket on Denys's bed. It doesn't look so clean, but it's better'n the floor."

"You take the bed. I'll take first watch," I said. "I need to eat. The adept had something on the fire."

"Fire's out."

He laid my hand on a low stool near the hearth. The lingering heat of the stone hut scarce held back the winter night. The wind rattled the shutters, and threads of frost shifted my cloak and the blanket Andero threw over my shoulders.

"If you could give it a boost with your—" My abrupt shake of the head cut him off. "Well, I suppose I can poke up the ashes."

"Doesn't have to be hot," I mumbled, but Andero went ahead anyway.

Power—even the rites to raise the dead and reive the Veil—had never frightened me. Not until this night. Magic had been my light, my salvation, but tonight I would eat Denys's pottage cold rather than relight his dead fire with spellwork.

As my brother puttered about with the embers, a new mania rose in me. Blindness and sentiment had made me weak. This cursed enchantress had been able to manipulate me, and a whining adept who couldn't bind a true spell had driven me to heedless murder. I could not allow that. Not ever again.

"What is that? I've seen you diddling with it on and off these past days." Andero's question yanked my attention outward. "Is it like your staff—summat to help you with spellwork?"

"No. Though it is enchanted." My fingers had pulled Anne's pendant from my shirt. Strangely, the bit of silver scorched as if it had fallen into Andero's blaze. "Is it—? Does it appear different from before?"

"I've noticed it glowing, but never so bright. Looks like a star fell into your hand."

Though we were too far apart to speak, I was sorely tempted to touch Anne's presence in the aether. But I couldn't. Wouldn't. Not with murder on my mind.

I looped the slender chain from my neck and stuffed the little bundle into my pocket. "I don't know exactly what it is. But it has naught to do with dreams or emeralds or rescuing Portier. Tell me, is there an oddment lying about in here? Some kind of device that would make a click. Denys used it as he read. It would likely be left beside his books or on a table." Depleted as I was, I could detect no enchantments nearby.

"There's no books, and no device of any kind I can see."

The adept must have taken the books and the Gautier device downstairs. I sent Andero down to look for it, but he found nothing. "Naught left but splinters and ash down there."

"Nothing?" All those books . . . priceless books . . . other devices . . . Saints' mercy, for that alone I deserved hanging.

After we devoured Denys's turnip soup, Andero rolled up in his blanket and dropped into his ever-easy sleep. I settled down to watch. I leaned my head on my staff, my senses stretched into the windy night. I wished I could shut off thinking.

The taint of cold fury lingered in my veins and sinews. Never had I experienced anything like, not in the darkest hours of my double life, not on the other occasions my temper had skewed toward madness. I had never claimed to be other than ill-tempered and violent, but I had learned early that my best magic flowed from cool-headed patience, rather than the heated frenzy others described. Never had I so lost control of my power. But for that spark of reason, I would have brought this house down on my head.

I could not separate the night's experience from what I had learned over these past days. First there was Portier, my stubborn friend who would not stay dead. Then, a sneering enchantress who wielded a green

Stone whose heart was corruption, who controlled people through dreams and thought to bury Portier where he could not be found, as if someone might find something other than a corpse in his grave. And now there was this tale of a noble king who wielded green Stones and conquered an empire, and who allowed himself to die only when his work was finished. A man whose enemies believed he could speak in dreams and might return from the dead to threaten them again. Connections undeniable. Anne always said that legends must illuminate some truth, even if it was not the truth the tale spinner believed.

If truth permeated even these outlandish things, then what of the other thread of these days?

Denys's words: *From the Three shall rise the Righteous Defender, who shall battle the Daemon of the Dead on the doorstep of Heaven.*

And my father's and his prophet's: *Tha'rt Fallen, Dante. Darkborn in frost-cold blood. Suckled on pain. And so will come the last battle of the War for Heaven and guardianship of the Living Realm, when the Righteous Defender will rise from the ashes and battle the Daemon. He waits for you.*

Andero believed I had killed Denys while defending myself. But instead I had howled in triumphant rage, incidentally murdering a fool whose only crime was greed. What did that mean?

As the hours of the night passed and the bitter wind wailed, images of those dying in the cages along the road haunted me. Their misery settled in my gut like lead, offering power to kill them all in the name of mercy and kill their captors in the name of justice. My hands shook with the need to do it. Rage. Murder. Magic. Inextricably bound.

Gods save me, what if *I* was the evil at the heart of the woman's green Stone?

Anne

CHAPTER 12

23 ESTAR, MIDMORNING
884TH YEAR OF THE SABRIAN REALM
MONTCLAIRE

"Damoselle Anne!" The girl stopped halfway down the hillside path waved her arms excitedly. "Visitors!"

I waved back and reluctantly packed up my writing case. For one glorious morning—the best of Aubine's mild winters—I'd chosen to escape account books, vintner's agonies, and my father's spotty memory by sitting in the meadow to write letters, one to my dear friend the Queen of Sabria and one to Dante.

I had to smile at Kati. Everything excited the girl since I'd hired her on at Montclaire to help Melusina with the house and the cooking. Since the day I had mentioned to my father that Kati and some of the tenants' children could scarce read, he had gathered them together in the afternoons for schooling in reading, history, geography, and mathematics. Sometimes Papa called them by their own names; sometimes he believed they were Ambrose, Lianelle, and me. No one minded.

Yet my joy in Kati's excitement was fiercer than shared pleasure at a child's enlarged prospects or my father's gradual emergence from the shadowed realms he had wandered for so long. The quicker I could get Montclaire functioning smoothly, the sooner I could leave. The most beautiful demesne in Sabria was no longer my home.

As slow, steady water droplets on a prisoner's forehead, each innocent and painless in itself, can become a torment, so was every day apart from Dante. I feared his brooding melancholy. I grieved at his stubborn refusal to believe that we shared much more than a house and a singular gift. And though he had warded Pradoverde well, I fretted about his myriad enemies. Offering the full story of his activities while king's *agente confide* might win alliances that would leave him less vulnerable, but I'd learned quickly that to suggest overtures to the king, my parents, the Camarilla Magica, or the Temple was to raise a firestorm.

"I did what was needed," he would bellow. "We were victors on Mont Voilline. If the cowards mislike the result or quibble with my choices, let them hang me." Then he would retreat to hammer molten iron or dig in the dirt for the rest of the day. Cowardly, I let matters rest and bided my time. Only when he was teaching me sorcery did he come alive. Yet even that was fraught with argument. I believed we should expend all our energies in solving the mystery of Ixtador before my sister's soul was leached away. He insisted I must plod through ridiculous spellwork first. And to my heart's pain, it seemed that only the magic raised his spirits, never the student.

Latching the case and throwing my discarded cloak over my shoulder with the blanket, I began the long trudge up the hill.

Mostly I just missed Dante himself. Every hour apart, no matter how busy, seemed vacant. Every person I encountered, including the gracious, well-educated, temperate young men who just happened to arrive every few days to introduce themselves—all recommended by Papa's friends or Mama's kin in Nivanne—seemed shallow as the dust on a tabletop.

I should have considered myself fortunate that I could perceive Dante in the aether—a distant, tumultuous eddy in the mindstorm that I'd come to recognize as his presence. But my chest just ached the more. Even if we were close enough in distance to speak in our minds, he refused to engage in that way.

"Who's come, Kati?" I said, huffing the last few metres up the rise.

The slim, fair girl was red-cheeked and near bursting as she fell in beside me for the rest of the hike to the house. "It's one of the tenants, Buiron, and his son. They asked for the lord, but I told them you took all business as yet. They seemed a bit fretful. Thought the son might puke when I had 'em come out the kitchen and into the business room as you've told me."

Probably a new baby on the way or perhaps a petition to expand their leasehold. I had let it be known that tenants were welcome to bring their business whenever it came up, rather than waiting for the conte to make his quarterly rounds.

The two touched their foreheads in respect as I hurried into the whitewashed room off the steward's office.

"Divine grace, Goodman Buiron. And you must be Pev, your father's eldest." I motioned the large, hairy man and his blotchy son of fifteen to sit on the wooden bench that lined two of the whitewashed walls. "How may I help you this fine day? Such a fair new year we've seen already."

They remained standing. "Divine grace, my lady, but I feel— My lady, is there no way to speak to His Grace?" Even hesitant, Buiron's hearty basso filled the small room. "All know he's not yet back to his robust self, but I saw him ride out with you and the mistress on the New Year's feast and thought he might— We needs must show summat we've found this day. But it's no sight for a gentle lady."

"Bless you for your concern. But my father has asked me to continue the responsibilities I carried through the years of his absence. Honestly, goodman, I cannot imagine anything happening about Montclaire to match the terrible sights in Merona two years past."

Though indeed both man and youth were about to crush their hats into pulp. The boy's hands trembled. I prayed they'd not spotted some blight or pest on the vines. Our vineyards were only just coming back to full vigor. King Philippe had granted us a goodly stipend, but his own treasury was not bottomless. Such land as Montclaire must produce revenue, not only for my family but for the innumerable others who depended on us.

"Then come, if you would."

I grabbed a hat and my cloak and followed the two as they traipsed out behind the well house and through a tangled juniper thicket. A steep slope seamed with gullies and washes plunged downward toward the tenant fields and Vernase village.

" 'Twas this morning we discovered a fox took one of our piglets. Pev and me thought to track it down and make sure it couldn't come back for second helpings. But down the gullies we come on summat we never thought to find on this land."

A quarter hour's scramble took us into a rocky notch in the north-facing hillside. The chill of winter nights had already settled into its permanent shadows. Yet a taint I associated with summer hung on the still air. "Something's died back there."

"Aye."

He'd been a big man, bigger than Buiron. Animals had scuffed aside enough of loose rock and dirt to expose one shoulder, one leg, and the back of his head. He'd not yet begun to wither in the dry chill. Dead mere days, then. Teeth had ripped clothing and bared flesh. A dark-skinned man. Black hair. A chill surged through my limbs. His ear . . .

"We must dig him out. Right now." I threw off my cloak. We'd need it to wrap him.

Buiron's protest died unspoken and he nodded at his boy. I was already on my knees, tossing aside the melon-sized boulders and scrabbling through the dirt to expose the man's face.

I sat back, arm thrown over my mouth to block more than the stench. *Calvino de Santo.*

Grief, horror, and denial collided. Such a good and decent man. What was he doing *here*? And in such a state . . .

Every squared centimetre of his skin spoke of prolonged and methodical violence. Back and shoulders a hatchwork of whip scars, some almost healed, some fresher. Teeth and nose broken; the bones about one eye crushed. Scars on chest, arms, hands, everywhere the animals hadn't touched. Skin curled back from a slash at his throat. Murdered. On my father's land.

I threw my cloak over the ruined face so my companions could not describe him.

De Santo bore a rightful grudge against Papa. Disgrace would ever follow his name because my father had rashly blamed him for an attempt on King Philippe's life. But even if de Santo had come here to settle that old score—which I could not believe—Papa had no strength to do this to any man. His mind spent half his days outside ordinary life and memory. But whispers would spread like plague. I could not allow that until I knew who in the name of all that was holy could have wreaked these horrors on a fine and honorable soldier. And why.

His shirt was mostly gone. His belt had been used to bind his hands. I drew my knife, gritted my teeth, and cut away the outer layers of his breeches. Pockets and folds had been emptied. Nor was anything tucked inside his boots.

Buiron and his son stood waiting.

"Surely thieves have done this," I said. "Hidden their victim here to disguise their crime. Perhaps he was one of them. My father must advise me how to proceed. Until he says, no one must know the body's found, lest we alert the murderers. Not your wife. Not even the verger at the deadhouse—not yet. Swear it, goodman, on your lord's honor, and you, Pev."

"Aye, we so swear." They dipped their heads and touched their brows and I prayed they were half so honorable as the man who lay here.

We rolled him in my cloak and buried him deeper, so that animals could not reach him again.

As they headed off to their work, I raced up to the house, for my earlier activities bore a connection to Calvino de Santo that threatened to collapse my knees.

Queen Eugenie wrote frequently, keeping me abreast of her joyous state of life . . . a long-awaited healthy pregnancy. Her last letter had come just a few days previous, and she had appended a query that I had dismissed as nothing. I burst into the steward's office, where I'd dropped my writing case and letters, scarce acknowledging Bernard, who had settled in with the account books. My eyes devoured Eugenie's query.

> Dante summoned Ilario to Pradoverde 18 Desen last. Have you any idea when my brother might be planning to return to Merona? I miss him so terribly with Philippe embroiled in Norgand. Yet I was heartened that Dante actually sought his help for some project. I know that Dante appears more ferocious than is truth. That your feelings for him are so certain and strong but affirms my instinct. It would delight me so if he could see the worth in Ilario, that our dear ones might find the joy in each other that we find in them.

18 Desen. Forty-two days ago! For more than two years running, Calvino de Santo had never strayed far from Ilario. That meant he'd likely gone to Pradoverde as well. If the captain lay dead in Montclaire's soil, then where, in the name of all gods, were Dante and Ilario?

Such a pall of dread fell over me, I could scarce move. Pressing fists to my face, I closed my eyes and lowered my barriers. The aether was turbulent on this day, disturbed as I'd rarely felt it so far out in the country as Montclaire. Dante was there. I felt the pulse of his life, but far away and strangely quiet. All his anger, wonder, guilt, joy, doubt were but echoes. Despite the bright sun, the touch left me shivering.

Within an hour I had penned a short message to Finn. One of the stable boys ran down to the village with coin enough to ensure Mistress Constanza's hire messenger would take it north to Pradoverde at once and bring an answer as soon as might be.

Only to Bernard did I entrust the truth. As I told him of de Santo, reasoning shaped a story. The captain could not have been so brutalized for so long anywhere nearby. Vernase was too small. Strangers would be noticed. His appearance—his own belt as a bond, the rifled pockets, the slash to the throat, the shallow burial—spoke of haste. Someone didn't want him to get to the house. Perhaps he had escaped his tormentors, and they had followed him here. . . .

With his ineffable calm, Bernard used a variety of ruses from missing cats to eradicating potential vine pests to ensure that one person or another visited every house, shed, gully, and grove in the neighborhood. No stranger, alive or dead, could possibly be lurking within five kilometres. I mentioned rumors of thieves to our captain of the guard; he knew how to heighten the watch without alarming anyone.

After eight long days, Constanza's bleary-eyed lad Remy rode into the yard. I tore open the splotched paper before he could pocket his tip.

> *Damozelle,*
>
> *This is Finn writing to you in answer to your letter. The Lord Ilareyo is not at Pradovairday. None is here but me. Certain he was here in Desen's month when he and his soljer rode north with the master to see to the master's da. The master said they would return in seventeen days, but is now running more than a month past. Mayhap his da refused to die as quick as the letter said or he's learned something more about the majical dream. Theres a few men new in the village say they just come from the north and the winter storms are feerce. So mayhap that has delayed him.*
>
> *Your horses are fine but oats are dear. I cannot buy more nor pay the New Year tax without you or the master unlock the box.*
>
> *Finn*

Dante's *father*? Dante had refused to share his blighted childhood. But I knew enough to judge that something more than his father's dying must have spurred him to set out for Coverge in midwinter, with an urgency that forced him to seek help from Ilario. Now one of the three who had gone north, Ilario's *soljer,* had somehow ended up tortured and dead. And Ilario was missing. A better friend and nobler spirit did not exist in this world. And Dante . . . My probe of the aether told me he lived, but distant and somehow . . . altered. *Where are you, friend of my heart?*

"Bernard!" I called, spurred to a decision unthinkable even a day earlier. "I'm leaving. . . ."

ONE THING AND THEN ANOTHER conspired to delay my departure. One of our tenants was found beating his wife, which required my father—with my help—to hold an inquiry and give judgment. A shortage of oak was threatening the vintage and new supplies had to be found.

Then Papa lost another unhealthy tooth. As ever, it catapulted him back into horror. He huddled in corners, believing he was yet held in his underground cell, body and mind disintegrating as his captors repeatedly drained his blood to feed their magic. To draw him out again required constant comfort and reassurance, long walks outdoors, and unceasing talk. My mother was immensely strong, but she could not tend him every hour of every day. An old military friend of Papa's who often came to share memories and news agreed to stay over in my absence.

I never questioned my decision to go. My spirit would not be settled until I knew Dante and Ilario were safe, and I could think of nowhere to begin the search than the place they began their own mysterious journey.

For the sake of speed and secrecy, I decided to make the five-day journey to Pradoverde alone. I informed our guard captain that Queen Eugenie had summoned me to Merona and would send companions to meet me in Tigano. I had Mistress Constanza dispatch a trunk to Castelle Escalon, ensuring my story would be widely propagated.

Only Ella and Bernard knew my true destination, just as only they knew I could summon magic to protect myself—raw magic, not wrought spells as Dante could work.

After two years of practice, I could control, shape, and release power enough to foil an attacker, while retaining control of my emotions so I didn't kill anyone without intent. That was all I had ever wanted from Dante's lessons. Magic had destroyed my sister, crippled my family, and come near bringing the ruination of the world. Its creeping energies in my body still left me queasy and ill.

Dante didn't understand that. He seemed convinced that if I learned enough about spellworking, I would embrace the wonders of sorcery as he did and work some grand rite to finish what we had begun on Mont Voilline. I didn't believe it. I didn't want it. Our shared gift meant he could draw on my blood-born power, and I would ever stand ready to give what he needed of me. He feared that blindness would destroy his own talent, and I grieved at his pain whenever some small failure seemed to confirm it. But if any man was born for one great purpose, Dante was born to wield magic. Neither gods nor nature could be so cruel as to steal it away.

But for now he'd won our argument. I trusted that he had not forgotten Lianelle and the depleted dead, and I embraced the discipline that was his only joy. Through our shared experiences in the aether, I had touched the beauty, the harmony, the rich spirit buried beneath his anger and self-doubt, and I would not it give up. Not ever.

AT LAST ALL WAS SETTLED enough for me to go. I was stuffing a few last things into my traveling bag when Ella called out from my window. "There's riders come into the yard. Five, six, seven of them in green-and-white livery."

I joined her at the window, prepared to fly down the back stair to avoid yet another delay. But surprise held me as Bernard stepped out to greet the newcomers. They were Temple servitors.

The visitors dismounted, deferring to a man of middle height who waited for Bernard to come to him. A man of rank, then. Why would a high-ranking Temple servitor come to Montclaire? My father had always been the king's man, a champion of science and reason, no enemy of the Temple, but no more its devotee than he was a partisan of the Camarilla Magica.

Bernard bowed and turned for the door, glancing up at my window on his way. Had they come to see *me*? Fleeting guilts suggested they'd come to accuse us of Captain de Santo's murder. But that was ridiculous. The Concord between Crown, Temple, and Camarilla Magica left religious crimes alone to Temple jurisdiction. And my arrangements with Dante were known to only a very few.

I pulled off my cloak and passed it to Ella. "Take this, my riding gloves, and my bag to Bernard's office. I'd best go down."

She nodded in understanding and headed for the back stair. I descended the main stair and met Bernard in the foyer. "What are Temple servitors doing here?"

"One of them's a tetrarch, damo—"

"A tetrarch!"

"Aye. Name of Beltan de Ferrau. Begs an interview with you on a 'matter of grave import.' Says Mistress Constanza told him you were off to Merona today, so he risked arriving early. I could tell him you're sleeping."

"No, I'd best hear him out. I can't have him bothering Papa. Bring him to the grand salon."

I sat in a cushioned chair beside the tall window in our best room and took some of Melusina's embroidery to hand. Though I detested needlework, I felt the need to let a Temple man find me engaged in innocent occupation. My mind was entirely too fixed on murder and a missing necromancer.

The door swung open. "Lady Anne de Vernase, His Excellency Beltan de Ferrau, Tetrarch of the Jarasco Temple Minor."

"Excellency." I rose and dipped a knee slightly as the clergyman strode through the doors. Court and Temple protocols would rank my father, the conte of a *demesne grande*, equal to the Tetrarch of Merona's Temple Major, and thus well above the administrator of a Temple Minor of a city small enough I wasn't sure where it was located. But I was a woman, and daughter, not wife. I well knew what protocol deemed my *own* rank. "Welcome to Montclaire on behalf of the Conte and Contessa Ruggiere."

I dabbed my thumb on my forehead as a gesture of respect and exposed my marked hand on my shoulder as the law required. He would not find fault with my deportment.

"Lady Anne, please forgive me intruding on your home and your peace." His voice was pleasant and solid, neither prim nor self-aggrandizing. Indeed, when I raised my eyes I was astonished to see quite a young man for his elevated office. Fair-haired, with rugged features, and strongly built, he more fit the image of soldier than of priest. Indeed, even his garments, though bearing the rich green hue and the white-embroidered symbol of the three pillars, were simply fashioned of common kersey. The blue of his eyes was so clear as to be visible across the room.

"We delight in visitors at Montclaire. Unfortunately, my father and mother are yet abed. They're in fragile health."

"I am fully aware of your parents' ordeals, my lady. And I understand that those of your brother, your young sister—may her Veil journey be swift and true—and you yourself were no less horrific. But it is you I've come to visit this day, early, as I've told your man, so as not to delay you on your travels."

"Then, sit, Excellency." I waved to a chair facing mine, bypassing such politenesses as refreshments. This man had no more interest in politeness than would a battering ram. Well and good. I knew how to build walls.

"I don't believe in dancing around subjects to make them more palatable, my lady," he said as soon as I'd sat down again. "I've come to speak to you about the sorcerer Dante."

I blessed Melusina for scattering her needle projects around the house. It gave me good excuse to keep my eyes fixed on her intricate design of a golden-leaved azinheira. My fingers pushed the needle deliberately through the stretched linen, no matter the warning trumps sounding inside me.

"A dark subject for a bright morning," I said. "My family's ills are, in some part at least, attributable to that mage."

"Very dark. I've come seeking your help to apprehend him."

"Apprehend?" I refused to let my voice heat and deliberately pushed the needle through its next position before continuing. "I understood he was paroled two years ago by order of the king."

"Only the Temple can absolve a man of blasphemy. And the sorcerer has not been brought to trial for his newer crimes."

Blasphemy. The needle stabbed my finger and I curled it for a moment so as not to stain the linen. Necromancy was blasphemy of the highest order, punishable by torture and burning.

Rumors of Dante's deadraising had been rampant throughout Sabria. But if any beyond Eugenie and me had actually witnessed the things I had in the palace Rotunda, they had never stepped forward. So we had believed. And what *newer crimes*?

"Naturally, I've heard rumors," I said, waving my needle in the air, "but I assumed them naught but gossip from a fearful time. I leave such weighty judgments to my goodfather, the king, and to others wiser than I. As to newer crimes, I've no idea what those might be—though everyone in my family and in Sabria, for that matter, could believe any wickedness of that man, true or not."

De Ferrau's posture did not shift, as if I'd said only what he expected. "Many of my fellow tetrarchs, older and more experienced than I, have seen fit to accept the king's judgment in this matter. Perhaps it displays my youth and ignorance to believe that rumor is often founded in truth. Perhaps those of us from the northern demesnes where life is harsh are more like to pay close attention to sacred matters—and require their strict distinction from civil law. Or perhaps it requires younger eyes, like mine, to observe that the rumors of necromancy coincided with very visible and well-described daemonic occurrences in the royal city, and that these same incidents and same rumors ceased entirely on the day Master Dante was exiled from Merona."

Though his body had settled easily into his chair, the young tetrarch's pale eyes did not waver from my face. A frisson of fear feathered my spine. This man was Dante's enemy. My enemy.

He leaned forward slightly. "After the dreadful events of four years past, which neither king nor Camarilla has ever explained to us, Sabrians properly turn to the divine Pantokrator and his Temple for answers. We tetrarchs are required by our vows to provide them. It is abomination to me that Master Dante has not been brought to any Temple for questioning. I intend to change that."

In a long, slow motion, I drew the gold thread through the linen and poked the needle back through the fine weft, while words raced and whirled through my head like dry leaves in a gale.

"Why come to me? Of all people I have reason to despise the man."

"I have witnesses who claim you have maintained contact with Master Dante these two years since."

"*Contact?* I'm not sure what you are insinuating, sirrah."

The only people who both knew of Pradoverde and had been in any position to witness Dante's deadraising were people we trusted. Yet neither had we hidden ourselves. I dared not deny the association.

With all the composure I could muster, I raised my eyes to de Ferrau. "Two years ago I was made a pawn of Germond de Gautier in his conspiracy to assassinate King Philippe and topple the throne of Sabria. I witnessed horrors. I was subjected to vile enchantments and poisons. My family was brutalized, my sister murdered. No one could emerge from such events unscathed. My symptoms—screaming fits, nightmares, uncontrolled frenzy, which many residents of Castelle Escalon can substantiate—induced me to confront the man who was responsible for them. He was the only living person who might unravel the illness I suffered. He did so as a condition of his parole. Our association was not pleasant, nor is it something I wish to relive for a stranger. Suffice it to say, I now reside here with my beloved family in the home of my childhood, helping my parents recover from torments far worse than my own. I cannot help you."

I laid the sewing aside and rose.

"Creator's peace, Tetrarch de Ferrau. And I will ask that you refrain from disturbing my parents with any mention of Master Dante."

He dropped his gaze before I did, but I suspected it was not from embarrassment. I could almost hear him assessing and evaluating my answers. At last he rose briskly and snapped a bow. "Thank you, Lady Anne. I appreciate your candor."

I showed him out of the salon. As Bernard opened the outer doors, de Ferrau swung around. "Perhaps you would be interested to know that these new crimes I spoke of include a sorcerous explosion that destroyed one of Jarasco's town gates, a fire that leveled the stable of one of our local hostels, the incineration of a Camarilla adept, and a rain of deadly arrows that slew a dozen of my Temple's bailiffs. Civil, magical, and sacred crimes, and he is implicated in the direst form of murder this side of Heaven's gates—that of one's own father. I have brought witnesses to Merona. Whether you choose to hear their testimony or not, Dante de Raghinne is an abomination. I strongly recommend you take any further symptoms to a different physician."

Incineration . . . explosive destruction . . . more than a dozen murders . . . And now de Santo, too, dead. Dante would never— But did I believe that?

Tetrarch de Ferrau and his servitors rode out before I could move from the doorway. Breathing away a wicked fit of the shakes, I grabbed my small traveling bag, bade farewell to my parents, and raced away from Montclaire on a track through the vineyards and hills that no Temple servitor could possibly expect.

Dante

CHAPTER 13

6 ESTAR, AFTERNOON
DEMESNE OF ARABASCA

Winter chased us south and west and into the new year. The three of us rode as long and hard as the winter roads and care for the horses permitted. Though we glimpsed no signs of pursuit, we took precautions. I hid my collar.

Midmorning of our tenth day out from Castelivre, Andero brought us to a halt atop a shallow rise. "I'll tell you, Master Mage, I've seen the ice barrens and sea cliffs of the northland, and every sort of hill and mountain you could imagine, but never such a road as this one lies below us. It's got neither curve nor blemish, as if it could take us right over the rim of the world without us meeting another breathing person."

My heart raced. "The Syanar high road. Be sure, we'll encounter blemishes enough along it—caravans, thieves, Cult shrines, and enough pilgrims to choke a priest. Mattefriese lies only a few days east."

"And there we turn south to Carabangor?"

My back stiffened.

"Be easy, Dante; the hoptoad has lagged again to dig his mushrooms or roots or whatever. I just need to understand what's going on with you. You've not spoke three words of explanation since we left that blighted ruin."

"There's naught to explain. We're going after Portier."

"And if he's not to be found? I know you don't want to think about that, but what if? If this Jacard and the enchantress are as wicked as you say, perhaps someone else ought to know what you're about. Perhaps your lady?"

"She's not my lady, and I've naught to tell her as yet. You wouldn't understand."

"I understand you've not worked a smat of magic since we've been traveling. I understand you've not sent word to those who might care about you. Something happened that night at Castelivre and you've locked it up inside you."

"I told you that's none of your concern." I spat it through my teeth, then yelled over my shoulder, "John Deune! Get back here or I'll boil you in your own pots!"

Cantering hoofbeats brought the little weasel back, babbling: "Pardon the delay, Master, especially as it was all for naught. 'Twasn't dock I saw, but blisterweed. I'm attempting only to give some variety to our fare. . . ."

Fortunately for him, Andero took out right away, and I had to mind Devil and my seat. Would that I could break the damned tether that linked Devil to Andero's mount. "Lag behind us again, John Deune," I shouted after them, "and we'll send you back to Merona afoot."

I forced my hands to unclench, lest I bruise poor Devil. I wanted to hit something. To hammer something. To twist something until it broke. Anything but lay my mind to what Andero had said. I'd spent these days on the road reviewing every word, every circumstance, every action that I could recall since the day Masson de Cuvier had arrived at Pradoverde, trying to figure out why the sky over Jarasco might have been bulging and what connection that might have with white-gowned enchantresses and legendary emeralds and tales of the war for Heaven and the madness that had risen in me in that ruined cellar. Going over it again would feel like shaving my skin with a rasp.

By afternoon, the intermittent snow had yielded to a dry chill, and we joined a stream of travelers heading eastward. Patching sounds, smells, and snips of conversations into a moving landscape was a welcome distraction.

A heavily guarded caravan hauled tin and silver to trade for silk and porcelain.

A large family drove a rattling wagon eastward, hoping to reclaim their family holdings in Aroth. Their axles ground, spalled most likely, and would surely break down before too many more days on the road.

A large group of Cult penitents ventured the pilgrim way in winter as punishment for their faults. They nattered at each other about proper badges on their clothing and whether one could drink wine when fasting. An argument about the requirement to stop at every one of the fifty shrines along the way put them to blows.

A few days' sharing encampments and wells with these myriad strangers and I began to distinguish individual travelers. One of the penitents peppered her conversations with wholly irrelevant quotations from Cult holy books. A soldier, who forever stank of spirits, had a wicked case of the shakes. A woman with five bodyguards and an older female attendant was riding to her wedding. Would her bridegroom smell the seductive smoke of *synoise* lingering on her garments? Did she deaden her senses in anticipation of his attentions or to erase the time they were apart?

It was about this same time I began to suspect we were being followed.

"Odd," I said to Andero. "Weren't those two ahead of us yesterday?"

"Who?"

"The two riders we passed not three breaths ago."

"Naught but a clump of scrubby locusts at the edge of a field three breaths ago."

"Then they must be hiding behind the trees. They stink of pipeweed and have likely not bathed since their birth washing. Their horses are lively and light, but they never make ground on us, and never talk but in mumbles when they're close by. How odd is that? One of them wheezes like a leaky bellows. The other has a nose that runs like a river. Surely you can pick them out."

"There's a deal of riders about, Dante. None odder than the next."

A day out from Mattefriese, the traffic grew heavier. The roads were dry. We shed our wool mufflers after sunrise and welcomed the sun's blaze at midday. Three times that day I noted the two, once ahead, twice behind.

"I've peeled my eyes," said Andero as we made camp at a caravan stop outside the city walls, "but I've seen naught out of the common way. There's thirty campfires hereabouts, and travelers always ride together in the lean seasons." Andero's great bulk leaned closer. "Not my place to say, but you're blind, if you recall. And now your collar is exposed, and your scraggle of a beard makes you look like a dying scarecrow, none dare lag anywhere near you."

"Tell me how a man who smells like a wet dog looks better," I said, a grin threatening. My brother could find my better humor, even when I thought it entirely lost. Still, those two riders were up to no good.

Andero sharpened his pen, unstoppered his ink bottle, and went back to scratching at his map as he did every night when the weather was dry. John Deune fussed with the fire and his pot. The manservant had maintained an exceptional quiet since we'd joined the other travelers.

"What of you, John Deune? You must have been accustomed to watching for thieves when you traveled with Lord Ilario. Have you noticed anyone suspicious?"

The thwup and splash of a dropped water flask marked him. I'd never heard him clumsy or so fluent in his cursing. "No! Certainly not! If I did notice such villains—and indeed I was always most careful watching out for the chevalier—you can be sure I would mention it right away. Many a time I saved his lordship's purse from a snatch. He refused to go about without his jewels and gold chains and silken kerchiefs, as if every man and woman might own such things and not desire them. It was certain his privilege to display his riches so."

I didn't like having John Deune around. He didn't know when to be quiet. And I'd never taken enough notice of him in the days when I might have learned to distinguish his truth or lies. But to abandon such a silly, preening cockroach on this road would be like offering him up to bandits. He was Ilario's man, and Ilario had given his life for me. I owed him something. But I couldn't make myself trust him.

Not wishing his knife so close to my throat, I didn't allow him to shave my chin, but indeed, he wielded a pot and spoon with worthy skills. Using his leather packet of herbs and spices, he could have made a decent meal from dead grass and sticks. Yet I would have welcomed his dead master the more. Guilt and regret were hollow company.

"Perhaps you could work some magical thing to detect those two," said Andero. I clamped my teeth against the curse I wanted to bellow at him, emptied my mind of the reasons, and rolled myself in my blanket.

MATTEFRIESE

Andero reported a large number of Temple bailiffs hanging about the gates of Mattefriese, so we took to the road as soon as Andero and John returned from the city. Andero brought information about our route, and John Deune brought supplies along with complaints about rancid bacon, stale bread, and the high cost of water.

After only a short distance on the high road, Andero slowed, allowing a wagon to rattle past us and out of hearing. "Five metres and we turn south," he said.

"What are you doing, fool of a smith?" said John Deune. "Abidaijar is straight east on the high road. The librarian . . ."

"Plans have changed," my brother said. "We're not going to Abidaijar."

The winds cut deep as we headed south. I drew up my hood, wrapped my scarf about my face, and retreated into a drowsy half sleep. . . .

"Halt!" bellowed Andero, dragging me back to full alert. "Where is the blasted prig? How are we to make any speed at all if he keeps drifting so far out of sight?"

I held tight as Devil followed the other beast's lead and came to a stop.

"I'll go back. You wait here," said Andero, detaching my tether rope.

"We should leave him," I said. "He's likely decided it's time to collect the Temple's price on my head."

"If he didn't have most of our food and all the extra water, I'd agree. From what I hear, we can't afford to go ahead without. But I see the least thing suspicious, I'll break his neck."

My ever-genial brother made me believe he'd do it.

Surely it was half an eternity till the two of them returned.

"My profound apologies, Master. It was only after we were on our way that I realized I'd left all our extra water at the caravanserai."

"Then why didn't you say something instead of vanishing?" I snapped.

"Indeed, Master"—he was near choking—"Goodman Andero had emphasized how we dared not risk this road on a meager supply. Shamed, I thought it best to slip back quickly before we'd gone too far."

I could not judge if he spoke truth. Yet no one had brought the Temple down on me in Mattefriese, and Andero wouldn't have brought him back if he'd seen a risk. We shared out supplies equally and warned him that next time he fell behind we'd not stop for him.

"Certainly, Master. Certainly."

"I think I know the two stragglers you spoke of, Master," said Andero as we rode onward. "Glimpsed them in the marketplace buying sausage and water flasks. Two scrawny, pasty-faced fellows in ill-fitting clothes.

One wheezing; one about to drown in his own snot. But they strike me as shop clerks more than highwaymen. I don't—"

"Why would anyone be interested in us?" burst in John. "Well, of course, I know there's a price on the mage's head. But how would *they* know of it? Not that I noticed them. But none would ever guess that a ruffian on a leash"—he sniffed like a lord himself—"could ever be a court mage, certainly not one so clever and dangerous."

Clearly John Deune believed blind men were necessarily deaf as well.

"Exactly so," said Andero. "Indeed, they ducked away when a Temple bailiff came poking his nose about the market, elsewise I'd have had a serious word with them. Sure, if I should see them along this road, I'll gut them both."

I believed that, too.

DEMESNE OF ARABASCA

For days, we encountered neither man nor beast on the road south. As the steep ground leveled out to high plains, sere winds sapped moisture from our bodies and life from our spirits. Even Andero grumbled.

We traveled what Andero's comrades in the Coverge legion called a ghost road. Our narrow dirt track centered a wide, shallow, grassy trough, the evidence of repeated invasion. For centuries, armies had marched across this land. My imagination conjured pockets of colder air in the wind, naming them hollow-eyed dead men who whispered, *Lead usss.* To be locked in one's own head oft made for poor amusement.

No one followed, not even our sausage-eating tagalongs. Either Andero or I stayed alert during John Deune's night watch. But I set no wards. To imagine reaching for power set my hands trembling like an old woman's.

On our fourth day out from Mattefriese, the road brought us within sight of a village. Andero described it as a cluster of ramshackle huts huddled together like scrawny cattle with their backs to the wind. Though the daylight waned, he urged us to keep moving. "They'll want to feed us," he said, "but I've never seen folk could make a life from so much nothing as out here. Taking aught from 'em would be thieving."

But it was already too late. "Welcome, travelers, be ye men or spirits!"

"It's four of 'em come out," murmured Andero. "Elders. A scrawny lot, but grinning wider than a pawner when a lord walks into his shop."

"Rest ye this night 'neath our roofs," said a breathless man who sounded older than the road. "We'll spit a lamb in celebration of thy company, then share a cup and a tale of the wide world."

"We've no wish to put you out," said Andero. "And we need to be on our way."

"There's naught before thee but the haunted heights and the sea of sand. The dead will wait. We get few living travelers along this road. What news and stories thou might share will sustain us longer than the bits of sustenance we provide."

"Have you seen travelers ride through since the change of season?" I blurted, as another cold pocket of air gave me a shudder. Easy to understand how people living here could imagine ghosts on the road. "Perhaps a party with a prisoner?"

"Only the one group, some two cycles of the moon since," said a rasp-voiced woman. "Maybe a dozen riders. They didn't slow. Didn't even look our way. We thought they might be dead."

Perhaps Portier and his captors. Two months . . . The timing could be right. Not dead, though. Surely not dead.

"We'd be grateful for whatever you can spare," said Andero. "My name is Manet de Shreu. This is my master, Mage Talon, and our servant, John Deune. My master travels south to ply his work in desert climes."

"A sorcerer!" The old man's voice grew wary. "This land aches from magework. . . ."

"But he is welcome, anyway," pronounced a woman, chiding. "He Who Wanders the Stars bids us welcome wanderers of all kinds."

"I've no business here, elder," I said. "Just a need to sleep."

The villagers paraded us to each house in turn. Most were occupied by women and children, their men out with their animals. They sustained a small herd of sheep and goats by spreading them far out on the plains to graze, companioned and comforted in their lonely nights by their god or angel or whatever *He Who Wanders the Stars* was thought to be. The women produced woolen cloth that they colored with dyes distilled from the highland plants. Every other year, they took their cloth to Mattefriese to trade. They spoke of the journey with wonder, as if it were one of King Philippe's voyages of exploration, a dangerous and exciting adventure from which one might or might not return with riches untold.

The colors and weaving were quite fine for starveling villagers, so John Deune declared aloud, as if poor folk might be as deaf as blind men.

Yet, indeed the villagers did the same. Whispers trailed us like dust in our wake: . . . *he wears bruises from the Hungry One's rod. Hide the children. Is he dead? Daemon.* From Castelle Escalon to this village at the end of the world, I could not seem to escape the name, the same in every myth. It had never bothered me until Castelivre.

Claiming recent illness, I excused myself from the lamb spitting, tale spinning, and further mumbling. They provided me tea and the porridge they kept on the fire for infants and elders, and did not ask me to reconsider. Andero insisted we not crowd their cramped homes, so they offered us a lambing shed to bed down in. Stomach satisfied, grateful for a windbreak and the deep straw, I rolled up in my blanket and forced urgency aside. Andero would watch.

As sense played chase-and-hide with oblivion, a solid mass manifested itself a few centimetres from my head. Perhaps with a touch of a wheeze. My hand crept to my staff.

"Soft." The old man's words weighed in the night like gold amid feathers. "Thou'rt safe with me. I recognized thee from afar—a wanderer who cannot choose what realm he walks. Who crosses boundaries no man is meant to venture."

"You're more right than you could know," I said, exhaustion slurring my words. "Sometimes it's hard to find the way."

"Arise, Daemon. Walk the road of the dead. But be wary of thy companion, required to speak truth, though his meaning is ever lies. And though wary, stay with him, for he leads thee to thy unhappy destiny. Thou'rt other, born in darkness, gifted with strength that can quench the light of Heaven."

My body near stood up of its own self, ready to bellow a denial. But my limbs would not answer and I decided I must be asleep. *Born in darkness.* How else could he know that?

"DANTE, ARE YOU STILL AWAKE?"

"No," I muttered into my arm. "There's no wind. No rocks. No more wheezy old men with doom on their tongues. King Philippe sleeps no better."

"I need to speak with you." My brother's voice was troubled, and when I didn't answer right off, he didn't go away.

"So speak."

"It's middle-night."

Gods, my turn to watch. I groaned. "All right, all right, I'll get up. Are you drunk?"

"Nay. The shepherds said they'd keep watch. I told them bandits tried to steal your collar at Mattefriese and might be after us. It's— I've been drinking tea with the headman and his wife."

"Then, what?"

"I don't like to trouble you."

I sat up, trying not to grind my teeth. "I'm awake. You're not troubling me, and I don't eat large men more than once a year. What is it?"

"There's a man and a child been herding sheep in the hills out east. A boy went out this morning to take them supplies and found the little one half dead and the man bashing his head on the walls of his hut and tearing his skin away. They've no healer in the village."

My spirit froze. "I'm not a healer, Andero."

"I know that. It's just that—well, it really sounds more up your line. The headman's wife had them brought to a hut where they keep the sick, but she saw no signs of illness. No fever. No flux. Nothing. They're thinking it's a curse and are afraid to go near them. Maybe you could tell them what's what."

"They don't want me near them. You heard them mumbling about sorcerers and daemons. It's naught but bad water or sheep fever."

"But the two will starve if their own people won't care for them. The boy's naught but a nub."

"I won't. I know what you're trying to do, but I can't. You heard them. They don't want magic. And so wary of it, they're like to blame me even if this fellow's broken his head or eaten poison."

"Just asking that you *tell* them whether it's magic or no. I'll vow you don't have to use magic to do that much. After . . . if you can't do for them, then that's the way it must be."

The stubborn oaf was setting up to argue until dawn. If I wanted to sleep again, I'd have to look. "All right. All right. If they agree to accept my word, I'll take a look. Make sure they understand."

After a few hours under a roof, the cold was fierce and hungry. The wind slammed my chest like a battering ram. As we made the long trek to the hovel where the shepherd and his son had been abandoned, I didn't dare ask Andero to look at the sky. Dread rode the winds that night, outside me as well as inside.

"If you see that dotard who barged in before you did, tell him *he's* the Daemon," I grumbled. The old man's words trailed after me just enough to roil my gut, but not enough to mean anything.

"Didn't see him."

Maybe he was another dream. Gods, I was ready to be done with dreams forever.

Someone had built up a fire in the healing hut before running away. The room was unbearably hot and smelled of burnt sheep dung. I sent Andero to discover if there was one person in the village who might assist me. I didn't want my brother in the room if there was sickness after all.

They had laid the burly shepherd on a pallet and tied his limbs to spikes fixed in the dirt. He fought, moaned, growled, and whimpered, spewing curses in what hoarse voice he had left. When I placed a hand on his forehead, he near bit it off. The boy lay beside his father unbound. Still and limp, skin clammy and breathing shallow, he was too wasted to be a threat.

Neither showed fever. The man was sweating profusely and stank of sheep, not drink.

Raghinne's healing women had used a litany of symptoms to gauge illness: *sweet and sour, tongue and teeth, stiff and soft, pulse and palpitations*. The shepherd's breath and his puddled urine smelled normal, neither sweet nor sour. His blood-pulse raced, as one might expect, but was strong. His joints flexed almost too much; as I struggled to rebind his arm, he tried to choke me in his elbow. Squeezing his head in the crook of my arm, I fingered his tongue. Disgusting . . .

The door creaked. Light footsteps hesitated, as the wind swirled the dust and smoke.

"Who's there?"

"Dorothea," she said in a breathy whisper. Her fear was like a fifth person in the room.

"I don't see," I said, "so I need your help. Tell me about these two. Does the man smoke blisterweed or something like?"

"Jono be an ill-luck man. But he's my sister's man and this her only babe . . ."

The sister had died birthing the boy, five years past. Then Jono had lost two sheep the next summer and one more the next. And only in the last tenday he had returned from Mattefriese market with scarce half the full price for two years' worth of cloth.

". . . but he's a good da, and neither drinks spirits nor smokes any pipe-weed. I can't let them lie here, less'n you tell there's no hope."

"Can't say as yet," I told her. "Come tell me how his tongue looks. . . ."

We stepped through everything I knew of mundane healing without finding a hint of the problem. The man's fingernails near pierced my skin, and he screamed as if the bed were made of iron spikes. The child scarce breathed. I'd naught left but magic. Gods . . .

I was not so stupid as to mistake why I'd worked no magic since Castelivre. Andero had seen it. Some people have a terror of snakes, imagining them in their beds, transforming every tickle in their shoe or up their back to a slithering whipsnake. Some people feel spiders everywhere; some see bears in the shadows on moonlit nights. I had ever feared the dark. Jacard had seen it; thus his gleeful selection of my ruin.

But down there in Denys's cellar, fear and anger—madness?—had taken me to a place so cold and so dark, my sightless state seemed but eventide. I had lost control, lost my self, and stolen life from a man who likely did not deserve it. Worse, I had murdered him with magic, my lodestone, my center. I had thought that feeling my skills deteriorate through sensory crippling was the worst torment the world could wreak. But to corrupt the work that had given my life meaning was far, far worse. And now they wanted me to raise magic next a child. . . .

Gifted with strength that can quench the light of Heaven. The old man might have spoke his words anew in that moment. Cold sweat drenched my clothing.

"Are you well, mage?" The woman touched my shoulder, and I near jumped out of my skin.

"Well enough. What's the boy's name?"

"Luz. He is a cheery boy."

Luz . . . *light.* I almost laughed. Or sobbed. "And the father is Jono?"

"Aye."

A cheery boy and an ill-luck man who were going to die if I couldn't help.

I curled my dead fingers about my staff and laid my left hand on the shepherd's forehead. A simple detection spell. I could at least leave these people with an answer. I summoned every discipline I knew, then applied a miserly smat of power. "*Maleferre,* Jono."

Stars exploded; cannons thundered, blistering, ripping, shredding. . . .

"Damnation!" I yelled, rubbing palm and fingers on my cheek to convince myself my sole useful hand was neither bleeding, nor charred, nor fleshless. Dorothea moaned and crashed against the door, letting in another gale to choke us with blowing ashes.

"It's all right. It's all right," I said, breathless from pain, surprise, disgust, and a smat of relief. "Come back. It's just . . . the fool has gone and bought himself a gheket!"

Every marketplace had a gheket seller. Maybe the bone man, maybe the silk merchant. But always there was one who would note an idiot who was down on his luck and whisper in his ear, *I've got my gammy's luck charm* or *my da's cure-all* or *my mam's everheal. All it will cost is a quarter of what's in your pocket.* Or a half.

Outlawed by the Camarilla—one instance in which I agreed with the prefects—ghekets were luck charms constructed from fifty to a thousand elements, from shark's teeth to pine needles, without regard to keirna, formulas, or good sense. The good ones were entirely inert. The rest, bound with some smattering of true power, could be a disaster. As they comprised so many things, there was always a possibility that the random combination would make a difference in the buyer's life—about the same chance as a star falling on one's head. But in general they were so ridiculous in composition that they caused much more trouble than they could possibly help. This one had been bound with a hefty dollop of true power, but the conflicting energies had shattered. The bits and pieces of spell-laden junk were literally ripping this man's mind to shreds. I could not ignore it.

Holding my power, I touched the boy. "*Maleferre*, Luz . . ."

Relieved, I called Dorothea in from the night, where she had retreated in terror.

"The boy's not ill, and there's no curse on him," I said. "He's hungry and overheated, and his father has most likely harmed him without meaning to. Look for a bump on his head. Get someone to carry him out of here, and send my companions to me."

She fetched Andero and John Deune, and then picked up the boy herself and carried him out, crooning to the child as Anne did to her horses.

I told Andero and John what I'd discovered. "I can likely take care of it. I've done it before. But I'll need a decent fire, lots of strong sweet tea, and someone to see the man doesn't tear his limbs off or mine. And someone to see that I don't . . . forget what I'm doing. Get carried away."

"John will take care of the fire and the tea," said my brother. "I'll see to the rest."

"Good." Andero knew why my hands were trembling. "Watch carefully. Be quick. And do whatever is needed. *Whatever.* I mean that."

The task I faced was daunting. It was as if a creature the size of an elephant, having the thickest, curliest wool of any sheep, had rolled in a field thick with briars. I had to remove each single briar, as well as every tiny spine of the briars that might have broken off, from that creature's coat. There was no general sweep that would do it, and no partial solution. If the man was to be helped, every spell fragment must be dealt with individually. And I had no time to waste; he would be dead or irreparably damaged in another day. There was no choice.

Dragging my staff around the pallet, I scribed an enclosure in the dirt floor; then I knelt at the shepherd's bedside and laid my hand on his forehead. Taking a deep breath, I willed Andero to be strong, opened myself to the aether, and reached deep to summon power. . . .

The spell fragments abraded my senses like burrs, bee stings, needle pricks, and ant bites. I destroyed each with a tiny burst of power. One. Then another. Then another. With utmost care.

From time to time, I stopped, resting briefly by John Deune's tidy fire, drinking his tea and eating honey cakes villagers left by the door. Only then did I hear Andero straining to keep the giant shepherd from harming himself, speaking as gently as if Jono were some outsized babe. Yet I felt the burn of my brother's eyes on me. Good. I nodded his way, then knelt and began again.

Fortunately, as each spell fragment was removed, the man settled a bit. By late afternoon, he slept peacefully. John Deune slept on the dirt floor next the remnants of his steady fire. Andero and I sat outside the door in the sun, too drained to speak. All three of us had done well. I felt clean again, or as if the hangman had withdrawn the noose a few centimetres. I had kept control. Hadn't murdered anyone. The lingering intoxication of true magic warmed my blood.

Dorothea reported that the boy had indeed suffered a blow to the head and a sprained ankle. He was now awake and eating a hearty supper. I told her to bring him to sit with his father, so the child could see that all was right with him. Perhaps it would restore the lunatic father's faith in his luck to see his boy on waking.

Andero sighed. "I suppose I'd best saddle the horses so we can be off."

I croaked a laugh. "You'd have to stuff me in your baggage to get me traveling today. But I do need Devil. I've got to visit the hut where they found these two. A gheket is always bound to an artifact of some kind—a twig circle, a twist of cloth, or some such. If someone else finds it, we'll have to do this all over again."

He groaned. "Not in this life!"

The boy who had discovered the raving shepherd volunteered to take me to the hut. He had escaped the curse once, so I supposed he thought riding on a horse named Devil with a nasty-looking sorcerer behind him could do no harm.

The artifact was blessedly easy to recognize, a small paper cone, totally unremarkable unless one could visualize the tangled knot of spell-lines that dangled from it in garish disarray. One by one I detached each tendril and destroyed it. When all was done, I crumpled the paper and stuck it in my pocket.

I fell asleep in the saddle, as my young guide was telling Devil how fine it would be for the two of them to ride beyond the horizon to discover palaces and kings. On our return to the village, he elbowed me to get off. Trusting him to care for my horse, I crawled gratefully into my nest in the lambing shed, ignoring the horrendous clamor of Andero's snoring. It had been a very good day's work.

Yet, as I sank into the straw, my satisfaction was blighted by imagining Portier captive . . . buried, perhaps, for another whole day. The voices of the aether wailed in wordless hunger, as if my magics had reopened the wound in the Veil.

Surely through the next hours I walked the road of the dead. Every breath tasted of rosemary and ash. Fingers pawed at me like whispers: *Daemon, daemon, daemon.* One clearer voice spoke, too, gentle and firm.

Pay them no mind. Thou'rt my worthy companion, stronger than you know. It matters not that you were born in darkness to another fate. His silken hair and long coat shifted colors with his stride, gold and gray. His smile that was not quite a smile soothed my fears. But when I woke once again to the everlasting dark, I was screaming.

CHAPTER 14

DEMESNE OF ARABASCA

The old doomsayer did not come to bid us farewell. Too bad. I wanted to tell him that this journey was about greed, arrogance, political power, and the truths of nature, not anyone's myths of daemons and angels. He certainly wasn't all that vigilant about his beliefs, as he hadn't stopped me, the daemon, from helping Jono and his boy. Yet, locked in the dark with Anne's image of the starving dead and my own nightmares, it wasn't so easy to dismiss his words.

As we mounted up, the shepherdfolk showered us with gifts of honey and bread, and a barrage of hints and warnings about the road south. It was dreadfully difficult to sort out such busy conversation without being able to see the various speakers or judge which comment followed on another. Thus we were half a kilometre along our way before their meaning penetrated my thick head. "God's teeth, we're headed into Kadr!"

Kadr. The realm of the witchlords. A rugged, two-hundred-kilometre-long rampart that marked the boundary of Sabria and the remnants of Aroth. Certainly I knew Carabangor, the last refuge of the witchlords, lay in the deserts of the ancient empire, but somehow I'd assumed the route from Mattefriese would bypass the haunted realm. No wonder the shepherdfolk believed dead men walked this road and that the land *ached* from magework.

Nineteen years previous, Philippe de Savin-Journia and Michel de Vernase had chased the witchlords from their rocky strongholds and down to the ruins of the ancient city, completing the subjugation of the Arothi. Since then, King Philippe had repeatedly been forced to roust bandits or Arothi rebels from the caves and gullies of the witchrealm. It was in the aftermath of that earlier battle, of course, that Masson de Cuvier had first encountered the woman in white.

"Be careful," I said. "Everything the shepherds said about water sources and not straying from the track, you must believe it. Untriggered spelltraps don't just wear away through the years. The witchlords knew what they were doing. They considered anyone not of their own blood nonhuman and had no qualms about discouraging them in vile ways."

The shepherds had told Andero and John Deune to watch for red markings on any water source and avoid any area that appeared blighted. Now I knew using magic wouldn't necessarily transform me into something worse than a witchlord, perhaps I could do more to shield us.

"The whole place looks blighted to me," growled Andero. "Looks like daemons gnawed away all the softness of the mountains and left only these rock bones. It's no solid cliff, but a honeycomb where you'd never want to go. The creatures know. Haven't seen a bird light anywhere."

"Salvator—my teacher—told me that the witchlords would devour a land to feed their magic, and then move on. Supposedly they settled in Kadr because it was beautiful and fruitful, and corrupting it was particularly satisfying. I don't know if that's true or not."

"I'm not averse to adventuring—like it for the most part—but damned if I would choose this land to explore."

We used our water sparingly, but the road was steep, and though the air was cool, bright sun and dry wind left both men and horses thirsty. We stopped at every seep and mudhole to water the horses but dared not use any for ourselves.

As thirst sapped strength and spirit, my nightmares leaked into waking. Devil plodded onward, while in my dark world spectral beings pressed gaunt faces to walls of emerald glass. A never-ending tide, pushing and shoving each other aside, licking their colorless lips, their eyes wild and hungry. They licked the green glass as if their tongues might wear it away.

By our third night on the Kadr road, despite our care, three of our waterskins hung flaccid. One held only a few mouthfuls. One held perhaps a litre. We broke camp before dawn, unable to rest.

At midmorning, John Deune spotted a well a few metres off the road.

He and Andero ripped away the weedy overgrowth to expose its crumbling stone. "There's no red marks!"

"Wait," I said when John Deune's pot rattled. "We have to be sure."

I touched the warm stone and dived into the aether. Spellwork enveloped the deep well. A clean-water spell, slender threads like dew-laden spiderwebs reflecting the rays of the morning sun. Spells of abundance, thick lines that frayed into a million parts all looping back on themselves. Spells of protection to prevent children and the feebleminded from falling in. All common, benevolent things one might find at any ancient well.

"I think we're all right," I said. Yet, just as I was about to release my inner seeing, I glimpsed a small gray thread tangled deep in the tracery of well magic. A single touch set my teeth on edge.

"Stop!" I snapped. "Don't!"

The pot clattered to the ground in a splash.

"Don't drink it. Don't touch it. Leave the pot where it is. Something's not right."

"But we must have water," said John. "There are no marks."

I plunged once more into the well magic, peeling away the layers of spell threads that lay between me and the gray line, disentangling the energies that created it. When all lay exposed, I felt sick.

"Not this water, John Deune. Drop anything that's touched it into the well."

I'd seen the spell before. It was a particularly virulent form of a memory block, exactly the kind Finn had read from my notes back at Pradoverde.

"It doesn't kill you," I said. "You're alive but with no memory of yourself. No memory of your past or your friends or why you do what you do. No memory of what makes you laugh or weep, or what books you enjoy, or what you consider good or beautiful. Only the knowledge that you cannot remember. Better to be dead."

There was little to be done for the victims of such witchery. In my first days after collaring, I'd tried removing such a block from an old pikeman who had survived the Kadrian wars. Arrogant, stupid, I was sure I could manage what Salvator's hedge-witch friends could not. And indeed, I had removed the block. But excising it had destroyed so much of the man's underlying nature that he was left only a hollow shell, no person at all. Naught could repair my error. A terrible lesson.

"It would take me days to counter a witchlord spell," I said, "and undoing them often triggers another layer of traps. We cannot delay so long."

John Deune took the news hard. He fidgeted and moaned, digging in his packs until he'd spread pots and linens everywhere. "How in the wide world are we to mark the well? Some unwary traveler will have his mind destroyed, all for the lack of something red. It's kin to murder."

"There's always a solution." Andero piled rocks on top of the well and drew his knife. I laid a spell of stasis on his blood offering to keep it fresh and red. It seemed fitting.

KADR

None of the water sources along the Kadrian road were drinkable. We watered the horses at the least questionable spots, then dismounted and led them to preserve their strength. We limited our own intake to a few drops every two hours and blessed all gods it was not summer. Another day or two should see us off the mountains.

On the second evening from the poisoned well, the road curved round a cliff or high embankment and the land fell away in front of us. The fragrant smoke of wood fires drifted past.

In the space of a moment, I might have been coming in from a day of fence mending at Pradoverde, ready to set Anne a new lesson. Or she might have been waiting to pounce on me with a passage from my notes, insisting I explain about *aerogens* or *magical spheres of influence* or itching to talk about why all spell keywords were Aljyssian. Anne's mind was her truest magic, sparking and pricking as brilliantly as her sister's enchanted pendant.

Silly that such a common scent could rouse such vivid memory . . . and the associated weaknesses of mind and body I had worked so diligently to banish. It was not mere concern for Anne's reputation that had kept me sleeping in the guesthouse these two years.

I hunched my cloak tight against the settling cold and summoned words from the dust of my mouth. "What's down there?"

"A tidy place," croaked John Deune with palpable excitement. "I'm sure I see a pond."

"A vale a quarter the size of Raghinne's, green and shallow," said Andero, his parched bass scarce more than a whisper. "A dozen buildings scattered. Plowed fields. A few sheep. A few cows. They've trees that aren't stunted, and the grass is dormant, but not gray and patchy as that I've seen on the way."

"Good. Very good." Andero's reports must have been invaluable to his legion.

We descended slowly, so as to give the residents fair warning. A dog picked up our scent, his bark as excited as John Deune. Three persons came out to greet us when we reached the settlement.

"Who might you be traveling this road?" The young woman's greeting felt much cooler than the shepherds'.

"Manet de Shreu," croaked Andero, "my master, Talon, and our servant, John. Foolish inexperience has left us short of water. A supply for ourselves and our horses would put us forever in your debt, though we could offer reasonable payment as well. A shelter for the night, even barn or shed, would be welcome. But we're willing to move along so's not to disturb your peace."

"Polite spoken," said another woman, older and more authoritative. "Travelers are rare in Hoven. Caravan routes go round the longer way. But we welcome strangers who bring no evil and promise to move on within a sun's turn. Subsistence is yet too fragile to support any but our own." She sounded a well-educated woman.

She introduced herself as Zophie and her companions as Krasna and Tesar. The settlers had built their homes around a healthy spring, and they invited us to drink our fill. One of their boys took charge of the horses, promising that he knew how to keep thirsty beasts from gorging on water.

Krasna said they were accustomed to travelers arriving thirsty. "From time to time one who's drunk of the poisoned wells wanders through here. It's terrible to see."

I was content to let Andero carry on the introductions and our business. He could make easy conversation with strangers as if he'd known them all his life. As we sipped their sweet water, dipped from the stone font they'd built to capture the spring, he introduced me as a teacher of history, bound on a tour of ancient ruins in the desert.

I squirmed a little and hunched my cloak higher at the lie. But enforcing the Concord was unlikely to be important in such a remote place, and the omission of my true profession certainly kept matters simpler. Indeed, it was Andero who caused a sensation.

"Five families settled Hoven four years ago, five more in the year just past," said Tesar, a man whose voice rumbled through a chest that must have rivaled Andero's. "But all who knew aught of smithing died that first winter."

"If your forge is in decent repair, I'd be pleased to give you a few hours' work in exchange for the water." The words were scarce free of Andero's tongue when Tesar bundled him off to examine the forge, talking excitedly of coal supplies and broken wheels and worn-out tools. Our welcome assured, Krasna and Zophie hurried off to consult the other families about a meal. John Deune filled our water containers and carried them off to wherever the boy had taken our horses.

Left alone in the heart of the settlement, I spun in a slow circle, reaching out to learn what I could. There was no trace of enchantment about, no Kadr magic, but also none of the small wards and benevolent blessings one found about any farm community. It was curious. No matter Camarilla penalties, no matter the reasoned explanations of alchemists, physicians, and biologists about what benefited plants and animals, old ways died hard among those close to the land.

Yet, indeed, the peace of Hoven was profound. A meadowlark trilled and chirruped, and nightmare and terror receded. Would I could just stay somewhere like this.

I bent to dip my cup once more, only to discover the font was not where I thought. Extending my staff failed to locate it. I removed my left glove and felt the earth for dampness. Nothing.

I spun one direction, then the other. The burbling spring could have been on any side. Distant voices, the clatter of pots, hammering, bounced off the surrounding structures. Five steps could impale me on a fence or send me plummeting into an abyss. On the verge of panic, I planted my staff, touched my copper bracelet, and summoned power. *"Oraste."*

My seeing spell came together with all the speed of frozen honey. Ghostly blurs and blotches—trees? houses?—rose all around. Black ridges between might be walls or hedges or rivers or distant mountain ranges for all I knew. I shoved more power into the spell. . . .

"Daemon!" The scream was cracked with age and vitriol. As it scorched the dark, something large and heavy slammed breath from my chest. The next blow struck my head, toppling me into a bottomless chasm.

Appropriate that straw scratched my face, for a cow stood over me making cow noises. Surely an entire herd of cows had been dancing on my head. Back. Chest.

I tried to tell the beast to speak more slowly, but the words spilling out were not at all what I intended. "Mmlrff."

"Dante! Earth and sky, are you all right? Never saw a woman could throw so straight and so hard. And she's as old as Tark's Spine. Must've gotten off a barrow load before I could get to you."

"Mmlrff. Sppttt."

"Here, sit up and mayhap your wits'll settle into place. You've the face of a rotten turnip."

He plumped me up like a chair cushion. The black world spun, and my arm flew to my mouth to convince my stomach to hold onto its contents. Every bone and muscle wailed. "Night's daughter!"

" 'Twas rocks."

I squinched my forehead in question.

"Rocks. A whiskery gammy who ought to be dandling her children's children's babes clobbered you with a cartload of rocks. She didn't want to kill you right away, though we've a deal of convincing to make sure killing's not next up."

My crime floated atop the murky slops in my skull like a broken branch. "My collar. Are they Camarilla? Temple?" How unlucky could we get?

My brother crouched in front of me, his breath tight and harsh. " 'Tisn't that you hid your collar, but that you used it—used your magic. Sorcery is anathema here. They've vowed to kill *anyone* who works spells."

Truth glimmered. ". . . no spells . . ."

"Well, they say you did."

"No. It was— They've no spells here. I wondered."

"Gather your wits, little brother. They've locked us in a barn and swear they'll slay us all should you so much as blink your eye. I hope you've no such ideas; they're quite serious-minded."

Anger rippled through my veins, sweeping away some of the muddle. "Might not have much luck with that."

"I've mentioned so, but they're saying your magics likely won't work as you expect, neither. Zophie says they've spent years fixing this valley to block spellcraft."

Certainly there were things one could do to interfere with spellwork.

Hedges of whitebud laurel, fences of cypress wood and iron. The lack of enchantments should have told me. Anger yielded to relief. It wasn't my own incapacity crippling my spellbinding.

Andero pressed a clay mug of strong beer to my mouth. I drained it.

"So what now?" I swiped my sleeve at my mouth, nearly missing it.

"I've got to convince them you're not a danger."

"I can explain. I got lost. Dizzy." Humiliation bled from my pores like liquid fire. "I panicked. You've seen it. I've made this wholly ridiculous little spell. . . . Gods, I was trying to see. That's all."

"Not a chance in Dimios's caves they'll let you speak, little brother. Some are biting crazy that your corpse is not already burning."

A leaden mantle pressed me back to the straw. My head weighed like a cannonball.

"I'll have to convince them." He sounded remote, as if he'd fallen into a barrel. "Here, have another swallow."

I pressed my lips closed and shook my head. My thick tongue blocked words.

"These are not bad people, Dante, but they've this fury about sorcery. They're ones who lived here and managed to escape the witchlords. They're determined to make this land clean again. But more than that, the very reason they've come back here is that wicked sorcery is on the rise to the south. Most have lost kin and friends to a sorcerer they call the *Lord Regent of Mancibar.* They talk of evil dreams, bleeding. . . ."

Bleeding? Dreams? A thousand questions dribbled away unspoken. Something was definitely not right with me.

" 'Dero"—my tongue might have been a lump of cheese—" 'ware the beer."

"It's only to make you sleep, Dante. I'd not let them give it till you'd waked from the stoning. 'Tis the only way they'd let you live another hour. You've got to trust me, little brother."

A mighty blackness rose from my gut, cold rage that choked off my breath. "No!"

I reached deep, but the world fell apart. . . .

IT WAS GOING TO BE a wretched death. Ribs and gut were crushed onto a giant post that rippled and bulged. My face bounced against some contraption of leather, iron, and scratchy wool, my skull ready to disintegrate from the pounding. Without wit enough to conjure a curse, the only word I could squeeze out was, "Stop."

To my astonishment and gratitude, the rippling, bulging, and bouncing stopped.

"Blessings to all saints, Master!" Footsteps brought busy hands that quickly loosed the straps holding me—holding me to a *horse*, so returning faculties and the beast's pungent release told me.

Getting my feet to the ground was another matter entirely. It required moving my head, which set off cannons and earthshakings. Using the beast's mane and loops on the saddle for handholds, I lowered myself gingerly, as the entire contents of my skin rushed wholesale to my feet. The world spun like burnt stew in an iron pot.

"Devil," I mumbled, grateful for the beast's good behavior as I rested my forehead on his neck.

"But this wasn't my idea, Master! It was your brutish man who threw you over the beast like a sack of washing, rousted me from a deep sleep, and threatened to twist my head from my shoulders did I not take you into the woods in the very middle-night."

I didn't bother to correct John Deune. He'd figure out I spoke to the horse, not him.

The angle of the weak sun on my face named the hour early or late. Early more likely, from the feel of the cold air. Feet and hands were numb, and I wished the rest of my body so blessed.

"Have we wine or water? Food?" I'd not eaten anything since somewhere between the bone well and the slimy spring, a full day at least. And I'd not drunk anything since— I rummaged in the murk, trying to understand where we were and why I'd been tied over a horse feeling as if I'd been pummeled with bricks. The stoning . . . the beer . . .

"Where is Andero?" I'd kill him.

"Behind us, Master. He persuaded them to let you go free. We're on the road south again. We've a bit of cheese yet, and the last of the olive paste. We could stop for a while and build a fire if you wish, but I assume you'd rather be on our way."

"When will Andero be here?"

"Let me fetch the food. Two days you've slept; you must be ravenous. I filled the water—"

"Two *days*? And we've been traveling all that time?"

"Not speedily. The trees have overgrown this road, so your man bade me lead the horses afoot. And certain I had to sleep last night, being not so strong as the mighty Andero or a powerful mage. But we set out again at first light. The farther we get from Hoven, the better for all."

Gods, it was dark. Enough memory filtered back to make me wary of using magic. How long did I need to be under that ridiculous ban? Surely two days' journey . . .

"So, the Hoveni sent no guard? No watcher?"

It made sense that natives of Kadr would have people trained to detect enchantment, a skill that required little innate power beyond acute senses and meticulous observation. There was no other way they could have reacted so quickly to my attempted seeing.

John knew exactly what I meant.

"Master," he said, "Goodman Andero instructed me to be very clear about this. You are under his most serious bond not to use any magic until we leave this land. Those people claim they'll know. I've no idea how. Naturally you are wise in these matters as a poor manservant is not."

The leather loops on Devil's saddle were empty, leaving a void in my spirit as would a missing limb. "Is that why my staff is not in its place? Am I being protected from temptation?"

"Your stick is stowed quite safely on my own mount. Goodman Andero thought it best our hosts not see it depart with you. I'll replace it on your beast if you'd like."

His every comment ended abruptly, without his customary digression. Something was amiss.

"Give me the whole truth, John Deune."

"I cannot tell you more right now, Master."

"Cannot or will not?"

"I'm avowed. Goodman Andero swore me on my poor dead chevalier's honor not to reveal more until we were past the Uravani River that marks the border of Kadr. By this second evening, he estimated."

Dimios's ice caves could not be colder than my anger. Fully awake now, I stepped closer, his quivering guiding my steps. "I relieve you of your vow, John Deune. Surely he assumed I would sleep the whole way, for you've no possible way to prevent me discovering the truth. When you see him next, you can tell him I beat you, strung you up by your scrawny neck, or embedded my knife in your quivering craw. Whatever you like. I once set a man spinning in the air in a scarlet flask. *Where* is Andero, and *what* in the depths of the Souleater's maw is going on?"

"He has stayed behind." His croak was scarce audible.

But he stood within my reach. My hand found his bony wrist. "Whatever for? Have they harmed him?"

"I cannot—" Deune tried to twist out of my hold, but he had no strength to match mine. I drew him into a fierce embrace, his neck in the crook of my arm. Then I jerked my grip tighter yet.

His feet came off the ground. His free hand clawed at my arm, at my sides, and flapped at my face. "Master, please. I had nothing to do with it. He promised he would crack my skull like a nut if I failed to do exactly as he said. Take you. Keep walking. Keep silent. Someone would know, he said. Someone would report our progress to him. He swore he'd call down a curse on my . . . my family."

"If he's dead, you'll join him in Ixtador this day!" I roared and tightened my arm until his choking silenced his protests. "Tell me!"

"Not dead, no, Master," he rasped when his choking relaxed my hold. "Not at all. Just given his word, his bond. They will let you and me go as long as you work no magic until we cross the Uravani bridge. And—" His reluctance was palpable.

"And?"

"He will stay with them."

"Stay?"

"It was the only way. You were a dead man. They would listen to no reason, until he offered to stay. But they were desperate, for they've only three grown men left and none a smith. They'll do him no harm, if you honor his pledge."

"How long? A few days? A month?"

"Five years."

"Five *years*! And you *left* him? You let him *do* it?" I threw John Deune into the dirt and raised my arms skyward. My hands trembled with pent magic. The earth . . . root and vine and deep-buried worm . . . stirred. "You damnable, cowering, ignorant . . ."

He whimpered.

I wrapped my arms over my head, trying to crush the frigid rage rising from my gut. I needed to wield wild magic until the everlasting dark blazed like summer sunrise. But I could not. Dared not.

If Andero had given his word and five years for our lives, he'd not thank me for turning back. I believed I could get us both away, despite the protections of Hoven. My brother had no real concept of my skills. But I could not betray this . . . honor . . . he so prized. And, as he well knew, Portier was waiting, and the world's safety, the mystery of Ixtador and starving souls and terrifying dreams. There was simply no time to fight this battle.

With all the strength I could muster, I shoved the cold blackness away. "Not this time," I spat through gritted teeth. To whom I didn't know. My arms fell to my sides and my fist uncurled. "Not this time."

Faithful de Santo would have reached Anne by now, told her of her danger. Between his tale, the journals I'd left at Pradoverde, and her own determination, she would investigate and likely learn more than I had about the Maldivean Seeing Stones and Saints Reborn and what, in the name of all gods, my rending of the Veil had done to the world. The good captain would convince her to be wary and he'd watch out for her. But I feared it would be only for a time. More and more I was convinced that the next great battle must fall to Anne, no matter what I found in Carabangor.

I was broken. More than half-mad. Whatever this cold darkness that lurked inside me, roused by rage and linked to my magic, frightened me more than anything I'd experienced when probing the realms of the dead. Everyone I cared for in the world was at risk, and I, so talented, so powerful, the master mage who raised the dead and opened the rent in the eternal Veil, was helpless to aid any of them.

So I would go on. Find Portier. Set him free.

My breathing calmed. My heart stilled. I extended my hand and waited, until the man at my feet grasped it. I hauled him up and released him. "Pardon my anger. The confusion . . . I cannot—"

"No matter, Master. You were injured. I hope no harm comes to you or your friend. It's why I've tried to follow his instructions so carefully." John's voice was flat. I didn't trust him any more than before. But we'd seen no more of pursuit, and I had no choices. The old shepherd's warning about trickster companions would have made me laugh did I remember how.

"You've done well. I could not ask for better service."

"We had best get on with things, then. I'll fetch something for you to eat."

"The world is still in danger, John. The chevalier understood that, better than I knew, and he'd be pleased with your service. Get me to Carabangor and I'll see you rewarded fairly."

Unlike Andero, John Deune didn't bristle at the offer. He brought me cheese, olive paste, and a biscuit that could drive nails into oak. Starving, I ate it all. When all was packed away, I hauled myself into the saddle, not daring touch the staff that was replaced reassuringly at my knee.

"Now, I suppose you must lead me out of here."

"Yes, Master." Dislike and resentment were thick in the familiar drawl. Sarcasm dripped from the honorific. I'd not sleep easy while we were together. John must want something awfully to put up with this.

The lead rope strung from his saddle to Devil, John Deune clicked his tongue and we moved down the last slopes of Kadr's ridge toward the Uravani River, the desert, and Carabangor's mysteries.

I believed I could fall no lower.

Anne

CHAPTER 15

15 ESTAR, EVENING
DEMESNE OF LOUVEL

I rode like the Souleater's own legion, stopping only to relieve the horse or to sleep. The demesnes of northern Aubine and southern Louvel were as familiar to me as my own hand, so I could hold to private lanes and vineyard tracks that spies were highly unlikely to watch. Yet, I took no chances. The first night I bedded down in the Marques Piafort's riding school, deserted since the death of his wife and daughter of summer fever. Cranked tight as a crossbow, I couldn't sleep.

The second night, I huddled in a wayside shrine dedicated to Sante Ianne. Ilario believed Portier was Sante Ianne reborn to serve the world yet again. Outlandish, I would have said three years before. But Portier's extraordinary history had set me questioning. Even Dante had confessed—albeit grudging—that something extraordinary had occurred with Portier on Mont Voilline, something beyond his own magic and our joined power. *Fates keep them both safe.*

On the third day, determined to remain unpredictable, I rode west out of my way to the Ley and the small harbor at Villefort. There I paid a bargeman to carry me upriver past Merona and into northern Louvel. I told him I was slipping away from a cruel uncle in order to meet my lover while he was on leave from the Guard Royale. The man reduced the fee and recruited his two grown sons to provide extra hands at the poles.

From our landing at Leynoue, it would be two hard days' ride to Laurentine and Pradoverde. I would need to take care on my approach. If de Ferrau's witness knew I had lived with Dante, then perhaps he . . . or she . . . knew *where* as well. And if Dante wasn't there, then by the Creator's mighty hand, I'd follow him to Jarasco and into the wilds of Coverge.

PRADOVERDE

Duskborn plodded along the cart track. Both of us were about done in. Cold, relentless rain had made the two days from the river a misery. The rain had slacked only a half hour past, as the invisible sun nudged the western horizon. But mist had risen in the clefts and hollows, stealing what remained of the light.

I'd been sorely tempted to take a room in Laurentine. But even through cold, sodden weariness, I had judged that a mistake. Beltan de Ferrau of the Jarasco Temple Minor had traveled a very long way to question me, and I had gone to a great deal of trouble to avoid being followed. It would be idiocy to walk into a public house and risk alerting one of his spies. Besides, answers lay only a few kilometres more. I needed to be home.

Duskborn balked and snorted, his ears alert. I soothed and hushed him, urging him off the road and into the lee of a hill.

Dante, friend . . . I urged the words into the aether. But I sensed him only as before . . . a distant, stonelike presence, entirely unlike his usual fiery knot. Yet such was the immeasurable nature of the aether that unless he answered me, he could be one metre distant or ten thousand, awake, asleep, or insensible.

No threat materialized. Somehow I coaxed the last of Duskborn's strength to life, and I soon dismounted at the hornbeam copse that marked the edge of our land.

"Stay here, brave heart," I whispered for no sensible reason. "I'll come back for you soon and you'll spend the night with fine Louvel hay and Ladyslipper and Sonata for company. And Devil, too, if the gods are kind."

But there was no kindness in earth or Heaven that night. I crossed Pradoverde's boundary, past the small cairn I'd placed so Dante could find the cart track on his own. A raw screech sirened through the aether.

I kicked over the cairn, silencing the noise only Dante and I could hear. The tripped ward signaled that an intruder had violated Pradoverde's boundaries and that Dante wasn't available to cut off the noise.

My feet moved faster up the swale that hid the house from the road. When an orange haze suffused the sky above the grassy slope, I took out running.

"Finn!" I screamed. "Finn, where are you?"

There was no more purpose to stealth. Flames enveloped the kitchen building and the wooden sheds and steps at the rear of the main house. Orange tongues spurted from the front windows of the lower floor. A dark mass exploded from the door and splintered itself. The larger part darted back inside. By the time the dark figure emerged again with another armload, I had reached the pitiful pile of books he had dumped on the damp ground.

"Mistress!" Finn dropped his current load onto the pile. "Stay back!"

"Is anyone else here?"

"None." He vanished into the smoke curling from the front door.

My cry of caution was swallowed by a thundering burst from the rear of the house—Dante's laboratorium. I ripped off my cloak and the sleeveless gown layered over my riding trousers. Arm shielding mouth and nose, I followed Finn inside.

The heat near sucked the life out of me. Despite frenzied flames dancing in the workroom and licking the walls, thick smoke left me near as blind as Dante. Wood snapped and creaked. The walls were stone, but the upper floor . . . the roof . . . We had little time.

Heartsick, I groped through a jumble of furnishings toward the small painting of a lighthouse that had hung in Dante's rooms at Castelle Escalon. It blackened and curled before I could reach it. So I changed course. Finn knew the only things truly worth saving: Dante's books or . . . Oh, gods, his journals. Everything he knew of magic was written down in his awkward angular hand. Losing it all . . . Angels' mercy, it would destroy him.

The library, too, was a jumble, shelves toppled, volumes scattered across the floor. Many were already burning. Loose papers floated on the heated air, bursting into flame like swamp lights.

"Which ones?" croaked Finn, coughing as he picked through whatever volumes lay atop the piles.

"His own first. Anything in his hand." Frantically wiping my eyes, I spun around. Nothing was in its place. "But where?"

"Here, I think." Finn waded through the ash-covered debris and thrust leather-bound journals and stacks of paper into my arms. "Now go on. I'll bring what else I can."

"Hurry."

I stumbled through the door into the blessed air, dropped my burden on the pile, and whirled around, intending to go back for more. But the roof had caught, lighting the yard with garish orange.

"Finn!" I screamed between hacking coughs. "Get out!"

He emerged on the heels of my words, staggering under the load. I thrust my arms under his and together we lowered the treasures onto the pile. So little . . . all that remained of a life's work.

Thunderous flames geysered skyward, as the roof collapsed into the shell of the house. I sank to my knees in the mud, coughing. Flooding tears eased the smoke sting in my eyes, but naught else.

Finn collapsed beside me, long arms dangling over his knees as he coughed until he could scarce catch a breath.

The firelight dimmed quickly inside the blackened shell of stone.

"What's left standing?" I said. "We need to get these under cover." The mist was thickening. My face and neck were slick with moisture.

"The guesthouse and stable weren't fired," he rasped, getting slowly to his feet. "I'll fetch a barrow."

As he slogged around the smoky ruin, I stacked pages with bound books atop and underneath to preserve what I could from the moisture. Finn brought a sheet of canvas along with the barrow. I used it to cover the remaining pile. He pushed the loaded barrow and I carried an armful across the muddy yard and garden to the guesthouse.

"What happened?" I said, numb. Dante had woven fire wards about Pradoverde, but they could merely warn those under its roofs. It was impossible to weave protections against every possible source of fire.

"I'd gone down the village for a stoup. Come back round the lake and through the wood. Surprised someone creeping round the house. Guess I should be grateful he didn't want to kill no one. I'm no good wrastler. Woke up face down in the muck with the house afire."

"You're a hero, Finn. Bless all saints and angels you're all right."

He pushed open the guesthouse door. "Badger balls!"

The smaller dwelling where Finn and Dante slept had been ransacked. Beds and tables overturned, lamps and ink bottles smashed, clothes chests emptied. We had to lift a heavy oak chest and move it aside to get the barrow through the door. What were they after?

Finn threw a broken table and the torn pallets into a corner so we could unload the barrow. Three trips more and we had all we could salvage under the guesthouse roof. Rain hissed on the fallen timbers, sending acrid smoke billowing into the mist and choking us with the stink.

While Finn tended Duskborn, I laid a hearth fire, shoved debris aside, and assembled beds. By the time Finn stumbled inside, we had water boiling for black tea, all the provision Finn and Dante kept.

We gulped it until we stopped shivering. Now we had light enough, I insisted Finn let me clean and dress several nasty burns on his arms and back with the ointment of aloe Dante always kept nearby. Only then could I pose the question that kept me on my feet: "Have you had any word from Dante, Lord Ilario, or Captain de Santo since they rode north?"

Finn shook his head, too tired to speak, and collapsed on his pallet. I soon followed. Everything else would have to wait for morning.

"Who did this?" I said, when Finn stumbled out of the guesthouse door into the rain-washed sunlight. A thicket of hair framed his bony soot-smudged face.

I sat on a bench in our little orchard, my back to the ruined house. Idle, for the moment. One glimpse into the blackened carcass of my home had convinced me there was nothing in the steaming black soup within that could possibly be salvaged.

Finn joined me on the bench. His grimy fingers gripped the seat's edge. "Didn't see him well, as it was dark early and fogged in. And he wore a kerchief covered his mouth. But he had a swagger about him very like a fellow I met down to Nelli's taproom. One of the three that come from the north I wrote you about."

"The ones who told you of the winter storms on the road to Coverge?" That's where Jarasco lay—Tetrarch de Ferrau's sacred demesne. Now I could envision the city on the maps my father had hung in our schoolroom. The pale-eyed tetrarch had not left my thoughts all morning. Papa had always said that righteous holy men were the most dangerous enemies.

"Aye. Mayhap I talked too free. . . ."

"Common thieves, do you think, looking for charms or silver or gems a mage might own?" Or had they been more purposeful, as someone hunting evidence of necromancy?

"Never met a thief, save me and other lads snatchin' lemons and such." Finn glanced out from under his wild shock of hair. "These were friendly—at least two of 'em were, as one kept always to himself. Yet I'd not think of 'em as common. They was clean. Tidy, you know, not like someone's been working in the vineyard, nor even draymen. Fingernails clean, too, as you're always onto me about. They said they'd come south looking for work where it weren't so cold. I didn't ask what as I'd no work to offer, but mayhap I ought to have."

"No reason you should. Were any of them in the taproom last night to see you there?"

"Don't know. I was down there, but . . . with Nelli . . . out back. Not inside. That's where I am mostly in the village."

I nodded as if I'd not noticed his cheeks scarlet under the soot.

His whole posture softened, while his earnestness redoubled. "But mayhap someone heard talk of the grenadier's dream. That fellow, John Deune, said three emeralds so large would be worth more than Pradoverde."

"Grenadier? Emeralds? I thought Dante went to see his father."

"That come later—the message from his brother. From the day he got that, I knew he'd go. It talked about the angel, you see . . . the angel in the dream that was still preyin' on his mind."

Clearly Finn had a much longer tale than I'd imagined. "Come, I've got some cheese and biscuits in my saddle pack. You can draw some water. After we eat I'll sort through this mess while you tell me everything that happened from the hour I left Pradoverde."

He heaved a great sigh and leapt to his feet. "There's a deal to tell. I had to write it all twice . . . but it's likely burnt up now."

As I sorted books, blotted pages, and spread them near the hearth to dry, Finn replaced the spare furnishings, gathered the scattered clothing, and recounted the tale of Masson de Cuvier and his terrible dream, and of the day Dante received the unexpected letter from his family.

"So he believed this woman—this enchantress—caused his father's accident?"

"Drove him half loony, it did. He ran me off and spent the whole day in the forge. Never heard the like of his hammering."

I had heard it before, whenever Dante's temper drove him to violence.

"You ought to leave when he warns you," I said, though it felt like a betrayal, like admitting de Ferrau's accusations. Yet I had experienced the ferocity of Dante's rage in the aether. Dante's wonder at the universe, his keen, ever-questioning mind, and his passion to make sense of what he found made him an incomparable teacher—and a companion worthy of a lifetime's knowing. But whatever drove him—whether his desire to know, or to set the world to rights, or to overcome the scars of a past he refused to share—fed both his passion and his fragile, frightening temper.

"The way he was, I didn't know but he would burn the place down and himself in it." Finn glanced up from his bundle of muddy garments. "He had me write the letter to the chevalier that very night. . . ."

"And the three of them rode north—Dante, Lord Ilario, and Captain de Santo—and you never heard from them after."

"Aye."

What had happened to Dante and Ilario? And John Deune, too, who was supposed to meet with them along the road? How had Captain de Santo ended up dead at Montclaire?

Where did I begin to make sense of all this? I felt less certain that heading for Coverge was the right course. Dante was not dead, so I couldn't imagine him remaining long with a family he despised. Such a magical mystery would drive him hard, especially if he saw some remnant of Kajetan's hand in it. His blindness necessitated a companion. That he had asked Ilario to do it—angels comfort the chevalier for enduring *that* task—was a powerful measure of his urgency.

I could not come up with any hypothesis that would connect this dream enchantress to the Temple. The Temple had no argument with magic, save when it impinged on their particular view of the divine—as necromancy did. Neither did they use magic in their practices. But perhaps de Ferrau's investigation had turned up evidence relevant to this *inquiry*, something that might tell *me* where to look if not the tetrarch.

Merona, then. I would accept de Ferrau's invitation to hear his witnesses. And I could, perhaps, ask the zealous tetrarch if he commonly burnt the homes of those he accused. Or tortured soldiers . . .

Having a plan got me moving. I did what I could to dry and sort the books and papers. Many were ruined, charred, or the ink hopelessly smeared. The scant information Finn recalled about the emeralds had me sort through the small stacks of surviving books to see if the particular volume he'd read had survived. I didn't see it. Nor did I find any useful history. Papa and my goodfather had always talked of the Maldivean Hegemony as a model of good governance, but it had been such a slight interruption in the brutal history of Aroth, I'd never paid any attention to it.

Finn fetched supplies from Laurentine and verified through Nelli the tap girl that the three men from the north were yet hanging about. "I'd like to talk to them before I go," I said. "But I don't want it known that I've been here." I decided to wait until I was ready to ride for Merona.

FINN AND I DUG THROUGH the cooling ruins and found our iron money box under the stone floor of the kitchen. Before I left, he needed money to pay our tax lest he be hauled off to debtors' prison in our stead.

"What's all this?" I said, as I opened the iron box to see a heap of folded paper.

"I threw the post in there till the master came back," he said as he wrung out a shirt and hung it over a chair next the hearth. I had suggested that Nelli merited a shirt that wasn't black with soot. "Figured I wouldn't lose it that way and have him yelling at me."

"But you needed me to unlock it."

He shrugged. "After I wrote you the letter, I thought to look in the master's pettibox, where he keeps that ring and the silver locket and such at night. Sure enough, he left his keys there. Now they're lost in that stew of the house."

"Well done, though." I riffled through the stack, disappointed to find nothing in Portier's scholarly script or Dante's oddly angled one. I tossed the tax notice back in the box, along with a small stack of responses from booksellers and libraries regarding some general inquiries. One large fold of stiff, cheap paper bore the seal of Castelle Escalon's steward, the usual wrapping for a forwarded letter. I set it aside.

"You should leave Pradoverde, Finn," I said, as I counted out the tax assessment and his wages. "Leave Laurentine altogether. This Temple inquiry means mortal danger for anyone connected with Dante and me."

"Nah. You trust me to take care of things. The master does, too, though he does give me the frights, I'll confess. And it's . . . interesting. I'm not just doing sweat chores here. Besides, Nelli is close and willing. Wherever am I going to find all that again?"

Despite all, I had to laugh at his practical view of the world.

Once we'd hidden the money box in a new location, I ripped open the packet from the palace. Inside was a stained fold, sealed with the cheapest wax. The letter was addressed to *Lady Anne de Vernaze at the Palace in Merona* in a big, loopy script like that of a child. Curious, I perched on the table edge, rising to my feet again as I read. . . .

Lady Anne,

I am writting this to tell you of events that have brot the man you know as Dante to a wild and forrin land. Stubborn as he is, he will not. Nor does he know I do so.

I wuld prefer to speak as he wuld address you, but his words are like to be bigger than I can spell, and I just have a difficulty enuff as we have not even met, you and me, and you being the nobul lady he values so deeply. Come to that, Dante and I have not met in so many years until this month past that it would be awkward writting to him! So, first to tell you whose pen is addressing you. I am his elder brother, called by name Andero, of late the Smith at Raghinne.

Our father is dead, exploded by a dream. I ween that you are more customed to such doings than I, but there it is. Words spoke in Da's dream, and the fearful vision of it, now lead us south to a ruin called Karabayngor. My brother is beset with worry over his frend, the man who cannot die, and guilt over your noble frend and others dead by his doing. He feels portents that an old enemy plots some great evil he cannot guess. You likely know enuff of my brother to heed his portents, as I lernt to when I was but a nub.

A manservant has come with us, one John Doon by name. He is a sneaking sort and sorely dislikes Dante, but seems a useful companion. He says he serves us as honor to his dead master. I watch him carefully.

"No, no, no!" Ilario, dead? *John Doon . . . his dead master.* The words could mean naught else. "Gods, no!" My arms crossed my breast as if to hold him in . . . the lean, rangy grace, whether dancing or fighting . . . his silliness . . . his charm, utter devotion, and solid friendship. Such life he exhibited in his most ridiculous posturing . . . and in the quiet, whimsical, honorable person so few in the world were privileged to know. The gaping hole in my heart, as raw as if the tissue had been ripped away in that moment, could not . . . could never be . . . eased. Holding a fist tight to my breast, I read on. . . .

I asked Dante to come home when Da got exploded, so as maybe to fix up the badness between them, but Da was hard beyond what I even knew. Dante is grown hard, too, and stubborn, as I said. But I am equally stubborn. He lets me see for him.

Excuse my boldness, my Lady, but I think that if you care for my little brother as much as he cares for you, you will want to know how he fares. If he travels with me, then he does not miss as many meals as he might otherwise, and though he frets a deal about you and his frend and those lying dead, he feels a rightful purpose. But since some terrible events in the northland, more troubles him than he will speak. He is feared to work magic, even as he knows this task will require it. It is a death to him, and I know not how to ease it.

I will do my best to send another report from the south. This fine tavern lady, Marga Tasso, says she will send this on and hold whatever further papers I dispatch to her.

My highest regards and looking forward to meeting you in person on some future day,

Andero, at the town of Mattefreese
8 Estar

8 Estar. Almost a month past. Atop grief worthy of a lifetime's weeping, I had to imagine Dante headed to Carabangor, the ruin in the dream, the place where the enchantress waited with her terrible jewels. And *an old enemy.* Stars of night, could he mean *Jacard*? Of course he would be driven to pursue such a mystery. But to venture so far without sending for me . . . Stubborn did not begin to name him. Why could I not make him understand that I would venture any danger, any risk, at his side? We were two halves of the same whole; I was so sure of it.

Yet in all the wrenching emotions the letter evoked, the most frightening was imagining what *terrible events* might make Dante afraid to use his magic. How could he breathe, how could his heart even beat without it?

This must explain what I felt in the aether . . . how closed and tight and cold his presence.

"My plans have changed," I said, crumpling the hard-traveled page. "Tomorrow at dawn, I ride for Carabangor."

LAURENTINE

"I hate leaving you behind, lady," I said softly, combing Ladyslipper's coat. "But you've gotten fat here at home and I'll have to ride hard. Besides, I'd not risk you. I've no idea where this road will take us."

To wherever Dante was. That was my only goal.

The horse next to the vacant stall where I hid with Ladyslipper whinnied in a curious note, as if asking who had intruded on the Laurentine hostelry so early.

Some disturbance had waked me in the dark hours that morning, and I would have sworn Dante was sitting on the floor beside my bed. I had stretched my arms, trying to reach him. When my hands came up empty, I had to dash the tears from my eyes, whether from the failure to touch his solid presence or from a lingering sense of despair, I could not have said. *I'm on my way, friend. I'll not leave you alone again. Not ever.*

Duskborn, waiting closer to the stable door, snorted and blew. Footsteps crunched on the dirt. Two sets?

I made sure my hood covered my hair and ducked behind Ladyslipper.

"Here we are," said Finn. "Give me a moment to explain. My lady"—he hurried into the stall—"the men from the north are gone. Picked up and left yesterday, saying they were headed south where there might be building going on. But there's something else. . . ."

Finn's urgency quenched my explosive disappointment.

"Nelli told me a lone woman came in yestereve, asking where to find *the lady of Pradoverde* as she had information of great importance for her. Nelli did as we'd agreed, saying you were gone back to Aubine months ago and weren't coming back. But Nelli was just feeding her a bite before she rode out, so's I stepped up and said I could send on her message if she liked."

"And you've brought her here?" I snapped, recalling the extra footsteps. "I told you we needed to be secret." Of a sudden, the stall felt much too confining.

"Had to. She says 'a friend of yours' is in terrible trouble with the Temple, and she's taken a terrible risk to bring his message. I figured"—he swallowed hard—"a lone woman was taking more of a chance meeting up with you than you were with her. With your . . . you know." He widened his eyes and waved his hand at me in a way that could only signify magic. "But even yet, I would have put her off and come to ask you first, but I asked her what friend, and how was I to know it was even someone you cared for. She said he gave her this to show you . . ."

He held out a small bundle of black string, seashells, scarlet beads, and silver bangles.

Impossible. My breath halted—as suddenly and painfully as if I'd fallen from a rooftop. The bundle was entirely unmistakable. "You were exactly right. Bring her."

Grief and rage battled for my heart. But I pressed my back to the wall just inside the stall gate and drew my zahkri, the Fassid dagger my grandfather had given me when I could never imagine killing anyone with it. When Finn led the woman through the gate, I stepped into the doorway and blocked her way out. "Who are you and what have you done to the man who owns this?"

Only one person in the world carried a charm to protect himself from crocodiles—Ilario de Sylvae.

CHAPTER 16

LAURENTINE

"My name's Rhea Tasserie, healer in the service of the Temple."

She retreated to the corner post of the horse box, poised as if ready to climb over the wall into the next stall to get out. She was almost a twin to the post—tall, bony, all knots and knobs, brown hair cut short for use, not beauty, skin rough from wind and weather. Her brown eyes were young, though. And fearful, maybe.

Her gaze darted from me to Finn and over my shoulder to the quiet stable behind me.

"Go," I said to Finn. "Watch."

He vanished into the dusty gray light. I waited for the woman to speak.

"You're the one, then? Lady Anne, the conte's daughter?" She bent a knee, little more than a jerk, almost as an afterthought. "He said you were small and beautiful and . . . fierce."

"I was told he was dead." And if she was responsible, she'd soon follow him into Ixtador. "Why have you come?"

She folded her long arms across her breasts. Her plain, sturdy traveling clothes displayed no mark of the Temple. Her mouth twisted and tightened, as if resisting an answer on its own.

"He's not dead. He lies in the hospice at Merona's Temple Major," she said, at last. "We only moved him there a half month since, as he's been very ill. He's under strict guard at all times."

A Temple prisoner . . . brought from the north. Great gods, was he Ferrau's witness? Relief was quickly overwhelmed by fear. Ilario knew the truth of Mont Voilline, of how Dante had saved his sister and his friend Portier and the world from unimaginable horror. Of necromancy. He was wary of Dante but would never betray him, unless . . . Calvino de Santo's wounds flared in memory.

"What kind of *illness*? What have you people done to him?"

Her long body bristled. "If you're thinking to accuse me or anyone at the Temple of harming him, you'd best think again. He'll tell you himself, he was as near dead as a man can be this side of the eternal Veil. He suffered a belly wound, pierced clear through. We Temple healers saved his life."

"Forgive me for being argumentative, Rhea Tasserie. But I don't equate saving a life with the right to hold a man prisoner or to torture or murder him."

"The Temple has every right to protect the people from daemonic evils." But her gaze faltered and slid off in Ladyslipper's direction as she spoke.

"Daemonic?" I shook Ilario's odd little charm at her. "There is no nobler soul in this world than the man who carries this." Having just mourned Ilario, I would battle the Souleater himself to reclaim him.

But which Ilario had they seen, the lighthearted dandy the world knew or the man who had devoted his life, his reputation, and his considerable intelligence and skill to his royal sister's protection?

The woman's bony shoulders twitched under the brown wool. She riveted her gaze to the horse. "That's why I've come. Someone's got to persuade him to answer what's asked of him."

"So it wasn't your prisoner, but Tetrarch de Ferrau who sent you here. His Excellency didn't believe me when I said I couldn't help him."

"No! I mean, it was neither one of them sent me. He—the prisoner—had told me about you, and I thought maybe an intelligent person that he respected might make him see sense. So I told my superiors that my mother was ill and only I could ease her, and I took his silly charm and came here to find you. But yes, it's the tetrarch's questions he needs to answer, elsewise he's going to be linked to horrible things—blasphemy, necromancy, murder. He'll be *exposed*. And his kin will be linked to those things, too."

Danger hollowed my stomach. Eugenie, so recently maligned as the shadow queen. The king. Their long-awaited child. This woman certainly knew who Ilario was. But did de Ferrau? "Does the tetrarch understand the consequences of his threats?"

"How could I know that?" She pressed one long, slender hand to her brow and scraped her wisps of hair backward, holding tight as if to gather her thoughts. "I'm but a minor healer who's not even supposed to know this prisoner's name. Tetrarch de Ferrau is trying to persuade the senior tetrarchs to arrest the daemon mage. He is a *most* persuasive speaker, a good and *holy* man, the youngest tetrarch there has ever been, so he *will* convince them. And then this prisoner will have no choice but to testify. If he refuses, they'll judge him equal in guilt with the sorcerer."

Discipline held me steady. I sheathed my knife.

"Why do you think I can persuade him to a course he does not choose of his own? I could go straight to his family and reveal everything you've just told me."

Eugenie would do anything for Ilario. That would reveal the Temple's despicable use of her brother to the king, and the tetrarch and the Temple would inherit a powerful, implacable enemy. Perhaps de Ferrau believed that Anne de Vernase, corrupted already and hoping to avoid condemnation for her own deeds, might succumb to threats and save them a pot full of trouble.

For a while, I thought Rhea Tasserie wasn't going to respond. She bit her lip and stared at the stable ceiling—the very portrait of exasperation . . . or misery. Perhaps she prayed for guidance. But eventually, she hugged her middle again and met my gaze.

"I heard something I shouldn't, and to speak it—" She shook her head, jaw and mouth clenched. "I should be forever exiled for revealing a Temple secret. But I cannot— If the slightest word leaks out to the prisoner's family, he will *disappear.* No one will be able to prove he didn't die of his wounds in Coverge. Ask anyone serving at the Temple hospices in Jarasco or Castelivre. They'll tell you about the swordsman companion of the daemon mage and how he died of a belly wound back in Desen's month. No one who tended him in those first few days ever saw me. No one else knows he survived."

"He would *disappear*?" Bless Dante, who had taught me to leash my power for magic, else anger might have propelled me all the way to

Merona to crush the Temple Major on its tetrarch's murderous head. "How dare you claim Ferrau is *holy*? By this measure, your own life is forfeit."

"His reasons are not petty," she said urgently. "It's the mage he wants. The necromancer. None of the rest of you. Certainly not me."

"*No* reasons suffice. You're speaking of secret execution of a good and decent man. Murder."

"A man complicit in unholy rites—and in the murder of a dozen servitors! Though"—I could feel her retreat from her charge as soon as she'd spat it out—"not necessarily deserving of a charge of blasphemy or its severest consequences."

Holy angels, severest consequences . . . not just death, but excruciating death.

"Again, healer, state why you've come to me. If the chevalier will not spew whatever falsehoods your tetrarch demands to save his own life, then what can I possibly do?"

She folded her arms and turned away. "I could get you inside the Temple walls. He says you are 'eminently resourceful in matters of seeing.' I've no idea what that means. I don't *want* to know. I am trying to convince you to persuade him to confession. That's all."

I gaped. Released a slow breath. Ilario knew of Lianelle's potion. Part of my young sister's legacy was an enchanted concoction that left its user unseeable. He would never have even hinted of such a resource to this woman if he didn't trust her . . . or was desperate enough he had no alternative.

I picked up the brush and resumed grooming Ladyslipper, letting the rhythmic motion and the feel of her, warm and living, settle my agitation as thoughts shaped themselves into this new pattern. Rhea was offering to help me rescue Ilario. Or leading me into a trap.

Rapid, shallow breaths jerked her shoulders. Fingers wrapped around her sleeves tapped and squeezed. Excitement? Fear? Or a war going on inside her?

"How can I possibly trust you?" I said. "How will you not be tainted by our wickedness? How will you reconcile your conscience?"

"Your friend trusts me. Everyone else at the Temple thinks him a fool. But I was with him when he was out of his head and said things . . . he wished he had not said. Eventually, when his position became clear, he allowed me to know that charm would be recognized by his friends. I had thought it nothing of worth." Her trembling hands rubbed her upper arms. "If my superiors discover I've come here, I'll tell them that I hoped to gain higher status in the Temple by persuading the prisoner to speak what he knows. They already believe me hopelessly naive about how the Temple must navigate political waters. As to conscience, I am damned if I do this and damned if I do nothing. But I am a healer before all, and I would not see this man dead."

Her voice cracked as she spoke this last. I wanted to believe her. Perhaps de Santo's fate had bruised her conscience. Saints' mercy, if this was a trap, I had no choice but to leap into it. Dante would have to wait a bit longer. I could not allow Ilario to be murdered, too.

"Come along, then," I said. "We'll ride together. You will follow my lead until we get to Merona. And if one hair on my friend's head is harmed, I swear I'll see your tetrarch hanged by his thumbs as fodder for crows."

LEYNOUE

Mud. Thick, sticky, sloppy mud everywhere. The rainstorms that lashed northern Louvel in late winter were legendary, and those that came near paralyzing Rhea and me must have been recorded as the worst in living memory. I had chosen to return to Merona via the river route, lest Rhea have Temple allies awaiting us on the main road. But I regretted the choice bitterly as we slogged our way to Leynoue, only to find no bargeman willing to challenge the swollen river's dangerous currents. Entire trees hurtled downriver. It didn't help to know the road from Laurentine to Merona would have been a similar sea of mud.

The delay gave Rhea time to draw a detailed map of the Temple hospice and write down the daily schedule for guards, attendants, physicians, and interrogators. I memorized them and gave them back. She burnt the notes and acted as if they had never existed. Indeed, she scarce spoke outside necessity. We shared a room to save expense at the inn, but naught else.

At least she no longer pretended she'd fetched me to persuade Ilario to testify. We acquired clothes for him—no easy matter, due to his height. Rhea had a spruce green wool cloak that she said was common among lower-ranking Temple servitors and I paid a seamstress to add to its length. I didn't tell Rhea that my sister's potion should enable Ilario and me to walk out of her Temple without need of disguising cloaks. Would de Ferrau dare mount a search?

If Ilario was well enough, perhaps we'd join Portier in Abidaijar. Portier might have new information, and the three of us could set out to find Dante and his brother.

On our third morning in Leynoue, Rhea and I sloshed back to the inn after another fruitless trip to the barge landing. Actually, we hadn't even made it so far as the landing. The lower streets of Leynoue were awash, the landing submerged. Both of us were strung so tight, a pinprick would have us bursting.

Rhea halted abruptly at the foot of a mucky path that led up the hill. "When you— If you were to— You must take all the medicines sitting at your friend's bedside," she said. "He isn't fully healed as yet inside. Few people survive a penetrating belly wound. It's just a blessing that those who cared for him chose not to put him through the agony of pouring hot oil into the wound."

"Hot oil . . ." I'd not grasped the severity of Ilario's injury. My father made sure to know everything he could about battlefield surgery and had taught me enough to understand the deadly risks of sepsis. "Then how did you keep him alive? The Academie Medica says—"

"I didn't attend the academie. When I took over his care, I treated his wound open for a time to keep it draining, repeatedly cutting away the dead tissue. It's a new idea, well proved thus far. However, it prolongs the recovery. He should be fine eventually, but he must keep taking his medicines."

We resumed our climb, mud squishing inside my boot.

"Where did you learn such a technique?" I said. Papa had also never called in Temple healers when we were ill. He didn't trust their training and said that one must assume they had divided loyalties, if they thought Heaven was a finer place than this side of the Veil.

"My mother is a Temple healer in Heville. She's a widow with none to keep me while she worked, so I grew up in the hospice. Watched. Helped out. Asked questions of everyone. The academie physicians and students came to Heville to practice, as we treated such a variety of wounds and sickness. So I learned from them, too. By the time I was old enough to enter the academie, I was already teaching." She cast a glance my way, averting her eyes when they met mine. Her cheeks glowed scarlet. "My best student is caring for your friend while I'm gone. The method of wound care is my own idea."

Students? Altering healing practices that had been used for decades? And I had judged her no more than my own four-and-twenty years!

"How old *are* you, Rhea?" My own cheeks heated the moment I blurted the question. "Pardon, I didn't mean to pry."

She shrugged her bony shoulders. "No matter. I'm nineteen."

Which answer threw me over completely. "Saints! You must be very good."

"My superiors find me useful." Her attention was firmly on the slick cobbles winding up the slope to the Street of Innkeepers. Her long legs kept her ahead of me. "I've a good memory. I can recall everything I see or hear."

"I was schooled at home, too," I said, hastening to keep up. "My father was an exceptional teacher, with wide-ranging interests and a great deal of wisdom about the world. I wish I could have absorbed them all on first hearing."

"Your father was truly—?" She bit down on the question and cast such a fearful glance my way, she must have thought I, too, was a daemon necromancer.

Guilt sent its creeping little fingers through my anger and mistrust. If she was telling the truth, she was risking everything to help Ilario.

"Understand me, Rhea." I lowered my voice so that a man and boy traipsing past us down the hill would not hear. "I owe Ilario de Sylvae my life three times over, and my brother's life, and a great deal more. To hear of him imprisoned and condemned without defense by those who claim to speak for the Creator of the universe makes it very hard to trust anyone from the Temple. If you want to free him, we are allies. Speak freely."

"I just wanted—" Her wide brow wrinkled. "Your father was truly the Great Traitor, condemned and then reprieved?"

"Yes. The man I honored most in the world was condemned on my testimony. I was as firm in my belief in his treachery as you are of your tetrarch's holiness. And I was absolutely wrong."

"The daemon mage could have obscured your mind, and your friend's mind, to believe in your father's crimes. To hide his own dealings. He could have obscured the king's mind to give him parole. Powerful sorcerers can do that, so I've heard. The holy tetrarch says the mage torments our dead, destroys souls. . . ."

She sounded sincere, as if striving to understand. But she was a child of the Temple, and believed in Beltan de Ferrau's virtue, and could recall anything she saw or heard. Any attempt to explain the Gautier conspiracy and Dante's actions would only tie me closer to him. I could not let her trick me into spewing confessions.

"I believe the mage capable of much wickedness. But my judgment of my father was made on facts and evidence, not compulsion. It just happened that the logical interpretation of the facts was flawed, because the crime was so much greater and so much more complex than anyone could ever imagine. As for King Philippe, I was present on the day he paroled the mage. He believed what he did was right and just. There are few people in the world whose judgment I would trust more."

She swallowed my words as the night devours the light, and asked no more questions.

By evening the river had receded. By the next morning, my friend the bargeman welcomed us aboard his boat. By sunset, Rhea Tasserie and I parted under a linden tree on Merona's Plas Royale, after going over our plan one more time. Though the thought of further delays near ground my bones, Rhea was adamant that we could not attempt the rescue right away. For the prisoner to disappear on the very night of her return would point an accusing finger directly at her.

A day or two would give her time to report on her mother's lingering illness from a winter grippe, fend off any contrary reports, expound upon the delays of travel in such dreadful weather, and ensure that Ilario was fit to travel. When all had settled back to normal, she would hang a red scarf out her window in the hospice at sunset for an hour. On that night a small gate in the hospice garden would be left unlocked, and she would wait for me in the southeast corner of the garden. By the time she realized I wasn't joining her, Ilario and I would be gone.

CHAPTER 17

MERONA

At last! I counted again. Fifth window from the right in the second of three rows. The hospice was a newer structure, built to house Temple servitors, traveling officials, and the infirmaries, as well as all manner of official activities. Long and low, its ranks of simple pediment windows sat orderly and pleasing in a style revived from before the Blood Wars. A number of casements stood open, and an irregular shape was draped over the sill of the one Rhea had indicated was her private bedchamber.

Fog had rolled up from the river, dulling the colors of evening. The Temple pennant that flew from the staff above the hospice roof was more mud brown than ivy green. But the rag hanging limp from Rhea's window was surely scarlet.

Three days of skulking about the royal city and I had near given up on Rhea's signal. Every sort of imagining had flown through my head. She was under arrest herself. Ilario was dead or dragged off to their dungeons, while the girl and her holy tetrarch prepared a trap. All still a risk. And while I twiddled my thumbs, Dante was getting farther and farther away, in search of an enchantress who spoke in dreams and emeralds that showed visions of a devastated world. I needed to be with him.

Hefting my bundle of Ilario's clothes, I strolled through the evening bustle—royal guardsmen hurrying to change the watch, mounted courtiers, ladies in carriages, students and scholars hurrying to supper from the academies and collegiae that lined the broad boulevard. I had to give Rhea time to leave off her afternoon's work. She was accustomed to sleeping for a few hours before returning to sit with Ilario through the night watches. But on this night she would sneak out to meet me in the garden.

Clutching the cold glass vial in my pocket, I stepped into an alley and breathed deep. Peace reigned in the royal city, both in the streets and in the aether, since Dante had undone the hauntings and plagues he'd worked for Germond de Gautier.

Two days previous, I had talked my way into the palace stable and fetched one of Ilario's own horses. Guillam the stable master believed I was arranging a secret hunting party for the chevalier's birthday and had agreed to keep my presence and my acquisition secret. Though he looked somewhat askance at my bedraggled turnout, he recognized me as the queen's onetime maid of honor and Ilario's friend. As every night thus far, the horses were waiting at a private hostelry just off the Plas Royale, a lad paid well to hold them ready.

The bells of Sabria's royal city clanged in calm and reassuring timbre. Seventh hour of the evening watch. It was time.

Eight drops of the potion on my tongue. The world blurred, as if the fog had thickened, smearing the faded colors and winking lamplight. But soon the brick walls of the alley, the horses and carts and passersby returned to sharpened clarity, a faint blue halo about their edges to hint at the magic enveloping me. As I stepped out of the alley, a hurrying post messenger near bowled me over. I pressed my back to the wall with grim satisfaction. None could see me.

A side lane separated the hospice garden wall and the wall of the Collegia Musica. A few steps along and the sounds of city business dropped away. The hospice precincts were not easily broached. Birds chittered in trees planted well away from the high walls. The ivy grew thicker the farther the wall stretched from the Plas Royale, but certainly not thick or strong enough to climb as romantic poets insisted. Thick enough, however, to mask an iron door kept solidly locked.

But on this night, the opening lever, wrought in the shape of a grapevine as thick as my arm, yielded smoothly to my touch. I held back, waiting for bailiffs to jump out of the dark masses of shrubbery within. Quiet conversation carried across the lawn from the direction of the hospice. Lamplight spilled from one and then another window as evening deepened into night. But no alarms sounded. Not so much as a leaf stirred.

Rhea's diagram had shown a service door at the rear of the building. A bailiff stood guard there at any hour, she had told me, always an experienced man who recognized the Temple servitors allowed to use the entrance.

I halted a few metres away near a thick tangle of lilac bushes and launched a pea-sized bit of gravel at the liveried bailiff. It struck him on the cheek. He spun around. Thanking my brother for pestering me to compete in endless throwing competitions, I aimed the next for the man's thigh. One more, and he was trotting across the grass in my direction.

"Hey now, what're you about out there, rascals? Hiding, are you?"

Wishing the guard would keep his voice quieter, I skirted around him, darted through the doorway, and pressed my back to the wall inside. After a few moments, he poked his head through the door, saw nothing, and harrumphed.

The door snicked shut behind him. Blotting the dampness from my forehead and tucking my shoes more firmly in my belt, I reminded myself to keep a moderate pace. It would be stupid to betray my presence by panting and heaving or bumping into a servitor. Heart pounding, I ventured onward.

Ten metres in, branch left. Take the first stair to the right, to the uppermost floor. First obstacle. Three or four women—cleaning women from the look of them—lingered on the first-floor landing chattering about babies and the advantages of hiring out to wet-nurse instead of cleaning. I could not pass.

To retreat and find an alternate stair meant passing through lobbies and reception areas, still busy so early in the evening. *Do not run. Do not run.* At least the stair was wider and I could get around the groups of servitors or visitors who dawdled. At the first opportunity I returned to my original path. The third-floor chamber where Ilario lay was accessible by only the one stair. And then there would be guards.

Fortune smiled as I reached the last door at the end of the third-floor passage. The two guards were peering out of the window, pointing and chuckling at something on the lawn. I was able to slip past and through the single door behind their backs.

Most of the small, bare room lay in shadow. A single candle burnt on a bedside table, illuminating a clutter of jars, bottles, and spoons. The candlelight spilled onto a bed shoved into the corner and the untidy sheet and blanket that draped a huddled form, facing the bare wall. Tears welled at the sight of pale hair tousled on the pillow and the feet hanging off the end of the short, narrow bed. After all, I'd been afraid Rhea had lied.

I closed the door softly.

"Naught to say to you, interrogator." The words from the corner were slurred and faint. "Succor me, Santa Alis, Santa Claire, Sante Ianne . . ." A Cult prayer litany.

"Hold still and quiet, my fair chevalier," I whispered, touching his shoulder. "A friendly ghost has come to steal you away."

He didn't move. But his pale slender hand reached over his shoulder to grasp my hand. His flesh was cold and damp.

"Be this another fever dream?" he said softly. "Or shall I begin my litany of thanksgiving right off?"

"Not until we're out. I've brought clothes your tailor would wholly disapprove of."

He shifted, shoving ineffectively at the bedclothes. I dragged them off and helped him roll over. He wore only a coarse wrinkled shirt that might once have been white. His face remained firmly pressed into the pillow. "Head's an iron pot filled with porridge."

"We must do this," I said. "We'll find a safe place for you to rest as soon as we're away."

"Small problem." He raised his left wrist, bound by a metal band chained to the iron bedstead.

I roused a short blast of Mondragon heat from inside me and shattered the damnable chain as far from Ilario's hand as I could manage it. The raw and ugly bit of magic left the bedclothes smoking. My stomach curdled in disgust. How could Dante love this so?

"You've practiced." Ilario coughed, stretching his hand and its shattered remnant of chain away from his head. "Might warn a fellow."

"If I think about it, I can't make myself do it. Now, up." I slid an arm under his shoulders. We eased him to sitting, small, strained sounds in his throat rousing my dismay. Ilario had always been the very image of life, even when dealing death with his sword.

Arms rigid, hands pressed against the bed, head drooping, he exhaled slowly. "'Fraid you've picked a bad night, ghost. They infuse me with diabolical potions to loosen my lips."

"Unfortunate." I dropped the clothes in his lap. "Get these on, Knight of Sabria, or I'll take you out of here naked. And imagine what that would do to your reputation."

His shoulders spasmed . . . and then shook.

"Great heavens, Ilario . . ."

He glanced up, his blue eyes heavy lidded, his skin scoured by pain and blotched green with fading bruises, but sporting a grin as wide as Ocean. "Anne de Vernase," he said, squinting as if he might see me did he try hard enough. "My beloved lady. Unseeable as grace. Irresistible as an avalanche."

He pawed at the pile on his lap and pulled out the ugly green tunic we had bought for him in Leynoue. He sighed heavily. "But no appreciation for fashion."

I knelt in front of him and pushed stockings up his long bare legs. Then baggy trousers. He squirmed enough to get them over his underdrawers so I could fasten buttons and ties. It must have looked very strange, as if his clothes were dressing him all of themselves. He couldn't reach high enough to get the tunic over his head. I did that, too, taking care to prevent the chain dangling from his wrist from rattling.

"No boots till we're away," I said.

"Barefoot. Mercy . . ."

His mocking dismay raised a smile as I pulled the vial from my pocket. "I'm going to give you a few drops of my sister's magical brew, and we're going to walk right out of this place with none the wiser."

"I'll be a ghost, too? Delightful! Ghosts couldn't have guts that feel as if they've been stitched by a sailmaker. Though I'll say . . ." His brow creased and he peered into the shadowed corners. "The healer. Where is she? The time . . ." No mockery when he spoke of her.

"She's in the garden." There wasn't time to probe his opinion of Rhea. "Now, open your mouth." Four drops for him. It was going to take us a while to get him out. Surely . . . I hadn't thought about the possibility Lianelle's potion wouldn't work on someone else. "It will feel strange."

"Saints and angels!" Ilario stretched his eyes wide . . . blinked . . . gaped . . . threw his arm across his face . . . and then faded into nothing. "Strange medicines you dish out. But alas, sweet ghost, I'm still here."

"No more than I am here. Trust me."

The bottles and jars on the bedside table glared at me. Gods, what were they all? I scooped everything into my pack and slung it back over my shoulder, blew out the candle, and returned to his side. Laughing in relief, I found his head, not quite poking him in the eye. "Now, onto your feet like a good fellow. Lean on me. Right foot first. We'll take it slow, but you and your ugly jewelry must be absolutely silent. Save all groaning and whining for later."

Supporting an invalid when we couldn't see each other was incredibly awkward. Three times, tangled feet came near tumbling us in a heap, and twice an aborted groan told me I'd moved too quickly or too far.

Our shuffling progress was brought to an abrupt halt by clicking footsteps and gruff voices outside the door. "Did you mention the time?" Ilario mumbled into my hair.

"Near eighth hour."

"Saints . . ." He retreated to the bare wall behind the door, dragging me alongside.

When the door opened a few centimetres, Ilario set up such gagging, hawking, spitting, and groaning as near made me vomit in sympathy.

"Go 'way," he croaked. "Leave a man . . . bit . . . dignity to heave . . . patchwork guts . . . privacy. Queshions later . . . won't answer anyway . . ."

"Where's the healer?" The man with the steel-edged voice wasn't pleased. But he didn't push the door farther open as Ilario drowned out a mumbled response with more retching.

"Well, fetch her," the man snapped. "Tell her the prisoner is puking."

Rhea, who wasn't in her bedchamber, but in the garden.

Iron bars crosshatched the single window, and we dared not move through the door. It remained open but a few centimetres, and the murmur of voices in the passage did not abate. Fire and destruction might be the only way. . . .

"What's happened? Why are all of you here?" Rhea's clear voice interrupted the mumbling. "He was resting peacefully when I left him. Move aside, please!"

The door opened slightly wider.

"Clean him up," said the man. "But give him none of your pills or potions. Perhaps a sour gut will persuade him to answer."

"I wasn't told he was to be questioned tonight."

"His questioning is the tetrarch's concern, servitor, not yours."

"Forgive me, bailiff. I'm just concerned with keeping the man alive. Let me see what's wrong and clean up the mess."

The wider view through the opening door told me we could not push our way through the men crowding the passage. A disheveled Rhea grabbed a lamp from the passage, marched into the dark room, and shut the door firmly.

"What in the—?"

Holding the lamp high, she tweaked Ilario's rumpled bedclothes, and then whirled about to stare at the bedside table. Ilario took a breath as if to speak, but I squeezed his arm and pressed my other hand in the vicinity of his mouth.

"Bailiff!" The healer darted to the door and flung it open, raising a curse in my heart. "The prisoner's gone. Someone's moved him."

"That's impossible. We all heard him. Step aside!"

Rhea held the door open and the men swarmed inside, a short man with tight black curling hair and beard in the lead. "What have you done with him, woman?"

I swore under my breath. There was no way to get past the men.

"Your own men, Teil and Geroux, were on duty when I left. They took away his dinner tray and ensured his chain was locked, yes?"

Two other men nodded.

"Where were you, girl?" snapped the black-bearded bailiff. "Not in your bedchamber."

"Why do you question *me*? Hadn't you best be finding out who took my patient before Tetrarch de Ferrau finds out he's missing?"

The mention of the tetrarch's name prodded the men like a spear in their backsides. The bailiff took one moment to examine the broken remnant of chain dangling from the bedstead. Gray as the sheet, he pelted from the room and down the passage.

I nudged Ilario toward the open door, hoping to make it through before the woman closed it, but he wouldn't move. I caught it halfway as it swung closed. We could still make it through. . . .

"By the angels." Rhea raked fingers through her spiky hair. "Where have you gone?"

"Not far, my healer," said Ilario.

I wanted to slam my head into the wall. Or his.

"Has she killed you?" Rhea tried to retreat from all directions at once. "I never thought—"

"She's come to my rescue," said Ilario. "I told you she was extraordinary. But unfortunately she's the size of a seahorse, and I fear we'll take nine years to get out of your happy home if you can't lend me a hand yet again."

"You are . . . corporeal?"

"Wretchedly so. Here beside the door."

As she approached, squinting, I felt him extend his arm. Rhea stared at her own as if it had demonstrated clear signs of leprosy.

"We need to go," I said, giving her another start. "So tell me truthfully, are you friend or foe?"

"Healer."

She gathered the sheets and blankets from Ilario's bed, hefted the bundle on her shoulder, and yanked open the door. "He did vomit earlier this evening," she said to the remaining guard, who barred her exit with a drawn sword. "Likely from the interrogator's poison. I need to haul these down to the washhouse. Unless you want to do it. . . ." She thrust the bundle at the guard.

He retreated to the wall, clearing a nicely wide path for us.

"I'll be back in an hour with clean linen."

With Rhea bearing at least half of Ilario's weight, we proceeded slowly down the passage to the stairs. I seethed at Ilario exposing my secret to the woman, yet I had to confess the wisdom of it. She had done well. And I could not support his shoulders without him stooping. His belly would surely be an agony.

We made it down the back stair and halfway across the lawn before the hospice bells rang in noisy anxiety, summoning all servitors into the Great Hall.

"I have to go," said Rhea. "Wait in the corner we agreed on. The lord can rest. If I don't attend this summoning, they'll know I've betrayed them."

"If they've discovered him gone, they *already* know," I said. "We can stay hidden, but you . . ."

"I'm a loyal servitor and will not be suspected. I'll help them search. Stay here."

"We need to be away from this place!" I tried not to shout after her.

She stepped back in the deeper shadow of a lilac tree. "He's going to collapse if you don't let him rest, damoselle. Their fine little potion will keep him knobbled for at least another hour. And I've had no time to write a list of his medicines, and you've no idea how they must be given. I've not got him this far only to let you kill him. Lord, can you make it a little farther with only the lady?" she said.

"Anne and I shall stagger onward in good order, Captain." He straightened as if giving a salute. "Neither bailiffs nor dogs nor small ferocious children shall deter us from our objective."

"I'll be back as soon as I can. Then I'll take you to a house I know. Safe enough for a few days and I can see to your medicine." In moments, the pale blur of her bundled laundry vanished into the hospice.

"You trust her," I said.

"She saved my life, Ani. Ten times over. I smelled the dry fields of Ixtador so often, I came near calling myself one of the Reborn. So, yes, I do. Never doubt she is a most devout adherent of the Temple, but she's a healer first and has protected me from the worst of their questioning. And she brought you."

"They want me here where they can watch me. This Tetrarch de Ferrau came to Montclaire asking questions."

"Ah. The hound of Heaven hunts our friend. That's good. It means they don't have him. He and Calvino are likely on their way to find Portier . . . or those cursed emeralds. . . ."

Ilario told me everything of their journey from leaving Montclaire to the escape from Jarasco to the fight in the rift where he'd stayed behind. I told him of de Ferrau and the burning of Pradoverde and the letter from Dante's brother. I didn't tell him about Calvino de Santo. I couldn't do that until he had more strength to grieve.

"We'll find Dante, Ani," he said, as the Temple bells rang ninth hour. "But I've got to say, he frightens me. He is so angry, and great god of Heaven, this magic drives him so hard. I'd swear he traveled in a different world half the time on the road. That night, surrounded by the column of light, so beautiful and terrible, he could have been the Souleater himself. I'd not like to see him with more power than he has already."

We were silent for a while after that. He laid his arm about my shoulders, the battered prisoner offering *me* comfort.

"So we wait for Rhea," I said at last.

"She's an odd sort, but then, who am I to say? I've lived eight-and-twenty years as a mindless idiot, and I'm sitting here invisible with a beautiful, intelligent enchantress who fancies a madman. Give me a few days in her care, away from the tetrarch's potions, and we'll ride for Carabangor."

Dante

CHAPTER 18

23 ESTAR, EVENING
AROTHI DESERT

By the time John Deune led me across the ancient stone bridge that spanned the river Uravani, we had shed our cloaks and wool shirts. The warm, dust-laden air, the sweet rot of an old riverbed, and the snappish energies of the aether signaled we had truly traveled to a different place. And there was more. . . .

Once we reached the Arothi side, I called John Deune to halt. "Tell me of the bridge."

The flood of enchantment flowing over and through me spoke of something massive and very old.

"It's just a bridge. Looks odd to me. The river's naught but a muddy trickle that a man might ford without so much as a plank to walk across. But the span is as wide as a boulevard and built like a fortress with gate towers on the ends, as if someone might actually want to conquer a country that looks as lively as a rat with a broken neck."

"Are there markings on it? Carvings?" Conquering legions had traversed this bridge since the days before writing. I'd swear I could hear the surging power of the great river and feel the ground shiver with the tramp of their feet.

"Don't see any. No carvings at all save the Cult statues on each end. Oughtn't we be moving?"

"Cult statues?"

"There's the statues atop the gate towers." John sighed and spoke louder and slower, as if I were an idiot child. "It's the Righteous Defender and the Daemon of the Dead as you might see at any Cult shrine, though you'll not see them so large as these. These are quite shabby, though, noses and ears ground away . . . the Daemon's claw broken off, the Defender's sword missing."

Ghost prickles raised the hairs on arms and neck. "I thought the tales of the Righteous Defender were just Temple stories, not particular to the Cult of the Reborn." Adept Denys had also called the Defender's opponent the Daemon of the Dead. "You must know a great deal about Cult legends, serving Lord Ilario so many years."

"I'm not a Cultist myself, but, as you say, my lord was . . . devoted." John Deune's servile superiority set my teeth grinding. "The Temple believes the Righteous Defender of the Gates of Heaven to be an angel. The Cult says he will be one of their Saints Reborn."

"Naturally they would. And what of this daemon?"

"The Souleater's Chosen, the strongest of his champions. In the last battle of the War for Heaven, they say the Daemon will battle the Defender before Heaven's Gates, trying to take the unworthy where they don't belong."

Free of Andero's bond, I touched my copper bracelet and looked backward. A small advantage to me, that I could not see the flaws John Deune described. Instead, through the charcoal veil of blindness, I saw the figures as they were meant to be seen, towering, fearsome shapes silhouetted against the clear gray sky, no shoddy details to reduce the majesty of their grappling. For no reason at all, my breath came short and my throat swelled to choking.

"So we go on, Master?"

Unable to speak and unable to explain why, I jerked my head.

Throughout that day, we traveled the ghost road away from Kadr and into the hot, dry wastelands of Aroth. The sun hammered and bent me as if I lay on my father's forge. Again I fell into waking dreams: emerald walls and gaping spectres, a flashing sword and a daemon hand . . . scarred and clawed. Once I glimpsed the fair young man, his sword tucked under his shifting coat. He tossed his long gold and gray hair over his shoulder. When his eyes met mine, his fair face lit in greeting, he pressed a long finger to his mouth as if to hush my fears. I jolted awake, chilled to the marrow.

Three times on that day, cold shudders prompted me to ask if we rode through some gully or streambed where fog lingered. Each time John Deune denied it. The third time, his irritation burst its bounds. "There's naught but trampled ground as far as I can see. Why would I lie about it? Sometimes we pass what looks like long furrows and holes like pockmarks on the land. There's a few broke-down wagons far from the road. Naught but brush growing. So is this where you're meant to go or not? I'm just following your man's orders as you said."

"Yes, I'm sure this is right." We were close.

Indeed the land of Aroth seemed bound by enchantment—every noise too loud or too soft, the very earth beneath my feet unsettled. The world felt thin, day and night and season leaking into one another. In one hour the desert heat seemed like to bake me. In another, the dry chill set my bones shivering.

I swallowed my curses lest John abandon me in the wastes. I used no magic. Surely I would need all the power I could muster for this meeting.

I COULD HAVE NAMED THE moment when Carabangor came into view, for a shadow fell over my spirit that no tree or cloud could explain. As a dawn wind blew across the desert, my companion drew us to a halt and confirmed the appearance of broken towers on the horizon.

"I didn't intend to bring you here, John Deune," I said. "But I thank you."

"I'm sworn to serve you, noble master, though I know I'm weak and ignorant beside Goodman Andero." Weak, yes, though he held himself wiser. Likely he was.

The wind gusted and moaned about the piled stones and fallen timbers of an abandoned caravanserai. The horses were skitterish, so we tethered them in the shelter of a spindly locust tree and walked into Carabangor.

It was as if I had been journeying forever away from the life I knew and into the realm of haunts. Ancient voices and newer ones twined in the chaotic aether . . . layer upon layer of birth and death, affection, jealousy, murder, torment. City upon city had stood in this place.

Once through the gates, I paused, gripped my staff with both hands, and opened my true hearing. And she was there. Weeping, pleading with me to come and deliver her from her prison among the dead of Carabangor.

"There it is, Master, a ruin with six eagle statues in front of it." John Deune's whisper blared like a herald's trump. His hand on my arm felt like ground glass in a wound.

"Wait with the horses, John. If I've not returned by dusk, run to Andero. He'll see you safe until you can get home. Your oath to Lord Ilario is discharged."

Perhaps he obeyed. Perhaps he didn't. I moved forward as a sleepwalker might, drawn by the fascination of my waking dream. My feet were sure, unfazed by swirling sand that scoured the rubble as if trying to rid the desert of this blighted ruin.

The temple interior was cool and moist, just as de Cuvier had described it. The wind darted ahead of me down the winding staircase, and the fog muffled my steps as I descended into the great cavern. Imagination gazed upon the landscape of my dreams—the milky lake, the boat, and in the center of all, the phantom, the woman of dreams, her silken hair floating in the fog so you could not tell where one ended and the other began. I did not doubt the scene existed in truth just as I viewed it in memory.

"Help me!" The plea floated through the damp air. The glancing heat on my cheeks, on my shirt, on my arms, would be beams of green fire from the Stone resting on her palm.

Mind clung to the memory as my body found its way to the shore.

"Who are you?" My graveled voice bounced from the cavern walls.

"Oh, blessed stranger! I beg thee save me from this everlasting torment. I can pay. This jewel shall bring thee the supreme amongst all thy desires."

What game did she play, pretending not to know me?

"Your freedom will bring other things, too, will it not?" I said. "Things no one sensible would desire. Speak to me, phantom. Tell me why you've brought me here."

"I send the dreams in hopes of freedom, and I offer fair exchange. Why wouldst thou not wish passion's sorcery?" Earnest inquiry, as if she didn't know the truth of her green glass. "Hast thou no love? No art? No kingdom that drives you? I can attest to the Stone's beauty and worth."

"Desire for answers drives me. But you know that already."

Stupid to get into word twisting with an enchantress. I had to be careful. My purpose was Portier and the world's safety. I had to understand this woman's designs and the magnitude of power she could command to execute them. And then there was Jacard. . . .

"Where is your partner?"

"I have no *partner.* The other is a jealous fiend who tries to confuse and twist my sendings. I was always to stand first. I serve my beloved lord and no other, though he is so long delayed. Did the priests answer my pleas, I would never offer the Stone to strangers."

A jealous fiend . . . a beloved lord . . . priests . . . "But where are these others?"

"Set me free, gentle stranger. Take my gift and together we shall discover the answers you seek and I cannot give, prisoned as I am. Thou'rt comely, as is my lord, and I'll serve thee well."

Diving deep into the aether, I knelt and touched the mold-slimed paving, applying my best skills to decipher the magic. To little avail. The cavern in which I stood was real enough, but everything in it was so tangled in spells that it was impossible to judge truth from illusion. As if I were brushing sand from a buried pot, I cleared away the murk of emotion and history. The remaining spellwork was not so much a structure as a snarl of a thousand glassy threads, each pulsing with power, of such complexity it would take me days to pattern it. And at the heart of all was . . . nothing. A quiet emptiness. Nothing I could identify as the green glass in her hand.

Impossible, unless all had been one grand illusion. Gods, what I would give for one hour of sight.

"So long I've waited." Her voice wrenched the soul for pity. But I'd no intention of setting her free.

"Tell me who you are and how you came to be here," I said.

"I am Nessia, Keeper of Rhymus. To hold the Stone of Passion in time of trial has been my duty, ordained from birth, for I am of the clan of Tareo. When the barbarians came, the priests promised that my beloved lord would soon come for his Stone and deliver me. But I fear I'm forgotten. Have the barbarians won, great lord? Art thou one of them? Thy garments are strange, but thy shining neck collar speaks of your worth. . . ."

Her presence was soft as spring grass, as supple as willow, her call filled with desperate hope. Had I not unmasked her in the dream, heard her malevolent laughter, and smelled my father's charred flesh, I would have been at her side already.

"Please speak, lord. Is it some sin of mine keeps me here? I've offered the Stone freely, but all were afraid."

"You spoke in my father's dreams. Told him to forge a chain to bind me. He died in agony for heeding your command. You said you intend to bury a holy man alive."

"Nay! I would never—either one! I'm but my lord's servant, innocent of any crime save impatience. 'Tis Rhymus causes the seeing. I but touch its squaring facet, speak my need, and invoke the spell of dreams. To *shape* the dream is beyond anyone's skill save the Stone's rightful wielder, the priests who teach us, or the magic of the Stone itself."

Old anger and frustration gnawed at my gut. I was getting nowhere, shouting across the lake, incapable of reading her face. I needed to examine her prize, touch it, and judge its powers or whether it was evil in itself. I trained all my perception on reality. The copper bracelet was cold to the touch. *Oraste.*

Reality, imagining, and dream were inseparable in Carabangor. Though blurred and dim, all appeared as in my memory of de Cuvier's dream: the broken roof, the lake, the boat, the woman's slender shape on the distant islet. The boat was sturdy and felt as if new built that day. No smell of rot, no splinter marred the smooth finish of the oars.

Anne's pendant and Portier's ring went into my pocket. I bound my useless hand to the oar with their silver chain, a test of truth. I'd never had to do that in the dream.

I let the seeing spell lapse, lest it sap my power. The woman's weeping was a beacon more precise than any hilltop lighthouse. No sound intruded on my passage save the dip of oars, the soft echoes of her weeping, and the flutter of birds as they passed through the broken roof to the lost sky.

The prow bumped the islet. I detached my hand, took up my staff, and felt my way onto the rock.

Her gown whispered against the rock as she came to meet me. I towered over her. Astonishing, as she had loomed so large in the dream. A small, soft hand brushed my cheek, enveloping me in the scent of roses. "Maker's grace! I've offered prayers . . . vows. I thought none would ever answer. Bless thee and all thy kin."

Where was the venal laughter, the mocking, the murderous intent?

"The travelers feared your dream sendings." My voice grated like rusted iron beside her softness. "Though not at first . . ." What had de Cuvier told me?

She touched my lips with smooth fingers, sending ripples of heat through my flesh. The scent of roses . . . the enveloping fog . . . of a sudden I could not get a breath or shape a thought. The darkness closed in.

I backed away a step and tried to begin again.

"Have you a jailer? Someone who feeds you?" Perhaps one of these priests could reshape a dream. Or perhaps a renegade adept who knew of Portier's strange history and mine had learned enough to manipulate the girl.

"Nay. My body has no wants save a human touch. Stonekeepers drift in dream and sleep, waking when a living person crosses the boundaries of the temple. The priests know well how to manage such. Oh, please, great sir, may we leave this terrible place?"

Such longing. She could be no more than a girl in her teens. Her floating hair teased at my face. "Dost thou take me across the lake, this great treasure is thine. Please, I cannot bear its burden longer."

"Oraste," I whispered. Unable to resist, I risked the seeing spell again.

Against a world of charcoal and gray, the Stone rested like a green-plumed bird in the smooth nest of the lady's hand. A scarlet radiance beamed from its core.

"Rhymus the Red-Hearted," I said. "The Stone of Passion."

Her fingers closed, mottling the brilliance. "Once free, I am not permitted to keep it. Take me across and it is yours." With a sudden jerk, she twisted away for a moment, and then backed into my arms. "We must hurry before the other comes. Please. *Amiatro*."

The pale water lapped at the islet. Smeared stars in the blackness beyond the broken roof touched the night with silver. The fog and Nessia's hair and gown took on the luster of pearls. I could not think, could not breathe for the swelling in chest and loins.

The girl gave me her arm and waited for me to help her into the boat. She settled at my back, adjusting her position, slopping the milky water over the side as I bound my hand to the oar, hearing splashes behind us.

"Hurry," she said. "Please, before anyone follows us!"

My shoulders strained as I rowed toward the marble shore. The boat wallowed, heavy with the two of us as if I rowed the world's burdens across that lake. What was I doing? Who could follow?

Struggling to stop my arms, I shipped the oars. "What is this, lady?"

Nessia leaned forward. Her warm breath tickled my neck; her breasts pressed on my back. "You must keep rowing! Hurry!"

"Stop this!" But I could neither turn nor stop. My shout croaked back to me as the echo sought its resting place through the great cavern. As of themselves, my shoulders dipped forward and pulled at the oars.

"Too clever you are, blind man." This breathless whisper came inside my head. "You'll not believe what you cannot see, and, of course, you cannot *see* anything. Always thinking. Always probing. Too much thinking when one lives in the shadows."

No longer could I sense boat or oars or Nessia's excited breaths. I drifted in a yellow fog, the familiar voice teasing my ears. Surely a new dream vision had tangled my perceptions. "Who *are* you?"

"Did I not tell you? Nessia, Keeper of Rhymus. She who lures dreamers to free her from her cruel abandonment. Rhymus and I have waited a long time for someone to set us free. I cannot let you lag."

"You murdered my father. Why?"

"You are here, are you not? You defied me, and I was out of patience long ago."

"Where is the captive, the one you took—or lured—from Abidaijar?"

"The librarian? You must look into Rhymus to see your desires!" she said, and laughed the wicked laugh of the dream. "Soon the Stone of Passion will be free."

As abruptly as I had been caught up in the dream, I was once again in the boat, hand chained to the oar, immersed in a world of black and charcoal and gray. I should turn the boat around. This was a terrible mistake. . . .

Before I could dip the oars, the prow bumped the marble shore of the cavern, and before I could stop her, Nessia bounded past me onto the shore with a joyful cry. She spun and extended her hand, the Stone's emerald light penetrating my shadowed sight. "Take it."

Even after I was free of the boat and standing beside her, I refused to touch the thing. I dared not possess so dangerous an implement. But I looked. Though all instinct said no, the hunger was in me, and I was ruled by my desire and lost in my confusion.

The glass seemed to grow as I stared, until it encompassed the entire field of my vision. Its color deepened to the purest, richest emerald as I gazed on the vision—oh, glorious! What beauty lay there in its crimson heart: *moonlight over the ocean, a shining path of rose-touched silver across the luminous waves. Crimson dawn on snow-covered peaks . . .*

Behind me, the lake sloshed as if a storm was rising, splattering the shore, but I would not look away.

"See, blind man! Is it not a marvel?" The triumphant cry filled me with fear.

"How did *you* get here?" cried Nessia. "Go away. *My* freedom first!"

Her words signaled danger. But the vision grew with all its magic and mystery, and I could not relinquish it: *Illuminated lettering on ancient parchment, revealing secrets of magic . . . mine for the reading. The soaring arches of a temple housed a mother goddess and her son. A woman lay a newborn infant, red and wrinkled and full of ruddy life, before the goddess. The ground beneath my feet shuddered, and darkness enveloped the temple, as if a great fist had crushed it. A burst of green light, and he was there . . . the young man with gold and gray hair, worried, beckoning me. . . .*

My soul drank deep of the seeing.

"Oh, look at this!" she said, peering over my shoulder. "You are a kindred soul."

The young man led me into a darker place. Against a pall of midnight, Portier lay at the bottom of a metal-lined pit, limbs, chest, and neck strapped to the floor. His flesh was filthy, myriad wounds seeping blood. Dirt cascaded into the pit in thin, steady streams. His terror filled me as my own. Beside his grave—I could name it no other—blazed a fire worthy of my father's forge.

A shadowed figure stood beside the pit and as my guide and I watched, he pulled from the coals a great iron, glowing red at its tip.

"No, no, no!" I whispered, trembling with dread.

But this time the vision did not fade. *The figure in black raised the red-hot iron and knelt beside the hole in the floor, saying, "I give what you gave me. It's time you know my pain. Now you can grovel, powerless, in the everlasting dark."*

"No—oh, god—my friend!" cried Portier. "Dante, no!"

But I raised the iron and pointed the fiery end at my only friend's bulging eyes, and as I plunged it into the soft tissue, inhaling the odor of scorching flesh, his words melted into animal screams that set my own flesh afire. Flames . . . devouring . . .

My own eyes flared into hot coals, and my skin cracked and my flesh shriveled . . . and the voices of the aether burst free of their barricades. I tore at my hair, at my skin. I bellowed with agony and fury. Through fog and fire and shattering clamor, the woman laughed. What had I done?

In the tumultuous shadow world, the figure of gray gossamer yet stood in front of me, the vile glass resting on her palm. "What's wrong, sirrah? Take your payment! Your desires—"

In a frenzy to quench pain, to silence screaming, to make her *stop*, I grabbed her. "What did you make me do? Where is he?"

"Good sir! No! I've done nothing! You cannot—" She gripped the Stone hard.

"Despicable, evil, murderous witch! Throw it down. Your horrors shall not come to pass!" She weighed no more than a feather as I subdued her writhing, wrapped an arm about her neck, and squeezed . . . tighter . . . until the green glass clattered to the floor.

Yet as pain and madness drained from me, it came to me that though Nessia's struggles had ceased, the laughter did not.

"Free at long last!" crowed a woman's voice in triumph. "And Rhymus is mine!"

CHAPTER 19

CARABANGOR

Broken paving ground into my knees. The exultant woman stood at my shoulder, though Nessia yet lay still on the marble floor an arm's reach away, her cooling flesh draining warmth from my own. Flashes of memory: of soft pleading and harsh laughter, of sweetness and cruelty, of eyes of ebony and eyes streaked with silver . . .

"Two." I could scarce speak. "There were two of you."

"Indeed so. By bringing us across the barrier of the lake you set us free. And by slaying the poor worthless limpet, you've freed Rhymus, this most wondrous bit of glass which I now claim. And don't imagine I'll turn it or my own charge Orythmus to you or any other man comes asking! This day shall be writ in the stars forevermore."

Two blots of green pierced the everlasting sea of gray and black.

"La-la-la-li, those fine painted ladies must envy me! Too bad they're long dead, while in this new world I'll wear silk skirts of red!"

A soft rush of the air, clinking metal, quick breaths, punctuated her triumphal song. She was dancing. Her dripping gown sprinkled me with milky droplets. She must have clung to the boat as I rowed across the lake.

I ground a fist into my forehead, splayed my fingers and yanked at my hair. "I am not here. Not here. This is but illusion. Elsewise . . ." Surely I yet stood in the sand-scoured streets of Carabangor and was not kneeling beside another victim of this corrosive madness.

"Well, certainly you are *here*, magus." She knelt beside me, exuding damp, sweet-smelling heat. " 'Tis true I spread a bit of blandishment about you, but I was told your talents were mostly show, and 'twasn't till I met you in the dream, I knew that was not so. You near set my plan askew, recognizing that the dream sending was not entire of the limpet's doing. I dast not allow you to think clearly, or let her tell you sad tales of her wicked sister."

Blandishment. "Then the man in the pit . . . Portier?"

"I *saw* your vision! Lovely and wicked. Are not Rhymus's pageants marvelous? And now I shall be able to demonstrate them for more than dull-wit soldiers or muddle-headed blind men. I shall build me a great theatrium and require my subjects to attend. They'll shower me with flowers and jewels and bowls of cream and strawberries!"

"You took the librarian captive."

"How could I? I've been prisoned for seven centurias!" Quick as a moth she shifted to my left ear. "He languishes in the *Regent*'s chains, so I *could* arrange for you to do the deed in truth. My loyal servants could carry the tale of my cruelty into the land so all would fear me. I shall require your deepest respect and obedience in our new life. Now I'm free, possessing two of the Seeing Stones, even the Regent of Mancibar must bend to me. . . ."

As this noisome preening flowed over and around me, I grasped one smat of logic, and though I had not prayed since I was fifteen, I blessed the universe for its favor and begged one more boon. If I had not mutilated Portier, then what of Nessia?

I ripped away my gloves and examined the unmoving form that lay on the pavement before me. Found her soft, cool cheek. Her slender fingers. The scent of roses twined my senses, choking, nauseating, as I laid my ear on her warm breast. Stillness.

In a new frenzy, I groped about the floor to find my staff. Holding the girl's soft hand in my shaking left hand, the staff in my grotesque right, I reached for power and hunted deep. There was no life in her . . . nothing. . . .

"Leave off that! Good riddance to her," said the other, kicking my hand from the dead woman's. "I'll advise you, never spend seven centurias with your whining, perfect sister."

I maintained my position, despite a hard shove from the foot planted in my back. Bereft of anything truly useful to do for the dead girl, I wrapped her with a small spell locked into my staff, a charm of stasis that preserved gathered specimens from decay. Maybe in another seven hundred years someone would find her and marvel at her beauty, properly cursing the hand that ended it.

As the last of my power drained away, the gray world faded into blackness deeper than the void between the stars.

"You are mine now, magus." Only the voice remained. Eager, but not harsh. Harsh would have suited better. "You may come with me willing, or we can fight. The fight might be amusing, yet the outcome is assured. Though I've much to learn, no magus can match the power of the Seeing Stones. And besides, I know thou'rt curious, consumed with desire to know more of me and my precious baubles."

"I can provide no more amusement," I said, dully. My bones were sand; I could not have conjured a spider's tickle. "Pitiful, I believe you called me, and so I am. A murderer. A madman, as like to slit your throat as to serve you. Bring down the rest of this ruin on top of me and you'll do the world a service."

Not even the promise of magic could stir me. What use? The most magnificent gift the universe could grant a human mind, and I did naught but corrupt it. My true nature remained as it had ever been.

The woman touched my head, as if she were a queen and I a dog at her feet. "Pitiful, yes. And dangerous in your way. But I have plans . . . needs. The Regent schemes to dispose of you, and then seduce me into yielding my pretties to do with as he will. But I've seen more of courtly scheming than he'll ever know. My own magus . . . Yes, I'm thinking that would be wise. We shall create such mischief!"

My head was a muddle. She possessed Orythmus the Black-Hearted, the Stone of Command, as well as Rhymus. And this Regent of Mancibar, her collaborator, had Portier in chains and had told her about me.

"You must remain here while I send a signal. The Regent maintains an outpost a few hours away and left me a trinket to ensure a proper welcome should this day ever come. *Assergio de nom Maldeon! Stay.* And I think . . . I've seen blind men use a walking stick, but this one . . . watching how you used it with Nessia, I'm thinking it's more than that. You must not touch it lest I tell you."

My staff fell from my hand. I could not muster strength or will to grasp it or to force myself to standing, much less decipher how she managed it or even how far or in what direction she stepped away from me. But then, she was barefoot—assuming that any image of her I'd seen had actually been her and not the other—her dead sister. *Gods.*

Erratic jolts of magic shivered the aether. My instinctive reach to disentangle the magic felt akin to eating iron, a certain sign of depleted power.

In moments, she was back again. "You've a horse."

What need to answer a statement made with such certainty?

A tap of her fingers stung my cheek. "You have a horse."

When my hand refused to break her wrist, I knew I was truly bound. "Aye."

"Good. We can ride together. And we'll not wait for escorts. I cannot bear another instant in this dismal place. The Regent will be curious as to how you arrived here alone. He assumed a blind man would require companions."

The urge to glance up and assess her features was a vestige of sight that had not worn away. To try to hide my interest in her comment would likely be more noticeable. The Regent's identity was a critical matter, though I'd already guessed it. Of more immediate import: She didn't know about John Deune.

I'd lost all sense of time in the cavern, but the air didn't smell like evening yet. I'd told John to wait until dusk. If he had obeyed . . . Well he wasn't going to rescue me, but perhaps, in service to Ilario, he would obey and return to Andero. Every day since Castelivre, I'd told Andero that if aught happened to me, he must send to Anne and tell her everything. I needed to delay our departure long enough for John Deune to get away.

"Spellwork brought me," I mumbled. "My companions thought I was mad to come. Deserted me. And so I was."

"I knew it! The Regent says you're a coward weakling who does only what your superiors bid. But from that first glimpse in the dullard's dream, I knew better. 'Tis learning speaks to you. You pursue it as other men pursue empires. It gives you power, makes you brave, and sets you apart. You fear the Maldeona, yet still you came, no matter companions or dangers. A blind man alone."

"How is this possible?" I snapped, angered that she could know so much and I so little even yet. "To speak through dreams. To learn and manipulate minds through dreams. How could there be two of you? Who is this regent? I set you free, but I don't even know free of what!"

"Ah, my dark one, I am tempted to silence. To keep you ignorant would be a cruel torment."

She was even more contrarian than I.

I leashed my infernal temper. "You may do as you will."

"Exactly!" Her breath brushed my cheek. "I have waited seven centurias, locked away by those who beat and starved me, insisting the gods had given me breath for one reason only: that I might hold the world's greatest treasure and give it up to the first man who asked for it. Never again will I serve men. What do you say, magus? Tell me how you burn to know these things."

Just keep this up until evening, I said silently. "Yes, I burn to know all."

" 'Only a few days,' the priests said when they bound us in sorcery and put us in the Cavern of the Ancients. 'Mayhap a moon's cycle.' The barbarians were ravaging the city. Imperator Maldeon was already dead. Only when the roof fell and horrible wild men came to gape at the cavern and steal the gold and jewels did Nessia believe it.

"The priests had taught Nessia to use Rhymus to send messages in dreams, and she called to them repeatedly. No one came. I couldn't wield Nessia's Rhymus for myself, or use Orythmus to command *her,* but I knew how to make her dreamers see me instead of her. Once they saw me, they heard me, too, so I could put ideas in their heads about Rhymus. So angry Nessia was! Ever after she pretended I didn't exist.

"A few wanderers came in through the years. Cowards all. But at last the righteous soldier arrived, and I set to work. Let someone rescue the fair Nessia and set us both free."

"So you could control both Stones," I said, turning my head as she circled me. "But why ensnare some madman to slay her when you could command anyone to do it?"

"Because the Seeing Stones forbid it! 'Tis impossible for the holder of one to kill the holder of another, or to pay or ensorcel another to do the deed. The knife will not cut or pierce; the rope will not choke. Neither may the Stones be used or taken against the holder's will. Poor Maldeon tried it once, and his children died in the firestorm that resulted! The Stones must be freely given or claimed from the dead, as I did. That's why we of the Tareo were trained so harshly to surrender the Stones to their rightful owners."

Indeed, Adept Denys had told me the same.

"I needed the dreamer to destroy my sister of his own will or near enough. The righteous soldier was very close. But you're righteous in your own way; it was very easy to ensnare you. I just had to convince you she was dangerous."

Her fingers lifted my chin, her touch the tingling precursor of a lightning bolt.

"Tell me, was not it a wonderful plan? Come, come, thou'rt quite a somber fellow. The Regent, who is also a magus, says he and I shall wield the Stones together and create an empire of magic. His price is you. But if I keep you as my own magus, I can strike a harder bargain. You may come out of all this far better than you expect. Alive, even! And I can grant your deepest desire."

"What makes you think I would want anything you could give? You can compel me to walk or sit or stand on my head, but you cannot make me do magic for you. A sorcerer can only use his talent unbound." Bile stung my throat. No compulsion was required. Anger, confusion, and fear—my own corruption—had already driven me to murder.

"But you *will*, magus. I am Xanthe, not Nessia the Limpet. I'm not so shifty as to promise what I cannot give."

Laughing, she whispered a word and brushed her finger across my eyes. With a searing fire like the iron rod of her illusion, the world changed. . . .

The sun was at its zenith. Its beams shot through the broken roof like the arrows of Heaven. The white lake glittered like a sunlit snowfield, and the velvet green vines that blanketed the walls were laden with a profusion of flowers of pink, yellow, and red. The plumed birds that had screeched in the dark were scarlet and green, and soared on the beams of light, their grace and plumage mocking the ruins of human works.

Gods save me . . . I could see.

"Now let us begone from this place. *Assergio de nom Maldeon! Follow.*"

"Wait!" My head spun, disbelieving, but she didn't slow. But even without my cooperation, my legs pushed me up. One foot set itself before the other, taking me up the stair behind her like some juggler's trained dog. Her white gown swirled as she hurried up the stair, already drying in the desert air. She smelled of lemon flowers.

When my eyes were hit with unfiltered noonday in the sun-drenched streets of Carabangor, I'd no mind left to doubt. I cried out and threw my arm across my face.

The lady laughed, her delight wriggling into my bowels like gut worms that made eating repugnant to a starving man. Evil it is that can take our deepest desire and twist it so wretchedly. The sunlight held no glory. Beauty and color but infused my soul with acid. I hated Xanthe for the deaths I had wrought in service of her schemes, but more truly terrifying was a corruption that could make the world of light loathsome.

Impossible to kill her. Depleted as I was, the same finger that could open my eyes could surely strike me down. Getting my own self killed would serve no purpose but to silence guilt.

To stay alive long enough to understand the limits of Xanthe's power and what her partner planned to do with it would be the greater penance. To stop their schemes, or pass the knowledge of them to one who could, was the better choice. Yet how would such be possible when I could not take a step of my own will?

The notion that came to me then was abhorrent. As it hardened into conviction, I fought it with the same disgust I'd experienced when chasing vultures from my flayed teacher, dying in his cage. But the Syanese say life is a wheel, and we cannot escape those things that come around to us again and again.

I could not give life where I had taken it. I could not recall the names spoken so foolishly in a dream. I could not send my brother back to safety; nor could I teach Anne or Portier one more nuance of magic that might serve them in the dangerous future. Live a deception, though. That I could do.

Thus, fashioning an expression proper for the occasion, I bowed before those silver eyes and dropped to one knee in the dusty street. Taking Xanthe's hand and pressing it to my forehead, I infused my voice with unbounded awe. "Lady, for such a gift as you've just given me, I shall do whatever service pleases you."

CHAPTER 20

CARABANGOR

Xanthe laughed in delight, so I knew from the first that she could not read my thoughts outside of dream. "I knew it!" she said, grabbing my collar and drawing me to my feet, so close I could feel the heat of her beneath her flowing gown. "What magus could live crippled?"

She was, if possible, more striking than the woman of dreams. Though she was impossibly young, not out of her teens, her gown of white gossamer revealed a figure in the fullest bloom of womanhood. Her pale hair rippled like water and made a most pleasing contrast with her deep-hued skin. Silver glinted in her black eyes like moonbeams on the night sea, and any painter must sell his soul to capture the line of her brow or the flush of her cheek.

"Now, my slave, where is your horse?"

Run, John Deune! Ride! With utmost urgency I willed him to ride for Andero. Then I bowed to Xanthe again and stumbled forward slowly, pretending to lose my way, making sure to stomp my boots and curse at every street crossing lest he be nearby. Truly it was near impossible to find the path to the gates in the noonday glare, with tears streaming from my eyes and no magic to lead me.

A scouring lash ripped across my shoulders, dropping me to the dirt. "Stop this foolery, magus! I am not an idiot! You'll not escape my service so easily!"

"Lady, please!" I said, once I'd caught my breath and realized my shirt was neither aflame nor shredded. I wasn't even bleeding. The lady's hands held no whip, but only the two green Stones, flashing and sparking in the sunlight. "I used magic to find my way in, but I've naught left to discover the way out."

"Summon more, then." Another lash near drove me into the dust. "Do not dare disobey me. I can scourge you for a month and you'll never die. I can take back what I've given." Darkness fell over my head like a leather hood, then vanished again. Pain incised my eyes like a knife blade.

Swallowing rapidly to curb the urge to vomit, I bent so low around my hollow gut, my head near touched the dirt. "I serve you willing, lady. Your gift . . . I cannot explain the magnificence, but it's difficult— So bright after two years in the dark, and depleted as I am. Soon repaired, of course." I'd not wish her to deem me useless.

"What does it take to repair this depletion? I believed you exceptional." Her disappointment was that of Castelle Escalon's noble children refused sweets at table.

"Rest and food. That's all. An hour. Surely your master has told you how a sorcerer, a magus, expends power." Almost any magic working would deplete Jacard's power. An advantage to me, if her partner was my adept. "If we could just sit in the shade until the sun slips a bit lower and my eyes adjust to seeing."

"He is not *my* master. And he never visited us long enough to deplete anything. All right." She took my elbow and guided me into the lee of a wall. "Sit. We've no food, and I've no idea how to conjure it with my Stones as yet, but I know where water's found. Do not expect me *ever* to serve you again." Her voice receded. "Husband your magic more carefully. You must devote it entirely to my pleasure."

My agreement came out like the bleat of a dying goat.

She soon returned, marveling at the size of Carabangor and lamenting its ruin. The liquid she carried in a potshard was hot and stale but welcome. I drank half and bathed my eyes with the rest. The shade helped even more. Shocked by midday brightness and bruised from the stoning at Hoven, my head drummed like a legion on the march. A dull ache settled behind my eyelids.

"Tell me more of this *Regent*," I said when Xanthe settled beside me. "That is, if it pleases you."

Talking clearly pleased her. "He rules the Principate of Mancibar to the south of this wasteland. He came there two years ago, he told me, an exile from Sabria, where a cowardly wicked magus had ruined him with lies and scandal. Ah, the stories he's told of that wicked magus! Now, who might that villain be, do you think?" She nudged me and giggled a little. "Iaccar says you even murdered his kinsman!"

And so was my last remaining doubt put to rest. *Iaccar* was the Arothi variant of my adept's name. Jacard. And he believed I, not Anne, had killed Kajetan. I buried my satisfaction deep.

"Iaccar told me he'd had his eye on Mancibar as a good place to plan his revenge on this nefarious Sabrian mage and his king. It's a lax and easy sort of place, and small, only the one city and a few villages, without many soldiers to complicate matters. He spread rumors. . . . Well, in truth, once he wheedled sweet, gullible Nessia into helping him with dreams of spiders and blood sucking, he didn't have to spread so *very* many rumors. 'Twas hardly a season till the people overthrew their prince and raised Iaccar to rule them."

Her own thirst taking hold after her centuries of enchantment, Xanthe fetched more water. Convincing her it was necessary to access my full talents in her service, I begged her to bring my staff from the cavern. She did so but made sure I could not reach it. Once she settled again, I urged her to tell more of Jacard. She was willing to talk of anything.

"He told me he forbade his subjects to call him *prince*, claiming he was worthy only of the title Regent and would guide them only until a rightful heir could be found. At first I thought him humble, a pious man like the old imperator, though for certain mush headed, as why go to the trouble to raise a rebellion, if you're only going to give up the prize again? But I didn't say that to Iaccar, as it was a marvelous diversion to have someone new to converse with. Once he'd visited me a few times, I decided he wasn't humble at all."

Indeed. "Was it a dream sending brought him to you?"

"Nay, 'twas magical writings told him legends of Holy Altheus and the Seeing Stones. He taught me all about this marvelous age of the world. How life has changed since I left my own! 'Tis like scorpion stings that I must wait longer to see these ladies' court gowns and mirror glasses."

So Kajetan's notes, perhaps even information gleaned from Adept Denys, had led Jacard and me to the same place. "Why did Jac—Iaccar—not set you free?"

"Indeed I planned to induce him to slay me for the Stone—and have it be Nessia, of course." So casually she spoke of twisted murder. "But I soon discovered that would be impossible."

"Why so?"

"Why, because Iaccar holds Tychemus."

Gods in all heavens! In the span of a moment, a situation I'd thought wretched became infinitely more dangerous.

"He couldn't kill Nessia for me. And I certainly didn't want him spoiling my plan. So I told him it had to be a dreamer that took us across the lake. That's when he suggested you."

"I believed the third Stone lost," I whispered. "Buried."

Jacard had a source of true power. And wielding only one of the Seeing Stones, this untutored woman with no magic of her own could already drive my mind to madness and my body to painful groveling.

Xanthe untied a scarf from around her neck and laid the two green crystals side by side. "Iaccar said his gods led him to it. That may be true. The gods prevent the Stones from being truly lost. But they can be hidden. When the Earthshaker destroyed the kingdom of the imperator's brother—"

"The imperator." Only now did her use of the term stir up recollection. "Altheus of Maldivea?" A humble, pious man. The benevolent warrior who had won an empire. Who lay down and died when his work was done. Whose enemies feared he would return . . . like a Saint Reborn. Who had lived seven centuries in the past.

"King Maldeon—Nessia's beloved—was Altheus's third son. Maldeon began calling himself *imperator* after tricking one of his brothers into releasing Rhymus to him. Some said Maldeon caused the earthshaking to gain Tychemus from the third brother. Mayhap. Either way, Garif, who held Tychemus, died of the earthshaking, as did most of his subjects. But Garif's priests hid the Stone and sent a messenger to Maldeon saying it was buried in the rubble. Then they killed themselves, so he could not force them to reveal its hiding place. The priests believed the gods had sent the earthshaking to protect the world from Maldeon, who was a clever man, but very cruel. He searched for it every day thereafter, dismembered people, crucified them. . . ."

She chattered continuously through the scorching afternoon, speaking of torture and murder in the same breath that expressed her childish wonder at the construction and materials of my garments and the marvels Jacard had told her of—clocks and books, lace and silk and sailing ships. Her prattle revealed naught about the qualities of the Stones or Jacard's true intentions, but much of Xanthe herself. Those of her caste were not taught to read or cipher or allowed to see maps of the world or learn of it. They must desire nothing the Stones could provide and be ready to relinquish them instantly upon command of those who put the treasures in their hands. Xanthe had repudiated her training from the beginning, but had been wily enough to make sure that no one knew of her rebellion.

In midafternoon Xanthe willed me to my feet, tying the scarf pouch holding the Stones to her knotted belt. "No more stories until we are safely in Mancibar, my dark one. Take me away from this daemonish place."

With no more excuse to delay, I led her through the gates to the ruined caravanserai. Devil cropped at the dry grass under the locust tree. Alone.

Good. A first step. But relief at John Deune's absence was but a temporary balm. Would he go to Andero? For himself if not for me?

Devil nuzzled my hand in greeting. What a fine horse he was, a shining bay, sleek and powerful in the leg, with a lightning-shaped marking on his forehead and a spark in his eyes that spoke of wild and noble ancestors. I'd not have looked twice at any horse before this journey, much less accounted one of them noble. My hand apologized that I'd naught to give him.

"Where are we bound?" I said, as Xanthe shoved my staff into the saddle loops.

"South from the main gates," she said gaily, as I pulled her up behind me.

She clasped her slim arms around my waist. I did not allow myself to recoil from her touch.

With barely a nudge Devil raced through the streets of Carabangor and around, if not through, the collapsed southern gates. For a while, I let him have his head, wishing the rushing glories of color, shape, and open sky could lift my spirits as they did his. But heeding Anne's lessons, I soon slowed him to a comfortable gait. It wouldn't be for long. A rolling dust cloud was headed straight toward us. The ground rumbled with beating hooves.

A last chance to turn and ride the other way. Free, with full use of my senses, I *might* be able to learn of the Seeing Stones, spy on Jacard, and locate Portier. But I'd no water, and I could not doubt the lady's threat to rescind her gift of sight. It took no genius to understand that Xanthe's desire to be independent of Jacard presented me a better chance to find Portier and learn what was needed than proceeding on my own. Damnably risky, but better. I had to set guilt aside and work.

A small, focused heat stung my waist, as if a glowing ember had fallen into my pocket. I wound Devil's reins about my dead hand and investigated. As it had in Castelivre, Anne's nireal scorched my fingers, its gleam brighter than noonday. *Seeing* her gift made it so much more solid than I had ever imagined it. I could almost glimpse her tidy figure in the glare, almost hear her sober questions, her quiet teasing, her foolish sentiments. . . .

"We wait here," I said, muzzling a ferocious growl. I yanked Devil to a halt in the scant shade of a tamarisk grove and ignored Xanthe's prattle about the trinkets and delicacies Iaccar had promised.

The dust cloud disgorged a troop of ten horsemen clad in green and gold livery. A red-haired officer with wild brows, leather skin, and a neck as wide as his shoulders halted them and dismounted. "I'm Captain Hosten of Mancibar's palace guard. Have I the honor of greeting the most gracious lady Xanthe, the Mistress of the Maldeona?"

"Most assuredly you do," she said over my shoulder, giggling again. The sound grated already. Anne's laugh—

I squeezed the nireal in my fist and shut out the thoughts of her. What if Xanthe commanded me to spill my thoughts? Sabria's court ladies had done so all the time, even when they feared me. This woman reminded me of those empty-headed jennies in the queen's household, save with a touch of malice and cruelty that would shock even Sabrian aristos.

"The Regent of Mancibar has commanded me offer you his hospitality and transport, paying you all due respect." He bowed crisply and gave her a hand down from behind me.

As I dismounted, I stuffed pendant, ring, and chain into my boot, along with the distraction I could not afford. I took a position behind Xanthe.

Hosten's signal brought one of his men forward leading a yellow-gold mare, outlandishly outfitted with tassels, bells, and quilted satin. Xanthe examined the placid beast. Then she spun round, a smile teasing her rosy lips.

"My servant can ride this one. His stallion pleases me better."

"As you wish, Mistress," said Hosten.

There was no argument to be made. Under my breath I cursed the fact that this would leave my staff, as well as Devil, with Xanthe.

Silver eyes sparking in the sunlight, she whispered in my ear, "*Assergio de nom Maldeon.* Follow me. The rest of you"—the captain and his men paused as she raised her voice—"hear this: No one is to speak to my slave or heed his speech. His words are mine alone."

She may have been a servant, deliberately kept illiterate and uneducated, but she was clever and insightful. I underestimated her at my peril.

Xanthe took her seat on my horse, casting a sidelong glance my way. With a twist of malice to her smile and a clear augury of my immediate future, she laid into Devil with a whip she had appropriated from the red-haired captain. Her bonds tightened around me. I mounted the gaudy mare and rode after.

HOURS WE RODE ACROSS THE wastelands. Every shrub, every rock, every crack in the red, hard-packed dirt became fodder for my seeing. No matter how hateful the circumstances of my recovery, I needed to know this place so I could use its keirna in spellwork. The sky deepened from flat silver to purest azure.

Our desert track joined a wagon road, wider and well traveled, though we saw little traffic. As the shadows lengthened and our route bore farther south and west, the landscape became more benevolent. We no longer traveled in the rain shadow of the Kadrian highlands, but through grasslands of ocher velvet with patches of rich, well-watered green. Each rolling hill opened onto a more verdant scene of fields, small orchards, and an occasional sparse woodland.

Winter had not touched this land. Yet something did. The clean air of desert and field was tainted with smoke and char and something worse underneath. The third time Captain Hosten guided our party away from the route to avoid plumes of greasy black smoke, I asked Xanthe why. She passed the inquiry to the bullnecked captain.

"Those villages lie under the interdict of the Regent of Mancibar," he said. "Visitation is forbidden."

"Loyal to the old prince, I'll vow," Xanthe said, loud enough all could hear. "The Regent told me he was yet subduing a few parts of the countryside. 'Tis none of our affair."

Three villages in the space of four hours' ride struck me as more than a few. But I didn't contradict her. I wasn't sure if I could.

As the sky's azure deepened to cerulean, we approached a range of stark cliffs rising from the fields. My body thrummed with exhaustion, all focus and concentration fled. My eyes streamed with tears again, exhausted by light and color, and I felt neither here nor there. Mingled with images of squat mud houses and bony flocks were visions of arrows raining from the stars, of burning books, of a pregnant sky filled with ravenous faces. Emerald light limned rock and tree like the werelights in a bog. As the road steepened and led toward the cliffs, I clung to the mare. One untoward jolt would send me sliding from the saddle.

We passed into a great city crowded up to the bulky heights. Yet it seemed not a human city, for it lay in shadow while the rays of evening still shone on the green-gold grasslands and fields behind us. Ranks of burning torches lined streets crowded with fine stone houses but lacking people. No groups chattered their way to local taverns; no sausage vendors hawked their wares for a tradesman's supper.

The red-haired captain shouted unintelligible commands and dour-faced soldiers in green passed us along. Xanthe peppered Hosten with questions, but I grasped only snippets—*blood cadres . . . spiders . . . hauntings . . . disappearances*—and comprehended nothing.

Dirt yielded to cobbles and still we rode upward.

"Attend, magus! Are you deaf now?"

Xanthe's severity roused me from the murk. I shook my head like a wet dog. "Lady?"

She rode beside me—the dream. Her silvered eyes glinted in the onrushing night. "Behold the Regent's house," she said. "Remember, you are my servant and will not speak unless I allow it."

"Naturally," I said, dizzy and thick tongued, as overwhelmed as a pebble placed to hold back a roiling river.

The Regent's house stood on a horn of rock protruding from the heights. Red sand cliffs rose sharply behind it. Yet the house was no fortress, but a palace. I had never before seen so much glass in any building. Come morning, it must be a well of light.

"I know this place," said Xanthe. "Not the house or the city. 'Twas never Mancibar, the City of Moneylenders, in the days of Maldeon. Hardly even a village. We knew it as Sirpuhi of the Red Cliffs."

Sirpuhi was not a word in Sabria's common speech. Arothi, I thought. But I knew it. I'd read or heard it but could not recall where.

As I lowered my leaden bones earthward, Xanthe slipped from Devil's back and ran up the wide steps. She might have just stepped fresh from her enchanted lake, as her white gown and pale hair streamed out behind her in a balmy breeze. A green-robed figure awaited her.

"I've brought him!" she called. "Our bargain is commenced."

I discovered I could not move from the spot where I dismounted. Just as well, as I'd no wish to go closer. The waiting man's sharp features and dark wedge of a beard were unmistakable. Jacard.

Inevitably, Xanthe beckoned me to her side. I trudged forward, fixing my bleary eyes on her.

"Kneel, magus," she commanded, pointing her long white finger at the pavement. "The Regent of Mancibar is lord of all you see here, and all we have seen on our travels from Carabangor. My servants will offer him his accustomed honors."

Neither pride nor will, hatred nor disdain, was an issue. My knees bent of themselves before her words were completed, and my head touched the paving stones and stayed there. We can always fall lower than we believe possible.

"*Master* Dante. I cannot say what pleasure it gives me to see Philippe de Savin-Journia's hireling, the betrayer who ruined the greatest venture in the history of magic, brought to his knees. Though I am distressed to see my gift to you undone—even for this brief time. Did you enjoy the doom I shaped for you . . . creeping about in the dark like an earthworm . . . left ignorant and crude as you were at birth . . . books, charts, maps, all arcane lore out of your reach? Your power fades, doesn't it? I knew it would. Your corrupted approach to spellwork relies too heavily on sight."

Though I could not raise my head, no binding could have kept my tongue still. "Even blind, I heard you run gibbering in terror from Mont Voilline."

"Shall we compare the magnitude of our defeats, Master? Shall we ask my subjects to judge who's won and who's lost? I look forward to long talks in my dungeons, where we can compare the absolute divergence of our fates."

A thread of smoke rose from a dry grass blade that poked through the paving stones not three centimetres from my nose. The acrid stink seared my nostrils and caused my eyes to flood. The blade pulsed red-gold, blackened, and curled. But the blade next to it flared into a moment's blaze. And then the next. I blinked rapidly, but Xanthe's command held me powerless to move. Two more and my hair would catch. . . .

My bowels clenched. Burning bore a horror near that of blinding. They mustn't see. "Until my mistress chooses to surrender me, I serve her pleasures only."

"Surrender you?" Xanthe burst in. "Never! You have no claim to the magus, Regent Iaccar. Yes, we made a bargain, but you never told me he was so powerful."

In a billow of smoke, the little blaze went out. My lungs convulsed. Each spasm scraped my forehead on the paving.

"We shall see how things fall out." Jacard remained cool. "I would recommend you keep his talents under strict control, lady. We've a sorcerer's hole and inhibitors prepared for him, as I've explained to you. But eventually . . . Dante and I have debts of honor between us, and I shall demand possession of him."

Jacard's calm confidence wholly unnerved me. I had been liberal with derision, both public and private, making sure de Gautier and his fellows had seen my aide for the weakling coward he was. Jacard's persistence had surprised me, until I discovered that his uncle, Kajetan, kept his foot up the little prick's backside to keep him spying on me. The blaze under my nose had been Jacard's warning. He had learned something of magic in these years.

"I've done very well controlling my servant on my own," said Xanthe haughtily. "Though I shall certainly make use of these things you offer. The magus is clever, and I don't wish to play wet nurse."

Xanthe agreed that I should be locked up right away, and the two of them vanished into the house arm in arm. The sight left me more ill than I was already. The idea of Xanthe and Jacard forming some alliance with their Seeing Stones, including me as their magic-wielding slave, was the stuff of nightmare. I already had nightmares aplenty.

Captain Hosten quickly took me in charge. "March, magus. Know this: My men have three spears poised to ream your ass and a sword aimed at each of your nice soft flanks. Do you twitch or mumble or look elsewhere than your feet, you'll feel the sting of one or the other or mayhap all five at once."

The red-haired soldier delivered this speech with sober calm. He was a big man, near Andero's height, though not so broad, and had likely found posturing unnecessary since he was a boy. Unwise to cross him. His five armed minions formed up around me, while he clamped a giant hand around the back of my neck and moved me forward like a stratagems gamepiece.

Still fogged from hunger and magical depletion, I had no resources to resist. Up endless variants of wide shallow stairs, through courtyards and vast, brightly painted chambers trimmed with gilt and mirrors, along galleries open to the cooling night, we came to a less decorative gallery. From the stink, its open arches must have overlooked the midden. The interior wall held three solid doors inlaid with crosshatched strips of wood and iron. We halted in front of one.

A sorcerer's hole. I should have known. A normal prison cell was not effective at detaining a sorcerer of any significant ability. I hoped it was of some reasonable dimension and not the size of a coffin like some I'd seen. "Inhibitors" were unfamiliar. But having experienced Jacard's contrabalance, a device of ancient magic designed to prevent spellwork while burning a sorcerer's eyesight away, I had no desire to discover what an inhibitor might be.

After confiscating my knife, spoon, and copper bracelet, one of Captain Hosten's men performed a brisk search of my pockets, which turned up naught but my spare gloves, wool scarf, and a dirty rag. They found the second, smaller knife in my boot sheath. It was common belief that a metal object might permit a sorcerer to work spells in a sorcerer's hole. That belief was entirely unfounded; one could not bind spells inside a well-constructed sorcerer's hole. Nonetheless, I was pleased they failed to check deeper inside my boot, where I had stuffed Anne's pendant, Portier's ring, and the silver chain.

At spearpoint and without a spare word, they shoved me into the windowless closet lined with cypress and camphor laurel, turned the iron lock, and left me alone with no light. With every smat of will within me, I stifled rising panic. The place was not a coffin. Air, albeit ripe, lay just beyond the door. Darkness was no friend of mine, but at least I could function adequately in its demesne.

I felt around the space, then settled in the corner, huddled in a quivering knot. Only a few paces square, my new home contained but a few items: a straw mattress and blanket, a covered clay bowl for sanitation, and, of course, a sorry excuse for a sorcerer and the desert of his soul.

CHAPTER 21

MANCIBAR

Wild, confusing nightmares savaged that first night, as if stripping away the light again had stripped away my pretense of sanity. I walked a desolate road, cold and dry as death. From the corners of my eyes I glimpsed starving faces, and each time their cold hands brushed my skin, I wanted to be sick.

In a whirlwind change, Xanthe laughed as she affixed my hands and feet to an ice-glazed pinnacle with bolts of green crystal. The bolts infused my bone and blood with fire, so that I exhaled green flame, yet could not die. She licked my cheek and whispered of the Souleater's coming—Dimios, the First of the Fallen, whose lash of ice could flay the skin in layers so thin one could see through them. The torment would last for millennia.

Before me stood a forest of ice pillars, and frozen into each was someone whose death lay on my head. Ilario, Nessia, Denys, a dozen temple servants, my father . . . so many. Portier, too, stood in his frozen pillar. Unlike the others', his eyes were open—and living. His mouth moved, but I could not hear.

I woke repeatedly through the long hours, bathed in sweat and panicked by the dark, certain I was blind again. Though sleep would help replenish my power, I fought to stay awake. I pinched my skin and calculated sums, distances, and the number of stars in the heavens. But inevitably exhaustion would triumph, and I would slip back into nightmare.

Perhaps the dreams were naught but thirst. Perhaps they were more of Xanthe's play. They were not some ripple in the aetherstorm. The same energies that bound a sorcerer's hole to prevent magic working shut off the current of voices. The waking dark offered naught but my own harsh breathing and thumping heart. All else was unnerving silence.

In the middle of yet another grueling torment came an eruption of painful yellow brightness. This one was real.

"Up and out, magus. Your mistress summons you."

I could have kissed Captain Hosten's boots. I didn't care that he hauled me out by my filthy shirt or shoved me onto my knees.

"Drink. Please." I hated asking for additional favor when he'd already brought me morning.

"No. The lady wants no trickery before you're brought to her." Hosten motioned his men to clamp my wrists in bracelets of heavy wood, inlaid with iron and thorn and linked with a short, rigid iron bar. The inhibitors?

"Won't trick." My mouth felt like scabs. Likely it was a good thing, as I couldn't smile. Though dreadfully uncomfortable, these inhibitors were no artifact of true magic, but a popular device among country folk who believed all magic flowed through a practitioner's hands. Once I had rested, eaten, and drunk enough to replenish my power, they would not hinder me.

"I asked if you were to be fed or bathed," said the captain, wrinkling his nose as the soldiers dragged me to my feet. "The lady said she would decide."

I nodded with as much dignity as I could muster, then straightened my back and lifted my chin as if I were a court mage once again, and not a filthy, unshaven prisoner with dust for bones. For the same reason, I pressed my shaking hands tight against my belly, even if the thorn bindings poked through my shirt. I wouldn't want these men to misinterpret my condition as wreckage. No indeed, wouldn't want them to know I could likely not charm a bee to buzz about their ears as yet, with or without the prickly manacles.

Hosten bowed politely. "I bear you no ill will, magus. I've no concern but to see you safely brought where you are required to be."

That place was a good distance from my cell. I slowed Hosten's brisk pace to something more manageable for my trembling legs, by inspecting every centimetre of our route. The palace sprawled in open splendor, showing no evidence of war or defense works. Its corridors were a labyrinth of vast rooms, tall columns, courtyards, and galleries on a hundred different levels. Glass windows filled the walls—some tall and thin, some square or round or cut into small panes. Some sheets of small, gem-colored panes were fashioned into scenes of warring angels and beasts, like a grand mosaic of colored light, a marvel I'd not seen even in Merona.

Yet, indeed, Jacard's fine house seemed in sorry disrepair. Paints were dulled and peeling. The gargoyles and beast carvings had crumbled, their noses, snouts, and ears little more than rough patches. Some of the colored glass panes had been replaced with clear, and some remained cracked or broken. The thick draperies that closed off the arched doorways instead of wood had faded. Foul smells seeped through cracks in the floor tiles and the walls.

We found Xanthe ensconced in an upper-level apartment that bowed outward from the main structure, overlooking the city and the expansive lands eastward. She lounged on a soft couch amid an overabundance of pillows, hangings, mirrors, lamps, statuary, tables, and gold-trimmed dishes. It appeared Jacard had stuffed all such decorative foolery from the palace into the one vast suite of rooms. Bless all spirits, the lady had thrown open every window, bathing the clutter in morning light, else there'd have been insufficient air for the three of us.

"Did my servant behave himself, Captain?"

"Dragged his feet on our way. But he attempted no magic."

The lady had traded her plain white gown for a close-fitted court gown of scarlet. Her fingers sparkled with jewels and her bare arms were ringed with bracelet upon bracelet of silver, gold, and every sort of gem and colored stone. Unlike the chamber's, her personal decorations did not seem excessive or ill chosen.

"Good." Her sharp word forced my eyes from her bare feet, washed and rouged, toes banded with glittering rings. "In that case, magus"—her waving finger dragged my eyes to a tray of delicately fried fish, cheese, eggs, and fruit—"you may eat. When Captain Hosten told me he gives no refreshment without orders, I was distraught. Captain, unless I tell you elsewise, you will provide my servant with reasonable provisions in his chamber. Is that understood?"

"Indeed so, my lady."

"And take those ridiculous manacles off him. He's under my command here. They'll do only to make a mess when he eats. He's like to have trouble enough with that hand." Her mouth stretched in disgust. "A good thing I've already eaten. Imperator Maldeon did not allow cripples in his house."

Glaring at me in warning, Hosten unfastened the bracelets. I tried to appear unthreatening.

"And now you may leave us, Captain."

He whirled on her. "But the Regent said—"

"I've informed the Regent that unless he permits me the normal privileges of royal guesting, I shall take up my residence elsewhere. He has agreed. Now, go!"

"Yes, my lady." He bowed his way out, speeding his exit when Xanthe scowled at him.

"I already tire of this place," she said, as I drained a full pitcher of gloriously cooled ale. "Iaccar says Hosten is to be my bodyguard. But the captain clucks and scolds like a nanny goat. I've insisted he stay at a decent distance to give me privacy."

"I'd guess him to be a very capable soldier," I croaked, savoring a morsel of goat cheese. "Quick and strong." My arms had a whole layer of new bruises.

"When he says you must do no magic, you'd best heed. He can sniff spells."

I paused between more cheese and a handful of the savory fish. "He's a practitioner, a magus?"

"Nay. But he can sniff out magic. Iaccar swears to bury you alive if you so much as enspell a candle outside my rooms."

"A watcher, then." I forced breath through my constricted chest, blessing Xanthe for letting that bit of information slip. So I'd need to work around Captain Hosten as well as Xanthe, Jacard, a sorcerer's hole, and a mind shredded with nightmares that left a taint on the day. But I could see.

As I gorged, the lady chattered about anything and everything. Hosten had been a sergeant in the old prince's service, so Xanthe understood. He had tried to augment his pay by selling palace art objects to a caravan factor who happened to be the palace steward's brother. Mancibar's former prince had driven Hosten out of the palace naked through a gauntlet of his fellow soldiers. When Iaccar scouted out fighters willing to share in the prince's ruin, Hosten had been first up. The incident did not speak well of the captain's cleverness. But doggedness, physical capability, and a vengeful nature could make a formidable opponent.

Even when my belly felt near bursting, I continued to nibble at the remains of the feast. Xanthe smiled beneficently, though she might not have done had she realized what else I was working at—a slight illusion to fade my bruises. Something simple, just to see if I could. Something easy to justify if I was caught.

Magic flowed through bone and sinew, heating my joints like strong wine. No hammer fell on me. No footsteps thundered beyond the curtained doorway signaling a watcher's alarm. Xanthe's smile did not dim.

Another small working—a slight change in texture of the pear I ate. Simple, too, but purest magic, altering the fruit's underlying nature. Anne had refused even to try such works, appalled that true magic could so "violate nature's laws of growth and decay." As if such a working was somehow different from striking fire without flint and steel. We had argued until dawn. . . .

"What is it, magus? What makes you smile? I wasn't sure you knew how."

I glanced up from the pear, cold sweat popping out on my back. *Never, never think of her, fool. Not her name, not her talents, not her whereabouts.* Xanthe must not know of her.

"Only the wonders of your gift, lady," I said. "To see, even something so simple as a pear . . . its shading . . . its perfect shape so like other pears, yet unique to itself. But now that I've eaten enough food for three, tell me what use you'd have of me."

I had to set both guilt and magic aside for the time, allowing Xanthe to think she had me fully under her control. Earning her trust was my path to the Seeing Stones. The Seeing Stones were the key to Jacard's schemes and Portier.

Xanthe wished to rule a demesne of her own as absolutely and luxuriously as had her liege Maldeon. "Such spectacles and entertainments he ordered, and always the best wine, beautiful clothing, and the fastest horses. I forever put myself in his way, thinking he would take me as his mistress. But he teased and said I was too prickly and he preferred his women 'smoother.' Then he took *Nessia* to his bed. I survived and bided my time. Eventually, such a vigorous man must desire one to laugh, ride, and spar with him in bed."

Though her bracelets might *not* survive, as every mention of Maldeon or Nessia caused her to yank at one of them. Broken loops of silver and pearls already littered the floor.

"On one night the imperator encountered me in the fountain court. He yanked my hair and wrenched my gown from my shoulders, stroking and caressing and kissing me with magnificent urgency. I was sure he'd had enough of my *smooth* sister. Thus I demonstrated fully the pleasures of a prickly woman. But no sooner had he roused my fires to burning than he shoved me naked to the grass. 'I deemed I might have double pleasure on these cool nights,' he told me. 'Thou hast her same looks, but not the taste I relish. Thou'rt vinegar to her honey, and I need no woman to choose my pleasures for me.' "

Xanthe had popped up from her couch and wandered about the room, stroking the silk and caressing the alabaster. Now she whirled to face me.

"That was the night I began preparations in earnest, using all my wiles to learn of Orythmus. Come the day Fortuna Regina yielded the stone to my hand, I would be ready to use it. Such bribes I paid, such suffering and disgust to glean the words, the binding lore. So many long nights' practice. Even so, I mastered only three commands. You've experienced all: to move or stay, to suffer pain or not, and to see or not see. All useful, certainly. Imagine my delight when I realized that sight could be your leash. But I want bigger magics."

She dropped to the floor, so close the thrumming heat of her made my own blood pulse. "You are my bound slave, and I can cause you such pain as will make you devour your own flesh. But as you pointed out, I cannot command your use of sorcery, and now I've seen you— It would be far more pleasing if you help me freely. You are the Regent's enemy. He told me how he rejoiced in your blindness because it would be worse than death to you. I can protect you from his vengeance. Your eyes, your life, your future, and your soul are mine, are they not?"

"Indeed, Mistress, my fortunes are in your hands." But she could issue only a few commands. Potent ones, yes, she was right about that. But Orythmus must hold much more.

She leaned across the table, her dark eyes huge and sharp with silver, not at all smooth. The scent of lemon flowers wreathed my senses. "Teach me the secrets of the Maldeona."

"Teach you . . ."

"Iaccar insists he can read the Stones to learn of them, but I think perhaps you can do it better. Then I'll not be beholden to him."

"You wish me to study your two Stones and teach you what I learn—how to use them, control them."

"From the moment I heard your voice in the soldier's dream, I knew you were not smooth, either. You'll not rest until you understand all magic. Why else could we send you to see a man you despised and know you would go? Why else could we send warriors to beset you on your journey and know you would be there? It puzzled me at first when Iaccar told me how a mention of his prisoner would bring you halfway across the world, for he also said you would as soon kill any man or woman in the world as befriend one. But then I learned that this librarian is a magical mystery, too, as potent as the Stones. The two together would surely fire you beyond reason."

"Indeed, lady, I—" Conscience required denial, curses, or outright refusal. To teach this murderous child to access power that already shivered my soul violated everything I believed about wielding magic. Yet with one glance backward, denial died unspoken. I had flailed in horror and regret at murder, yet found reason to proceed. I had yielded to Xanthe's bondage, accepting her word that I could not strike her down. Did I pursue understanding of these mysteries for the good of a world I despised? Did I care for the starving dead any more than I had cared for Philippe de Savin-Journia six years past when Portier had drawn me from Bardeu? Or was it always the magic?

"Confess your sins, magus. Tell me I have not misjudged."

"Certainly you are correct, Mistress. I am neither smooth, nor kind, nor gentle, nor even civil, though as your servant, I shall . . . behave. Magic—learning, teaching, and wielding it—has ever been my sole desire, and, indeed, blindness was insupportable." The words Xanthe wanted flowed from me with disturbing ease. "If my sight is at your whim, then certainly I must do as you wish. What greater gift could I ask of any sovereign than permission to pursue the deepest secrets of sorcery? Of course, I make no promises. The Stones are ancient and complex. I may not be able to unravel their mysteries. . . ."

But I would. If anyone in the world could do it, I could. Gods, to know the mystery of these things, to be allowed unfettered access . . .

My fingers drummed on her table. A plan of study was already arranging itself in my head. "We'll begin here with the two Stones you control. Without writings or detailed history to guide me, I'll need to parse their magics on my own. That will take time, as I've no notion as to the most basic structure. Are the things enspelled or is their power intrinsic to their crystalline nature or are they something else altogether? As I go, I'll do my best to extract useful skills to teach you. Eventually, I'll need to understand how the three relate to each other, how they work together, as what little I've gleaned from writings says their power grows geometrically with their union. I'll need access to Tychemus."

Xanthe grabbed my chin, all her ferocious delight chilled, as if clouds had drifted across the sun's face. "It had best not take too long to give me what I want or I'll think you dawdling apurpose. Before all, though"—she scraped a fingernail along my unshaven chin, then reached for my braid and near twisted it off—"you must be cleaned, like it or not. You stink like the kennels. And this must be cut off. Slaves have no privilege to wear long hair."

I wiped my hands on my breeches and knelt up quickly, uncertain what had changed. "As you—"

"And I want that"—screwing her face into a knot of disgust, she pointed at my clawed hand—"covered at all times. I refuse to have such ugliness thrust in my face. Keep it gloved or I'll have *it* cut off, too."

I swallowed an apology and dipped my head instead. She didn't seem to want words from me.

She leapt to her feet and yanked a ribbon that dangled against the wall. A bell clanged deep in the house. I began to count.

Quick, heavy footsteps. The curtain whipped aside and the red-haired captain stepped in and bowed. "Lady?"

Thirty measured counts had elapsed. The distance to Hosten's post—a span of action, always useful to know. And he had not come running when I transformed the pear, so he could not detect minor spellwork at that distance. Also a useful measure.

Xanthe gave orders as to my grooming and commanded I be returned to her at sundown.

"Fed?"

"No. I've changed my mind. His sustenance will come solely from my hand."

"As you say. Up, magus."

I allowed Hosten to fasten the burdensome manacles about my wrists. Then I turned to the lady and bowed. Not too deep. I would submit, but must not allow her to think me cowed, even in the shadow of this mysterious pique.

"One more thing, Mistress. I must have my staff when we work. It will enable me to produce results much faster."

She cocked her head, frowning, assessing. "The Regent has been trying to wheedle it away from me. He said you would want it and that it would be a great mistake to give it to you. He said you had secret spells stored in it, enchantments that could drive me mad or make me ugly."

"It is not in Iaccar's interest to have me succeed, Mistress. You either trust me to do as you wish or we might as well end this now."

Her face hardened. My every muscle hardened awaiting her response. It took a long time coming.

"I'll consider it."

I nodded. Victory enough for now. She didn't look at all pleased, but I was yet standing.

"You are my slave, Magus Dante, naught else. Remember that your eyes are the price of disobedience."

"I cannot forget, Mistress. Not ever."

I RELISHED THE IDEA OF a soak in a hot bathing pool. My earlier glimpses from the palace windows had revealed a long, low building south of the main palace, holes in its foundation and roof emitting the telltale steam and smokes of a luxurious bath. I had experienced such a place only once in my life.

Instead, we returned immediately to the sorcerer's hole. The captain shoved me to my knees in front of the opened door, growling at me to be still if I didn't want my throat cut, and summarily sawed off the most of my hair. Before I had quite recovered from the surprise, he shoved me inside, slammed the door, and locked me in, leaving the pile of black hair . . . admittedly filthy . . . on the stone floor beside me.

A quarter of an hour later, the door opened again and, as Hosten watched, a nervous soldier set an earthenware bowl and pitcher, a towel, and an implement of some kind just inside the door. Another man tossed a pile of clothes at me. Hosten himself picked a few longer strands from the pile of my hair, wound them around one finger, and waggled it at me. An artifact so intimate could enable a watcher to isolate spellwork to a particular practitioner. He would know which spells throughout the palace were mine.

The door slammed; the bolts snicked; and I was left in the dark to make what ablutions I could.

I washed. Shaving with a bone knife and one good hand was more challenging. The netherstocks, shirt, and breeches felt like good cloth, but plain. No buttons. No ruffles or pockets. My hands knew what to do. I appreciated the improvements for the most part, though hair no longer than a centimetre was going to take some getting used to.

Once dressed, I had naught to do but think. Acquiescing to Xanthe's bargain, allowing her to understand that I relished what she offered, did not mean yielding my purpose. I would carve out a private laboratorium—a part of my mind where I could work without her influence, as I had in my previous double life. This wasn't so different. Xanthe was as ambitious in her way as de Gautier and Kajetan. Obey her, and I could learn of the Stones. Please her, make an ally of her, and I could find a way to plumb Jacard's purposes and rescue Portier. Whatever power my friend represented in this world must not be left at Jacard's service.

What had irked her so sorely? Negotiating such a precarious temper would be tricky. She wanted me to eat from her hand like a trained hound, whether it was food or the course of our partnership. I could do that. But it meant that she must never guess that I had interests beyond the knowledge she offered me.

I fingered Anne's pendant and redoubled my morning's resolution to neither think nor speak of her in Xanthe's presence. If Xanthe turned her power on Anne—

That could not, would not happen. I needed a way to prevent Xanthe extracting those things I would not reveal. I dabbled with ideas but came up with nothing sure enough and fast enough to bind in the time I was likely to have in an emergency. I couldn't count on more than a count of thirty to keep Hosten off me.

I pressed the heel of my hand into my forehead, where the dull ache seemed to have taken up permanent residence. A thousand other questions pursued each other through the darkness . . . what tactics to use . . . what to tell the lady of myself . . . what did Jacard really know of me . . . how to go about learning all I needed to know. And how in the name of all the gods was I to let anyone know what I learned here?

CHAPTER 22

MANCIBAR

"Much better." Xanthe circled me, brushing her fingers across my not-quite-naked scalp, a most . . . heated . . . sensation. "Drab, plain, and clean, as becomes my slave. Behave yourself and I might indulge you with better garments."

Kneeling—clearly, her favored posture for slaves—I nodded, dismissed my treacherous body's reaction to her touch, and remained silent. Beyond her windows the shadowed city and golden plains stretched eastward to a deepening sky.

"In Maldeon's house, only the imperator and his ladies washed themselves," she said, poking a tidbit of fish into my mouth. "I would sneak into the baths, pretending I was Nessia. But the little scorpion found out and tattled on me, which earned me a beating and made the guards watch out for me. She said I'd have to find my own king. And so I will. Till then, I've no desire to smell sour flesh."

Her complaints about Nessia might have been true or might not. They would not erase my memory of the girl's voice as I squeezed the life out of her. That memory must hold me to my purpose. *Hold patience. Gain her trust. Learn of the Stones and Jacard. Find Portier.* Gods, I was no good at patience.

Another bite of fish. Then grapes, one, two, and three. A slow way to take a meal, especially when the one feeding me was so distracted with her own talk.

"I'm glad they found you a clean glove. The priests told me that if I failed in my duty, the god would shrivel my body into purple and black wrinkles, like fruit left in the sun. In my dreams, my arms and legs looked exactly like your grueish hand."

She held a fragment of buttered bread far from my mouth, feinting, teasing. She wanted me either to rise to her goading, so she could punish me, or to beg. I refused to play.

"For certain no god burnt my hand. I was most diligent in my family duties. And I'll vow the heat was much fiercer than desert sun."

Xanthe dropped the bread and collapsed on a pile of cushions in a rustle of bright yellow satin and laughter that swept across the room like a tide of silver bells. Soon a pillow came hurtling straight at my head. And then another and another. "You're as stiff as a Tareo matron, magus! Perhaps I should call you Matron Dante."

When the first hard implement—a spoon—joined the barrage of lacework, silk, and tapestry, I redirected the conversation yet again. "Shall we begin our quest, Mistress? Two generous meals, a bath, and a nap have replenished me. I feel quite ready to serve you."

She sat up straight, instantly sober. "What do we do? Well, I know the first thing." She pulled a small bundle from under her canary-hued skirts—a silken pouch, which she emptied onto the table beside the remains of my supper. Emerald light beams darted from the two Stones.

To my surprise, she fetched my staff and laid it beside me. "You may sit, if you wish."

I did wish. Between Hosten and Xanthe, my knees bore more bruises than my face.

Curling my legs in front of me, I leaned in close to the low table. A visual examination first. There were many things to learn before touching the faceted crystals.

Color: a deep green. Easy to mistake them for emeralds. But flecked with gold that might be lamplight . . . or something else altogether.

Overall shape: irregular, of total dimensions perhaps seven by five by three centimetres.

Facets: at least ten polished surfaces, entirely irregular in shape and dimension, some at square angles to each other, some at more oblique or acute angles, the two Stones quite different one from the other. No scratches, nicks, or other markings on the polished faces, nor marring the crisp straight edges. The one who had cut and polished the crystal had been expert and meticulous.

Clarity: that of the finest gemstones in Queen Eugenie's jewel case. And yet the longer I gazed on them, the more opaque the center grew, as if storm clouds gathered there, the one with a bloodred hue, the other with green so dark, one must call it black. Rhymus, the Red-Hearted. Orythmus, the black.

I averted my eyes. I wasn't ready for visions as yet.

And so to magical structure. Closing my eyes, I shifted my perceptions into the realm of magic and dream.

I blinked. Puzzled. The Stones formed a dark, impenetrable mass, more like holes in the aether than objects of power. A tangle of spell threads dangled from them, as the gheket spells had dangled from the shepherd's paper cone. Attached to the artifact, not a part of it, they were most likely the wards that kept the owner of one stone from murdering the owner of another or charms to protect the surfaces from marring, explaining how they remained perfect after so many centuries. The innate properties of each glass were more compelling just now.

I held one hand a few centimetres above Orythmus and gripped my staff with the other, the better to focus my inner senses on the work.

Still I sensed no enchantment in or on the two crystals. Feeding a small amount of power into my efforts, I moved my hand around their sides and dived deep into the streams of the aether—

A bludgeon struck my cheek, toppling me sidewise. My head narrowly missed the edge of the table on its way to meet the floor. A boot threatened to crush my jaw.

"What is it you think to be doing here, magus?" Hosten.

I certainly couldn't answer.

"What is this about, Captain?"

"Spellwork is what he was doing, my lady. Magic. He's forbidden."

"Move your boot, Captain. I'll keep him still." Xanthe's scent near choked me as she crouched beside me. "Is this true, magus?"

Indeed, she had to modify her command before I could speak and wait for me to spit out wool threads, fishbones, and oil-soaked crumbs. "Certainly I was working magic. It's how I learn."

"The Regent won't have it," said Hosten. "The magus might interfere with other workings in the palace—things that protect us all from earth-shaking or thieves or our food from poison."

"He is my slave, and he'll do whatever I please while in this chamber—even magic. Anywhere else, you may stop him as necessary. But you will bring him to *me* for punishment. He knows the punishments I can mete out—and I can do them to you, as well, if I choose. I'll speak to the Regent about it tonight to make sure he understands."

"Aye, lady, please do that."

A kick in my side accompanied the release of my paralysis. Fighting for breath, I rolled to my knees and kept my forehead on the carpet.

Xanthe crouched beside me. "You will inform me whenever you must use your magic in my service. You are forbidden any other use of it. Wag your smallest finger outside this chamber and I will cut off your healthy hand. Do you understand?"

I did. Entirely. Moments later, I had resumed my puzzling examination of Orythmus's nature, having told her exactly what I was doing. Then I did the same for Rhymus.

I sat back, opened my eyes, and stared at the two crystals. They were a magical void, displaying no spell structure in the way I expected. What's more, they seemed to lack even the unseen energies that formed the basis of keirna—the essence of every natural object. If the streams of the aether were entirely emptied of individual voices, emotions, dreams, and visions, it would appear no different for the existence of these two lumps of glass.

How was that possible? There must be barriers hidden in the very material of the objects, physical barriers of unknown kind or enchantments buried so deep as to make them undetectable.

"So teach me," said Xanthe, bursting the quiet with excitement. "What have you learned? When can I command Hosten or Iaccar or my serving woman to attend me without ringing the bell or sending messengers?"

"Mistress—"

How could I explain to her that learning any new enchantment required care, precision, and time? And this one . . . it could be hours . . . days . . . until I knew the smallest thing to teach her. She wasn't going to like that.

"—though I'm quite capable with traditional sorcery, these Stones are entirely new to me. In fact, *you* are far more experienced than I. You know three commands for Orythmus. Even with my skills and experience, how could I possibly learn so much in a quarter of an hour as it took you months to glean?"

She creased her brow and twisted her mouth, not in a petulant frown, but in the way I had already come to know as her expression of deep thought. "A very good observation, magus. But my patience is worn thin by all these years. If you cannot serve, perhaps I should let Iaccar teach—" She straightened as if she'd pricked her finger. Her brow cleared. "What if *I* was to teach *you* what I know already? Then you could apply your own skills to my lessons."

"Good . . . yes, of course. Excellent." I had fully intended to ask what lore she had wheedled from her priests. I'd hoped to have developed some structure to interpret her information first, but this could shed some light on where I might begin—and would serve to keep her happy. Two worthy goals. "Certainly, that would speed things here at the beginning."

As a whirlwind, Xanthe darted through the room, closing draperies, dousing lamps, and setting one candle, a wheel of thread, and a silver ring on the table. Experimenting with several vases, cups, and other oddments, she at last positioned Orythmus on a dark blue porcelain plate sitting atop a cup. This placed the candle flame and the center of the Stone at exactly the same height at opposite ends of the long table.

"The clan priests told all manner of tales about the Seeing Stones: that only men could wield them or only those of noble birth, though Altheus himself was but his clan father's cousin. The high priest insisted the wielder must be someone of Altheus's own blood. After Maldeon scorned me, I felt free to trade my favors for secrets. That's when I learned that the wizard himself yet lived and I could learn the truth."

"The wizard . . . *Altheus?*"

"No, no. Tyregious was Imperator Altheus's First Magus."

The *Tyregian Emeralds* the Stones had been called in my book of gems. My blood heated. "He's the man who cut and shaped the Seeing Stones?"

"Aye. Maldeon kept him chained in a cellar that Tyregious might teach him how to use the three together on the day he wrested Tychemus from his brother. Though the wizard was old as the Spider God, he was a randy goat, and *most* ready to thwart Maldeon in any way he could. He told me the Stones did require a bonding with their users, but it had naught to do with Altheus's blood. For a . . . favor . . . he would tell me how to invoke the bond. So I pleasured him. He had me bring clay, so he could fashion a model of Orythmus. He taught me the binding, and about the faces, and how to invoke these few commands. We were but a few seasons into our lessons when the barbarians attacked, so I didn't have time to learn everything. Now I must bind myself to Rhymus, too, of course. He said it would work the same."

"Tyregious himself taught you— Great Heaven!" My excitement matched hers. I'd never imagined she'd been tutored by a true mage, much less the very mage who had studied the Stones and wrapped the ancient crystals in magic. "Tell me . . . show me . . . everything you can remember. From the beginning."

She slipped the silver ring about the candle. "He said that this exercise would tell me everything there was to know about the Stones, which was a ridiculous thing to say, else I would know all its commands already. But I'll show you anyway. We must use only one element with light shining on it. The wizard said he preferred a sunbeam shining on a statue of himself—who would ever own such a thing?—but that a candle banded in silver would do. Or the band could be gold or jewels or anything bright. Now, watch. . . ."

As if I could do aught else. *Everything* about them?

Xanthe strung a thread from the candle to Orythmus, turning the prism so that the thread met one particular face squarely, aligning the light and the receiving plane. "He called this the *squaring face*. You must move around and look at the candle through the glass."

So the candle was the source of light for the demonstration. That explained why the wizard preferred a sunbeam. The weak candlelight did not pass through the prism in a sharp beam as the sunlight had done at the Grand Exposition of Science and Magic. Not even a faint smear of light shone on my shirt as I moved into position. But I did as she directed and peered through the facet directly opposed to the one facing the candle.

All I saw was darkness. I took a quick look through the adjacent facets, to make sure I wasn't being fooled. I saw vague glimpses of the dim, cluttered room.

"Now look through this one." And she pointed at an entirely unlikely face, sitting square to the first. I looked . . . and there was the candle straight ahead of me. But when I glanced over the prism instead of through it, the candle remained exactly where she'd placed it, to my left. My seeing had traveled not in a straight line, but in a path that turned a corner.

As I marveled, she rotated the prism, using her thread to angle it as she wished. "This next one, he called the *doubling face*."

Again I peered through the face opposite the candle. "Snakes' teeth!"

Instead of one candle, I saw two. *Double images, skewed images, things round the corner,* Adept Denys had read.

Preening, Xanthe rotated the glass yet again. "You can tell me what he named this one."

"Vanishing face," I said, for the evidence of my seeing said the candle had disappeared no matter which other face I looked through. Even at the edges of my sight, the room seemed darker, as if the prism had gathered the candle's light and hidden it away.

"Indeed, so."

My next view showed the candle poised at a sharp angle, yet not toppling to earth as nature's laws would insist. The *skewing face*, she called it.

I could not but think of Portier on the day I had explained the Gautier lenses, the mystery that had led us to Mont Voilline. How he would laugh at an illiterate serving girl demonstrating such marvels to the pompous Master Dante.

"There are more. But these two together"—she turned the prism with a small triangular facet to the light and pointed to a larger triangular facet on the top of the glass—"he called the *seeing face*."

I knelt up and peered downward through the prism. The candle gleamed deep in its green-black heart . . . only it wasn't Xanthe's candle, ringed with silver. A guttering stub in a pewter holder sat on a small table. A grate in the wall named the room a prison cell. The candle's wan light pushed back a greenish gloom and shone on a dark head, bent over a page of writing. The words faded as quickly as the man—for it was a man's dirty slender hand holding a quill—could set them down.

> . . . found a scroll shortly before I was taken. So much explained. It said: Through the centuries of the Daemon War, the Living Realm grew darker, abandoned by its guardians, rife with ignorance, and plagued by cold and famine, magic lost. A pervasive sadness afflicted the world, for though they had discounted the worth of humans, Dimios and his fellows had learned that they could increase their own strength by draining the energies from the souls of human dead, a crime against the Creator who had set the order of

the world. He who had been the Pantokrator's First, was ever after named the Souleater . . .

"Aagh!" The writer threw down his pen and ripped something from his face, cramming his hands to his eyes. On the desk lay a pair of spectacles, lenses blazing with emerald fire.

"Portier!"

The dark head lifted, eyes bleeding, face bruised and gaunt. . . .

Xanthe snatched the prism away. "I daren't allow you to spy out his whereabouts. Iaccar and I have an agreement."

"How is it possible that I see Iaccar's prisoner?" This was no illusion; Portier had heard my call.

"Tyregious said the Stones' mystery was a matter of light and seeing, not spellwork. When I first looked, I saw nothing at all through the *seeing face.* He claimed it was because I was empty-headed. Did I mention that he was not at all nice, and that he smelled like a dead-pit?" She spat on the fine carpet. "But after I pleasured him again, he said it wasn't my fault that I had no power for magic to open the seeing face. That's when he taught me how to bind myself to Orythmus so I could use its magic. Then I'd be able to see, as well."

So a person must possess power for magic or be joined by some ritual link to see what the glass would show. Yet the looking required no expenditure of power. "A binding rite . . ."

"The next time I had to transport the stone from its resting place to Maldeon's chamber, I did as he'd taught me. I told the matrons I had fainted along the way and that my fall caused the wound on my hand. It was a great risk, as I was not prone to faints and the matrons might decide to replace me. But stonekeeper training begins at birth and no one else was ready. . . ."

"So you were linked to Orythmus before you took possession of it. Yet you could not wield it until Maldeon voluntarily yielded it to you as its keeper." I could not dwell on the vision's meaning. Xanthe's seeds of knowledge were sown when and where she would, and it was difficult enough to keep up.

"That's true. One cannot steal the power of a stone from its owner any more than one can take it by stealth or murder the owner to take possession. Not directly, at least . . ."

She licked her rouged lips. Even in the soft candlelight, her teasing sickened me. *Light and seeing.* This Tyregious had been speaking to one he knew would not comprehend. Had he hoped she might pass on his words to someone who might appreciate his work? Or had he merely wanted to flatter a pretty girl to soothe his captivity?

"And the wizard taught you how to choose what visions you wanted the dreamer to see?"

"No. He said that all I had to do was command the dreamer to see me instead of Nessia. I must invoke the seeing with words likely to rouse the dreamer's own nature—*desire, riches, fear, cruelty.* When the dreamer looked into the stone, Rhymus would show what it would, as the Stones were not gems, but pis-priss-pasras. Well, something like that. When I pushed for more, he insisted that he'd already demonstrated the entirety of their power with my candle. Which was a lie, of course, else how could Holy Altheus have used them to conquer Aroth?"

"Prisms. The word is prisms. Magic is all about seeing. That's what he was telling you."

She snatched up the thread, twisted it. "The dreadful, wicked, stinking old man laughed at me the whole time. He thought I was stupid. I was glad he was chained. Glad when I heard that the barbarians collapsed the palace on top of him."

My gaze explored the green glass, hungering to touch it, to probe it. "Have you bound yourself to Rhymus yet? I should watch—"

Acid . . . fire . . . lacerated my back. I crashed forward into the table. A green arc was Orythmus flying. An orange blur was the candle toppling to douse itself on the scattered cushions. Darkness fell like a river of tar, as another blow creased the backs of my legs. Another on my shoulders. Invisible chains tightened about my arms and shoulders, drawing them outward. The racked joints cracked, no matter that intellect claimed my arms lay limp amid the litter of fish and cheese and bread. Gods, how had I crossed her this time?

Xanthe stood over me. "Naturally, *you* would know the proper word. Righteous sorcerer, who dast wrinkle his nose at my scheming. *You* would not have had to stoop to duplicity and murder to get what you want, like stupid Xanthe did. Save I know that you *did.*"

"Correct," I croaked, stomach heaving. "I've done worse. Less reason. You don't know—"

Another lash. "I know many things. I know why you wish to watch me bind myself to Rhymus. You think I'm empty-headed, too. You've not even thanked me for showing you, and already you scheme to get the Stones for yourself."

Writhing, breathless, I could scarce answer. "Not empty-headed, Mistress. Never that. You've remembered these details for centuries. You outlived your king, his wizard, your mentors. Outwitted them. Taken what they desired. Your demonstration has only confounded me. A confusion I must work out, so I can teach you. I'll— Aagh!"

Her invisible yoke tightened, drawing a grunt of agony through my clenched teeth. "I swear to you, Mistress. Honestly. Whatever I must do to learn of them, the power of the Stones is not for me. Nor will it ever be." I spewed the words in desperation, yet their truth sank into my fiery flesh like a balm—the kind that only after contact begins to etch its own wound. *Dangerous*, the old shepherd had called me. Indeed I was no more trustworthy than Xanthe or Jacard.

"What man was ever honest? Not my king. Not my mentors. Not Iaccar. You lie to me at your peril, slave."

The pain faded and she left me sprawled across her table, heaving. Her skirts brushed my face and I heard the distant bell. I could not hold thought enough to count the interval until Hosten burnt away the dark with a torch.

"Put the slave back in his hole," said Xanthe. "Perhaps I'll let him out again in the morning. Perhaps not."

CHAPTER 23

MANCIBAR

She let me out. But not to work magic or anything else of use. Hosten and his five soldiers installed me in the corner of her grand apartment and shoved me to my knees. As Xanthe entertained a parade of seamstresses, jewelers, painters, and upholsterers, I was wholly ignored.

I neither moved nor spoke, and vowed to do absolutely nothing without her command. Certainly no magic, though to kneel there idle, knowing I could raise an enchantment to flatten them all or set the furnishings afire to mask an escape, near set me raving.

But I could not forfeit this chance. Nessia, Ilario, Denys . . . I recited the litany of the dead to remind me why I had to bide my time. The mystery of the Stones had scarce begun to open and already I could sense answers close.

The lady was indeed cleverer than Kajetan and his cronies had been. They, too, had wished to make use of my magic for their own schemes. They, too, had recognized my hungers. But they had never thought to test my resolve with utter boredom.

After a few hours, Xanthe summoned food. While I knelt, hands clasped behind my back, she doled out bread and fruit, a tidbit at a time, and gave me sips of sour ale. No meat. No fish. No conversation.

The day continued. In late afternoon, Jacard sent an invitation to go riding with him and several of Mancibar's lords and ladies—of whom there seemed to be a great number. Xanthe had me taken back to the sorcerer's hole. I remained there until the next morning, when it all began again.

She fed me and ignored me. Once she directed me to move a piece of furniture. No speech was required. When I completed the task, her finger pointed back to my corner. I went. And knelt.

That afternoon, she spoke with Hosten about finding me some unpleasant menial occupation about the palace. Nothing came of it. Perhaps she realized I would welcome hard labor.

Mancibar's lords and ladies came calling. Their garb was that of the desert—scarves and light flowing fabrics, entirely unlike Xanthe's replicas of Sabrian court gowns. No matter their politenesses as they shared tea and wine, their faces were wary and unsure of her. A few asked about me but turned away quickly when they heard I was a disobedient slave.

Xanthe noticed me watching. She pointed to my eyes and the floor. I fixed my gaze on the pocked wood.

At the end of the fourth day of this ridiculous posturing, when the door to the sorcerer's hole closed off the light behind me, I beat my hands and head on the wall and bellowed like a maddened bull. My rage bounced off the close walls, as it had in the cellar of the Gautier ruins.

Fear slapped me to my senses like a rain of cold mud. I shrank into the corner and fought to regain equanimity. This was but a game. The work yet waited if I could just hold patience and endure. Xanthe coveted the life the Stones could give her, but she was too clever to allow Jacard to hold her Stones with promises he had no intention of keeping. I just had to stay sane until her own patience ran out.

Think. Plan. For the hundredth time I pondered the vision of Portier and the passage he'd been writing. As did everyone in the world, I swore by the Souleater. But when had I ever considered what the name meant?

I did not believe in divine beings, whether angels or daemons, creators or saints. But then there was Portier and his unexplainable life. No matter what faith I had in my own magic, I had lost him three times on that terrible night when he was submerged in a pool for hours. Three times I had retaken my hold on his keirna. Three times I had found him still alive.

I did not believe in the Souleater. But then there was Anne's assertion that she'd heard her sister's voice among the spectres in Mont Voilline's pregnant sky, claiming that the souls of the dead were being leached away.

Now this vision had laid the question of belief square in my lap again.

My glimpse of Portier in Orythmus had rung of truth, and I could ignore Portier's witness no more than I could ignore Anne's. Had Portier concluded that the energies drained from the spectral dead were feeding some single being . . . mortal or divine?

I pulled Portier's ring out from the tiny rip in my straw mattress and slipped it onto my finger. Thanks to the sorcerer's hole, its annoyingly cheerful pipe music played only in memory. A pure, perfect little bit of magic had created the music and attached it to the ring—Portier's magic, worked purposely to irritate me, who made no secret of how I detested piping. Yet I weened he had also made it to thank me for shattering his barriers to magic—a foolhardy risk at the time. Four years he'd kept my success secret because he believed me Fallen, yet it had taken only a word from Anne for him to place his life in my hands at Mont Voilline.

Gods . . . what was the measure of such trust? And here I sat idle, believing that somehow this submission to a half-mad child-woman was my best hope to save his life. What if I had gambled away the chance for naught?

I pressed quivering fists to my temples. *Hold on, student. I will come. If I have to wear her chains until death or grovel to Jacard himself, I will.*

THE DAYS RAN ONE INTO the other. Five, then six, then ten. Despair nipped at my shoulders. What if Xanthe had truly given up on me and thrown herself into Jacard's hands? My body hungered to release fire and destruction; my soul craved the energies of spellwork to give it direction and purpose.

On one morning as I was released from the hole, one of Hosten's soldiers—a young fellow, freckled, a shock of light brown hair sticking out from his steel cap—winked at me. Without a clue as to his meaning, I ignored him. It was burden enough to discipline myself to kneel quietly another day.

Midafternoon arrived without Xanthe feeding me. To avoid the gnawing of my belly, I spent my time stretching my senses through the palace, trying to detect signs of unusual magic. Xanthe was engaged with one of Jacard's cooks, insisting the woman produce some concoction of sheep entrails and barley that she had relished when a child in Maldivea. They couldn't even agree on the names of herbs.

Without my staff's embedded spell or a larger infusion of power, my range of hearing was limited, but the palace seemed a subdued and argumentative place. Quiet disputes touched on horse exercise and grooming. Wordless yelling accompanied the shuffling of pots and kettles and whacking of knives in the kitchens. Murmurs traversed the intricate passageways along with the hurried footsteps of servants and guards, late to their posts. No screams today.

Closer footsteps brought an abrupt end to the exercise. A soldier—the freckle-faced one—carried in a tray.

"Set it on the table," said Xanthe and returned to her argument with the cook.

As the young man removed the linen covering, he glanced over his shoulder at Xanthe's back, and then stared directly at me. Raising one clenched fist in front of him, he nodded slightly.

Strength? Brotherhood? What was he trying to say? And who was he?

All sorts of notions raced through me as he left the room. But all came down to one . . . Andero. Hope and dismay battled feverishly. I was nowhere near accomplishing my purpose. To leave here without understanding . . . without Portier . . .

Xanthe spun sharply enough that her scarlet gown fetched eye and mind from my thoughts. Heart thumping at the idea I might have missed a signal from her, I inclined my head respectfully.

As the cook marched out of the room, Jacard arrived, garbed in rich black, trimmed in silver.

"How lovely you look, lady! Stars and Stones, has your mentor retreated to the corner to pout or is he hatching some treacherous magic to upend our harmonious household?" The sniveling fool played every nuance of royal host and magical advisor. "Best watch him carefully. He is an expert sneak."

"On the contrary," said Xanthe, "my slave's mind is constantly on me. I'll rip out his eyes and throw him in your kennels does he let his mind wander."

Her objective was assuredly accomplished.

This was the first time I had seen the sharp-chinned weasel since my arrival. He'd changed little in two years, save in the self-control I had noted before. Was it the Seeing Stone made him confident? Power for magic could do that, especially if one was too thickheaded to assess the consequences of its use. A dangerous combination. And these two together . . . gods save us.

They sat on her balcony for a while, gossiping of this lord who had come in from the country, or that one who had put his wife aside. Jacard had brought her a gift of a purple silk mantle, beaded in silver—which delighted her. Before very long, heads together, my mistress and my enemy departed. Neither looked at me, much less addressed me on the way out. I felt very like a ghost.

LATE IN THE NIGHT WATCHES, suffering from a surfeit of sleep for the first time in seven years, I sat in the dark fingering Anne's pendant. I wished I could speak with her about these things I had learned, my birth in the dark, the old shepherd's warnings about the way of the dead and my unhappy destiny, my vision of Portier, even the cold dark that so frightened me. *Pervasive sadness* . . . Was that what I had felt when looking on the Uravani bridge—on the images of the Righteous Defender and the Daemon of the Dead, locked in their divine grappling?

Anne did not get overwrought or blithering when speaking of difficult matters, even if they had great meaning for her. Her passions ran deep, but gloriously quiet. Perhaps she could help me sort out my fear and guilt and, yes, jealousy of her secrets with Ilario and Portier.

Yet, I'd hate for her to know about Denys and Nessia. She had told me more than once that she could not and would not judge me for the terrible things I'd done as *agente confide*. But these new crimes . . .

Fortune grant she was safe in the care of her friends and need never come to this dark place.

The muffled snap of the door latch brought me to my feet. I crammed the locket into my glove, chilled at imagining that somehow Xanthe had detected my straying thoughts.

A faint glow leaked from a shielded lamp. One pair of booted feet accompanied the lamp.

"Are we playing night games now, Captain?" Night summonings were ever dangerous.

"Sshh. Hurry!" A shadow much too small to be Hosten took my arm and drew me toward the gray rectangle of the door.

I yanked my arm from his grasp, startlingly easy. "Who are you?"

"Come, if you wish to see him alive. He'll be buried before morning."

My breath caught. Yet, I dared not trust. "Buried? Who? Has my mistress commanded my attendance?"

"Your friend, the scholar. If we hurry, we might prevent what they plan." The clipped words dripped urgency and secrecy.

"Tell me who you are and who's sent you." I injected as much menace as I could into a whisper. I could not risk my work with the Stones for a game.

"One who'll not see a holy man murdered for no reason. No saints' litany will erase such a crime."

Saints' litany . . . "You're a Cultist?"

"If you can free him, I can get him out of Mancibar and into Cult hands. Everyone says—he says—you have power for magic beyond telling. So will you use it for good or not?" He lifted the lamp and showed his face. Sprinkled with freckles. Very young. Worried. Frightened. "It has to be now."

What certainty could he offer that I would believe? But he spoke of Portier. He spoke of living death. No matter doubts, I had to go. "Show me."

The shuttered lamp led me through passages I had not yet traversed. Down a wide stair, deserted on this night save by statues of angels in every posture—contemplative, engaged, wings spread or furled, bearing books, messages, or lyres. Even in combat. A narrow, older stair led into a warren of musty passages and gaping rooms. Old stone peeked out from crumbled lath and plaster. Vermin feet skittered and whispered beyond the pool of lamplight. The dark closed in behind us. I refused to quail.

"So tell me who you are," I said again as my companion unlocked an iron-bound door.

"I guard him, yet he's done naught but bless me and join me in the litanies."

The comment struck a note as dissonant as a duck playing a harp.

Portier was quiet, sober, a gentleman born. But none would call him a pious man or one who doled out blessings beyond the politenesses his birth had instilled. I wasn't sure he believed in the divine any more than I did. He had deliberately sought out a Cult mentor with a scholar's credentials, not a priest's. And in his sparse correspondence, I'd heard no evidence of sudden or miraculous conversion to Cult devotions.

What small trust I had in my guide dissipated rapidly. I redoubled caution. No footsteps followed.

The young man drew open the narrow door. The iron bands in the thick wood and the scents of camphor and heated iron bespoke a cell unfriendly to spellwork. I made sure he left the door open, lest my own magic be fatally crippled.

The large chamber was mostly empty. But the scene in its center near took my breath. All appeared as I had seen in Rhymus's vision—the black hearth, the blazing fire, the iron rod protruding from white-hot coals.

I blinked. Inhaled the stink of fear and heated iron. Folded my arms across my chest, pinching and poking. I was awake.

A few steps farther. What appeared to be a simple grave incised the floor. A pit scarce big enough to contain a man had been hacked from the slick, dark stone and lined with iron. Beside it lay a slab of iron exactly the size of the opening. Dirt had been heaped at its foot.

Portier, the King of Sabria's cousin, the man who had given my magic a purpose and honored it even when he believed me Fallen, was bound to the floor of the pit with leather straps. Someone had scattered a handful of dirt over him. Unwashed skin streaked and smeared with blood, he writhed and strained within his bonds, exactly as I had seen him in Xanthe's vision. It was the exactitude of that scene, its perfect horror, that screamed warnings. And I'd swear that others in this labyrinth were breathing. . . .

I hated what I was about to do more than I hated any of the vileness I had wreaked in my life. Even after so brief an exposure, I knew the Seeing Stones were my puzzle to solve. Any chance of preserving my deception and discovering the truth, and likely any hope of rescuing Portier, depended on my actions here. This was my trial. Somewhere, I believed, Xanthe watched and waited.

I stepped into the soldier's pool of light. "Ah, Portier, you do get yourself into wretched fixes."

"Dante!" His croaking greeting wavered. His deep exhale shook. "Knew you'd come . . . heard your promises . . ." His heavy eyelids drooped with sleep or drugs.

My foot nudged a loose fragment of paving stone. It bounced and clattered into the pit and against his bound leg. "Do you learn nothing, librarian? You've let them take you again."

"Woman made a fool of me. But had to come. They mentioned *Sirpuhi of the Red Cliffs. . . .*" The words slurred, tumbling out one atop the other. "Been here 'fore . . . recognize it. Afraid to believe. You won't, but *must. Must.*" He grasped the word, as if dragging himself up a well. "Scroll explains about the fire . . . about me . . . about you. . . ."

Explained his dreams of multiple lives? What did *I* have to do with his delusions? Gods, I dared not ask.

"I helped you out of similar trouble once. I could likely do so again."

"No. Must listen. Was coming home to tell you. The Seeing Stones, the temptation . . . The danger is *yours*, not mine."

I crouched beside him and tweaked the strap at his ankle. "I disagree. Which of us is in the pit?"

He dropped his voice even lower and tugged fitfully at his bindings, fighting for the words even as his eyelids sagged. "Your strength. Gifts. You are born to do the unthinkable." Fear beyond mortal comprehension was bundled in those whispered words, all courage, all pretense drained away. "Must not fall. Must not yield . . ."

His words trailed off as I bent closer where I could view the perfect horror in his eyes and he could see my own, void of sympathy or hidden meaning. Though more than anything I wanted to comfort him, to ask what in the name of sense he was talking about, I dared not waver or misstep.

"I never thought we'd meet again, librarian." I spoke loud enough that anyone in the dark corners of the chamber could hear. "I did my best for you at Voilline. How could I allow such a valuable asset to be lost to Gautier's bungling? But you thanked me by running away on your own private quest, leaving me crippled. You and the rest of those cursed aristos . . . You've kept secrets, haven't you? You never trusted me."

"Secrets?" For a moment, he was naught but bewildered. And then he looked on me with such sympathy as must be lunacy from a man half starved, half mad, and strapped into his own grave. "Worried about you . . . so angry, so empty. That's the danger. I wrote to—"

"I don't think I can bring myself to help you this time," I interrupted. I could not let him talk too much. Or think too much. "My new mistress would not approve. And I owe her *everything.*"

"Mistress?" He squinted. Stared. Grew still. "Heaven and earth, you can see. How—?"

"Be silent, holy man, and hear me. The Lady Xanthe and no other has given me this gift, and so for her will I do service, and no other. Never again for those who've cost me everything I've reached for in my life. What kingdom is worth what I lost?" I let my voice rise in anger and madness. I knew well how to do that. "Think on the life you made me lead and you'll understand what I do."

"What—? Spirits, Dante!"

His eyes darted wildly as I rose and snatched up the iron. Its tip glowed red, pulsing as I waved it in front of his face.

"You lured me into your plots, Portier. *You* are responsible. And here you are trying to do it again—to wreck my life that is just now being rebuilt. Perhaps you should share the agony I suffered because of you. Two long years in the dark, no moment of which has been without pain. Do you understand what that means?"

I heaped curses and accusations on him. I drew the glowing iron across his brow, singeing his eyebrows, and I feinted so close to his eyes, he surely felt his tears seared dry. But when his throat could not voice another plea, and he had shrunk back against the plate iron beneath his back as if it might absorb him, I threw the rod back in the fire and kicked dirt onto his face.

"You'd best return me to my room," I said to the freckled soldier. "I will not steal my lady's pleasure."

"Dante." The harsh whisper floated on the heated air. "He's going to come for you. You are the Daemon."

Flesh and spirit froze. But I did not, could not, ask what he meant. Instead, I turned my back on my only friend and walked away.

CHAPTER 24

34 ESTAR, THE NIGHT WATCHES

The door of the sorcerer's hole slammed. The bolt shot. I wanted to tear down the walls with my teeth. Yet I dared not allow the freckled guard or anyone else to hear my rage, lest my unholy play be proved a lie. I had to settle for silent curses, heaping every malediction I knew upon myself as an execrable, cowardly, inhuman wretch. Imagining what might be happening to Portier at that very moment emptied my guts into the night jar.

As I ground my head on the wall, trying to erase images of suffocation, our exchange played out again and again. His first thought had not been to beg for help, but to warn *me*.

"Mayhap Saints Reborn don't need help," I spat.

But as reason penetrated self-loathing, the magnitude of his declarations overwhelmed me. He'd claimed some scroll might explain *about the fire.* His writing in Rhymus's seeing face had mentioned a scroll. Was Portier de Savin-Duplais, a man of relentless logic, of science, of scholarship, a man who withheld judgment in any investigation until all evidence was in, now telling me he had been chained to Mont Voilline millennia ago as punishment for stealing fire from Heaven? Gods save us.

I slid to the floor.

. . . Sirpuhi of the Red Cliffs . . . been here . . . recognize it. You'll not believe, but must . . . So he believed he was Altheus, as well, the Holy Imperator? I was near dizzy with the imagining. Continuing rebirth . . . the

fire of Heaven brought to humankind. What did that even mean? I had ever reminded Portier that combustion was an entirely natural process that any alchemist could explain.

Yet somehow in the dark, stripped raw by guilt, I could not call Portier mad or deluded or idiot as I would any other man in the world who told me such. And if he was right . . .

My back curled forward and my hands splayed on the floor, as if to ensure the Stone had not dropped out from under me or become water, sand, or silk.

. . . then what of the rest? *Your strength. Gifts. Your are born to do the unthinkable.*

The unthinkable what? Another voice echoed in the dark, one hoarse with age and prophecy. *Thou'rt other, born in darkness, gifted with strength to quench the light of Heaven.*

He's going to come for you. I doubted Portier was speaking of Jacard.

I curled up on my pallet and begged the night for sleep.

You are the Daemon. . . .

HOSTEN DRAGGED ME FROM THE dark the next morning without word or sign to indicate he knew of my trip to Portier's hell. The soldier with the freckled face was not among my five escorts.

"Put him here beside the table," Xanthe said, when the captain removed the bulky bracelets. "I've work for you today, my magus." She was wreathed in smiles, and patted my head as I knelt to receive her bounty. She acted as if the days of my exile had not happened.

Blood hammered in my veins. I wanted to bring the walls down to crush us all. Instead, I ate.

I did not believe in fate or destiny—unhappy or happy. Our lives were what we made of them hour by hour, day by day. It was the only way I knew how to live.

Begging had not yielded me oblivion in the night just past. So I had relied on practiced discipline, instead. I set Portier and destiny aside and worked on the problem of the Seeing Stones. I had devised a theory about their magic, then buried hate, conscience, and urgency and slept ferociously. I could not indulge petty vengeance. I needed power. I needed information.

"I wish to have a new command for my Stone by the end of the day," said Xanthe, wiping her greasy fingers on a towel of yellow silk. "Do not displease me again."

"I shall do my best, Mistress." I touched my forehead to the carpet, then knelt up and crossed my arms on my breast. "But first I must beg forgiveness. These days of exile have given me pause, as you so wisely understood, giving me occasion to recall my life as it was. I was born in ignorance and poverty to a man who crippled me. I was scorned by those at Collegia Seravain, who resented me for earning a master mage's collar without licking their feet. For six years I enslaved myself to ambition, serving those born to power in Sabria. Like you, instead of my lord's favor, I earned his disgust. I am barred from the circles of power, exiled from Merona, forbidden to cross paths with the elite. Blindness made me see what their proffered friendship meant. I was but a crude and ignorant commoner of no more use to them."

I swallowed bile and subdued all thought and feeling save the part I had chosen to play.

"You judged me rightly, Mistress, perhaps because we are so much the same. Ambition is a part of me as much as it is a part of you. But what I desire most is knowledge of magic. You have earned the right to lead our partnership, and I must and will yield to that right. For the gifts you have given me, I swear to serve you honestly from this day forward."

I waited for her invisible lash to sear and crush. But instead, her hand ruffled my shorn hair, then pinched my ear to lift my head. She did not quite twist it off.

"I'm not sure I believe you," she said. "Time will tell all. Earn my trust and your life will be better than any of these other people could give you."

A cage of silver wire hung about her neck, holding Rhymus and Orythmus captive. She removed Orythmus and laid it on the table. Then she shoved my staff into my hand. "A new command to please me. You have today. Remember the consequences of misbehavior."

"Always, Mistress. I cannot forget." I *would* not forget.

Gripping my staff and setting my focus, I set to work to test my new theory. Tyregious the wizard had told Xanthe that his little demonstration told all that was needed about the Stones. My own examination had found no spell structure within them. So perhaps he meant the Stones themselves were just as I saw, complex lenses—prisms—that enabled sight in varying, if mysterious, ways. In that case, the *command* Orythmus embodied lay not in the crystal itself, but in the spell threads attached to it, the bits I had assumed extraneous.

I plunged into the aether and this time turned my attention to the clustered enchantments that surrounded Orythmus. The first thread I chose to examine was exactly the command to *move* or *stay* that Xanthe already knew. The spell held numerous additional complexities Xanthe had not yet demonstrated. The command to move directly into danger, as to step off a cliff. The command to move in ways the body was not designed to do, as to bend an elbow backward. The command to move in ways designed to kill another. I preferred she not test these on me, so I moved on.

Much as an anatomist dissects a living animal and creates a map of veins, tissues, nerves, and bone, learning how they interconnect and incite each other, I pulled each spell thread into its component parts—words, objects, sensory details, logic—and sketched them in simpler patterns of color and light that I could recall and manipulate. Removing, rearranging, or replacing the elements in the spell and observing the resulting patterns taught me of its structure and suggested its nature. All remained in the realm of theory and logic, however. Without being linked to Orythmus, I could not test what I found.

I lost track of the passing hours. Though I craved to alter or destroy the vilest enchantments, I dared not. Modifying such complexities took an immensely long time. My freedom to learn would be measured solely by Xanthe's resolve to remain independent and Jacard's inability to undermine that resolve, and neither was so certain as I would like.

Hosten was a more immediate concern. Destructive magical energy was entirely different from even the most complex spell construction. *Noisy*, one might call it. Or *dissonant*. Hosten or any trained watcher could detect it and guess I was destroying some component of the Stone.

And, too, Orythmus as a whole was a marvel. Even the most terrible of its individual commands could surely be turned to good purpose. How many lives might be saved by sending a barbarian general over a cliff? I felt in no fit moral state to judge, save in what pieces of its whole I would entrust to Xanthe.

A twisting thread of yellow gossamer held the spell to command *obedience* or *rebellion*. Xanthe already used her control of pain, seeing, and immobility to enforce her wishes. With the more direct command, she could force Jacard's subjects to defy him, or ensure my own obedience without damaging me. Neither were skills I wished to give her.

As weariness bled my concentration, I feared I'd have nothing from the day's work I could entrust to her. Yet the very next thread, a thin clear strand of scarlet glass, seemed harmless enough. I crafted a keyword and linked it to the spell thread.

"Silence," I said, raising my head as I returned my awareness to Xanthe's rooms.

"How dare you command me! I've been silent this entire day, watching you do nothing but grip that stick and stare at my treasure. I've said not a word!"

"No, no, my lady." I jumped in quickly, raising my hand before she could punish me. "I've found you a way to command a person's sense of hearing. Far better than wooden stoppers."

To my dismay, once I'd told her how to invoke the little spell, she took away my staff and summoned Captain Hosten. "I'll not have you working spells alongside as I play, thinking to deceive me that they are my own. The Stone's power must be in my hands alone."

Xanthe was no fool. The thought *had* occurred to me.

Reckoning by the fading daylight through the gallery portals, I had spent ten or twelve hours at the work. My muscles and joints felt stiff as new boots, and I had scarce begun unraveling Orythmus's myriad enchantments. As Hosten locked the door behind me, I crawled through the dark onto my pallet and fell instantly asleep.

"OUT, MAGUS." THE RITUAL OF the wooden bracelets and readied swords and spears awaited.

I'd not slept for long. I could scarce focus my eyes on the route to my mistress's rooms.

"Oh, my slave, good work! Most *excellent* work!"

Xanthe flew across the room as I entered and threw her arms around me from the back, deftly avoiding the thorny manacles. Before I could accommodate the shock of her embrace, she danced away, spinning and whirling, until the caged crystals dangling from her neck made rings of emerald in the lamplight. When she collapsed on the divan, her cheeks were rose brown and the silver streaks in her eyes sparking and glimmering.

"Such chaos I set off in the kitchens when no person could hear any other. And when I threw a blanket of silence over the aviary, the birds flew into a frenzy, crashing into each other and tangling themselves in the trees! And my serving girl screamed so delightfully, clawing at her ears until they bled. Of course, I undid the spell quickly and soothed her with wine, but she was still weeping when she left me."

"Good," I said, dropping to my knees and bowing my head without being told. Hosten removed the inhibitors and bowed his way out.

"I want more," she said, shoving my staff into my hand. "Work all night, if you must."

"Honored Mistress, I regret that I've done all I can manage in a day." I laid my ancille aside. "Depleted as I am, I could go mad or die."

Only one lash, not hard enough to knock me over. Then she pouted and began to wheedle. "Come, magus, only a small taste more. You've left me—"

Heavy, hurried footsteps stopped her.

"Do you mock my courtesy, damoselle?" Jacard stomped through the doorway in midrant. "Have I insulted you, interfered with you establishing your household or managing your slave?"

"Certainly not!" said Xanthe. "Come, what's wrong? Such a delight to have you here. Sit."

"Not until I understand with what authority and what motive you moved the librarian."

Gods, Portier. I remained quiet and unmoving beside the couch.

Xanthe giggled. "Oh, dear friend Iaccar, we should dispatch my burrow rat back to his hole before discussing my wickedness. . . ." Xanthe rang the bell to summon my jailer.

"Your—" Jacard whirled about in my direction, growling.

I bit my lip to prevent baring my teeth as Hosten locked the inhibitors on my wrists. Portier yet lived. Jacard had said *moved.* Not *killed.* Not *buried.*

"Give the slave three choices for his supper," Xanthe told Hosten. "Feed him whichever he chooses. He must repeat your offering exactly."

With a wicked grin, she whispered a word and touched her lips. Instantly, my ears felt as if plugged with mud. With laughter I could not hear, she turned away.

There were no delays in getting me back to the sorcerer's hole. And, of course, I could not hear what choices were offered and I went hungry. It was another long night.

On the next morning, we began again.

XANTHE'S EXUBERANT PURSUIT OF SPELLWORK left me increasingly uneasy. It became difficult to find things that would please her, yet not lead her into serious sorcery. No one should have the breadth and depth of command Orythmus provided. The Stone allowed its bound master or mistress, even one with no intrinsic talent, to control a considerable variety of powerful magic. Not that those with talent were in any proportion more likely to be wise in the use of magic than those without.

Preoccupied with tricks and games, I had no chance to explore more of Orythmus's intrinsic nature. I hoped that studying Rhymus, comparing and contrasting the two, would give me better opportunity. But I had learned my lesson. I waited for the lady herself to suggest we move on to her second Seeing Stone.

On one evening seven or eight days after I'd seen Portier, Xanthe was amusing herself feeding me while altering the flavor of each morsel to something other. Fish that tasted of dirt. Olives flavored with mint. Pomegranate that reeked of burnt fat.

"Command is all very well," she said, waiting as I gagged on an almond that tasted like a clot of mold, "but I'm chafing to learn more of Nessia's Stone. And Iaccar is impatient that I learn to . . . enhance . . . his subjects' dreams. Gossip rumbles about his hauntings and vanishings, and more of his subjects lament the old prince, which angers him terribly. 'Tis not so terrible a way of maintaining order. Maldeon's ways were very . . . messy. So much screaming and bloody entrails everywhere. Iaccar claims you withhold the most powerful magics apurpose."

A good thing I was flushed already. Her accusation hit too close to the mark.

She threw down the food and dipped her hands in a basin of water. "Last night I bound myself to Rhymus. I decided not to show you how I did it."

"As I told you before, Mistress, I've no intention of wielding the Stones." In truth, my aversion to the Seeing Stones had grown more firm as the days passed. My hands felt dirty after touching them—something I'd never before experienced with a magical artifact. Yet, indeed, the disappointment stung. "May I ask a question before we move on?"

"You may ask." Implying with her tone that she might not answer.

"On the day you enslaved me"—she relished it when I referred to my servile state—"I looked into Rhymus and saw . . . and participated in . . . the librarian's torment. It wasn't a dream. How could I see so specific a scene?"

She shrugged, her dark blue gown slipping off her shoulder. "Perhaps it was the words I used to invoke the dreams. I just wanted you distracted and confused."

"But Iaccar had told you of my blinding. He believed the librarian my ally. Perhaps he suggested the scene? Or the scenes in the dreams, when Rhymus showed the rivers of blood, the pervasive gloom . . . and sadness?" And Ixtador's spectres walking among mortal men, a comely young man as their shepherd.

"Inside the dreams or outside, Rhymus chooses what to show through its seeing face. I saw those visions first when I peeked over your shoulder."

"And the dream of the meadow, where you learned of my father and Portier?"

"That was invoked with words!" Xanthe laughed, practicing dance steps with an invisible partner. "Iaccar said that if I knew the names of people of importance to you, he could tell me more about them so we could fetch them or kill them or make our plans. So, I sang an old verse in the dream. '*The heart of man charts a four-legged course; father, friend, lover, and always his horse.*' And sure enough your dream showed me those people and a horse—though the beast was naught but bones." She shuddered. "I hated that part."

The Stones were all about seeing. About pathways. Connections. They were prisms, not gems.

"My eyes had never seen Devil. That's why the dream showed naught but bones."

The words fell from my lips before I could consider my folly. Xanthe paused in her dancing. I glanced up. Her brow crinkled in the way I'd come to dread.

"And so one of the men was your father. And the friend was this librarian, whom you said was not your friend. . . ."

"An *unfaithful* friend," I said urgently. "He pretended friendship while he used me. Just as my father ruined and discarded me. What kind of father cripples his son to be rid of him? I rejoiced in his pain. All of them were betrayers."

"The lover, too? The woman? You never mentioned a woman. You refused to name her. . . ."

"She is the worst traitor of all. Her care was naught but pity. When I would not fawn upon her as she wished, she returned to her aristo parents. I could not bear her presence in my dream." I drew on all the bitterness festered from Anne's leaving. She *was* a deceiver. She had certainly deceived herself these two years. "She kept secrets with other men."

"Like Maldeon." Xanthe crouched before me, enveloping me in her warmth and sweet scent. Her flowing sleeves tickled my face as she stroked my cheek, smiling like a benevolent queen. "And even your horse is a betrayer. I indulge him with apples and sweet hay and he loves me dearly. He does not pine for you, magus. No one pines for you, I think."

I bleated a laugh. Terror of exposing Anne lined my airways with thorn. "You are surely correct, Mistress."

Before another day passed, I had to devise some triggering spell that would prevent me revealing Anne's name. Then, perhaps, I could work without this persistent distraction.

Xanthe returned to her dancing, her laughter like music, her form voluptuous as she dodged the darting sunbeams. She was so like a child, sunlight and shadow, pleasure and fury, each quickly raised and each quickly dismissed as long as one paid close attention and took quick action. There were certainly more difficult traits in a companion.

I wrenched eyes away and returned to the puzzle of Rhymus's visions. Jacard had told her that Rhymus itself transformed her words into its visions, drawing on the observer's desires or fears. But the Stones were magically void, and none of the attached spellwork touched the Stone itself. Which left . . . what?

Was someone else influencing the Stones and their visions?

Orythmus gleamed jewel-like in the lamplight, its facets taunting me. Squaring. Skewing. Doubling. Vanishing. Altering one's view of what existed already. Its *seeing facet* had shown me a different candle . . . and

Portier . . . and his fragment of writing that stuck in my logic like a fly in butter. Was that seeing in the present or in the past? Either seemed possible, for an intrinsically *im*possible thing. Yet I believed the vision true, and that wherever and whenever he had been writing the history of the Souleater, Portier had heard my call.

Was it possible that the energies of depleted souls nourished some divine cannibal? Though I had put the questions of Portier's nature . . . and mine . . . aside in the daylight, I could not ignore evidence. If I could but see more of Portier's writing . . .

"Did the wizard say if all the Stones have the same facets as Orythmus?" I said. "Doubling, skewed, and all."

"He said they did. Should we set up the demonstration for Rhymus? Though nothing you've taught me seems to use the facets at all." Xanthe's sunny presence dipped into cloud again.

"It would be helpful," I said. "The more I know, the sooner I can teach you to influence dreams." The sooner I could learn what in the name of all gods was going on.

"Oh, yes!"

It made sense that the optical properties of the three would be the same if they were cut from the same larger piece. Yet the facets differed in shape and angle, which must also affect their behavior.

We set up the candle and the thread and she turned the crystal this way and that. Indeed, similar facets caused similar effects. We even found a *strengthening* face that bolstered the candle flame until it was as vivid as a sunbeam, which reminded Xanthe that Orythmus had one as well.

On this day, at the least, Rhymus's seeing face showed the past.

The candle stood on a wide table in a room that could only be the library at Pradoverde. My own books were among those on the shelves. Two heads were bent together over a book on the table. One head was my own . . . the ragged mass of black hair untamed. My clawed hand rested on the table, an abomination. The other person wore a thick braid, the escaping curls sporting all the hues of autumn. Her small, capable hand turned the page. From time to time she turned her head to me—the one who was sitting with her listening to her read, not the one who looked down on her from this unbridgeable distance. And once . . . ah, gods . . . her two fingers touched my disgusting hand ever so gently, my nerveless hand that could feel naught but the memory of agony. And she did not turn away.

Xanthe and I worked long hours after that. But the seeing haunted me all through it. And never had I such a struggle as on that long night in the sorcerer's hole. My body ached. My spirit was desolation. Though I dared not call her name aloud, I bellowed it through the aether with all the hunger of a blind man longing for light. *Anne!*

CHAPTER 25

MANCIBAR

Over the next tenday, I explored both Stones. Whereas the spellwork of Orythmus gave its wielder the power of physical command, Rhymus's allowed one to induce laughter, weeping, or jealous rages, fright or devotion.

I chose Xanthe's gifts with caution, certainly more than I'd given the first. The command of silence was like an iron ball chained to my foot. She decided I was too curious, which distracted me from proper service. Thus, never was I allowed to hear any voice but hers. Never did I visit any part of the palace but her apartments and my dismal abode. I became a slave in truth and began to believe my bold deception had fallen flat. Jacard seemed in no hurry to use me. Neither he nor Xanthe spoke of Portier. Imagining my friend's state was all that prevented me from screaming halt to the masquerade.

Xanthe had begun to attract friends of her own from among the courtiers and city dwellers that frequented the palace. She glowed with youth and ambition like some lighthouse set out to pierce Mancibar's dark nights, and her strange history was a source of fascination. Aristos flock to centers of power like rabbits to gardens.

"I met three great lords last night, magus," she said one evening, as she fed me hard bits of winter apples.

"And did you bewitch them, or did you drive them mad with itching and sneezing as you did with Edane Mintierra last tennight?"

Hearing of her conquests, I felt quite like some mendicant brother along the pilgrim road, listening to Cult ladies describe sins in which he could have no part. Which made no kind of sense. I'd spent my whole life alone. Why did I feel as if I were shriveling into nothing?

"Mintierra would not keep his hands to himself. I choose whose hands will investigate me further, and it was not to be that foul-breathed scarecrow. And these were much greater lords, a consiliar and two warlords. Or that is what they would have been called in Maldeon's court. I cannot keep the modern ranks quite straight."

Well, of course she could. There was nothing of relevance to her ambition that she failed to learn the moment she was aware of it.

"Consiliar Ageric was dashing. Younger than you and quite merry. He whispered charming things in my ear all through supper tonight. His tunic was woven gold. Delicious! He's having me a cape made of the same material. He is quite exasperated with Iaccar and his grave robbing."

She fetched another bite. *Grave robbing* . . . She had mentioned that before. I considered my words carefully.

"But of course this consiliar would not elaborate on what he meant by an accusation of grave robbing," I said.

I had to let Xanthe talk as she would. Asking pointed questions ensured a topic would be closed off for days or my ears would be stoppered. Demonstrating frustration led inevitably to a lashing. Yet reticence was the worst offense of all. It was a most refined torture.

"Perhaps he said grave *filling*." She cocked her head and poked the wad of bread in my mouth. "Iaccar thinks to raise a legion of ghosts to conquer Sabria. Mayhap he slays the young men who go missing to fill his ranks."

I near choked. Likely a good thing my mouth was stuffed, as she took no note of it.

A legion of the dead. Fodder for the one who devoured souls. Was that Jacard's play? Imagining himself serving the Souleater in return for . . . what? Forgiveness for his own crimes? High rank in Dimios's icy demesne? Power to afflict the living?

The stuff of fables and preaching. Stories to induce submission to unreason.

Yet, inevitably, talk of myth and mystery took me back to Portier in his horror: *You are the Daemon*. Not *a* daemon, but *the* Daemon.

I forced my attention back to Xanthe. Hurry meant mistakes. Distraction risked exposure. Four years it had taken me last time.

". . . most tedious. As the moon wanes, Mancibar becomes plugged tight as a bunghole. What charming gentlemen wish to risk falling prey to the haunts for want of a hunting party? Only Iaccar is bold enough to feast through the dark of the moon. Once the moon grows back again, so do entertainments. It's all to do with Iaccar's ghost rites."

Ghost was an entirely unspecific term. It might refer to a spectre—focused energy left behind by the dying, like sun glare after closing one's eyes. Spectres could take on the appearance of the dead but bore no soul or life. True ghosts were troubled spirits—lingering memories, one might say—that manifested themselves more in feeling than in sight, around battlefields or sites of trauma or murder.

Souls that had crossed the Veil were a different matter. Only necromancers could give a revenant soul physical substance—as little as a filmy vapor or as much as a solid apparition. But that required an opening in the barrier that separated living and dead, complex, intricate spellwork. Only Temple Readers—those few who weren't devout cheats—could reach across the Veil without magic. While in a trancelike state, they could locate a dead soul and give some assessment of its state—its progress toward Heaven's gates, they claimed.

The Jacard I knew was no Temple Reader, and he could no more work the complexities of necromancy than an infant, even with some progression in these two years past. Yes, he could pour the raw power of his Seeing Stone into an enchantment. And he had escaped with his uncle's journals and the nireals, which could lure a revenant spirit into a human body, instruments that had taken me years to perfect. But Anne and I had shut down the tear in the Veil that allowed a soul's true passage. Was that why he wanted me here?

"Surely, ghosts—even cadres of them—are but children's frights," I said. "I understood this was a cultured city."

"Ageric says that Mancibar was once the most civilized place in the Southern Kingdoms. The old prince bought himself sculptors and artists, and singers and dancers who performed every night of the year. At winter solstice the prince and his favorites would progress from one great house to another for a month or more, taking mummers and jugglers, actors and magicians, each pageant outdoing the last. Prince Damek himself would don masque and costume!"

She'd gone off in entirely the wrong direction. Unlike Portier, I seemed incapable of steering a conversation where I wanted it to go.

"At the Sabrian court, Iaccar was never known for patronage." In truth, I didn't recall. That life—everything before meeting Xanthe—was becoming so remote as to be someone else's.

Xanthe turned up her nose. "He is constantly putting on grand feasts. But a more dismal host I've never seen. Quareg the Torturer laid a better table, and *his* entertainments were unmatched, if a bit bloody."

"Surely this great lord Ageric does not encourage you to supplant Iaccar. Despite ghosts, and missing young men and women."

" 'Tis only *men* vanish, which is why they're all so ripe for pleasuring just now. A terrible, cruel queen might have great delight ruling over a city of frightened men. Oh, quit your scowling, *Matron* Dante! I was very careful, as you forever warn me. I twisted my face into a ferocious frown and told Ageric I was shocked he dared speak so kindly of the fiend who once ruled Mancibar. 'It borders on treason to our beloved Regent,' I said. He near strangled! He wouldn't have dared stand up just then, lest we all note evidence of his fright on his elegant pantaloons."

What chokehold did Jacard maintain that could so terrify young lords? Night's daughter, I needed to know!

Xanthe sighed and fondled a bite of cold meat. "Yet, dear Ageric was so delightfully handsome and so willing, and I do relish men less grim than you and Iaccar. So I reached under the table and squeezed his leg. My fingers traveled into his garments to places he did not imagine I knew."

"Perhaps he thought it was one of Iaccar's ghosts. . . ."

She giggled. "The ghosts steal your sons or brothers, not your virtue! Indeed my clan mother, Mutiga, would have beat me senseless and shut me in a closet for a month for my bold fingering. Stonekeepers could not lie with any but Maldeon's favorites—and they were always old, ugly men who cared naught but for their own pleasuring."

Xanthe gave up on my supper, already postponed until near middle-night. Humming a cheery valzi, she spun about the room in graceful glee. One might compare her to the painted figures in one of Queen Eugenie's dainty music boxes, save for the words she wove into her melody: "Mutiga, Fadra, and Gisra of the Cold Hands are dead, dead, dead. In the ground they lay. Worms in their eyes, beetles in their thighs, too-ra-li, toor-a-lay, lack-a-day."

She rang for Hosten, and then collapsed on her couch, her face flushed. "The consiliar and I retired to the garden. Ageric sang to me sweetly after. Someday, I must hear *you* sing. . . ."

Smirking, she held out her open palm. "Come, kiss the hand that gives you sustenance, slave. Show me you mean it."

Heat pulsed from her body as I bent over her hand that smelled like fennel, pepper, and good fat. And I remained ignorant of Jacard's purposes.

A FEW MORNINGS LATER AS Xanthe dispensed a last bit of roast lamb for my breakfast, she talked of her latest conquest, a rich landholder named Mercurio de Blase. A tedious man who talked of nothing but dogs and the haunting of the city by the dead prince. His wife was simple and had never before visited the city, so Xanthe had thought it great fun to flatter such a woman with her special and serious friendship, and then invite the husband up to bathe with her. De Blase was older than me, she said, perhaps forty or forty-five, rough and demanding in bed. "I shocked him with a taste of rough bed play. Do you wish to hear about it?"

"We've much work to do if you wish to learn to create illusions, Mistress."

"Such a hard taskmaster you are, magus. You must learn to give all kinds of pleasure." She yanked a fistful of my hair, grown out long enough to grab, and kissed me hard on the mouth.

When I did not respond, she shoved me onto my backside. She paced to the window, then spun round, her eyes glittering at me in a most unhealthy fashion. Dropping my gaze, I arranged Rhymus on the plate where we kept it as we worked.

"We should begin. . . ." My voice croaked as it had when I was sixteen and Salvator insisted I learn what a willing woman could do for a restless, ever-angry youth. My skin pulsed with heat.

I was not made of stone. The lady was beautiful and ripe and had demonstrated a number of times that she was willing. But despite the lack of outdoor labors or other exercise to deflect my body's heat, I could not, would not, consider it. I was far too inexperienced with such matters and had decided early on that the only thing more dangerous than being

Xanthe's enemy was to be her bed partner. The memory of her sister's cold flesh sufficed to cool nature's urgency.

Yet I was no fool, either. Someday my mistress would decide to prove her ultimate domination of me and complicate life beyond imagination.

"No work this afternoon," she said, curling up in a chair, catlike. "Iaccar has begged another audience. His hospitality has its price."

Jacard had been visiting Xanthe more frequently now she demonstrated the use of her Stones. He displayed only friendly interest, even when he brought a request that she not plague his palace guards with paralyzed arms, stoppered ears, or itching loins. But he seemed increasingly nervous. Behind his back or elsewise out of the lady's view, his fingers clenched and clawed. His nails were chewed to the quick. He would never allow Xanthe to become a threat to him.

"Tell me about the Regent, my lady. I live a hermit's life here. What kind of ruler is he? Has the Stone of Reason given him enlightenment? Or even talent? Your skills already surpass any that I ever saw of his."

Xanthe was pleased at that. She was a quick study and knew it. Of course, she created no magic and provided no power for binding sorcery. She wielded spells already worked, an entirely different skill.

"Was he truly wretched? He claims you corrupted his workings and made him look a fool to elevate yourself."

"He needed no help to look the fool." I told her of some of Jacard's more ridiculous failures, finishing with the occasion he set out to rid Queen Eugenie's gaming rooms of ants and instead introduced a plague of rats.

"It was you! *You* did it, you arrogant shitheel!" snarled the Regent of Mancibar, who had slipped in quietly in the middle of my account. Xanthe did not stop laughing, though Jacard's face grew redder and his breath came faster. Quicker than he could cast any spell, he whipped the back of his hand across my face, knocking me flat.

"It's time we put an end to this farce, lady. I've watched this jackleg teach you juggler's antics while storing up knowledge for himself, assuming he is even capable of reading the Maldeona, as you call them. I propose we put him to the test."

I fingered the painful gash his rings had left in my cheek. Jacard was still trying to have it both ways. Either I was incompetent, which saved his pride, or I was devious, which left him my moral superior and Xanthe's defender and protector. In either case, the lady Xanthe had best hire someone to watch her back.

"Never touch my slave, Iaccar!" A furious Xanthe descended upon me, not to lift me up or examine my bloody cheek, but to swipe some of my blood onto her palm so she could wave it in Jacard's face. "You've damaged him."

"Let us learn if your slave has given you all to which you have a right. He's taught you how to make a shopkeeper dream of vanishing pennies, but has he taught you of living dreams—scenes you can play out in your rooms here, the rooms of your friends or your *enemies*?"

"Living dreams!" Xanthe glared at me. "Tell me, magus, why do I play with night sweats if I can do such things?"

Xanthe had about driven the city wild with nightmares and bouts of frenzied bed play. But we both knew Rhymus could do more.

"We were to begin work on illusions today, if you recall," I said. "As I've told you from the beginning, the lore of the Stones is new to me, and I present what I find, as I find it . . ."

Truly it was only the Stones' greater purposes that yet eluded me. To see them dangling from the necks of these two set my teeth grinding. The three together had enabled the Holy Imperator Altheus to bring down an empire fifty times his strength. They didn't belong with a half-crazed serving girl or a sneaking, murderous, bumbling coward.

". . . but certainly, Mistress, have Regent Iaccar teach you what he will. What he can."

Jacard, all pleasantries again, gathered Xanthe and faced her to the window, sweeping his arm toward the spreading landscape. "Touch your Stone of dreams, my lady, and repeat the words I tell you. . . ."

One hand over hers and one hand on the Stone glinting on his own breast, he recited a sequence of Aljyssian words—spell keywords. With each word, the enchantment built—a surge in the aether that brightened the sunlight and twisted it in knots. My teeth ached with the pent power.

With a concussive release, the spellwork shattered the glass of Xanthe's windows. Balls of searing brightness bounced on her carpet. Flames sprang from the fireballs, soon roaring, searing skin, charring fabrics. All false. Illusion. But the thick smoke set us coughing, until it curled into storm clouds that obscured the painted ceiling. A cloudburst pummeled us with rain. Billows of steam shot upward as the cold raindrops hissed on glowing ashes. My garments flapped wetly in the wind, and then froze, as a frigid blast whirled snow. My teeth rattled like a dancers' heels.

"Too cold!" shouted Xanthe, squealing with excitement. "But I love the rain . . . warm rain! And fire! Could I truly set the stables afire? How I'd love to surprise that rude stableman and his ever-sniveling boy! Or houses . . . Those women who think I'm too stupid to see their scorn. Their men . . . oh, yes!"

Jacard shouted the words she needed to shift the snow to rain again. More words warmed the shower and yet more quieted the wind.

This was no weatherworking. But vivid illusions could drive men or horses mad. Though no man in Jacard's stable claimed my loyalty, Devil did. Xanthe's vengeful lust warned me yet again. I dared not delay protecting the people and things Xanthe must not know.

I'd had no chance to do any spellwork of my own in these rooms. I was never out from under her eye. There was certainly no opportunity to stop and lay out a spell enclosure between here and the sorcerer's hole. And even if I could get free, Hosten spent his nights on a chair outside my door.

But Xanthe's chamber rippled with so many enchantments at that moment, the captain could never trace one more. Jacard continued to spew one word of binding after another for her to use. He and the lady were wholly engaged in their play.

There was no place for fear when working magic. So I throttled misgiving and dragged my staff around me, charring a circle in the thick carpet. Then I pulled out Anne's pendant that I'd taken to wearing inside my shirt and laid it at my feet. A cup of water from the table to draw in what I had learned at a well in Kadr, a red silk towel, my own self, and vivid memory yielded keirna enough to work a small spell that I could trigger with a thought. I'd spent so many nights considering it that it settled into its pattern very quickly.

The resulting spell was brutal. Entirely a last resort. Now to attach it to . . . something. I must be able to access it quickly, so that only a smat of power would bind it, no matter pain, illness, or confusion. But what did I have that Xanthe could not take from me? She could burn my staff on any day or force me to go naked. Using Anne's pendant or my own flesh, especially as I was the focus of the spell already, introduced risks of backlash or simple failure. *Gods . . . hurry. . . .*

Jacard's flow of command words shifted their illusion back to rain.

Thunder rolled and lightning set off more fires that consumed chairs and cushions and melted silver cups . . . only to move on and show them intact, undamaged. Silver . . .

I touched the band about my neck. It had been a part of me for so long I rarely thought of it. With a surge of my own power, I bound the spell and linked it to my collar. And breathed relief. Xanthe would never get Anne's name from me, nor any other secret that might betray her or my brother or Portier. To every fragment of the universe, I prayed I would never need use it.

Quickly I returned the pendant to my shirt and erased the circle by starting a small fire that charred a large splotch of rug. Unlike the illusion fires, it did not heal itself when the two perpetrators moved on to other pleasures. I extinguished it with the red towel.

As I dumped a carafe of water around the area to further mask the residue of my work, strange shapes emerged from the thunderstorm. Nightmare creatures of slime and rot, they looked like casualties of a century-old shipwreck rising from the seas outside the window and slogging toward us through the shattered panes, across the soggy carpets, and through the walls. Ridiculous. And yet . . .

Striding through the windowpanes, among the monstrosities yet not with them, was the young man from my visions. His long coat and gold and gray hair floated in the illusory wind. Head thrown back, he let the false rain splatter his face. When he reached the wall, he glanced over his shoulder and waved his hand, as if summoning me to his side. It was all I could do to stay still. But he passed through and out of sight with the rest, trailing the faintest scent of rosemary and ash. What was he? No illusion—of that I was certain.

In part to shake off the odd compulsion to pursue him through the solid wall, in part to rescue my position in Xanthe's esteem, I laid my mind to Jacard's enchantment. Illusions were relatively simple enchantments, a projection of a thought image into onlookers' minds. They could appear as a veil overlying reality or substitute for the surrounding truth. Either way, nothing of nature was altered. They were ephemera . . . the scent of supper cooking, the day's heat lingering in a stone wall, the recitation of a story.

For Jacard and Xanthe's collaboration, the true measure of success was not the illusion's elaboration, but its length and intensity. A huge flow of power was required to maintain it. Jacard had learned to summon the joined power of his gem and Xanthe's into his work—a triumph, to be sure. But it spewed forth unshaped and undirected, like water rushing through a pipe. And evidently, he still couldn't create anything beyond illusion. Naught of this storm would remain once they stopped, no speck of moisture, nothing melted, burnt, or broken.

In my mind I touched a spell pattern I had created from one of Rhymus's spell threads and gave it a name, a simple word of binding. Then, with reckless hope that Xanthe would respect skill more than humility, I ripped Jacard's spellwork apart. The convulsion in the aether near knocked me insensible. But in Xanthe's chamber, all was silence and stillness. Not a hailstone or raindrop remained. All was dry and tidy. I sat on a large footstool that covered the only destruction, the sodden, charred spot where I had worked true magic.

Xanthe and Jacard whirled on me.

"You make it hard for her, Regent Iaccar," I said as if bored. "My mistress is much more accomplished than you give her credit for. As always you just cannot see."

I crossed the room and knelt humbly at Xanthe's feet. "If you will touch Rhymus, good lady, imagine what you have just seen, and whisper the single word I shall give you instead of the catalogues of words this gentleman provides . . ."

A smile teased at Xanthe's perfect lips as she bent close to whisper in my ear. "You play dangerous games, magus. Dangerous."

I nodded and gave her the key I had bound to Rhymus's illusion spell, *Praesti*.

"Now, lady, as we have done before," I said. "Simply consider whatever changes you wish and they will manifest in the illusion."

She fingered Rhymus and whispered the word, and in an instant we were engulfed in another illusory storm. Not an intrinsically better illusion than the one Jacard had wrought, but far simpler to evoke and manipulate.

"Magnificent!" she shouted over the rolling thunder. "I was beginning to fear my power would be too tedious to use. Why would you want to burden me with so many words, Regent Iaccar? So I might depend on you alone to remember them? I think I've chosen the better teacher, though perhaps he's not so honest with me as he might be."

"You're a fool, damoselle!" Jacard snapped. "Let the daemon dole out his tidbits, and you can lap them up like some kitchen dog, but you'll never wield true power at his hands. He'll see you dead as he saw your sister. As he saw the great men who rivaled his power in the past. But not me. There shall be a new order in earth and Heaven, and you can either join me and be a part of it or suffer the fate of my enemies."

His boot met my belly with all the hate and fury he'd stored up since his first day as my adept. Even as I curled up retching, I was satisfied.

Xanthe's storm ended as abruptly as it had begun. A heavy silence fell, marred only by my choked heaves as I forced my breakfast to stay down. My mistress knelt beside me in a swirl and swish of satin.

I glanced up. Jacard was gone, but so were Xanthe's smiles and excitement. Spider fingers tickled my spine and I scrambled to my knees.

"You've held back, slave." Her menace pressed on my gut like a spear's point.

What were the right words? Another apology would surely enrage her further.

"You must choose," I said between choking spasms. "You're not the ignorant serving girl he imagines, but a woman clever, shrewd, and determined. Consider, lady. If I teach you all I know in an instant, then what am I worth to you? I wish to live. I desire knowledge—and power. If I didn't, I'd not be here or be able to do the things I do. If I am to be your slave, as I have been, I'll do the least that I must to avoid punishment and continue living. If I were to be your hireling, however, and be granted some measure of freedom, then we could bargain like free people for what I will share with you. If neither plan is to your liking, you can join Dimios the Souleater in the frozen netherworld—or trust your Stones and your fortune to Iaccar, whichever suits you best."

My mistress didn't like a second man serving her an ultimatum in the same hour. She carefully laid a command of immobility on me and proceeded to take her turn at my already throbbing cheek. On this day she used her shoe. Once she had vented her displeasure for a sufficient time, sufficient at least for my free-flowing blood to leave puddles and trails on her fine carpet, she burst into exuberant laughter.

"Oh, you are a fine one, magus. What fire burns in you! I have the power of your life, of your reason, of your sight, of your soul, and you presume to bargain with me like some peddler in the marketplace. 'No, no, girl. Two coppers for the fish or I'll let it rot!' I knew I was wise to throw in my lot with you and not with that stupid, greedy oaf and his ghost dances. He is mad to get his hands on the Maldeona. But we'll not let him touch them, shall we? Me and my hireling."

And while I lay there unable to move—from the beating, her command, or sheer astonishment that she had apparently accepted my bargain—she licked the blood from my lips, a kiss not filled with any lust for me, but for power and magic and all that they could give her. Then she rang her bell and my jailer herded me stumbling, trembling, back to my hole.

Along the way I did not take my eyes from the sunlight and the glories of the world beyond the palace windows. I feared, when given time to consider, that she would never let me out again.

Hosten shoved me into the hole roughly, as if my battered face were testimony of some violation of our mistress. But it was neither the beating nor the confrontation with Jacard nor the postponed shakes from my risky spellworking that disturbed me most as the dark, silent hours crawled past. It was the young man with the radiant face and the gray and gold hair. He had no place in Jacard's illusion. I had seen him in de Cuvier's dream of Rhymus and the world's ruin. He had appeared in my own dreams on this long road, but I was coming to think he was neither illusion nor dream. It was easier to consider myths, legends, and impossibilities in the dark.

This time I knew the meaning of his enigmatic smile. Recognition. He understood me . . . and the fear Portier's beliefs and warnings had buried deep inside me in those places thought and reason could not enter. The tall young man had tried to warn me, too. *Thou'rt my worthy companion,* he had said in my dream at the shepherds' village, *stronger than you know. It matters not that you were born in the dark to another fate.*

This time I understood the scents that always accompanied his presence. Families sprinkled rosemary in graves to keep insects away. And on his deathbed, my father had quoted a bit of Temple script: *And so will come the last battle of the War for Heaven and guardianship of the Living Realm. The Righteous Defender will rise from the ashes. . . .*

But it was the entirety of the passage I could not shake off. *The Righteous Defender will rise from the ashes and battle the Daemon.* Not *a* daemon. *The* Daemon. The one portrayed on the Uravani bridge. The Daemon of the Dead.

Anne

CHAPTER 26

27 DUON
MATTEFRIESE

"We've ridden ten hours today," I said. "Perhaps we should call a halt."

As the border town of Mattefriese grew ever larger on the dusty horizon, Ilario drooped in the saddle, his face pinched. "A real bed would be a boon divine," he said. "But I can go on."

The brevity of his answer and the tightness of its delivery reminded me yet again that no matter what he claimed in the morning, Ilario was yet half-invalid. The speed we had made since leaving Merona had cost him dearly. But we'd spotted Temple hounds at every stop and dared not linger—a bailiff among the guards at town gates, servitors patrolling markets, even Readers lounging outside the deadhouse walls, eyeing strangers.

"Be sensible," I said. "I'll need my hero later."

"We should stay here an extra day. He needs to build up his reserves again." Rhea shifted uncomfortably in the saddle. The poor girl must have a case of saddle sores for the ages. Yet she never asked for respite. If Ilario rode, she rode.

The world felt gray and bleak, stretched thin, as if the cool, sunny weather were but a facade of no more depth than a painted screen. The travelers on the road seemed but players in a mime, their speech meaningless jabbering. I'd not been able to sleep the previous night for the dread that infused the aether, weighing on my shoulders like a cloak of lead. Yet

I must have done, for I'd heard dreadful screaming that neither Rhea nor Ilario had.

I offered Ilario a waterskin, but he shook his head. "When we stop next."

Rhea hunched her shoulders and eyed the jagged ridges spiked from the dry country, before dropping her gaze to the hard-packed road. She had never been so far from the pastures and vineyards of Challyat and Louvel. I had tried to explain what we faced when she awkwardly broached the idea of accompanying us. But for Ilario's vigorous encouragement—a measure of his illness, I thought—I would have left her behind. He had worried that she would reap the whirlwind for his disappearance.

Ilario had dispatched a brief note to Eugenie, telling her he'd met a young woman who enjoyed travel. Eugenie was not to worry unless he decided he needed rescuing and sent her his crocodile charm. He vowed to return before her child was born in the spring. A risky promise, I feared.

The streets of Mattefriese blistered our feet through our shoes. Most shoppers had retired to somewhere shadier. We separated, Ilario off to seek beds for the night, while Rhea and I prowled the torpid market for food supplies and cooler garments. Now we didn't need cloaks, Rhea's green dress and apron spoke clearly of the Temple, and Ilario's tall frame and pale hair were too noticeable. I could do nothing about his height, but bulkier clothes and a good hat would help.

Rhea had proved worth beyond her care for Ilario. She was expert at finding good food for little money, whether picking through lean markets or speaking to hostlers about what might be found in their kitchens when they claimed their pots were emptied. We'd no time or resources to cook, so we ate what we carried. Ilario, though one of the wealthiest men in Sabria, had neither coin nor weapon with him, and my purse was not bottomless.

We found nothing suitable laid out. *"Meste,"* I said to a wrinkled Pytharian woman, touching my brow to thank her for her help.

She crowed. "Sabrian lady knows Pythari politeness!"

"Not so much a lady." I felt like a rag sale.

"Come, lady, friend." She motioned Rhea and me inside her shabby wagon. "More."

It was dim and stuffy under the canvas roof. The old woman's gold bangles clinked as she pulled items from an ancient trunk. First, a skirt of rust-colored leather. Rather, the garment hung like a skirt but was split and sewn together in the middle like trousers. She pointed out a slit pocket in the skirt where one could sheath a knife. *"Parfeta!"* I said, and pulled my zahkri from my own slit pocket.

She grinned and held the skirt to Rhea's waist. Tall and sturdy, the woman said she'd worn it when she rode the plains with her brothers chasing kingbucks. Ground-up kingbuck horn would make a man virile and a woman fertile. About my neck, she hung a leather thong with three brass disks and a bit of horn dangling from it, then waved off payment. "No coin. Make you luck."

We rifled her trunk and found white shirts, embroidered in red and green. Rhea gasped like a child on her birthday when she found a filmy scarf of deep rose to keep the sun off when we reached the desert. It drew out a youthful bloom in her cheeks. In friendly rivalry, we snatched up scarves and shawls, and a light mantle and woven cap of braided scraps that might do for Ilario. I pulled out a fine old-fashioned sword and a scabbard tooled with eagles. I glanced up, and the woman nodded. This meeting had been more than lucky.

She bit our coins with brown teeth and laughed in delight. *"Oistra en chiano."* Go, in joy.

"And you, Mistress," I said.

The westering light stretched across the market, as we stowed our purchases on our pack horse. Ilario trudged slowly down the alley. Sweat beaded his forehead.

"We found you a cooler mantle," I said when he joined us. "And a hat to mask your hair. And something else you'll need." I patted the sword hilt, tucked into loops on the saddle.

He raised his right arm and made a sweeping gesture, only to let loose a muted, "Ow. My physician best have a poultice ready. But the gift, little seahorse"—he rested his heavy head atop mine—"is dear. Without one—and without my captain—I've felt naked."

I knew that. Every time we glimpsed Temple green, his hand brushed his hip. And every night he offered prayers for gallant Calvino de Santo, who had no other family to mourn him.

As we settled our belongings in a smoky little garret in the nastiest little inn I'd ever walked into, Ilario passed me two papers, one rolled and tied with string, one a scrap scarce large enough to fold, sealed with resin. "I have a gift for you as well. Care of one Marga Tasso."

"You found her! Oh, my beloved chevalier."

"Ah, for that, dear Ani." A wistful note was belied by his mocking bow.

I laughed but could scarce rip the packets open, my hands trembled so.

Lady Anne,

The man who offers to take my message frets to be off. Travelers are rare, so I must use this chance quick-like or risk waiting a month or more.

It is a sorry fact that Dante and I have parted ways. When we stumbled in here, sorely thirsty, my brother got himself into a bad sichuation, trespassing the law. He did no harm, but our difficulties required my staying here, while Dante was sent away. John Doon accompanied him, and as far as I know, they took our original course south from here to Karabayngor. I do not have the highest confidence in John Doon. I caught him traffiking with two unpromising fellows who were following us on the road.

Worse are the tales I hear from this traveler and the settlers here of a petty prince to the south. He is a sorcerer who calls himself the Regent of Mansibar and wears a great green gem about his neck on a silver chain. There are bad goings-on in Mansibar, haunts and bloodletting and vanishings. That sounds like doings that my brother might get himself mixed up in. Powerful as he may be, Dante might have need of some reliable help. It chafes me greatly that I cannot go. But I have given my bond for his life. I would not be much help to him to put a price on his head, if he were not really in danger after all!

I know not what to recommend. I must admit to having a bad feeling, but you ween more of sorcery and mysteries than I.

Here's a map of our route with sources of good and bad water marked. Gods willing, my little brother will be safely on his way home soon with the answer to his mystery in hand.

Ever your servant, Andero
at Hoven in Kadr

Haunts, bloodlettings . . . and Dante with no help but Ilario's scraggy little manservant. Certainly I knew why Ilario had kept on a servant who despised him, a necessity of Ilario's lifetime masquerade. But in such danger . . .

Ilario had collapsed onto the wide pallet, his head propped on his fist. Waiting. I passed the message on to him and read the second. . . .

Lady Anne,

Troubling news. It is said that a cruel sorcerer now partners the Regent of Mansibar and holds "a beautiful lady of strange history" in thrall. This sorcerer comes out only now and again to fright the citizins, burning houses and shops for the pleasure of it. They name him daemon. I don't like to believe it is Dante.

Find me at Hoven, and I will tell all I know. Again I urge caushun. Though otherwise good and generous, these people will slay any who work magic here. I am under heavy suspicion still and cannot leave without trouble. I await more news before I can judge what course to take. In short, I don't know what to do, being unaccustomed to sorcerus adventures.

Andero

Fear settled in my bones like a leaden mantle. How had Dante gone from *feared to work magic* as Andero told in his first letter to burning houses and shops, holding ladies in thrall, and frightening the citizens of a remote principality?

"John Deune?" said Ilario. "By all saints! He's never traveled more than fifty kilometres from Merona. And he loathes Dante almost as much as he loathes me."

"You don't think he'd betray Dante . . . sell him to Jacard . . . or the Temple?"

Ilario shook his head. "He's never done me true ill, but you could rebuild Pradoverde with what he's stolen from me all these years. And he's dogged as a hungry goat. If he gets something in his mind . . . Trafficking with unsavory men following them? Maybe that's why we've Temple bailiffs and servitors everywhere we step."

"You need to sleep, lord. I've your digestive, and I should examine your urine." Rhea forever startled me, quiet as she was and prone to shrinking into corners. How had she ever summoned the nerve to seek me out?

"Egad." Ilario sighed deeply. "Here I'm bedding down with two lovely women, who have the combined intelligence to surpass that of the Royal Library, and my most exciting invitation is one to pass along my piss. Doesn't seem right."

As Rhea pulled out her medicine box, passed Ilario a glass beaker, and mixed her medicines, I took Andero's messages to the grimy window and tried to read beyond the ink. I could not believe Dante would ever partner with Jacard. Yet he couldn't be playing *agente confide* again. He'd never be able to fool Jacard a second time. What made Andero willing to believe Dante's connivance in these crimes? Had he witnessed Temple murders, perhaps, or explosive destruction? A new fear began to creep in with the rest. Dante was so angry, so bitter. . . .

DEMESNE OF ARABASCA

Andero's map was invaluable. Five days out from Mattefriese we came upon the place he had noted as *shepherd village, good water, hospitable folk.* Indeed we'd scarce come in sight of the place when three elders came out to greet us, offering a bed for the night and a feast in exchange for "tales of the wide world." Hovels of stone and sod, bony faces, and the bleak, rocky plain spoke of grinding hardship. But their eager smiles and the bright weaving of the elders' worn capes said there was more to be found here than poverty. We could all use a bit of cheer.

The letters drove me hard. I'd spent half the time since Mattefriese looking over my shoulder and half the time seeking Dante in the aether. His presence felt ever more remote.

Ilario had begun to practice with his sword in the evenings when we halted, but could not work half an hour until collapsing.

Rhea fretted that Ilario was foolish to push himself so and asked was he trying to undo all her work. On the previous night she had snapped entirely, yelling about why in the Pantokrater's creation were we chasing after a devil mage. She was very near tears. It struck me that the plain, brilliant healer could easily be infatuated with the gallant chevalier. I debated whether to ask him, but it seemed wrong to talk about her behind her back. She had proven herself trustworthy.

"We poor travelers would be pleased to share your hospitality," Ilario said, bowing to those who'd come out to greet us. "We've had good reports of your village from a friend who passed this way sometime after the turn of the year.

"Dead or living?" said one of the women.

"Living," said Ilario, matching her serious demeanor.

"Three of them, there would have been," I blurted.

"Ah, you speak of the sorcerer, the giant, and the blind thief," said a short man with eyes as bright blue as the weft of his cape. "All living. At first we thought the sorcerer was dead, and his companions just didn't know. But then he saved Jono and his boy, and, of course, dead men cannot give life. It was beyond our understanding. Likely old Otro saw more, but he spoke to none save the sorcerer. Come, let's see to your beasts and brew tea while the women roast a kid. Spring winds are sharp so near the stars."

Their casual talk of death and life was curious, and I wanted to ask why they thought Dante dead, and what this Otro might have seen, and who was the *giant* and who the *blind thief.* But I could not meet such hospitality with rudeness. We sat in a crowded, overwarm house drinking tea for two hours, hearing the tally of every person in the village, those who were present and those who were out tending sheep. They told us of their flocks and weaving and dyes.

In return, Ilario introduced himself as a wounded soldier, myself as his sister, and Rhea as his physician who had recommended the desert air for his healing, as near truth as could be spoken. Then he smoothly diverted the conversation, asking about He Who Wanders the Stars, who was so often mentioned in their talk.

I'd listened carefully to all the names of those present. Otro was not among them. I leaned to the quiet woman who sat next to me. "Your elders thought my friend, the mage, was dead. I worry that he may be ill. This Otro sounds like one who sees deeply. Where could I find him?"

"Otro wanders," she said. "He could be here or there, on the land or among the stars. If your spirit draws him, he'll come."

"Is he a holy man, then?"

"Some say."

Not so helpful. But she described Dante's companions for me. Andero, a giant man. And, curiously, the *blind thief* was John Deune. "The thief did not see us. Spoke as if we were not here. Thought us too stupid to see him pack away the blanket we lent him. The sorcerer saw more with his ears than did the thief with his working eyes. And more with his heart."

"Exactly so." I could scarce speak. Only Portier had ever believed me about Dante's heart.

The headman then proceeded to introduce us to the rest of the villagers as friends of the blind healer who had traveled through the village two months before. "Though Mage Talon was a great and noble personage and clearly beloved of the gods, he labored mightily through a night and a day to save the lives of two of our own. In his service, the giant wrestled the cruel spirits that tormented Jono while the enchantments were being done. And even the thief obeyed the healer's direction that night, keeping the fire lit to chase the dark away. Always will friends of the healer be welcome here."

Talon. I had to smile. Dante continually scoffed at the adventures of the beggar who became the councilor of a king. But only after I'd read aloud an hour or two.

We stayed later than we intended in that shabby, sweltering room, talking of weather, of the measure of the sky, and of the varied lands we'd traveled in fact or in story. As the evening grew late, and the smoke of the elders' pipes thick, I returned to Dante's story. "Why," I asked the blue-eyed headman, Ertan, "did you say Mage Talon was so clearly beloved of the gods? Sadly, that would not be the judgment he would put on himself."

The elder nodded seriously. "Then you must tell him, so that he will understand the wonder of his life. It is because the guardians left us so long ago, and speak to us no more. We have learned that when comes one who cannot hear our foolish noise, why, he is one to whom the guardians speak. And when comes one who cannot see, then that is one to whom the guardians will show themselves. It tells us that the guardians and He Who Wanders the Stars live, even though they live with us no longer."

"I'll tell him," I said. "But why have your gods—guardians—abandoned you?"

He shook his head, sadly. "We know not. Our ancestors must have offended them terribly. The guardians lived with us from the Beginnings, and roamed with us across the plains, teaching us to hunt and fish. We gave them honor, with dancing and stories and always the first kill of the hunt, and they in turn brought the rains when it was dry, and made us strong and enduring. But they began to bicker among themselves and would not tell us their arguments and visited only rarely. Some said they were jealous of us—which seemed unlikely. But when came the unending winds, and the mighty rivers dried up and the land withered, they sent no help, so that our people withered also, until we are as you see us. We've heard rumors of holy ones who've taken on the duties of the daemons, but they've not come here."

Seldom had I heard such grief expressed so simply.

"Their story is very like our tales of the Daemon War for Heaven," said Ilario as we walked out to the house that had been vacated for us. "The angels fought among themselves about whether to tell humankind of our place in the Pantokrator's heart, for Dimios and his fellows believed us not worthy to share the gifts of Heaven. But, of course, we of the Cult"—he glanced at Rhea, walking on his other side—"believe that Ianne, the first of the Saints Reborn, stole Heaven's fire and brought it to the Living Realm, incurring the particular wrath of Dimios forever after. If ever I should encounter Ianne Reborn, I shall speak to him about this place."

He squeezed my arm. Though I knew what he believed of Portier—and what I had come to believe—I wasn't ready to accept that other men or women were reborn to help the sorry world. For certain there were not enough of them. Nor was I ready to accept that some fallen angel ate the souls of the dead. Though, indeed, Portier, and my sister, and Dante had shown me there were many truths beyond science.

Rhea stayed late talking to the women. With only a few words on her part, she drew them into telling everything about the patterns in their weaving.

While Ilario slept, I could not. Instead, I wandered to the top of a low rise and sat to test the aether yet again. The stars were sharp and brilliant in the moonless sky, the air as pungent as fresh lemons.

"He Who Wanders has swept his house this night. Expecting guests is he, do you think?"

I near leapt from my skin, brushing the solid body sitting beside me. But I knew whose the rasping voice had to be.

"You're Otro," I said.

"Aye. And you follow the Daemon's road. 'Tis a dangerous way, the Way of the Dead. He was sore beset by spirits already. He screams in the night. I think he wrestles them."

"He's often screamed at night since he was blinded." Finn had told me.

"Mmm. This was not fear or grief. For one born in the dark, such terrors are but echoes. No"—his head bobbed against the scattered stars—"he fights for his soul. The Great War has never ended for the daemons."

"Why do you call him daemon? I *know* him. Your own people honor him for this healing he did here. He is human-born." Very human.

"*Daemon* is a very old word," he said, laughing and patting my hand. "You see him. So help him."

"How? Where is he?"

But the old man had gone as quickly and quietly as he'd come, leaving me mystified . . . and more worried than ever.

THE NEXT MORNING, AS WE loaded our packs and bade the villagers farewell, a burly, bearded man in a long tunic and ragged breeches approached me. A small boy hid behind the big man, clinging to him shyly.

"Name's Jono," he said, tugging his forelock. "I be the one what bought the luck-spell. 'Tis my boy, this one here, my only son, and me, that he saved from the madness. I thought I was an ill-luck man, yet he worked magic for the likes of me. . . . There're no words to speak the wonder of it. But I never had no chance to thank him."

"He'll be pleased you're doing well. That's thanks aplenty."

"Nay, words is not enough. You must tell him that Jono has his blood-debt, and if he's ever in need of aught that a poor man could serve, then I will do for him, be it near or far, or tomorrow or fifty years from tomorrow or when we walk the stars with He Who Wanders."

"He will be deeply honored, Goodman Jono."

The shepherd dipped his head in satisfaction. He pulled the boy out from behind him, and nudged him toward me. "Show the lady, boy. My boy, Luz, has summat for the sorcerer. He's a gift with his hand."

The child passed me a small roll of leather, tied with a strip of green rag, and then darted back behind his father.

"You made this?" Expecting some childish scrawl, I gasped when I unrolled the page. A few charcoal lines rendered Dante's features with astonishing likeness. But they reflected so much more. The wariness that years of loneliness had left on him. The little twist in the side of his mouth that was the prelude to his rare gift of a smile. The lines about his eyes that were etched by his longing to see. This was the man I knew.

"Oh, Luz," I said, "this is a precious gift. You've brought my dear friend very close. I'm in *your* debt." I curtsied to the boy as was proper when acknowledging a debt.

The man was pleased, and the boy hid a broad grin in his father's tunic.

Resolute, I shoved aside doubt and rode out with my friends on the Way of the Dead.

Dante

CHAPTER 27

25 DUON
MANCIBAR

"Burn this house?" Surely I was only dreaming that Xanthe had dragged me out of my hole, dressed me in black leather and a purple cape, and taken me down into the city. "Whatever for? Surely there are people inside." Criers had long called middle-night.

Neighbors had begun to gather in front of the fine house, gaping at our guards and torches. And at my collar that shone like a lighthouse beacon. Unlike me, Xanthe was anonymous, hooded and masked, her Seeing Stones tucked under her mantle.

"After sharing my bed this very morning, Lastegiere dared turn his back on me as he pranced through the market with his wife. I want everything he owns in ashes. Show me how to do it." Her voice brooked no quarreling.

"Certainly, Mistress, yes. But having wreaked a deal of unpleasantness on the people of Merona, may I suggest"—I grappled for the right words, the right tone—"that burning the man in his bed teaches no lesson. Whereas if he watches beside that proud wife and his neighbors, to whom he's bragged of his conquest . . . Think of his helplessness. His shame. Make it sudden, so he comes from bed naked. . . ."

She liked that very much. Indeed, the wine merchant burst from his house bare as a shorn sheep, trailing wife, near-grown son, five smaller children, and servants, as Xanthe's green flames devoured the House of Lastegiere.

Vengeance and humiliation became Xanthe's new passion, the price of my bargain with her.

My life had changed since the day I ripped apart Jacard's illusion. Most definitely better, but most definitely riskier. I had to yield her more complete magics, some dangerous, some cruel. But in return for my forthcoming, Xanthe no longer stoppered my ears; I was now allowed to feed myself; and I spent far less time on my knees.

Nights in the palace yet meant confinement in the sorcerer's hole, and I was now locked away before the sun descended behind the red cliffs. Jacard would not hear of me being loose after dark, now my mistress gave me more freedoms. But in daylight hours, when I was not working with Xanthe on the Stones, I was allowed to enjoy a limited array of other amusements: a walk in the gardens, a game of stratagems, or a run down the palace road and back with Captain Hosten. By my reckoning it had been almost two months since I had last breathed the air of the world outside Jacard's house. I began to feel alive again, and not the strange ghost I had become. But then she learned the pleasures of ruin.

In the space of five days, we burnt another manse and flooded the shop of a dressmaker who had failed to sew enough pearls on Xanthe's newest gown. I snarled and let fire belch from my staff to keep the onlookers at bay. She giggled at the spectacles beneath her enveloping cloak. Easy to guess her strategy. The evils would be laid at my feet, not hers.

Indeed, as we walked up to Jacard's house, whispers of *daemon* followed. I stirred up wind to blow sand in their eyes. My own, too, perhaps. Smothering conscience was easy.

Patience, I told myself. *Great gods, patience.* Unraveling the Gautier plot had taken me years, and I'd come very near failure at least once every month. Even such limited freedom as Xanthe allowed meant information, the thing I had lacked most sorely. My participation was necessary. Xanthe did not trust easily.

New activities and better prospects were not enough to banish the wild imaginings that plagued me in the sorcerer's hole. I would have given much for the chance to talk with Portier about why in this godforsaken world he could believe he had stolen fire from Heaven. And why he had named me the Souleater's champion.

But, bathed in Mancibarran sunlight, I recited my own litany. *I am a free man. I choose my own course. I do not believe in fate or destiny or saints or souleaters*. Clearly there were depths of magic I had not plumbed. Someone else beyond the owners of the Seeing Stones could speak in dreams and insinuate prophecies into the mind. I just had to watch, listen, and find out who it was.

THE FIRST DAY XANTHE TOOK me to morning market had me as foolishly excited as Ilario with a new coat. I relished the sights and sounds of commerce, the smells of teas and spices, frying meat and baking bread. I listened to news and gossip, and, whenever it was safe, asked questions.

Both market and city were dismal places, quivering with unspoken anxieties. Sellers snapped at customers. The tables where one might expect people to linger drinking mezhalin, the thick bitter tea favored by the Arothi, were deserted and layered with dirt. Passersby kept eyes averted, not just from *the Regent's lady and the daemon mage*, but from each other.

Even the goods seemed poor quality and cheap, despite the city's fine houses. The faces haggling over rotted fruit and coarse linen were pinched and gray. Save for Xanthe's. Her complexion shone like polished moonlight over shiny beads and bracelets of lead and copper that no Sabrian lady would so much as give her servant. She lavished praises on the sellers and complimented their work and, having no idea what things were worth, was profligate with the coins Jacard had given her.

"A plea, beauteous lady!" A gaunt woman in ragged silk darted from an alley and threw herself at Xanthe's feet. "My son's gone missing last Blood Night, but I've none more of family to feed me, nor to earn me through Ixtador's gates. He was never a cheat. Nor was his dead father. I beg—"

Xanthe laid a gentle hand on her head and whispered in her best imitation of Nessia's sweetness. "Forgive me, sonjeura, but I am only a guest in the Regent's house, scarce more than a prisoner myself. You see my fearsome guardians."

Xanthe's hand masked her giggling as Hosten's men threw the woman back into the alley. Casting sidewise glances at Hosten and me, she brushed off her skirts and continued her mission to a shoemaker's stall.

By our third trip to the market, it didn't surprise me in the least to hear the whispering that the beauteous lady was but a gentle dupe.

"I'VE A QUESTION, MISTRESS," I said to Xanthe as she pawed through her myriad purchases on our return to her apartments one midday. "I've heard that Mancibar was a great banking center under Prince Damek. Caravan money, ship money, all was exchanged and held safe here. And yet you told me it had only a few soldiers and was an easy place for Regent Iaccar to conquer. If a city thrives on money exchanges, that makes no sense. And its location out here at the edge of the wastes, far from the seaports and well off the caravan routes, is wholly illogical."

Xanthe drained a wine cup and draped a deep blue veil around her pale hair. Her cheeks glowed from the wine and the excursion. "Well, of course it is because Mancibar was built upon Sirpuhi of the Red Cliffs. None would dare steal or cheat at Sirpuhi."

"But half the shops are closed. The exchanges deserted. What happened?"

"Iaccar had Nessia speak dream words about a Spider God and his sticky webs, and about trapped children, sucked dry of blood and entrails. Spiders and scorpions appeared everywhere about the town, especially at dusk. Then he spread rumors that Prince Damek and his family and his cronies cheated on their accounts, and that their crimes drew the Spider God to feed on their bloated evils. The caravan dougas and ship captains lost faith and took their business elsewhere . . ."

". . . and so the people killed their prince and his allies." I finished her thought and carried it further. "But the nightmares didn't stop, nor the spiders, I'll vow. Men say it's because the prince yet haunts the city—a sign that this mysterious Spider God is not yet appeased."

"I cannot speak of that. Iaccar made me promise." Xanthe's lips pursed, teasing.

Ghost rites. And people went missing on nights they called Blood Night. Even strong young nobles like her suitor Ageric were terrified to offend the Regent of Mancibar, who perhaps claimed he could appease the Spider God, who perhaps could direct this Spider God's wrath upon those guilty of conspiring with the dead prince.

I stood at Xanthe's expansive windows, relishing the dry air and devouring the sunlit prospect of the gardens and lower town, and the vast fields and plains beyond.

All of this foolery about haunts and spiders masked Jacard's true purpose. He had come south to find the Seeing Stones, a source of magic his uncle had hoped to use to upend nature. I could not believe my glory-hungry adept would use such power solely to create himself a little fiefdom at the edge of the wastes. And this elaboration of dreams and murder to lure Portier and me here for naught but petty vengeance seemed excessive, even for a petty mind like Jacard's.

I could accept his desire to conquer Sabria—the kingdom that had proved beyond his uncle's reach. But why here? He could have chosen the teeming cities deeper in Aroth where the warlike people yearned for past glory and vengeance on Sabria. And I didn't yet understand what made Mancibar's history so powerful that it could protect fortunes, yet keep its legion so small.

Sirpuhi. An Arothi word. In Castelivre, Adept Denys had read it. . . .

"Holy," I blurted, whirling on the lady. "Sirpuhi—Mancibar—is deemed a *holy* place. This is where Altheus, Maldivea's Holy Imperator, was born."

"And where he came to die." Xanthe looped a string of copper disks about her veiled hair and examined the result in a gilt-framed mirror, a gift from Jacard. "The wizard said his master was yet a vigorous man after more than seventy summers. But one day he lay down in a coffin in the navel of the world, closed his eyes, and stopped breathing."

Burial places, holy places, battlefields, ancient vineyards . . . no matter what one believed about gods or heavens, angels or saints, power dwelt in the land. As I had taught Anne, history and rumor and belief were as powerful as sensory truth or mineral deposits when it came to determining the essence of a stream . . . or a place. No wonder my first impression of the city, on a night I was in the throes of exhaustion, had nearly flattened me. The keirna of Sirpuhi must be tremendous.

And Portier believed he was Altheus reborn. Jacard's uncle had believed it, too, and Jacard had secured Portier early on.

Jacard could not possibly think to duplicate the Voilline rite. No matter the innate power of the land and of the Seeing Stones, he was one man alone. And I certainly wasn't going to help him this time. Even Orythmus could not force me to work magic, for spells were bound by the will of the practitioner. And before all, he would have to open the Veil to draw the dead soul.

Dread writhed in my gut. I had been so sure I'd repaired the rip in the Veil at Mont Voilline. Yet, both Anne and I had been exhausted beyond life that night on Mont Voilline, and my ruined eyes had felt like molten iron. . . .

I closed my eyes and pressed a fist against their incessant ache. Creeping doubt opened terrible possibilities. Did Jacard know that Portier had regained his ability to work magic? And if this was a reborn saint's birthplace and deathplace . . . Gods, what would that mean?

"Altheus's enemies feared him," I said softly. "When Maldivea fell, they reduced it to dust and poisoned the land so that the Holy Imperator wouldn't rise from it again."

Xanthe twined a string of coral beads about her fingers. "I don't know about his enemies, but Maldeon certainly feared his rising. His brothers came to Sirpuhi every year hoping to speak to their father, but Maldeon always made excuses. He said those who were dead should stay dead. Now *he* is dead!"

Xanthe beamed as she played with her treasures. She, of course, lived. There was something admirable about the way she so relished every morsel of her renewed life. She reminded me of a kitten. With very sharp claws.

Cultists believed saints could not die unless the work that had brought them back to humankind was done. But even for a Saint Reborn, was the work always successful? Answers, for better or worse, lay so near I could almost taste them.

"I must know what is this great making Iaccar attempts," I blurted. "He's worked elaborate schemes to lure the librarian, a man who is magically interesting, and me, a man who is magically capable, to this particular place. Clearly, Tychemus alone does not yield him the power he needs, and your strength and wit have foiled his attempts to woo the other two Stones from you. Why do the townspeople fear the dark of the moon? What happens on Blood Night?"

The whispers of missing sons and bleeding had struck my ears like poison-tipped arrows, raising festered guilts I did my best to bury. Surely owning Tychemus, Jacard found no need to bleed living victims to feed his power.

"Stop this fretting!" Xanthe wagged her bead-woven finger at me. "Iaccar's games are none of your concern. I'll not let him have you or my jewels. Now, teach me something new."

I knelt to her and bowed my head to the carpet, masking the dread that weighed on my back like a cape of cold lead. "As always, Mistress, I am grateful for your mercy, your favor, and your protection. What shall I look for today?"

"Iaccar told me the Stones can detect enchantments. That's what I want."

Of all things I didn't want her to notice when I worked magic. But she was adamant.

Thus I did as she wished. And I dared not exclude my own enchantments. As expected, she tested the thing on me repeatedly through the next few hours. She promised me a fine reward for the skill.

"And one more thing," she said, dandling a sweet Jacard had sent her. "I know the Stones protect me from Iaccar's knife and the knives of his hirelings, but . . ."

". . . you would feel more comfortable with some additional protections against people like that woman at the market this morning?"

"Yes. That's it."

Rightly so. Jacard was straining to the breaking point. Anxious sorcerers are dangerous, especially with so much power and so little control as he had shown with Tychemus.

I worked her a few small charmed potions that would enhance her ability to fight off sepsis, insects, snakes, and poisons. With more time, I could have provided her a Gautier spell to warn her of many kinds of threats. Anne's sister had worked such a marvel, but it would take days to reconstruct the spell. Xanthe hated me spending time on magic other than the Seeing Stones. She was young and inexperienced and believed her treasures would make her invincible, if I only taught her enough.

Nothing in the world made one invincible. For two-and-thirty years, I had tried.

27 DUON

Two evenings later, we burnt another house. Xanthe gave no reason but that she wished it. No argument of mine could change her mind.

The air was turgid, the falling darkness charged with dread, the voices of the aether disturbed as I had not perceived since Castelivre. Few townspeople even came out to watch as we dismounted and called out the lordling and his family. I could not tell if it was fear of our presence or something else that had the city and its residents awash in panic.

Xanthe's expression was lustful as always, yet furtive, too. She used Orythmus to command the lordling's own wife to pour oil through every room of their townhouse and set it afire. The lordling tried to stop his wife, not understanding it was impossible, and the maddened woman bit a hole in his cheek. Afterward, as city magistrates dragged her away, she wept and screamed that she loved her husband and why did the Regent not banish these daemons.

As before, I provided the public face for the unpleasantness. Cruel deeds were the necessities of a double life. Experience had made me expert at twisting my conscience into submission. Only . . . not this time. I despised myself.

Xanthe didn't giggle that night. As we walked away, she hugged her cloak tight and murmured that she might have gone too far. Once back in her apartments, she rang for Hosten straightaway.

"Damoselle Xanthe!" A snarling Jacard, draped in purple and crowned with a modestly imperial diadem of gold leaves, shouldered his way past the captain into her salon.

"You and your daemon burnt out Rodrigo de Cerne." Fury twisted and darkened his flesh. "How *dare* you attack my steward? And how dare you have this skulking wretch out of his hole on this of all nights? You and I made an *agreement*!"

The devil in her rose to full height. "Do you fear he'll laugh at your ghouls, Regent? Or do you think he might point out what you do wrong that makes your ghost rites so dreadfully bloody?"

Jacard's pointing finger shook with rage. "You will stop these burnings, damoselle. And if this daemon is not locked away in a quarter of an hour, he will be dead. I don't need him. I never needed him."

Xanthe curled her lip. "You've not power enough—"

"Good Mistress," I interrupted. Jacard meant what he said. No doubt at all. "The heat and smoke have left me ill, and I'd not like to foul your apartments. Perhaps it would serve you best if I retired, unless you've chosen such public humiliation as fit punishment for my faults."

Left with the prospect of challenging Jacard before she was ready and my vomiting on her beloved carpets, the lady retreated, motioning Hosten to take me. She had, indeed, gone too far.

For once I was pleased to leave the tumultuous aether behind. I lay on my pallet in the dark and the lingering heat, unable to sleep, worrying at

Xanthe's increasing wildness. I ought to have an escape plan. The spells attached to the Seeing Stone would make it easy.

Tyregious had been a master of spellcraft and had left a wealth of spells attached to the Seeing Stones. I ought to be able to replicate them for myself. Unfortunately, Tyregious's work was very different from my own.

When I created a spell, its structure—the bones of logic that gave it the shape of my desire—contained the keirna, the intrinsic power, of the natural objects I used in its creation—the muscle and flesh. When I infused it with what power that lived in my blood and bound it with my will, the spell took on life.

Tyregious had created incredibly intricate structures, connections and logic I had never conceived of. But his spell threads were merely the bones. I could detect no intrinsic power bound into them at all—no keirna from *any* object. The Stones lacked keirna of their own. Without keirna to provide muscle and flesh, even my own considerable gift was not enough to make the spells work. They seemed to depend entirely upon the fonts of magical energies that flowed not from, but through the Seeing Stones, empowering magic far beyond my skills. Impossible, I would have said. Most definitely humbling.

Even magic was crumbling underneath me. What would I find when everything I believed had been stripped away?

I pulled out Anne's nireal and pressed it to my brow. Another mystery. How rock headed I'd been to ignore it for so long. As ever, I cursed the sorcerer's hole that prevented the *use* of magic, as well as its shaping. For now, its touch, the reminder of Anne, was all I had to soothe the cold, dead rage smoldering in my gut.

"You say you can see what lies within me, lady," I whispered. Aloud, because I could not bear the silence on such a night. "Tell me I am not going to destroy the light. Not that."

CHAPTER 28

27 DUON, ELEVENTH HOUR OF THE EVENING WATCH

"Out, magus." The thrumming aether flooded my skull, and a faint light resolved itself into a shielded lamp. But the voice . . .

My head felt much as it had after the stoning at Hoven. Thick, dull, and wholly disoriented. Hosten sounded like a woman.

"Get up, hireling. Has someone put iron in your breeches?"

I blinked and her form took shape against the dark. "Mistress?"

"Again, your teaching has served me well. My new detection charm revealed that a serving man had hexed my balcony rail. I cut off his hands for it."

"Hexed? Cut off his *hands*?"

Gods, had she even used the charm properly? Could she have misinterpreted its signal?

"I promised you a reward. So come. Leave your boots behind, as I've done. And hurry; Hosten's seeing to the mess and taking the mewling boy to his parents. I've insisted the captain do these things himself, but be back at your door before middle-night or he'll need to tend his own children next. Because, of course, none can suspect I took him away from guarding you. He looked quite like rancid butter."

I pulled on my shirt and breeches, sickened by her smirk as she watched me. What reward would she give me for providing her another excuse to shed blood?

I padded down the passage after her. "Where are we bound, lady?"

"I decided to answer your curiosity. Iaccar says he works to appease the Spider God and contain Prince Damek's spirit. On Blood Night, after a great feast, he performs some tedious chanting and gesturing in the public square. The spiders diminish and the dreams fade as the moon waxes. No more young men vanish. But spiders, dreams, and vanishings return as the moon wanes again."

"Public rituals wouldn't be the ones important to him," I said. "His real work—"

"—takes place on other nights," she said. "Tonight."

My pulsing blood thoroughly cleared my head, and I needed no urging to keep up or to memorize the turnings. We descended a great stair into a gilt-trimmed rotunda, equally deserted, and then another that took us into a sprawl of dark and empty rooms. Down a long hallway that changed character halfway along . . . lower, narrower, older. And then down again. No servant, no aide, no dog or courtier was to be seen in the passages and galleries.

With every descent, the aether quieted, as if we traveled far from the peopled city and its cares. Yet a breathless weight pressed me to the earth, something different from my childish fear of the dark and suffocation. This was awe. Dread.

More turnings. Always left. Always downward. Pressure that made my teeth ache. Power so rich and deep my bones throbbed. And threading all, the burnt-iron taste of blood.

"Hsst." Xanthe signaled for stealth. I ducked under a lintel to join her in a room crammed with rolled carpets. Dust layered them so deep, they mimed the dune seas beyond Carabangor.

Xanthe set down her lamp, shuttered it completely, and cracked open a low door. We slipped through onto a narrow gallery high up the wall of a vast natural cavern—deep inside the red cliffs, I surmised. A thousand candles blazed in niches on the cavern walls, yet they scarce pushed back the shadows. I doubted a bonfire in each niche could do that, so oppressive was the gloom. The roof rose at least six stories above us, and I could not yet see the floor, thanks to the iron grating that rimmed the gallery.

We ducked and scuttered left along the gallery, invisible to someone whose brisk footsteps bounced off the walls from below. Neither could we see the man babbling in distress. ". . . please tell me what I've done, Lord

Regent. My catch is legal, not poached. I'm honest in my trade. Never cheat the weight. Never cut the eyes out to hide the rot. Always gift the tails to the poor. Pay my taxes. Honor my family, living and dead, and curse the old prince. . . ."

The gallery ended in a wall of rock. Two uprights of the grating were rusted away in the dark, damp corner, and Xanthe motioned me toward the gap. Kneeling, I peered through.

Directly in front of my eyes dangled four large silver eggs, suspended from the ceiling on fine cords—my nireals, a hugely complex variant of the pendant magic Anne's sister had worked. These were the soul mirrors I had spent more than a year devising for the rite at Mont Voilline—the promise of a living soul we had used to lure a dead man back to life.

Below the hanging nireals, four carved angels at least five metres high marked the corners of a rectangular depression in the cavern floor. Simple, elongated, perfect in form and grace, even wingless they would never be mistaken for awkward humans. Two serene faces gazed upward, two down.

The shallow depression was but three steps below the cavern floor. In the center of the space a catafalque supported a simple stone coffin. Altheus's? What would one find inside? Bones and dust? Emptiness? *If any being heeds mortal prayers, let it not be Portier.*

Beside the sarcophagus sat a small square bowl filled with fresh blood, as if someone had sacrificed to Duonna the Mother within the past hour. The blood's use was clear. Two brushes lay next the bowl amid brownish spatters, and hundreds of Aljyssian words covered the floor of the rectangular pit, the steps that bounded three sides, and the wall backing the fourth side.

And there was the gibbering man. Young, well formed, and naked, he was bound to the wall of words at wrists, ankles, chest, and neck by loops of leather affixed to pegs. The sobbing wretch stood on a jutting step as if he were another statue. Jacard was painting a few more words on the wall beside him.

Tossing his brush beside its fellows, Jacard picked up a sponge and water bowl from a cluttered table outside the enclosure and began to wash the squirming man. Oh, gods, gods, gods, what was happening here?

"Be still and stop your sniveling." Jacard's reprimand echoed from every side, as he dipped the sponge and swabbed the man's legs where he had fouled himself. "This is a holy rite and we cannot have you filthy. Would you not offer whatever help is necessary to protect your wife and children from daemon ravaging? If we are successful tonight, you shall be worthy to walk with divinity, no matter your fleshly sins. If only for a moment . . ."

Pouring the remaining wash water over the man's feet and the step, he sluiced the filth into a drain.

"Please, Lord, please." The victim could not produce any other response.

Stepping up again, Jacard blotted the man dry and slathered him with oil from a gold-banded vial, focusing intently on the man's privates. Only when the poor panting, whimpering devil was roused to full heat did he stop and wipe his hand on the towel.

Jacard unbuckled the second set of leather bindings fixed to the wall, currently empty, then jumped down from the step and consulted a book lying open on the table.

I wanted to stop this. But the prisoner displayed no wounds but terror. The blood was not his . . . not yet, at least.

Jacard, the greedy fool, was planning something huge. Though he had no partner practitioners or assistants to enunciate ritual words with a living voice—a fundamental part of a magical rite—he had scribed the words in fresh blood, which carried a gruesome taint but similar magical significance. If the blood was taken from someone involved in the rite, all the better. A screaming victim purposely roused to heat provided a potent energy to add to the nireals, the febrile atmosphere of the cavern, the Stone Tychemus. . . .

Xanthe tapped me on the shoulder and jerked her head back the way we'd come.

I shook my head vigorously. It was much too soon to leave. She pinched my ear.

I grabbed her hand and drew her down beside me. "I need to see this," I said, scarce breathing the words. Gray smoke billowed from the pit below us.

"Hosten," she mouthed, glaring in warning.

Yes, we were ended if I was discovered outside my cell. But to be so close . . .

I peered through the gap, trying to register everything at once: shapes, materials, doorways, the stair that led from the cavern floor to our gallery, the empty bindings, anything that might help me understand what Jacard was about. A ritual enclosure, formed by the four angels and the pit. The nireals. The overpowering scent of incense from a small brazier, the apparent source of the thickening smoke. Green shafts of light streaming from Jacard's Seeing Stone.

The adept had left the enclosure and was unlocking a grate in the far cavern wall. If only I had time to read the words—

Xanthe yanked on my ear yet again, and the sticking pain in my back felt very like a dagger's point. I restrained my impulse to throttle her and ducked my head in submission. Like rats we scurried back the way we'd come.

But before stepping through the door to the carpet room, I slipped over to the rail and took one last look. Every time a coil of smoke touched the naked man, he shrieked and shrank away, as if it carried the heat of its source. Or perhaps it was not pain but sheerest terror, for a giant figure was taking shape in the billowing fog: torso, limbs, head limned in emerald green. Its smoky hand was stretched to the prisoner's naked flesh, stroking, fondling, caressing. Hungry.

Gods! My hair stood on end. This was no illusion.

Features began to take shape on the face in the smoke. A clanking gate and green fire signaled Jacard's return and someone else with him, invisible in the murk. I raised my hand. I could snuff the candles and slip down the stair, fetch the prisoner before something horrid happened. . . .

But of their own insistence my feet retreated through the door. Orythmus, the Stone of Command, gleamed in the dark.

"Are you mad?" Xanthe growled through her teeth as she shut the door behind me. "I'll not suffer for giving you a favor. There are many things short of murder Iaccar can do to me."

"Please," I said, breathless, furious, frustrated. My body followed her without my doing. "The answer is so close. And, great gods, we cannot leave the prisoner to whatever—"

"The prisoner might die or might not. I *will* not."

Xanthe ran. Which meant I ran, retracing our long path, up and right, up and right.

A guttural scream tore through the darkness behind us, long and throaty, shriveling into mindless bleats before falling silent. And beyond it came another man's cry of such pain and despair as set my spirit bleeding. The second set of bindings . . . a second victim?

We'd not yet reached the grand rotunda, when a concussion of power through the aether near popped my eyes from my skull and the rising tension of massive spellwork ended. No gradual release. No sigh of completion. Jacard's great working had aborted before it was done.

My soul felt laden with grease, as if someone had smoked a pig inside a closed house. We'd scarce climbed the grand stair when Hosten bellowed at one of his men to relieve the watch. "I'm off to the magus gallery by the back stair. Report as soon as you've done."

The middle-night bells were already pealing. Hosten was going to arrive before we did. If he checked on me . . .

"Set me loose, lady," I said, breathless, matching her every step. "I can delay him." Raw power could bring down a wall of plaster on his head or shatter a lamp. Hands quivering with pent rage, I'd just need a touch.

A grinning Xanthe paused, fingered Orythmus, and spoke a word I'd given her. "He'll have to take the long way around unless he's a much more stalwart fellow than any I've ever met."

Thunder rumbled from the distant corridors. Wind howled, and hailstones clattered. No guard captain greeted us in the magus gallery. As the middle-night bells fell silent, I dashed into the sorcerer's hole. Xanthe slammed the door behind me and shot the bolt.

MY HEART HAD SCARCE SLOWED when a haggard Captain Hosten dragged me off my pallet and with his men and their spears marched me to Xanthe's rooms. Though his leathers were soaked with sweat, he said naught of his night's activities. "You're to examine her balcony railing," he said, shoving me into Xanthe's chamber. "Don't think to take advantage. We stay till she returns."

Fighting for composure, I stepped into the cool night. The air smelled deliciously of rain and dust. Though my spirit yet felt tainted with death and torment, the oppression of the night had eased. I dragged my hand idly along the half-painted wooden balustrade. To my astonishment, I encountered a barb in its smoothness—a plain, simple, nasty little spell attached to a small carving. Lean on the rail at that spot with even a slight pressure and the solid wood would splinter, catapulting the unfortunate leaner three stories onto a garden walk. Someone was trying to kill the lady.

"I was right, wasn't I, magus? You didn't believe. I saw it on your face." Xanthe stood in the doorway, her long hair damp, a gown of sheer silk sticking here and there to damp, bare skin. Any man in the world who wasn't holding images of mutilated prisoners and manifesting revenants in his mind would think her a girl of seventeen, willing and ripe for the plucking.

"Certainly, you were right." Though who knew if her unfortunate servant was responsible. "I can destroy the spell tonight if you wish."

"Tomorrow. I've other plans for tonight." She glanced behind her. "Hosten and his minions are gone. So did you enjoy your reward?"

"Iaccar's raised a revenant," I said. "He's trying to give it a body. I didn't believe . . . Well, Tychemus and the . . . virtue . . . of this holy place lend him a great deal of power."

She crinkled her brow and leaned against the door arch. "I told you—a ghost. He brags that he plays with souls better than you ever did. *You* told me Iaccar was incapable of great magic and that ghosts are but memories. So I assumed the ones I've seen were illusions made to frighten me. Was I wrong?"

But I hadn't known about screaming victims and words written in blood and the potent keirna of Sirpuhi of the Red Cliffs that seemed to have left its weighty imprint in my body. "I confess to foolish arrogance, lady. What else would I have seen if we'd had more time? Please, we must know . . . to protect you from such wickedness."

She sighed and rolled her eyes, vanishing inside. Settling herself on her favored couch, she pointed me to the carpet at her feet.

"I saw the face and figure of an old man in the cloud, little more than we saw tonight. Iaccar lifted Tychemus high, as if to offer it to the ghost, turning it this way and that. The face mumbled things I couldn't hear. This went on interminably until they were yelling at each other."

Kajetan, almost certainly. Jacard had raised a revenant who could speak. I didn't *want* to believe him capable of such. The abrupt discharge I'd felt signaled that Jacard had exhausted his power. But he had only one Seeing Stone as yet.

I scrubbed at my face, trying to decipher what I'd seen. Why was he bringing a second victim to the wall?

"Did you hear anything Iaccar said to the revenant? What were they arguing about? Was anyone else present?"

Xanthe clutched the green Stones suspended from her neck. "I couldn't hear anything. The prisoner would not stop screaming, though there were no hot irons or pincers or knives or anything but the ghost. It was a different prisoner than tonight's, a beautiful young man. Iaccar bound the librarian up beside him and began to invoke Tychemus—"

"The librarian!" I leapt from the floor as if struck by a pistol shot.

"Yes, though he's so scrawny and damaged he's not at all pleasant to look on. When Iaccar began chanting his lists of words, the other prisoner's skin just swelled and . . . cracked. He started bleeding from his fingernails and from his mouth and nose. And his knees. And elbows."

"Not the librarian," I said, "but the . . . beautiful man."

"Yes. All the bottles and jars exploded and the table collapsed. The ghost vanished as if Duonna the Mother's great mouth had swallowed it. Iaccar screamed and cursed and kicked over the bowl of blood. The tomb was shuddering and the walls bleeding . . . so I ran."

Truth burnt in my soul, a stain no washing could remove. The damnable, arrogant lunatic was not just trying to raise his uncle's dead spirit for an hour, but to instill it into one of the bodies he'd stolen from Mancibar. He wanted Kajetan to live again, in a strong young male body that would endure many years, a face unrecognizable to those who had known the vile mage. And I had given him the idea. That's how I'd put an end to Germond de Gautier. To keep the vessel living was much more difficult, requiring practice and many young men.

But far worse than such grotesque murder of an innocent . . . If Jacard had gotten so far as to destroy the hapless victim, that meant his uncle's spirit had actually *existed* this side of the Veil, in such solid presence that it was crowding into a physical body. That meant that the tear in the Veil—the rent I had worked as I strove to disentangle de Gautier's conspiracy—remained open.

I paced to the windows and stared out at the night. My fingers dragged through my shorn hair, digging into my scalp as if the truth lay just beneath.

"What is it, magus?"

"I've got to think." Eyes closed, I combined the gruesome scene I had witnessed and that Xanthe had described. Candles, nireals, Portier, the doomed victim, the looming phantasm . . .

No. This was not the same rite we had worked on Voilline. Elements were missing, the positioning wrong. Yet neither was it so simple as retrieving one dead soul. To keep a balance in the cosmos, those who had written the Mondragon's *Book of Greater Rites* had said an exchange must be provided to accomplish true necromancy—one living man killed just *before* the dead was transferred, not as a result of the transfer. But any death would suffice, and I could not believe Portier had been captured for that. If their object was simply Kajetan's retrieval, they'd not need Portier to keep the passage through the Veil open permanently. So, then, what was my friend's function in this rite? Was it his blood on the wall? If so, why? And why had Jacard held Tychemus up to the spectre, turning it, arguing . . . ?

The night wind shifted the draperies. Xanthe scowled at me unhappily. Pouting, she drew a shawl over her revealing garments.

"He can't read it!" I said, one small truth bursting free of confusion. I raked my fingers through my hair again and laughed in sick pleasure. "Iaccar's thick wits may give us time."

"What could possibly be laughable, magus?"

"I think Iaccar is working some ritual written in his uncle's journal—possibly to raise his uncle from the dead to live again in another body. He's done things I didn't believe him capable of. But you, lady Mistress, have shown me that he doesn't have the power to do it on his own. He cannot understand how to use Tychemus. His revenant uncle has to learn the Stone's properties as I do and teach him how to use it."

Though not so powerful as de Gautier had been, Kajetan was a learned sorcerer. But what did he know of the aether, of keirna, of the truths of magic I had studied since boyhood? I had seen Kajetan's work, and he was lacking in these basic understandings. Or did death provide enlightenment?

"Give a dead man a new body?" Xanthe had developed an unwholesome glitter in her eyes. "Could I learn to do that?"

"I've no idea. But I know now that we've some time, though not enough to waste. I must examine Tychemus before Kajetan can teach Iaccar how to use it more effectively."

"So what if Iaccar plays with ghosts? I think I'd rather have you teach me to do the same."

Gods, why could she not understand?

"Heed me, good Mistress. Before, we were in a tug of war with Iaccar, a sometime adept whose incompetence forever makes his workings go awry. As long as it was Iaccar, I had every confidence we would be able to wrest control of Tychemus from him as soon as we understood enough. But now I discover that the idiot is sucking the life from Mancibar to get assistance from his family—his dead uncle, who very nearly succeeded in upending the very laws of nature that make arrows fly where we aim them or stones fall to the ground when we drop them. Kajetan is a wholly different and more dangerous adversary. He has set all this in motion, first with his notes and journals and books, and now through these rites."

And another consideration I could not ignore. "Iaccar in his pride and ignorance most likely believes his loving uncle retains some blood loyalty and will do whatever he, Iaccar, wishes. But Kajetan is a creature of blood no longer. And he is not a man who will like being dead. So you can be absolutely sure he will get great satisfaction from wreaking havoc on the living. Your life, as well as your power for magic, is not worth a pile of dung if Tychemus can tell Kajetan how to circumvent its protections."

Kajetan would be in a hurry to escape Ixtador. He would wish to retain his own mind, his own purposes, and not become one of the starving spectres we had seen. And already Jacard had enough power to make Altheus's tomb shudder. . . .

I believed I had her worried. Gods knew I was. But I had learned one thing of infinite importance.

Hold on, student. I know where they keep you. The grate in the cavern wall.

CHAPTER 29

MANCIBAR

A few days after the bloody adventure, Captain Hosten delivered me to the stable instead of Xanthe's apartments. "Pleasure riding?" I said, astonished.

"Never fear, I'll be alongside you. And I've archers posted all over the mountain to take you down do you choose to ride off somewhere on your own." A tenday past, Hosten would have grinned at me with his warning. But the big man's easy, soldierly confidence had yielded to rigorous obedience. Dealing with the bloody evidence of Xanthe's rage and the monstrous indoor thunderstorm that had put his family in the way of it would bring anyone up short.

"The lady's chained my cods to Mancibar," I said as I inhaled the bright morning. "I'm not going anywhere."

He squinted into the crimson sunrise. "You're a crafty one, mage. I've a mind you've chose to be here. So I'm watching for the day you regret the choice. You'll not get away." As always he spoke this without anger, threat, or hostility.

"You're a fine jailer, Hosten," I said. "You've done your duty fair."

"Don't presume. Don't test me."

I bowed to him. I'd known that from the first.

The morning birthed cool and sunny, the dome of clear blue promising a searing noonday. Xanthe said it would never get any colder than I'd seen. Her home had not been far from here. She seemed to feel no regrets or even any strangeness at knowing that all her past life, including everyone she had ever known, lay in long-buried ruins. My former life felt much the same.

The lady was late. Hosten got involved in a long argument with the head groom over the care of his horse, and I wandered into the stable, thinking to have a word with Devil. Did the day come I *could* shed this place, perhaps in a hurry, I'd not want him to have forgotten me.

A pale, scrawny youth was grooming Devil. The boy mumbled and sniffed, pausing every so often to wipe his nose on his sleeve. An overwhelming odor of pipeweed filled the horse box.

Pipeweed . . . skin the color of paste . . . ill-fitting clothes . . . Gods!

I came up quietly behind him. Devil nickered and bobbed his head. Under the cover of the horse's greeting, I grabbed the boy's wrist, clamped my right arm about his throat, and shoved him hard into the corner of the horse box. "Who the devil are you? You've followed me on half a year's journey to the netherworld, so you know I can destroy you if you lie to me. Speak—and quietly and I might not hurt you."

"Followed you? I was born just a ways down—"

I pressed his face into the splintered wood and twisted his arm up his back. "Do not play with me. You were at the caravanserai at Mattefriese, and hung about us on the road for days before that, and though I was blind, I *saw* you, hiding in a clump of locusts. I need to know what you're doing here."

He was a squint-eyed, blister-faced boy still in his teens. His slack lips gave me no great confidence in either his intelligence or his goodwill. "If 'twere my saying, mage, I'd run my knife crost your foul throat and rid the world of a pestilence. But I'm not here of my own wish, and not to do you ill, but only to keep watch on you. To see what comes about. Go on. Kill me if you like."

Brave words, but his voice shook, his cold body quivered, and the odor of fresh piss wafted up his back.

"Why would I want to kill you? I don't know you. You're not Iaccar's man, I'd guess, not hiding out here in the stable. Who set you to keep watch?"

"My da."

"Angels' grace, boy. Who is your da?"

"One as saved your nasty skin. I'm Will Deune."

I let go of him and stepped back. Stupefied. "John Deune's boy! And the other one, too?"

He nodded. He didn't move a whit, but kept his face planted on the wall.

Excitement ruffled my spirit. "And your father, is *he* in Mancibar?"

"Not sayin'."

Tiresome beast. "Then, is anyone with him—a big man, built like a smith? Bossy."

"I know who you're talking of. Smith's not here." Sobs cracked his whispers. "So are you gonna kill me or no?"

"I'll not kill you, nor even cut off your cods. But you've got to tell me why. Why did you follow? Why are you watching? Your da never came back."

"We done you no harm," said the boy, on the verge of wailing. "You sent Da away."

"Yes, I told him to go. But why are you here?"

"Watching is all." The boy's shoulders shook, the flood of snot augmented by tears.

Outside the stable, Hosten was bellowing. "Magus?"

I pressed close, spitting in Will's ear. "I'm out of time, boy. Tell me a place where I can find you, should I wish to send a message to your da. I swear to you, I'll know if you lie."

"I co-come to the kitchens each morning at dawnbreak to carry breakfast to Wat, the head groom." He sniffled and stuttered. "B-but I'll not aid you in your foul plots! K-kill me if you want."

I pressed a hand on his forehead, as if to drill a hole straight into his skull. *The librarian is caged in the navel of the world.*

The stable door burst open. I'd no time for more or to aim this bit of information anywhere in particular, but I felt better that I'd passed it on.

"You're awfully ready to die," I whispered. "Don't. Now, get out of here."

I stepped back, and this time he scrambled away quick and quiet as a stable rat. I snatched up his brush and applied it diligently to Devil's hide, shaking my head in mystification at the workings of fate.

"Where are you, mage?"

Hosten came running and burst through the gate. He wrenched away the brush, flung it to the floor, and slammed *me* against the wall, much more effectively than I'd manhandled Will Deune. "Thinking of leaving us, are you?" he said in a deadly whisper. "Working spells?"

"I always dawdle about grooming horses before I escape," I mumbled, spitting out splinters as he maneuvered me into the stableyard and back to the palace. I took great pleasure imagining what I could do to him did I loose my magic along the way.

"Seems your mistress has come up ill this morning," he said as we trudged down the gallery to my rat hole. "Wouldn't be your doing, would it?"

"No." Dismay chilled my momentary satisfactions. "I wouldn't—"

"You'll have time to think over your story. You're to stay here until she sends for you."

The door slammed and the bolt shot. The dark closed in.

NO ONE CAME. HOUR FLOWED into endless hour, worry and then hunger gnawing at my gut. My mouth grew dry and dusty as Carabangor's streets. Nightmares plagued both sleep and waking. Asleep, I dreamt of emerald prisons and legions of the dead. Awake, I fretted that Jacard had gained the upper hand and chosen to let me wither in my dark coffin of iron and laurel—fit punishment for abandoning Portier in his.

When the door opened at last, I could scarce crawl to my feet. I stumbled into the light, shaking, but determined not to beg or weep.

Hosten passed me a mug of ale and a bun, which I devoured almost before they'd left his hand.

"Never thought it would go most of three days. But I dasn't come without orders." It was as near an apology as he'd likely ever made. That didn't stop him from pricking my side with his sword. We took the familiar route to Xanthe's apartments as if nothing had happened.

Hosten rapped on an inner door, hidden behind a curtain of yellow beads. "I've the magus, lady."

Bolts slid and snapped. A pause. "Send him."

Wrapped in a red silk bed gown and propped up by a score of fat, white pillows, Xanthe looked like a strawberry floating in a sea of cream. Though her complexion lacked its vibrant luster, she was entirely in command.

"Lock the door, magus." Never had I heard such determined hatred in so frail a voice.

I obeyed. As soon as I occupied a stool at her bedside, she grabbed my tunic and pulled me close. "He's tried to kill me again!"

"But the Stones prevent—"

"Oh, it was neither his hand nor a paid surrogate's," she snarled. "But it was his doing. 'Twas surely the same with my balcony. All these days he's fed lies to his subjects. That I'm a priestess of the Spider God. That I devour men. That my sinister magus is the Spider God's minion, who forces me to torture innocents."

"I thought all loved you." I said, my dry rasp no better than hers. "Who did it?"

"That morning I planned to take you riding, I woke early. As I walked in the gardens, a handsome youth brought me a lemon tart. You know how I adore them, and the youth was . . . quite . . . familiar, so I took it. Yet, two bites and I knew I'd not a moment to spare. I've witnessed poisonings of every kind. So I paralyzed the boy, dispatched Hosten to secure you, and locked myself in here. How I suffered! Your charmed potion and old Mutiga's hag-root purge saved me."

"Who was the youth? Why would he harm you?"

She waved her hand as if it was no matter. "He was the son of that wine merchant, Lastegiere. The vile creature spouted that I 'was never going to devour his soul.' What nonsense! It was Iaccar's lies spurred him."

It wasn't nonsense. Lastegiere was the man whose house we'd burnt for a public slight. Xanthe had taken the son to bed first, and then the father, and then played them against each other for a tenday. The boy had many reasons to feel his life devoured.

"Iaccar executed the boy and his father and sold the wife and younger children to a slaver who's already hauled them off to Syanar. Convenient, is it not? I've none to question and none to trust but you."

"What would you have me do?"

Her features were those of the beast masks that warded deadhouse gates. "I want Iaccar dead. And I want Tychemus. Alter the Stones; rip out their magic and reshape it so I can kill him and take his Stone. Do these things for me and I'll share all with you. I've promised you that which you most desire. Your sight, your freedom, those are important, but your life's blood is sorcery, and I can give you all three. As my sworn consort, you shall have the Seeing Stones to wield as my equal."

That some perverse triumph arose from a stupid boy's attempt to remedy his family's foolishness shamed me. That despite my constant avowals, apprehension, and deep-rooted fears, my soul yet quivered with desire at the power she offered disgusted me. But I was what I was. I relished the moment and swore to make use of it.

"A bargain to set my soul afire, Mistress, as you well know. But it would be the most dangerous work I've ever attempted, our chances of winning through so small as to be unseeable. Yet one thing I must have before I can agree."

Her grip near gouged my forearm bones. "What thing?"

"I must read Tychemus *before* we reveal our hand."

"He'll never allow that."

"Then you must find a way to separate him from the Stone so I can get to it. To subvert the Stones' protections will require time and preparation. I'll need to know everything possible about Tychemus . . . and the three together."

She laid back on her pillows. "I can separate him from Tychemus. Women always throw themselves madly on men after a narrow escape from death. And stupid men always believe it. He'll not refuse what I offer."

"And how will that give me access?"

"I'll tell Iaccar that I fear you've conspired with this boy to poison me. When I confess how ill I was and how terrified of dying when I've only just begun to live, he'll display great sympathy and invite me to dine with him. It is his habit. Afterward, we'll come back here. I'll arrange for someone to bring you here while I'm out."

"Hosten will suspect—"

"It will not be Hosten. Hide yourself here and you'll know when Tychemus awaits. You'll have until dawn. I'll not stomach the snake longer."

Somehow I did not doubt her.

"Then we've a bargain."

Once I'd downed as much food and drink as I could stomach, Xanthe summoned Hosten. By the time he arrived at her apartments, she had me on my knees, my back afire and near losing all I'd just eaten. "You arrogant, incompetent worm! I'll teach you not to hide things from me. Perhaps I'll lock you away for three more days. Perhaps I'll have your hole bricked up."

Hosten drew his blade and motioned me out.

"Do not succor him, Captain," said Xanthe, snarling. "Do not listen to his pitiful cries. Do not even stay near his door, else I'll blind you as I do him, and stopper your ears so they'll never again hear your children's voices."

She touched the Stones and spat the word that would remove my sight. Yet even as my stomach lurched, no darkness fell. She must have touched Rhymus instead of Orythmus. But I cursed and staggered forward at Hosten's shove. I knew well how to play this part.

THROUGH THE REST OF THAT sweltering afternoon, I forced myself to sleep. Trying to wrestle more meaning from the evidence I had would be no use, and I would need every smat of power I could muster. The key to Kajetan and Jacard's plan, to the use he planned to make of Portier and me, would lie in the three Seeing Stones together. I dreamt of emerald walls and firestorms and young men's skin cracking as Kajetan tried to wrestle his way into them.

When the door scraped, I leapt to my feet drenched in sweat, but instantly awake. Gold and purple wisps streaked the western sky. The young man with freckles, the same who had led me to Portier, guided me along a circuitous route to Xanthe's door. "She said to be patient," he whispered, waving me into the deserted salon. "This could take a very long time."

I settled into a wall niche behind a man-high statue of a winged horse. As the hour crawled past and the light dimmed, I wrapped my mind around all I needed to do. Nothing so different from my approach to the other Stones. Care. Precision. I could not allow the pressure of time to drive me to mistakes.

In our early days together, I had repeatedly set Anne urgent problems, requiring her to unravel some puzzle to stave off an unpleasant result. I would berate her and yell at her throughout the time. It had taken her months to learn to stay focused when I hurried her. But she had never complained. She had come to me to learn discipline.

At the first opportunity I must dispatch Will Deune to warn her. Compel him with magic, if necessary. Kajetan knew very well who had driven the knife into his heart. I pressed the heels of my hands into my eyes and tried to put her out of mind.

Xanthe's new clock ticked away an hour. One of her admirers had given it to her. Xanthe marveled that its hands could mark the sun's progress, and she was forever comparing it with the ancient sundial in the palace gardens. Xanthe did not lack admirable qualities. Many would say we two lunatics made a fine pair. But she would never speak to me of star patterns, or theories of nature, or her favorite books. She would never labor for two years with an embittered blind man just to ensure she could never use her power for ill. . . .

I had never feared death. My own life had ever seemed but an accident of nature, as like to end abruptly as to continue into interminable aging. On any other day, I would have welcomed one as much as the other. But something had changed in me. To end here, so far away from those evenings when Anne would read to me at Pradoverde, those times when I would think blindness not so wretched and her pity not so terrible if they induced her to share the books she treasured with me. Her voice had revealed a soul as deep as the roots of the mountains. . . .

I drew Anne's pendant from my boot and pressed it to my forehead. It burnt, as if left lying in the sun all day. Hosten was nowhere near here, and even at his usual post he'd not noticed the small things I'd worked. To reveal the secrets of Anne's gift, all I had to do was speak its key, the Aljyssian word for illumination. *"Luminesque."*

In the space of the word, I was returned to Castelle Escalon, walking its sprawling expanse while fearful eyes turned away, hurrying to my apartment where I could breathe in the light before plunging yet again into the fearsome web of murder and mystery. A heavy doom had shadowed those days, as it did this night. But Anne was there . . . so afraid, so alone . . . shattered by a bellowing anger through the aether.

But another voice offered her comfort and kindness, though that person, too, was alone and troubled. *Are you injured? In danger? There's been no one, ever. Trust me. One word . . .*

And all her fear was consumed in curiosity . . . and sadness. She had wept for her lonely comforter.

Before I could think what it was I experienced, my mind was assaulted by the garish lights and noise of feasting . . . singers, mourners, a journey feast with Queen Eugenie presiding. Interminable. Boring. And Anne was there, too . . . disgusted, horrified at the leering suitor thrust into her face.

But someone had challenged her to a game . . . and disbelieving, desperate for some sign of truth, she played: *You detest jolly pipe music,* she said, excited at the simplicity of the impossible.

Exactly so, said her companion. *Now you. Come, test me. . . .*

With the words, a wave swept through her. She named it *pleasure, relief, and a deep and resonant joy* . . . feelings not her own, yet vigorous enough to leave her smiling.

Gods . . . it was me! I had been so focused on her, so fascinated at that bright mind, at her quick acceptance, at the depths of her talent, I'd not realized what she had sensed from me—what she had sparked in me. Had I ever before experienced *a deep and resonant joy*? Passion, yes, for the glory of magic. Satisfaction, yes, in my relationship with Portier and the tasks we pursued together. But circumstance had forced me to push Portier away. And magic and riddle solving had but laid a blanket over my emptiness. Nothing had ever so transformed my life as had Anne de Vernase.

In wonder, I let the nireal's enchantment play out.

Our talks of star patterns and night-blooming plants.

Our fight to win the night's battle at Mont Voilline.

The moment she had opened herself to me completely, gifting me her power for magic, allowing me to wield it for the rightful end we pursued. Absolute trust. Uncompromising faith.

In sharing her experience of our joinings, she allowed me to see myself through her eyes. All these things had occurred in the aether. All was truth. And I had been too blind to see it . . . long before I was blind.

I am your reflection, she had said when she came to Pradoverde and gave me the nireal, offering all of herself. *My outward appearance is nothing like what lurks inside me. I don't despise you. I don't pity you. I* know *you. I* see *you, and everything I see, I value.*

And I had never believed her until now.

I hung the pendant around my neck and tucked it inside my shirt. Closing my eyes to Xanthe's room and the sordid deceptions that must go on there, I reached deep into the aether. Anne couldn't hear me speak, but I felt the pulse of her life. I would recognize her at a distance as vast as that to the moon. And I clung to that ferocious presence, allowing the river of feeling and voice, magic and dream, to sweep over, under, and through me, until a woman's giggles and a man's heavy breathing pulled me out.

CHAPTER 30

36 DUON, NIGHT

"I know it's bold to ask you to examine my inner room, Regent Iaccar, but while I lay so ill, I sensed a vile presence hovering about me." Xanthe's peppery manner could become Nessia's honey whenever she chose. "I'll not trust *him* to keep me safe. I've had the most terrible thought. What if the poisoner was *his* tool?"

"Your trust shames me, lady, especially after my appalling temper of late. Certainly Dante is capable of any wickedness. I've seen how he uses women, and you are so innocent . . . so lovely. . . ." Jacard's voice had dropped an entire register. I could easily imagine why.

Had I not known Xanthe, her seduction might have had me panting. Had I not known Jacard, his humility might have deceived me. He had once fooled Anne.

"On the table beside the window, you'll find honeyed wine," said Xanthe. "Pour me a cup—and one for you, if you wish—while I change out of this stifling gown. *He* says I look best in Sabrian garb, but I've had something new made. You can judge."

Soft lamplight bloomed beyond the statue that hid me. One cup was poured. And then a second. I bared my teeth and held motionless. Xanthe could not enspell Jacard with the Stones' magic. But her own would do well enough. And the spell of *vigor* she'd had me put on the wine would ensure no flagging energy on Jacard's part.

"You've been right all along. I've indulged him too much," Xanthe called from the bedchamber. "He's been getting ever more demanding, and says he will teach me only what *he* chooses!"

"Insolent."

"I am mistress of Rhymus and Orythmus, and I've given him his sight, and he treats me like a performing monkey. The burnings were his idea to make your subjects fear him. I was not allowed to succor his victims or even to show my sympathy! I was so hoping— Well, 'tis not at all what I imagined those long terrible years imprisoned." Her voice quavered. "Now, lord, tell me what you think."

"Stars and Stones, lady! You are"—he was hoarse—"the loveliest. . . . That gown. I've not seen the like ever, here or in all of Sabria or in any artwork or vision or fancy."

"I was saving it for my favorite. Come sit beside me, Iaccar. Is the wine not splendid as well?"

"Splendid. Yes."

"You're more generous with my folly than I've any right to expect. This evening has been so pleasant that I hate its ending. A thousand years of loneliness, and I just entering womanhood . . ."

Jacard was hooked in less time than a trout in a bucket.

More giggles. Their breathless exchanges deteriorated rapidly into elaborate sighs, much rustling of clothing, and increasingly urgent moans.

". . . not so shy as ladies in this day. I would view *all* of your manly strength, lord . . ."

Xanthe was very serious about her diversionary tactics. I focused my mind on my plan for the Stones.

". . . ah, slowly, sweet lord. Come, let's chase the frights from my bed . . . more comfort . . ."

They carried the lamp with them. The door snicked shut. The bolts shot. The Stones remained behind, their quiet secrets seductive beyond Xanthe's charms. It was difficult to delay even the brief interval I'd told myself was necessary.

When I could contain myself no longer, I crept out of my niche. A colorful pile of silks lay on the floor, topped by an intricately tooled leather belt complete with silver dagger. A lone candle, banded in silver, was left standing on the low table beside the couch, along with a wheel of thread and a familiar cup and plate of blue porcelain. Beside it lay the two neck chains with the objects of my desire held captive in their cages of silver.

Smiling, I set up the cup and plate at the opposite end of the table from the candle. I would begin with Tychemus alone—to understand its properties so I might better interpret the mystery of the three together.

I placed Jacard's Stone on the plate, aligning one face with the candle flame. Then I fetched my staff from its place beside the door and knelt. The Stone of Reason was like to its fellows. Irregular. Multifaceted. Similar in size, shape, depth of color, and clarity.

I closed my eyes, held my hand in proximity, and dived into the aether. Again, much like the other two. A magical void, surrounded by a corona of attached spellwork. I sorted through the dangling threads—a sensation akin to running my fingers through the fringe on a wool rug. The hundreds of spells displayed the characteristic leanness of Tyregious's spellcasting. Some were instantly recognizable from my work with Xanthe's Stones, while some . . .

I paused and sorted through a cluster of spells that dealt with substitutions—replacing a subject's spoken words, redirecting a person's attention from one idea to another—in search of a spell thread that had felt quite different from the rest. Bulky and awkward, as if the bit of fringe yarn was made of thick rope, rather than fine, combed wool, and was clotted with burrs, insects, and broken glass, its distinction was curious. I grasped the thing and began to disentangle its making. . . .

Jacard! I'd recognize his clumsy signature anywhere, but the structure itself, the more complex design and intelligence behind the formulaic magic, was more like Kajetan's work.

I probed deeper. Behind a confusing screen of circular word replacements and unlikely scenarios lay a simple filtering spell—an encompassing layer that would be triggered by any spellwork that incorporated names scribed in fresh blood. Whenever Jacard bound such a spell using Tychemus, his own name—and the personhood that name must forever represent—would be replaced with that of his uncle.

I blinked and sat back on my heels. Names writ in blood . . . it seemed aimed at Jacard's great working. But Jacard's name would not appear on the cavern wall. It was insignificant to the work. He was neither the revenant nor the unfortunate human vessel provided for it, but only the practitioner. So there must be some additional aspect of the rite I hadn't guessed. Perhaps Kajetan wanted something done that Jacard had refused. Thus their arguments . . .

I'd no time to sort out possibilities just now. So I left the consideration hanging and examined the facets of the Stone. Within moments I had identified the *squaring*, the *doubling*, and the *skewing* facets. A beam of yellow-green fire led me into the seeing face.

As before, the names in my thoughts seemed to shape what I saw. The candle that guided me into the vision was one of those on the cavern walls at the heart of Sirpuhi. As Xanthe had described, two naked victims were bound to the wall of blood-writ words, another robust young Mancibarran writhing in terror and lust, and on his left Portier, head drooping, limbs flaccid, drool sliding from his slack mouth. Above them, monstrous in the roiling gray smoke, leered Kajetan, eyes sunken and black, mouth gaping, gray tongue licking his colorless lips . . . hungry. Every touch of his smoky fingers evoked a silent shudder from Portier.

Jacard could not be thinking to install his uncle's soul in *Portier.* Portier's body was weak, wasted. He'd been cut repeatedly in hatchwork patterns—systematically bled with a ten- or twelve-bladed scarificator. And de Gautier's cruelty at Voilline had already left one of his legs a ruin. Why offer the revenant a crippled vessel? Even if Jacard and Kajetan believed in Portier's kind of immortality, surely rebirth was centered in the soul that passed beyond the Veil, not the mortal shell left here to rot. The younger, healthy male must be the chosen vessel.

Jacard tossed his blood-soaked brush aside and stepped up beside Portier, exposing the words he'd just painted on the wall. *Vosi Portier de Savin-Duplais au recivien, Matthei Pistor.* From Portier to the vessel, Matthei the miller. But he'd also scribed a second line: *Vosi Jacard de Viole au recivien, Matthei Pistor.*

Before I could comprehend what the addition meant, Jacard grasped the caged Seeing Stones—all three, blazing green—and laid his hand on Portier's head. . . .

A consuming brilliance erased the vision and left the seeing face blank.

Head swirling, I took up breathing again.

From Portier to the miller. From Jacard to the miller. What had Jacard said as I watched the beginnings of his last attempt? *If this works, you shall be worthy to walk with divinity. . . .*

Both souls to be transferred! First from Portier, who was half dead, incapable of resistance, and then Jacard's own.

Diabolical! My mewling adept would inherit a fine body and Portier's gift of rebirth. He could easily assert dominance over the remnants of a weakened Portier from the beginning. Save for one problem: Jacard's name was writ in blood. I stared at Tychemus and considered Kajetan's crafty little spell. The rite might not work as Jacard believed. . . .

Giggles and moans floated through the dark air. How much time had passed? I needed to move on. The other two Stones waited. Beyond Jacard's scheme and his dead uncle's nasty twist lay the answer to their riddle and my own need to understand the most profound magic I had ever seen. The three were meant to be joined, and I could not escape the conclusion that all the wondrous spells Tyregious had attached to them were peripheral to their true purpose.

Quickly, I placed Rhymus and Orythmus on the blue plate. A gleaming protrusion on Rhymus slid exactly into a V-shaped notch adjacent to the Stone of Command's seeing face. Turning Tychemus with its seeing face upward as well, I found the orientation that would fit the Stone of Reason into a wedge-shaped gap between facets of the other two. I pushed them together.

The edges flashed and sparked, until the three appeared a seamless whole. Emerald light swelled and then receded, as if the great prism were a living heart with but one pulse left in it.

Though tempted to seek further enlightenment in the seeing face right away, I held discipline and examined the joined Stones. As with the individual prisms, the conjoined three exhibited no magical structure of their own. Nor did they disturb the aether in the slightest. How was that possible? Unless . . .

If a man poured a bucket of water into the stream at Pradoverde, he might see ripples, splashes, or momentary diversions in the flow. But the water itself would be indistinguishable from the river. Perhaps the Stones did not alter my perception of the aether because their energies were of the same substance as that flow where I perceived emotion, magic, and dream.

Had time and secrecy not bound me, I would have laughed aloud at such a notion. And yet years of study and, indeed, the entirety of my life, shaped and driven by magic, provided me no other answer. As nature directed water to manifest itself as liquid, as ice, and as vapor so fine as to float in the air, perhaps it directed this mystical substance to manifest itself as both solid matter and as the energies Anne and I sensed and touched. It would explain my certainty of the truth the Stones revealed in their visions. Lies were instantly detectable in the aether.

Drunk with revelation and possibility, I looked closer, only to slam into another wall of impossibility. The wizard's myriad spell threads were no longer in evidence. No spells at all were in evidence. What Tyregious had shaped for the three individually was astonishing, glorious, intricate magic. How could the three together be nothing? I ought to heave the thing from the Xanthe's balcony, just to see—

My left hand—my good hand, which grasped the conjoined Stone—spasmed with pain, as if Hosten had speared it to the table with his dagger.

All right. Not that. Night's daughter! I stretched and clenched my fingers until the spasm eased.

Tyregious had told Xanthe that his little demonstration showed all there was to know about the Stones. The candle had dwindled, yet not so much that I could not use it to test the great prism. One by one, I peered into its facets. My seeing passed through the deep and richly colored glass but discovered no image of the candle flame. I stretched Xanthe's thread to check the candle's position. Turned the Stone. Checked again. Peered again. Nothing but glass and color. I was flummoxed.

Before examining the conjoined seeing face, I took a moment to prepare. My glimpses of truth in the individual Stones had each been fed by my own concerns. Assuming the three showed anything, I wanted nothing in me to influence what it might be, lest I miss some aspect of importance. I blocked out the sounds from the other room. Buried guilts, desires, and worries about Portier and Anne, and the terrors of blindness, necromancy, and unhealed wounds in the Eternal Veil. I went cold. Immersed myself in nothing. Became Dante, the *agente confide* who could not be moved by grief or joy.

Then, empty and impervious to compulsion, I knelt up and peered through the seamless seeing face. The candle appeared as flame only, a distant smudge of yellow in a world of rich-hued emerald light. Focusing entirely on the sea of green in front of me, I abandoned the world and opened myself fully to the aether. . . .

"THROUGH MILLENNIA HAVE I WAITED for you, Dante, Master Mage of Sabria, son of Raghinne, child of the dark."

I knew him before he rounded the angled glass corner, his long stride eating the distance between us. Cool, dry air moved through halls of glass, carrying scents of ash and rosemary, shifting his gold and gray hair and his ankle-length coat, offering glimpses of the sword belted at his waist.

His smile-that-was-not-quite approved of my arrival. For I was there, too. My every sense told me I walked in a green gloom bound by angled glass.

"Who are you?" I said. "Mage or god or . . . other?"

I had experienced strangeness beyond comprehension in my life, yet this surpassed all. Overwhelming wonder might have paralyzed me entire, had I not come empty.

"We have walked a long road together, friend. Some might say I met you in the dark of Grymouth Caves. For certain, I have watched you since your birth, witnessed your deeds."

He laid a hand on my shoulder, pressing slightly. My knees flexed, but in my emptiness, refused to bend.

"You are a stubborn man, clinging to disbelief. It stunts your ability to make choices."

"I explore. I perceive. And only then do I draw conclusions," I said. "I've rarely trusted anyone . . . including myself . . . and other sorcerers least of all. This is magic the like of which I've not experienced. I dare not abandon what's served me well. . . ."

Though somewhere in the place I had submerged desire, I wanted to kneel. I had ever been crude, ugly, and violent, while he was all serenity, all that was fair in speech, in form, in grace. But my body refused to succumb.

"This is not sorcery, Dante," he said. "And I am as real as you. Come. Let's walk." Inviting.

It was my dreams come to life, angled walls and ceilings of emerald. Each turning brought us into another hall or another room of smooth-polished glass. We ascended glass stairs, wide and narrow, that turned upon themselves, only to find ourselves below the room we'd just left. Doorways vanished behind us, subsumed in the translucent walls. The candle spark lit our way.

A spot on my chest burnt as if the spark's twin had taken residence there. At a distance so great as the sun itself, I knew what that heat was, but I refused to articulate it, even in thought.

"Here is the task you were born for."

We entered a hexagonal room. Six triangular panes formed the ceiling that reached its apex high above us. The view beyond the walls appeared as a turbulent sea. Only it was not.

Gaunt, hollow-eyed spectres, far more numerous than my dreams had revealed, crowded to the glass, pawing, licking, wailing with soundless hunger. This was no illusion, no vision of past, present, or to come, but the truth that had driven my actions for two years. Anne had glimpsed it through the rent in the Veil at Mont Voilline. Ixtador Beyond the Veil. Somewhere out there were de Gautier's victims, my victims: Anne's sister, Lianelle, her friend Ophelie, men named Gruchin, Denys, de Gautier, a dozen Temple bailiffs, Ilario de Sylvae, Nessia, my father. . . .

"Their souls are gone to feed one who grows stronger each day. He believes you will serve him, because the alternative is unthinkable."

"Who is he?" I said, knowing the answer already. "What does he want of me?"

"He has many names you will not accept, any more than you will accept my own identity. He is called First of the Fallen. Once Beloved of the Creator. The Lord of Gedevron. The Tempter. The Corruptor. The Souleater. He Who Longs for Release. Dimios, Son of Light and Dark. He believes you were born to be his champion in a very ancient duel."

"And so you name yourself the Righteous Defender?"

"That is one of my names."

"The Souleater is myth. The Righteous Defender is myth. I seek truth."

He smiled in sympathy and waved his slender hand to encompass the strange edifice we occupied. "Myth is truth, though one must learn its provenance in order to comprehend it fully. When the provenance is the Greater Truth of the universe, the learning can take many human lifetimes. But be assured, we can speak naught but truth in these halls."

Just as in the aether. Yes, as I suspected. But whoever this person was, I didn't want him trying to insert me into his myth. "I don't believe in destiny," I said.

"As well you should not. Choice is all. *Will* is all. A magus knows this." He stepped forward and a door opened onto an endless glass passageway. The dead swarmed both walls, atop the ceiling, under the floor. "Perceive: The universe is disordered. These dead are but shells, and they dwell in a place created by human ignorance and greed."

"What we call Ixtador."

"This aberrant intrusion into the wider universe set Dimios free to prey on the human dead. And so he has done, as you see. Now his deepest craving is to pursue this pleasure in the living world as well. You, my friend, gave him the opening he craved."

"When I opened the Veil." The vision in de Cuvier's dream had grown sublimely evil since Mont Voilline. The living world peopled with starving spectres. Eyes that had no souls. Eyes alien to the bodies they looked out of. No matter that the act had been necessary; I had opened the way to such a future. That was truth.

He nodded. "From the Beginnings, my choice has been to defend the divine from corruption, whether from my own kind or yours. But in this case, my power to intervene is limited, because the damage has been done by human works. Human gifts, human strength, must correct it. Yours, I think."

"But I failed to close it before. Even with all my power and more borrowed from . . . others . . . I failed. And I've no idea how to destroy Ixtador—remove the corruption."

"But this time you have the Fire. This." He touched the wall. The starving dead flocked to his hand on the glass. "The Fire is the universe's gift of light to humankind, a way for humans to espy reflections of the Greater Truth."

"The prism," I said. "The fire that Port—that Ianne brought from beyond the Veil was this prism—the three Stones joined together?" Altheus—Portier—had commanded his wizard to cut and polish the Stones the better to let the Creator's light shine through. They were a conduit. . . .

"More or less. This glass is the greatest treasure in the living world. To see these small minds—two living, one dead—playing with its pieces for their trivial purposes is abomination."

I had said something similar myself.

"Some will tell you that you were born in darkness apurpose to challenge me and that our combat risks destroying the prism, leaving the living world bereft of glory. But you wisely understand that your fate is your own choice, not some mythic destiny. You are not required to do such wickedness."

The old man had warned me: *Thou'rt other, born in darkness, gifted with strength to quench the light of Heaven.*

And Portier: *Your strength. Your gifts. You are born to do the unthinkable.*

The young man tossed his silken hair over his shoulder. "Can you not see, my friend? You have the strength and skill to wield the Fire as it should be wielded."

Tyregious had said the candle exercise demonstrated everything about the Stones. About seeing. About light. About magic . . .

Great gods of the universe . . . magic! I had witnessed the torrent of power unleashed by the Stones, purest magic that left both the formulaic practice of the Camarilla and my own plodding use of keirna unnecessary. No wonder Tyregious's spells had needed no intrinsic power—not when the Stones provided a flood of it—the whole of it. And what better gift to aid humankind in times of trouble, to create beauty, to reveal the face of the divine? Altheus, the Holy Imperator, knew. Portier knew. Magic was a hope that something marvelous existed beyond nature, beyond death and despair and decaying flesh.

Disbelief sloughed from me like a snake's skin. From youth I had scoffed at gods and daemons, while submerging myself in the most profound evidence of the divine—the Greater Truth of the universe, whether that truth be a benevolent Creator with messenger angels or the majestic precision of nature's order that scholars only now were recognizing. And this being who walked in dreams and mystery, who named himself defender of this Greater Truth, implied that my wrong choice could destroy it . . . destroy the Stones, destroy the very conduit that brought magic into the world . . . destroy the light. . . . *Unthinkable.*

Such a horror gripped me, such certainty that all the whispers and prophetic declarations meant exactly what they said, that I could scarce speak. Myth was founded in truth. And sometimes it *was* truth. Yet if I had choice . . . "Why would anyone, human or divine, believe I would *choose* to rob the world of magic?"

"A very long story," he said, his serenity veined with bitterness. "Dimios was enraged that such creatures as humankind possessed a gift meant for greater beings. He it was who punished Ianne by chaining him to the mount. And he punished the other daemons who gave Ianne such ideas. Dimios, in turn, was confined for that terrible deed, his lordship limited to a demesne of ice and gloom. In that great judgment, Ianne the thief pleaded that humankind be allowed to keep their bit of fire in perpetuity, the better to care for themselves and recall their place in the universe through glimpses of the Greater Truth. And indeed Ianne was given the Fire in this solid form, the prism, so that the light that you name magic could never be dimmed at the whims of daemons. None born to the wider universe can wield an artifact made for humans."

But now this conduit of magic, our window onto the wider universe, had been damaged by the excesses of the Blood Wars. We had seen magic failing in the two centuries since, but we never understood that the price of greed and overreaching was our own future as a part of that Greater Truth, our very essence that could exist beyond mundane life—our souls.

Truth. As clear as mathematics.

And still the Defender spoke, disdainful now. Indignant. "Some will say that destroying this aberrant Ixtador might extinguish the soulless scraps who languish there. Yet your gifts can set them free, using the Fire to give them their proper place in the order of nature."

He extended his hand. "Shun these bleak prophecies and accept the power that awaits you, Dante. Join me in fealty. Become my hand in the living world, and at long last we shall make things right."

Of all things I desired to make things right—to preserve the glory of magic, to protect and defend it from the corruption of those like Jacard, de Gautier, and Kajetan. I wanted to teach others to see. Surely my study, my searching, my skills, understanding, and desire had brought me here. Even the horrors of beatings and burnt flesh, of darkness and confinement, of lonely nights near the brink of madness had strengthened me, made me ready for difficult tasks—not just evil ones. And yet . . .

My mage collar itched as if a burr had been left inside it. I tugged at it and stared into the roiling sea beyond the wall. *Soulless scraps* . . . an unsympathetic description . . . *To set them free* . . . *give them their proper place* . . . What was their proper place? Would the destruction of Ixtador return a soul's lost essence or destroy it utterly? And what of the souls not yet devoured?

Green light penetrated blood, bones, sinews . . . beautiful . . . cold. Everything the Defender said rang true. Yet in the night watches at Castelle Escalon, speaking in the aether with a stranger I could not yet trust, I had learned how easy it was to hide the truth while speaking no lies. Which brought me around again to the old shepherd's caution: *Be wary of thy companion, required to speak truth, though his meaning is ever lies. And though wary, stay with him, for he must lead thee to thy unhappy destiny.* And the other, spoken by a friend abandoned and in pain: *He's going to come for you. . . .*

Oh, gods, gods, gods . . . I touched the glass walls. They were solid on every side and cold as ice. The dead flocked to my hand. Panic robbed me of breath. The walls moved inward . . . crushing.

Gritting my teeth, I shoved away fear. One answer would tell me. "How do we prevent this eater of souls from entering the living world?"

"I have taken my stand here," he said, drawing his fingers along the wall, causing a ripple in the ocean of spectres outside the wall. "And I will not be moved. Bring the three Stones together as one, and whenever you wield the Fire, your strength and my vision will be joined. We shall be as one, you and I—the Righteous Defender of the Greater Truth and his Hand in the Living World. Together we shall stand against corruption, remedy the wrongs that have been done, and reshape the universe."

What is the sensation when the desperately needed rain in a dry season pounds just enough harder that the mind comprehends the coming of a flood? Or when the snow that dances lightly in the air thickens and the wind swirling it rises just enough to speak the onslaught of blizzard? Such was my experience when he gave his answer. The world shifted, and I understood the course laid out for me, not by impersonal fate or daemon compulsion, but by my own irrevocable choices. By my skills. By my gift. To do the unthinkable.

This being, named in myth the Righteous Defender of Heaven, had taken his stand here in the conduit of magic that fed Rhymus . . . that sent dreams to Masson de Cuvier . . . to my father . . . to me. The Stone had shaped those dreams into *his* vision of past, present, and future. My father had seen him in the dream, the Righteous Defender, calling him the fairest of all the Creator's works. But months ago my poor sister had reminded me that the First of the Fallen was ever deemed the gods' fairest. The one named Dimios. The Souleater.

He awaited my reaction. "Great lord, this honor . . . to be your hand . . . I cannot speak. . . ."

Was it coincidence that Kajetan, who now existed in Ixtador, drove his living nephew to collect the Seeing Stones and wield them as one? Was it Jacard who wanted me in Mancibar even though I had no place in his simple rite? Or was it Kajetan? Or was it Kajetan's master? Kajetan plotted to take Jacard's place in a mortal body graced with Portier's gift of rebirth—one foot in each world, providing a passage for the One who wished to enter. If I became Dimios's bound servant, I could not stop it.

I did not believe in destiny. But I recognized truth when I heard it. Purposeful blindness was folly when you stood at the brink of the abyss and the road behind you had vanished. We had the myth entirely wrong. The Righteous Defender was trying to keep us blemished mortals *out* of Heaven—the Greater Truth—strengthening his arm by devouring our souls. It was the Daemon of the Dead . . . the guardian, the blemished mortal who walked the verges of the worlds . . . who was supposed to stop him. Arrogant, cocksure, dismissive, he'd so much as told me how to do it—to destroy the prism where he lurked.

Only I couldn't. I had walked straight into his trap, ignorant of those things I needed to know: how to wrest control of the Stones from their owners, how to destroy such things. Dimios would never have revealed so much if he was going to allow me to walk away. Sure, he had a grip on my soul already. The cold dark lurked in my depths, seething like the liquid fire at the heart of a volcano. And if I fell . . .

Desperate to find a way out, I gathered my wits. Perhaps I could buy time to set events in motion. I needed to adjust the spell Kajetan had left in Tychemus. That should prevent this abomination of a rite that could kill Portier and draw Kajetan, if not Dimios himself, through the Veil. Then I needed to find Will Deune and pass on what I'd learned.

Most of all, I needed time to invoke the spell I had prepared to protect those things I would not reveal—the truth of this mystery and the identity of those I loved, those who must now carry out what I could not. I would relish blasting the grate from Portier's cell, but that would expose me to Xanthe, precipitating the very collaboration I feared. Portier was hostage to my faith in Jacard's impotence, in Xanthe's stubborn nature, in Anne's determination and her power and her heart that would not falter at the deeds she must do. Me, a man of faith; it was laughable. But perhaps I could aid my friend's rescue, too, if I could just buy enough time. . . .

"It is time to choose your course, Dante." He whose fair hand awaited mine would not be denied.

I knew only one way to buy time. My hand gripped the silver pendant on my breast. Dimios knew me by my deeds. He could not see the rest.

My knees bent. I took his hand, kissed it, and pressed it to my forehead—the binding of submission and fealty. Emerald sparks leapt from our touch and I felt them settle like frost crystals in my bones. "I am imperfect in all things. But you have borne witness to my deeds. Magic, seeing, light, are life's breath to me. You are the Righteous Defender of Heaven and I will stand with you as long as I have a mind. As of the sun's next rising, I am yours. Tell me your will. . . ."

He bound me. And told me his will. And taught me that I knew nothing at all of pain. Laughing, he left me the hours until the sun's rising to contemplate the horrors of my future. Time . . .

Anne

CHAPTER 31

36 DUON, NIGHT
THE KADR ROAD

"Dante!"

I sat bolt upright, my head splitting, my spirit cracked. I could not breathe, could not think for the tearing, lacerating agony. An eternity, it seemed, until I knew it was the aether and not knives carving my flesh from my bones.

"Ani, love, what is it?"

"Are you ill?"

Ilario and Rhea spoke as one, their worried faces revealed by flashes of pink and purple lightning, their concern underscored by thunder that fractured the night and trembled the soggy ground.

I clutched my stomach, crossed an arm across my breast, and rocked rapidly in a vain attempt to prevent my heart from bursting its bounds.

"Don't know. Hurts." I squeezed the words between my teeth. "Dante." All his furious exuberance had returned, but buried in this horrific torment.

Ilario drew me into his arms, enfolding me in slender solidity. "Tell us how to help you."

But I could not think. We huddled under a shallow overhang on the Kadr ridge, soaked through by an endless drizzle.

Rhea laid her own blanket over us as she revived the embers of our fire. "Let me examine you, Anne," she said softly. "This could be some injury or joint fever. I've remedies. . . ."

"I don't think it's her own injury," said Ilario softly, holding me like a fevered babe. "She can feel . . . other things."

Not even in my murderous rage at Mont Voilline had I experienced such darkness tainting the aether. Icy malevolence. Wrenching, purposeful destruction. Memories of happiness were torn out of me—of my family's love, satisfying study, the beauty of Montclaire's spring wildflowers, of laughter and games and sweet sadness, of exuberant conversations with my unknown friend in the nights of Castelle Escalon. They blackened and withered as if the fires of Pradoverde had consumed them and left them as fouled scraps. My inner walls could hold against the onslaught no better than paper could hold back a lava flow. And Dante was at the center of it.

As the sun showed itself a ruddy bruise in the east, the ravaging stopped. As if the lion whose jaws had clenched me for so many hours had tossed me aside, leaving only the dry punctures of its deadly teeth. I dared not shift Ilario's steady embrace, lest it all begin again.

The aether calmed to a quiet turbulence more usual to a morning in the wild, but I did not close it off. Rather I pressed my face into the sodden wool of Ilario's breast and reached deep into the stream of emotion, dream, and magic . . .

. . . and Dante was gone.

"No, no, no."

"Tell me, Ani. Saints' mercy, is he dead?"

I shook my head. Even when he was so tightly closed, I had sensed the quiet echoes of his life—everything he was. But now . . . "Oh, gods, Ilario, he exists, but there's nothing of him there. *Nothing.* As if everything he is has been stripped away and only his bones are left." That did not, could not, mean he was dead.

"We'll find him," said my chevalier. "Never doubt. We'll find him, and through you and Rhea and Portier—saints grant *he* yet breathes—we'll have him back to explain all this. And, Ani, whatever has to be done about him . . . he will not burn. I'll not allow that."

HOVEN

The spring monsoon had struck as we ascended the Kadr ridge. No doubt the land of crags and seams saw little rain through the year, but we were convinced that it all fell on us. Though grateful we'd no dependence on the blighted water sources, we would have traded two days' thirst for an hour dry.

The steady drizzle made the steeps slippery and the flats a sea of muck. We tied ropes between us, so as not to get separated in the fog, and took turns in the lead, walking instead of riding so as not to lose the road. Even so we almost missed the settlement of Hoven, lost in a sea of cloud.

"Honestly, it's down there," said Ilario amid a flurry of hacking and sneezing. "I'm not leading you off a cliff. Trust—"

A cry accompanied a sharp tug on the rope at my waist. Rhea vanished down the muddy embankment to the side of the narrow road. Ilario's quick grab prevented me sliding after her.

"Are you broken?" Ilario called down into the fog where Rhea was spewing the first oaths I'd ever heard from her.

"No." The weight on the rope eased. "Just twisted— Oof."

Fortunately I was more prepared for the second wrench.

"Get a foothold and start climbing. We'll not let you backslide. If you need, I'll come down. . . ."

Centimetre by centimetre we took up the rope every time it went slack. "Careful of your gut, Chevalier," I said, feeling my own strain as a sudden weight told us Rhea had slipped again.

"To be sure."

When Rhea's head poked above the edge of the road, her cheeks blazed through a skin of mud. "Sorry," she mumbled. "Stupid. Lumbering cow."

Ilario offered a hand. She shook it off. "It's naught."

But as she climbed onto the mud-slick path, she was limping. Silently, guiltily, I cursed the thought it might slow us. Left to myself I would have ridden Duskborn into the ground and run the rest of the way. I had to see for myself. I'd sooner believe the aether itself broken before I would believe Dante so changed . . . or lost. I'd scarce been able to look at Ilario since his pledge to see that Dante did not burn. I could not bear to think what that meant.

Rhea pulled off her hose, and in moments, bound her left ankle, wrenching the bandage wickedly tight.

"As ever, you're much too hard on my gentle, glorious physician," said Ilario, touching her shoulder. She shook off his hand.

"You should ride for a while," I said.

"It's nothing!" Rhea gestured down the track. "Besides, we've greeters on the way."

"And dogs!" said Ilario, as two muddy pups pawed his already sodden trousers.

"Welcome, travelers." A handsome woman of middling age, almost as tall as Rhea, emerged from the mist. "Come out of the rain. Have a cup and tell us of your journeying."

Dressed plain, her dark hair bound atop her head in a tight knot, she sounded less severe than she looked. I tried to judge her on that, and on Andero's insistence that these people were kind and reasonable, rather than the fact that they killed anyone who worked magic. I knew of Kadr's terrible history. It was the only military venture my father had found difficulty speaking of, and the one that fixed his opposition to magic. That was long before he knew that his own father was a remnant of one of the most powerful and wicked of all blood families.

Ilario's silver tongue had the woman, Zophie, and her companions at ease within moments. The younger woman, Krasna, raced down the hill ahead of us to ensure us a roof, a fire, and a meal. We offered to sleep in the barn, but Tesar, a short, stout, and iron-hard young man near my own age, insisted on housing us with his family. "The rain is ever a blessing, but I'd not condemn anyone to sleeping on barn straw after journeying through it. Damoselle Tasserie, did the gentleman say you are a trained healer? A traditional healer, not a sorceress . . ."

Ah. Perhaps they were short on physicians as well as smiths.

As the villagers led my companions down the path, a bit of color caught my eye on the trail where Rhea had slipped down. The white embroidery told me it was a scrap of her Temple apron. Perhaps Rhea was leaving her Temple identity behind her.

"Goodman Silvio, Damoselle Madeleine," said Zophie, as we trudged the last few metres into the heart of the tidy settlement. "I've no wish to pry into your private business, but I must tell you, we do not tolerate any deviltry here—no magic, no enchantments of any kind. Our watchers can sense the slightest use. Trespass, and we'll see you dead. 'Tis harsh, I know, but the history of this land gives us cause enough. Some among us believe we should not warn our visitors, but I've been persuaded of late that such policy can pervert justice."

"Warning seems fair," said Ilario, "as long as it's the *use* you punish and not the skill."

"A person cannot help being born with the skill," she said. "I've come to see that, though I'd prefer to rid the world of the blight altogether."

No matter her conversion, I was not about to tell her I suffered the disease she loathed.

Villagers began stopping by Tesar's house even before we'd sat down to supper—this man with a stomach complaint, this child with an earache. . . . After the first few, Rhea offered to drop around to each house after our meal, so she could take care of what was needed in a more private setting. Everyone was pleased. As was I. We had purposely not asked after Andero.

As we devoured a savory pottage, Ilario carried the conversation with Zophie, Tesar, his wife, and the others, asking animatedly about the settlement, the prospects for the weather, the roads, and other travelers. Zophie asked him if he had a wife.

To my surprise it was Rhea spoke up. "He doesn't. But he has a lady. He told me he has room for only one woman in his heart, though hers is fully occupied with another."

Eugenie would weep to hear her beloved brother say such a thing. She forever lamented his lavishing his devotion on her alone. Loving as she was, even she had no idea of Ilario's true nature.

Ilario's cheeks flamed, and he quickly turned the conversation to Hoven's history.

I shivered despite the fire. Since that night on Kadr ridge, I had never been warm. Ilario's sober reassurance wedged in my throat like a fishbone. *Whatever needs to be done about him* . . . If Dante was mad, what in Heaven would I do? I would not believe he was corrupt.

I wanted to be gone from this place.

Once we'd eaten, Ilario and I accompanied Rhea and her medicine box on a round of the village's seven houses. Ilario visited with the men, as comfortable in the farm settlement as in Eugenie's salon. Rhea listened to coughs, doled out drops of medicine for joint fever and weeping eye. She excised a boy's warts, and lanced and cleaned a man's wickedly mortified cut made by a skinning knife. I helped as I could, while keeping my eyes and ears open for a sign of Andero.

The last house sat at the far end of the commons. Nan and Elio had five children, ages five through sixteen. As the gaunt farmer and his wife invited us in, Tesar mentioned that the newest settler in the village, a blacksmith, lived with the family, as well.

"He's down to the forge," said Elio, "but I think he's healthy enough."

"Ah, you've a smith!" said Ilario. "Mayhap I'll have a word with him when we've finished here. I've a worry about my mount's shoes."

Sadly, I could think of no reason to bolt just then.

As Rhea finished up with the children, the front door opened to the growl of thunder and a pelting rain. "Spirits and demons," boomed a soggy giant, "a deluge! Are we having a party?"

"Travelers," said Tesar. "A physician willing to examine the children in exchange for a night's lodging out of the wet."

"A good bargain at whatever the price. 'Tis a night to stay near a friendly hearth."

The newcomer appeared less wet, but equally formidable once he removed his great-cloak, and threaded the crowded room toward Zophie. He towered more than two metres in height, with shoulders and arms ready to shift boulders. His broad, handsome face sported a thick brown beard and enough lines to indicate he smiled more than he frowned. As Zophie murmured in his ear, he glanced up and caught me staring at him over the heads of chasing children.

Curiosity sharpened his glance. Juggling a steaming cup of cider, he soon joined me on the hearth rug, where I was helping a small girl with her apron.

"Don't believe I caught your name, damoselle," he said. His eyes were a deep, rich green, not so intense, but unmistakably kin. Recalling the awkward kindness of his letters, I felt that I already knew him very well. "Madeleine," I said. "Anne Sophia Madeleine, to be precise."

Pleasure blossomed across his broad expanse. " 'Tis an honor—a great honor—to meet you. I'm Andero. The smith."

No matter the crushing gloom these few days past, I could do naught but smile. It likely would have thrown him over if I'd embraced him as I wished. "It's reassuring to find such hospitality here."

"The good folk here have welcomed me kindly. One must be sure to understand and obey their laws, even for a brief stay."

"The laws have been clearly explained to us."

Andero nodded and sipped his cider.

I nodded toward Ilario. "My *brother*, Silvio, was severely wounded in a border skirmish in the north. His physician believes desert climes will aid his healing."

"A border skirmish . . ." He glanced sharply at Ilario. "A *swordsman*, is he?"

"Indeed so."

"Such a healer he must have!" The thicket of his eyebrows almost met his hair. So Dante had told him of Ilario.

"Most gifted."

Andero's gaze found Rhea, who took that moment to laugh at Nan's youngest, a rosy-cheeked babe who had a firm grip on the healer's ragged hair.

I finished tying the elder child's apron. She kissed my cheek and ran away. "We head south tomorrow," I said, "though I'm unsure of our route. We look for guidance."

"We can surely arrange for that."

Andero took my hand. As he helped me off the floor, he squeezed it hard. "Have a care in your journeying, damoselle. Things in the south are very worrisome. I'll hope to see you again before you leave."

"Sir smith," said Ilario, sailing toward us like a merchant ship into familiar harbor. "Would you consider taking a gander at my horse, the black gelding in the barn? I fear he's in dire need of shoes."

"I'll have a look," said Andero. "If I think work's needed, I'll take care of it tonight. Nan, Elio! Don't wait up if you see the forge lit. I could be late. Grace to all."

As if he'd bade them, the folk of Hoven and their guests braved the rain and headed for bed.

IT TOOK NO TIME AT all for Tesar's house to quiet. Though night shuttered the other dwellings, light flickered at the end of the village, where our host had pointed out the forge.

"The smith seems a stalwart man. Nan and Zophie had naught but good to say of him," said Rhea sleepily. "Will you see him tonight?"

"As soon as I dare."

Half an hour later, the rain had ended and I slipped out. The ground squelched as I tramped toward the light and the clank of hammer on metal. A blast of heat and Ilario's gelding welcomed me to the forge. But it was the smell of hot iron—the smell of Dante when he had soothed some bout of fury and come back to teaching—near brought me to tears. Save that I had no tears left since the night on Kadr ridge.

The smith had his back to the door. I moved around into the light where he could see me and waited. It was dangerous to startle a man dealing with hammers and red-hot metal.

He glanced up. "Mercy! Didn't expect you so soon."

Sweat beaded his broad forehead and dampened the shirt underneath his leather apron.

"I couldn't wait longer."

He threw the glowing horseshoe on a bed of rock, laid down his tools, and drew me into the shadows. "Appreciate your taking care. Me and the folk here get along well. But they don't forget I'm their bondsman neither." He cocked his head for a moment, appraising. "Dante's not forgot what you look like. I would have recognized you in more unlikely places than Elio's front room."

"I, too," I said. "There is a certain family resemblance."

"Honestly? I'd never have thought it."

"More inside than outside, perhaps. What's happened to him, Andero? Something's terribly wrong these few days past."

"Many things have happened, but I don't know much recent." He motioned me to a bench. "He's four days ride from here, in the city of Mancibar. You ought to know some things before you go."

"Anything. Everything."

"Pardon if I take up my hammer now and again, just in case anyone's noticing." He returned to his anvil. " 'Twas late in Desen's month he rode into Raghinne. Never saw anyone so lone. Didn't know then how scared he was. He'd ever been one to hide what he was thinking, frighting people off, even ones like me that never meant him harm. But I learnt a deal when I was soldiering. Understood him better, which is why I sent to him when Da went crazy. . . ."

He told me everything of their time together. Punctuated with the pumping bellows, the rumbling flames, and the pounding hammer, he laid out what Dante had told him of his father's words, of Dante's fears for Portier, of Castelivre and Adept Denys and how the healing in Otro's village had brought him back to magic. It would take days for me to put together the whole of it. But even that long story was not all. . . .

"I've learnt some of what's transpired since he left me here, but it's confusing and too long for tonight. Come morning, about two kilometres down the road south, take the track off to your left that crosses a little wash. You'll find a house a good ways in. I'll meet you there as early in the day as I can get away. You'll hear all there is to tell, and we'll figure out what to do. Now, you'd best get back before someone figures we're up to something here. 'Tis only a tenday past they've let me out of leg irons."

"Irons! I thought these were *generous* people?"

I wanted to snatch him away right then. Indeed, I had concluded that if ever some divinity had shown Dante favor, it was in sending him his elder brother. But it was very late. "We'll be there."

He straightened and heaved a deep sigh. "It's good you've come. He's needed you."

MORNING BROUGHT BRILLIANT SUNSHINE. The villagers were generous with tea and fruit, and effusive with their appreciation for Rhea's help. It was hard to believe they kept a bondsman in irons and had wanted to kill a blind man for trying to see.

Tesar's eldest son left us at a remote farmhouse, where Rhea examined a young pregnant woman. She'd had a babe stillborn because it was a footling. But Rhea was able to reassure her that this one was head down and unlikely to turn.

By midmorning we were headed south. Ilario and Rhea talked quietly of healing and Hoven. I lagged behind. The image of the pregnant farm wife, churning with fear and hope, haunted me. Andero had told me how Dante's mother, also churning with fear and hope, had birthed her children in a cave. She had allowed one to die there, sacrificed—*murdered*—another, and repeatedly abandoned Dante alone in the dark when he showed signs of magic. Such desperation was scarce believable. But the story explained so much about her son.

Yet, what had old Otro said? That it wasn't fear or grief that made Dante scream in the night. *For one born in the dark, such terrors are but echoes. . . . He fights for his soul. The Great War has never ended for the daemons.*

Had Dante told Otro he was born in a cave? I shuddered, despite the sunlight. *Daemon.* A very old word, according to the old man. What did that mean? The words of holy men were infuriating.

"One or the other of you, tell me of daemons," I said. "Who is this Panthia, whose worship demands infants' blood?"

"Panthia!" The name echoed like the crack of a pistol shot—from both the Cultist and the Temple servitor.

"*Infants'* blood?" said Ilario. "What are you talking about?"

"That's a forbidden name," said Rhea. "We should not—"

"Panthia's is a *holy* name," said Ilario. "Certainly no one here needs to be protected from truth lest their faith be shaken. To mask it is unworthy of a woman of your intelligence."

Rhea's cheeks flamed. "Such things are easily perverted into falsehood."

"What are you talking about?" I said.

"Ancient Temple writings name Panthia and Celeres daemons," said Ilario, "rebels. Yet Panthia brought humankind the first vine and taught us of its use. Celeres taught us the stories of Creation that we might understand our place in the Pantokrator's heart. His stories became the *Primordium*, though the Temple forbids mentioning his name, because you might get confused."

"But I thought the rebel was *Dimios*," I said. "The Souleater. Daemons are his followers."

"You see?" said Ilario. "Confusion. Yes, Dimios was the First of the Angels and was set to watch over humankind. But he refused to see us raised up, claiming he defended Heaven against the taint of our violence and corruption. He wanted to keep us ignorant and in our place—much like Temple tetrarchs do."

"That's unfair," said Rhea, bristling. "We do not deny Dimios's errors or Panthia's and Celeres's good teaching. Scholars believe those texts that name them daemons must be in error."

By this time we'd come to a halt. "Please, I just want to know." I told them of Dante's mother.

Rhea's hand covered her mouth. "His mother birthed in caves? Abandoned her child in the dark for *days*, all for magic? It's all turned around. . . ."

Ilario compressed his lips and shook his head. "Panthia and Celeres rebelled against *Dimios*, not the Creator. Dimios slew Celeres and Panthia, beginning the War for Heaven."

And *the Great War has never ended*, Otro had said. The *Daemon* War.

"It's all about words and texts and translations," said Ilario. "Those who hear the stories of Panthia and Celeres see only good in them. And so poor beleaguered women like Dante's mother take their worship into caves, thinking to offer blood sacrifice because that's how you get a *daemon*'s favor. I didn't know Dante had been brought up amid such beliefs."

"Is it over—the War for Heaven?"

"It is long over," said Rhea. "The Creator confined Dimios and the other Fallen in Gedevron. Anything else that's happened—" She bit her lip and glared at Ilario.

"The Temple doesn't like you to think that daemons are still scheming to wreak havoc," said Ilario. "Because you might start believing that saints walk among us, as Cultists do. Or you might doubt the divinity of the Pantokrator, which Cultists do *not*, as I've reminded my friend, the healer, many times in our discussions as she wielded her knife about my gut. Mercifully, she did not choose to correct my errors with her instruments, or chastise my cursing with her cautery iron. . . ."

Ilario bestowed a most appreciative glance on Rhea. Not many had ever taken Ilario seriously.

She didn't see it. Jaw tight, wincing at her sore thighs, she was urging her mount back onto the track. "You're a fool, Chevalier."

He jerked as if she'd slapped him. Foolish girl. If she was truly infatuated with Ilario, she could not have hurt him more.

Ilario and Rhea rode in stiff silence, while I pondered aged shepherds and the mechanisms of history and the dubious truths of myth and prophetic speeches. Dante, locked in the dark by vengeance, had been drawn south by an enchantress who could murder through dreams and who promised worse evils to come. He'd been pursued by a self-righteous tetrarch bent on gutting and burning him and was told by his own father, his sister, and a prophetic stranger that he was destined from birth to become the Souleater's minion. How could he not be crazed? Had it finally broken him? Was that what I'd felt? And if not that . . .

"I think we've found it," called Ilario softly. "Hold back for a moment." An hour's plod down the narrow track had brought us to a clearing and a ramshackle house of wood and stone. Smoke plumed from the chimney.

"Divine grace!" Ilario called as he rode into the clearing.

It wasn't Andero who stepped out of the doorway to greet us, but a thin, prune-faced man. Which man was more astonished, none could say, but Ilario spoke first: "John Deune!"

CHAPTER 32

THE KADR ROAD

"Master!" John Deune's complexion paled to the hue of Melusina's sheets. Knees buckling, he dropped to the muddy ground and shriveled into a weedy knot. "Save us, I never thought to harm. 'Twas only a trinket, a small gem long buried." His voice shriveled, too. "Were you sent to fetch it? Did I have it I'd give it over straight off. Who'd imagine the dead would care?"

"I'm not dead. Not this hour anyway." Ilario slapped his arms and cheeks. "But it was a near thing. Here you are in the wilds of Kadr—the last place I ever expected to find my valet."

Deune's head lifted. "To honor your memory, I assumed— The mage needed a guide."

"But how did you come to be in Coverge to see me fall? You swore to tell my sister where I was before going off to see to your— Ah, were your sons the *unpromising followers* Andero wrote of?" Ilario slipped off his horse and gave me a hand down.

John Deune squinted at his master in puzzlement, his anxieties forgotten for the moment. He didn't know. After eighteen years in Ilario's service, he had never heard his master speak as anything but the idiot fop, the laughingstock of Sabrian nobility.

Ilario glanced over his shoulder at Rhea and me and burst out laughing. "We've a number of things to clarify, John. My recent brush with the eternal Veil seems to have knocked some wits into my skull. Amazing things, death and healing, yes?"

John Deune scrambled to his feet, puckered gaze raking the three of us. "What's wrong with you, lord? Has this lady witched you?"

I could not enjoy his befuddlement. My throat constricted. My eyes fixed on the doorway. "Is Dante here?"

The manservant's seed-like eyes shifted to me, his lips curled. "The daemon mage haunts Mancibar nowatimes. We've parted company, now he's found what he seeks."

"That's it, is it?" Cutting disappointment made me snappish. "Did you think to steal the emerald from the blind man, John? Is that why you stayed with him?"

"Wouldn't be the worst evil. Not compared to cold murder. Not compared to selling your soul to get what you want. Not compared to torturing the man you've come to rescue.

"Torture Portier? Never." Spider feet tickled my spine.

Though yet eyeing Ilario uncertainly, the man stood straighter. "A witness saw Master Dante torment the librarian with hot irons till he could scarce speak for screaming."

"Impossible. Dante and Portier are like brothers." Then why did the hairs on my neck rise?

"There's much you'll not wish to believe, my lady. When you've given your heart to a daemon, it's not so easy to reclaim."

"You know nothing of my heart!" But shouting could not drown out fear.

"You asked." Snorting, John Deune tramped around the side of the house. He returned with an armload of wood that he dumped beside the door.

He eyed Ilario. "I suppose you're here to meet the smith. There's a fire good enough for cooking inside, and I'll put water on to boil. You were ever a fair master. I could do for you, as usual. For my regular pay."

"I've no wherewithal," said Ilario. "Not a kivre of my own. Naturally I'll pay your back wages once we're back to Merona."

I didn't want to hear from anyone but Dante. Or Portier . . . Holy gods. But John Deune was the only witness available. Gritting my teeth, I tethered Duskborn beside the other horses. "Forgive my sharpness, John Deune. I—we—need the rest of your story."

"But you'll believe only what you want of it? Call me liar?"

"I'm just tired and worried. I'll listen. Please."

"Come inside, then." A few scraps of leather and a tumbled pallet were spread on the cold dirt floor. While Rhea heated cider from a small cask, John Deune told his story, beginning with the day Dante woke draped over a horse.

". . . He near killed me that day, but I'd sworn, so I took him where he said, to the temple in Carabangor with the eagles out the front. Then I found me a place to hide, because yes, I saw no ill in taking a bit of glass whose owner had been dead a thousand years. I saw all that came about. The lady was like an angel, standing on a rock in the middle of that white lake. She keeps calling to the mage to come rescue her, and in her hand's a green gem the size of a bird's egg. Master Dante rows out to her. . . ."

"Just like the old soldier's dream." Andero filled the doorway. "Every detail he describes is just as Dante saw it in the dream."

"Well he didn't describe it to me," snapped John. "Did he tell you that after he gets her across the lake, he chokes the life out of her? Murder, pure and simple. A girl younger than you, lady."

"He wouldn't . . ."

"Heed him, damoselle," said Andero. "There may be an explanation, but you needs must listen. Wasn't the first time a madness took him to murder. As I told you."

I didn't want to listen. Murder and daemons, the horror in the aether . . . everything told me that the world was terribly wrong, and that Dante was at the center of it.

John Deune nodded, smug. "Just as I said. He was wild as he was with me when I got him away from Hoven, and as he ever was at Castelle Escalon. The angel woman lay dead on the ground. Then the other one arrived and I thought he might kill her, too."

"The other?" His hateful images clogged my thinking.

"Another woman the very twin of the first, ripe and beauteous as you've never seen, climbed out of the lake. She snatched up the dead woman's emerald and showed the mage she had another just like to it. When she came up the stair, I had to scoot out of the way so's not to be seen. But I'll tell you, lady, once the both of them come out of the building into the sunlight, I knew the bargain was made. He knelt to her and held her hand to his forehead. Even a servant knows what such a swearing means. As they walked out to where his horse was left, he had to cover his eyes."

He sat back in triumph. Ice crystals formed in my bones. "He could *see*."

"Clear as day. He sold himself to her. Some say he rules her now. He comes out from the palace and burns folk out of their homes, and there's hauntings and vanishings and bleedings growing ever worse in the city. She wears the two jewels, but he carries his white stick. And they live with the Regent of Mancibar, who is the very whinging, creeping sorcerer who worked for him in Merona. None could tell me the daemon mage has become a *servant* to that one."

Jacard! Dante had been right. And John was right that Dante could never serve Jacard. And whatever twisted logic might suggest Dante was playing *agente confide*, yet again, was erased. Jacard would never believe him. The woman had cured his blindness, given him light, given him a reprieve from his horror at losing his magic. . . . What would he give for that?

"Your sons watch Dante in the city?" My voice rang hollow and flat like a dead woman's.

"Alvy met some fellows at a tavern who serve at the palace. They say the mage teaches her magic, plays games with her. Maybe more. Eats from her hand, he does."

Every word brought another blow. Though my body was frozen, the room swam in the heat.

"One of Alvy's friends got called to the lady. She said he was to fetch the *librarian*, chain him in a pit just so, and leave an iron rod to heat in the fire, as she and her sorcerer were going to have some jolly fun. The guard did as he was told and said he watched as the mage come down and frighted the prisoner half to death. Yelled at him. Cursed him. Burnt him about his face with the red-hot iron. Threatened to put out his eyes as the librarian had let happen to him."

"Night's daughter, he didn't *do* it?"

"Said his mistress wanted to do it. But any man would be damned forever to treat his *brother* so. I thought to take the boys and go home. The jewels were out of reach, and Mancibar was nowhere I wanted to be with young fellows getting stole from their beds and turning up shredded or with no blood in them."

Bleeding? Shredded bodies? Angels' mercy . . .

Andero continued the tale, earnest, intent. "When they came through Hoven, I persuaded John to send the boys back to the city to watch Dante. Will got hired on at the palace stables. He's seen Dante ride out with the lady, friendly-like. He says there's no doubt Dante could ride away at any time—certainly using his magic. So he *chooses* to stay. And there's no doubt at all that he can see."

The room fell quiet. Their eyes were on me, waiting. I could answer the sympathy in Ilario's face no better than the accusation in John Deune's or the worry in Andero's.

"I'm going on to Mancibar," I said. "None of you has to go with me. You all know I've resources I've not even explored as yet. Yes, Dante has done dreadful things." Somehow saying it aloud set my back straighter. "He set out on this journey convinced that this woman and her jewels and the dream were connected to what we did at Mont Voilline and posed a danger at least its equal. Just look at the measure of his urgency. That he would ask for help from you, Ilario, and then allow you to save him, die for him . . . Nothing could be more alien to his nature. To return to Coverge *blind*, and then to ask you, Andero, a brother he's not seen in half a lifetime, into such danger as we faced before, I cannot imagine how difficult that was for him. To continue on with you, John Deune, to willingly submit himself to one who loathes him—that's the measure of desperation, not cunning. No matter what's happened to him, no matter what choices he's made—and I will not believe he's chosen some evil path until I hear it from his own lips—I will find him. But first, I think"—and this was my own dreadful decision—"I must find Portier. I'll not let Jacard bury him alive for any reason on this earth." I wrenched a deep breath, satisfied in my resolution. "So choose for yourself what to do. More than half a day's light remains. I'll not wait."

Ilario stood and stretched. "My hind end was just informing me that it needed the comforts of a sculpted leather seat and not these scraps on dirt." He bowed toward Rhea. "My kind physician: Soul's grace, damoselle, again and forever. Your good care is well taught, so I can likely manage dosing my lingering ills from here out. Clearly you'll be welcome in Hoven until we return to escort you home."

"You can't—oughtn't—be mixed up in this business," Rhea mumbled. "The danger . . ."

"Portier and I have saved each other's skin a number of times," he said. "I'll not leave him to Jacard's whims. As for Dante, there's more to this story than *any* of us can judge. I witnessed this urgency Anne cites; it was no brotherly love bade me do what was necessary to let him get away. But, of course, I am particularly unwilling to allow the ferocious Damoselle Anne to abandon me when I'm not in top fighting trim. So if you're yet fretting about my bowels, physician—or my soul—you'll have to come as well."

Rhea snorted and hefted her pack. "Stubborn still. Wouldn't trust you to take care any more than a hound."

Andero looked from her to the queen's bemused brother, and then back, as awestruck as if he'd seen a dove challenge a stag. It was always startling to witness the bold fire that shy, quiet Rhea brought to her profession.

"All right, then," I said. "Three of us."

In one fluid motion, Andero buried the fire in the little hearth and snatched up his own pack. "Not going to let someone else see to my little brother, now, am I? If he needs rescuing, I'll do it. If he needs killing, I can do that, too. As I've already left a message at the forge that I'll come back to fill my bond when I've done what's needed, I'd like to get on the road as soon as may be. What of you, John Deune?"

"I'm going to fetch my boys away," said John Deune. "They've been too long in the daemon's path already."

"So be it," I said. "Let's ride."

MANCIBAR

The iron sun hammered the slow-moving flow of travelers on the approach to Mancibar. Each one had serious business, as the ill repute of the city precluded frivolous visiting. The city gates floated in the sun shimmer, as vague and insubstantial as the gates to Heaven.

John Deune had left us the previous night, intent on finding his sons. Ilario was off keeping company with some of the other travelers. Rhea and Andero rode behind me, talking quietly of soldiering and healing. As ever in the long days since crossing the river, I was lost in a heat haze haunted by the image of the Uravani bridge.

According to John Deune, Dante had spent most of an hour contemplating the sculpted figures—the Righteous Defender of Heaven and the Daemon of the Dead. The figures were a powerful image, the serene Defender, sword arm upraised to Heaven, and the Daemon lunging forward, arms extended as if his wake might draw the lesser daemons behind him. When Ilario pointed out that the Daemon was missing his clawed right hand, Andero told us how his father had purposefully mutilated Dante's hand to mark him as the Souleater's Chosen. Such cruelty—like his mother's slavish ignorance—was incomprehensible. Whatever gods might be a part of this universe, I refused to believe they would countenance such works.

Neither Dante nor I subscribed to popular myths of the Beginnings. I was more inclined than he to believe that some benevolent hand had set the earth spinning and set it among the stars according to the perfect order mathematics described. Yet both of us had been shaken by our experience at Mont Voilline. A man who would not die. Spectral visions of starving dead. The winds of Ixtador sweeping the mountainside. And here amid Mancibar's patchy fields of vigor and blight, the universe seemed at once more capricious and more dangerous than in the high pastures of Otro and his prophecies. What was the truth?

Ilario returned, reining in at my side and motioning Andero and Rhea close.

"I've a plan." He grimaced as he blotted sweat from his face. Despite his hat, his fair skin was deeply sunburnt. "I met a jongleur who has hopes of getting on to entertain at the Regent of Mancibar's palace. He says that most of those who played or sang for the old prince have fled the city and there's opportunity for lesser-known folk to get paying work. Good, yes?"

"In what way?" My thoughts were sluggish in the heat.

"We need a reason for entering the city. And we need a way into the palace. Why would any sane person go there? But musicians, players, poets, they're all mad."

"But we're not jongleurs or . . . or anything," I said. "You can sing, at the least."

"Our physician happens to have a fine contralto—I was not entirely insensible for that first month of our companionship. Andero says he picked up a bit of juggling while he was soldiering. You're a graceful dancer and could learn more. And when the time was right, you could perhaps do a few magical tricks. *Vanishings*, perhaps?" His eyes sparked.

My head lifted. "We'd have to be very careful," I said. "Couldn't count on getting away with it more than once." My supply of Lianelle's powder was getting low. But if we could become familiar with the palace, the people, the defenses, and then get all of us inside, ready to strike . . .

Lingering at a caravanserai outside the walls, we picked apart Ilario's idea. Without any better alternative, we pulled out the scarves and shirts we'd bought at Mattefriese. I loosed my braid and tied my hair to one side with Lianelle's silver pendant, letting it dangle like an earring, and gave Rhea the necklace of brass bangles and kingbuck horn the old woman had given me.

Ilario donned the mantle of braided scraps and rubbed his hands on the fatty dried meat Andero had brought from Hoven. "With your permission, my physician," he said, grinning and wriggling his fingers in Rhea's direction.

Though puzzled, she shrugged assent. He proceeded to grease her short hair and curl it about his fingers until it stood out in all directions. "There, very like a Syan dancer I once entertained," he said, pleased with himself. "Only she smelled better."

Andero's glance could have pierced Ilario's fragile belly. Whether it was general disapproval or a particular pique at the lord's flippant teasing of a lady, I wasn't sure.

Thus transformed into Marco Flamberge and his troupe of jongleurs, come all the way from the coast of Tallemant, we talked our way past the gate guards of Mancibar and into the haunted city.

We'd scarce emerged from the gate tunnel when John Deune pounced on us, dragging along a blotchy, gap-toothed boy in greasy slops that could only be one of his sons.

"I've a need to speak with you, lady," spat the manservant, his complexion yellow, his hands trembling, "and find out what the daemon's done with Will."

"Discretion, John," said Ilario, dismounted in a graceful instant. He herded us into a busy lane well shielded from watchful guards and the beggars, cutpurses, and swindlers waiting to cozen bewildered travelers. "Now, what's the problem?"

The little man was seething and shaking, near collapse with fear and anger. "Tell 'em, Alvy."

"A tenday ago, Will came to the Cockatoo acting crazy, so scared he'd pissed hisself. Said the sorcerer had found him in the stables and witched him. He wanted us to run off. But I told him Da wanted him to stay, and he'd be in worse trouble if he weaseled out of it."

"What did he mean, the sorcerer witched him?" I asked.

"Said the sorcerer attacked him, near twisting his arm right out of its socket. He knew Will and me had been the ones following him, back when he was blinded. And he forced Will to tell his name and where he was certain to be in the mornings, so's he could find him. Said he might want to *use* him. Will didn't want to tell 'im naught, but said the sorcerer ate into his head with eyes like fire and said tell him or he'd cut off his cods. Will was mortal feared and told the mage that he come to the kitchen every day at dawnbreak. Next day Will never come back from the stables. Stableman says he must've got caught up in the ruckus about the daemon mage that morn. But the fellow didn't dare talk about it, and said maybe Will'd show up dead from it like the rest of them the haunts take."

"Dawnbreak . . . ten days ago," I said. "That's the day he disappeared? The day of this ruckus?"

"Tenday, aye," said Alvy, chewing his dirty fingernails.

The dawn when Dante vanished after a night of horrors. "The mage didn't tell him what *use* he might have for him?"

"The mage said he might want to tell Da a thing or two. That was all. Will was raving all night about the mage and the librarian. Said he couldn't get the words out of his head and out his mouth. Summat about a *cage in a navel*."

"But Dante didn't *say* this to him?"

"Nay. Will must've heard it elsewise."

It didn't make sense. The cage, perhaps. But naval? We were fifty kilometres from the sea.

John Deune wagged a finger at Andero and me. "This is what comes of dealing with the Souleater's own. We got to find my boy before they bleed him and throw him on the dung heaps."

We'd heard enough about the vanishing young men of Mancibar to understand his fear. But I wasn't going to tell John Deune of our plan. "We'll do whatever we can to learn what happened. You do the same. Watch for us in the market and we'll come up with a plan."

Andero paid Alvy for his watching. No smiles on the smith's face this day. The boy and his father hurried away.

Before the sun had set we had acquired lodgings in a poor district, the better to stay anonymous. Then we split up to survey the city.

Andero at my side, I strolled up the steep promenade, unable to take my eyes from the sprawling palace backed by the red cliffs. All day I'd held back, afraid. But seeing the place where he was, I paused, closed my eyes, and delved deep. *Friend,* I said in the voice only he could hear. *I've come to help you. What in the name of all stars have you done?*

The aether boiled around the stony silence.

CHAPTER 33

MANCIBAR

Rhea kicked a shoe across the cramped room. It didn't wake me. The rising heat had long convinced all four of us that whatever sleeping we'd done had ended.

"I'll fetch us something to eat that isn't noodles," she said, climbing over packs and pallets to the doorway. "And, yes, I can do it on my own. I'm not a child."

The healer had gotten testier every hour we stayed in Mancibar and seemed near unstrung this morning. Not even Andero could calm her.

"She's a Temple child," I said, once the paper-thin door had stopped quivering. "Maybe she's starting to worry about her soul now we're so close to Dante."

Maybe it was just sharing that nasty little room with three less-than-clean companions. The squalid Street of Beggars housed the most wretched residents of Mancibar. No reputable beggar would be seen there, as those who occupied its tin-roofed shacks and disease-ridden sniffing dens had nothing to spare for generosity.

Our lodging was a windowless lean-to at the back of a noodle shop. The nights were stifling, yet to open the door was to welcome flies, beetles, ants, rats, and the stink of the shop's refuse heaps. When the noodle maker fired up his pots for the day, the walls wept grease.

Yet, the room was a cheery haven beside the city itself. Mancibar's oppressive gloom gnawed at the spirit, fouling the taste of food and drink and evoking a sense that something horrid lurked in the alleyways alongside the piled-up filth.

Ilario scowled as he tied back his hair, newly darkened with black dye. "She's likely got actor's jitters. She didn't ask me to show her my urine this morning, and when I asked her if I was free of that particular duty, she yelled at me that she couldn't possibly *sing* in front of anyone."

I scraped up a grin. "She's likely ready for something more interesting than urine."

He glanced up sharply, flushed a deeper scarlet than his sunburn, which I'd not thought possible. "Oh, you mean—" His laugh was a bit thin. "No. She knows far too much about me for that."

The smith had followed Rhea as far as the doorway, watching her go. He swallowed the last of the ale from one of our flasks and wiped his mouth on his sleeve. His jaw was hard enough to crack nuts. "Damoselle, couldn't you speak to my brother in the way you do?"

"No. I mean, I've tried, but he doesn't hear me . . . or won't answer . . . or can't." Every hour, I tried.

He settled on his haunches and swiped at his tangled hair. "Wouldn't want to stay in this poison city too long. When you can't even get a smith to talk free, there's something rotten. Never knew a smith was feared of haunts or treachers either one."

Andero had spent the previous day hunting for work. Though my purse could use replenishing, his quarry had been gossip more than coin.

"I'll scout the walls and gates today," he said. "See if that channel gate the farrier mentioned would serve to get us out of the city. Don't like a place where leaving is so wicked tougher than getting inside."

"Nor I," said Ilario.

Every person, from noble to infant, was examined before being allowed to leave Mancibar. No man of fighting age was allowed to leave without written permission from the Regent.

"When we take Portier, Jacard will drop whatever might he has amassed right on our heads." I blotted the sweat already dampening my neck. "I'd like to think—"

A little explosive destruction might serve us well. But we'd no assurance Dante would or could come with us. Yet surely if he could rescue Portier—or wanted to—he'd have done it by now. I hated my inevitable conclusions.

Andero left abruptly with a promise to return by dusk. While I sewed cheap bangles on ruffled skirts Rhea and I had found at the market, Ilario dashed up and down the alley, dodging, spinning, and leaping as if he'd been bitten by a mad dog. Then he had me climb up a rickety staircase that led to the roof and drop wood shavings and scraps from the height, so he could thrust and poke at them with his sword, working to resharpen his eye, and then he dueled with the rats and wild cats that populated the lane. He was healing.

Rhea had not yet returned when the chevalier threw his sword on the pallet, donned his odd hat and cloak, and with a knightly flourish, kissed me on the head. "Offer what divine petitions you know, little seahorse. Soon we'll know whether Maestro Flamberge and his troop will be allowed to entertain the Regent of Mancibar and his guests."

"Every care, Chevalier," I said, squeezing his hand. "I'll not lose you again." By every right, by every medical judgment, he should be dead. Rhea was a marvel.

He bowed, scraping his hat's new feathers on the filthy floor. "Every care, damoselle. Save me comestibles, please. My body may no longer be that of a fifteen-year-old boy, but my appetite is."

Ilario de Sylvae was as gifted as any person I knew. How a man could draw a smile from me on that morning in that place was beyond imagining.

Rhea returned not long after he left, apologizing that she'd found only a few pieces of dried fish and some oversoft grapes. Sad to say, they were a tasty change from our landlord's soggy noodles.

The two of us spent the next hour practicing some gigues favored by Montclaire's tenants and a few more exotic dance steps I'd learned on my family's travels when I was a child. Rhea threw up her hands at every misstep. "I'm as graceful as a barge pole."

"With three of us we attract less attention. We need your good hands and good eyes, and if we find Portier and he's injured or ill . . ." Eyes swimming with tears, she joined me again, at least until the next time she stumbled or tripped.

We made masks for each of us from a silk petticoat we'd found in a rag box at the market. My every attempt at conversation fell dead. When I commented on Ilario's returning health, she threw down her work and retired to the alley. She couldn't undo the puffy redness around her eyes when she came back inside. But if she wouldn't tell me why she wept, I had no help to offer.

Only when the afternoon had fully matured into breathless heat did Ilario return. With a groan, he dropped onto his and Andero's pallet and threw an arm over his face.

My heart sank. "What luck?"

"Never have I been so humiliated," he said. "I've spent this entire day in one queue after another, answering highly impertinent questions from a legion of officious servants. "What is your entertainment? How long is it? Where have you performed? How many in your party? Despicable, flat-eared, bug-eyed, no-talent jog-wattles! As if bureaucrats could pass judgment on a true artist. They hated my piping. Said it sounded like Belphusian donkey horns."

"Your *piping*? Are you mad? I thought you bought the shawm just for show. It's broken . . . no reeds . . ."

"But I've always wanted to play. Music is food for the spirit as cavorting can never be. I thought I would add a bit of civilization to our performance."

"Oh, Ilario, what were you thinking?"

"Our application?" asked Rhea, biting her lip.

"Rejected."

I slumped against the wall. "Saints . . ."

"But then I tried to soothe my crushed heart by singing the 'Cancionero de Amiste,' and the other selectors decided we might be worth a tryout after all. At the next feasting . . . which happens to be tonight."

He popped up to sitting, his blue eyes sparkling like some mischievous sprite. Rhea caught it sooner and picked up the first thing to hand, a bracelet of bronze disks, and threw it at him, saying he was surely the most hopeless, ridiculous man on the face of the earth. A shoe soon followed, and then another. I joined in by beating him with the gaudy skirt.

Andero arrived just as Ilario called out a muffled surrender. The smith's expression declared we'd gone insane, perhaps from the heat and the stink. But Rhea's hiccup-laced explanation of Ilario's teasing cracked the smith's grim facade like a spring thaw at a frozen pool. "Thought you'd found us summat stronger to drink than ale," he said, with a wistful chuckle.

"Regent Iaccar is feasting tonight with at least three hundred guests," said Ilario, as we downed Rhea's fish and grapes and most of Andero's ale. "We are to be served somewhere between the soup and the meat. We'll hope the guests are enjoying themselves enough to pay us no attention."

Andero shook his head. "Doubt it. Folk say the vanishings come more frequent of late. Even the merchants and noble folk want to stay home, but the Regent bids them come, and if they don't they're fined or beaten. If any dares an opinion, they say it's the strange lady's mage who's brought them worse times."

The reminder instantly sobered us all.

"What could justify burnings and bleedings?" Andero slammed his great fist on the inner wall, likely shaking the noodles in their pots. "When Dante told me the things he'd done, I passed it off, thinking he exaggerated. Seeing that adept left naught but ash at Castelivre set me back. But then he near killed himself helping that hard-luck shepherd. But hearing all this . . . and about the Temple murders in Coverge and the ruination in Jarasco . . . They say these fellows taken here in Mancibar are found with their skin split open and no blood in them."

Germond de Gautier's screaming yet tainted my dreams—the terror and pain as the revenant of de Gautier's own grandsire tried to reshape the scholar's living body. Was Jacard merely clearing out those loyal to the old prince, or was he using the nireals and the Mondragon books to work some terrible magic? Dante had always believed a threat would come, but never from Jacard. Never from himself.

"Dante always has a reason," I said, not believing it at all, "even if we can't see it. But first we must find out where Portier is."

"What did Alvy say?" said Andero. "A cage in a navel?"

"*Naval* implies ships, water . . . which make no sense. We don't know for sure that the phrase had any meaning."

"Actually, it might refer to a *physical* navel." Rhea had retreated to the corner of our pallet. Elbows on her drawn-up knees, hands on her hair, her long forearms hid her face and left her quiet words almost unhearable. "I was told . . . learned . . . when I was out today that Mancibar was once called Sirpuhi of the Red Cliffs, a holy place—"

"The navel of the world," said Ilario, straightening, his tin plate slipping from his hand. "Saints Awaiting, Altheus was born here . . . died here. I'd no idea. Of course that's where they'd bring Portier. Kajetan would have known of this place . . . and told Jacard. . . ."

His gaze skewered me as if to implant what he knew straight into my head.

"Years ago, Portier and Dante spoke of places on this earth where the 'Veil was thin' because of certain meaningful events . . . places like Eltevire, where the first murder took place, like Mont Voilline, where Ianne brought us fire. Oh, yes, Ani. He's here inside that palace."

"Who?" said Andero.

"Portier . . . Altheus . . . Sante Ianne. And Jacard is planning to use him again. . . ."

Was it possible that Dante had passed us the message about Portier's prison?

The nerves I planned to have so firmly under control attacked me so hard I couldn't eat for the rest of the day. Naive hopes kept floating to the surface despite my best attempts. I would likely not see Dante. More than a tenday had passed since he'd attacked Will Deune in the stable. On the next morning, Will had vanished during a "ruckus about the daemon mage" and Dante's spirit had vanished in a flurry of agony. His presence in the aether had altered not one whit since that time. He could be dead. I tightened my grip yet again and continued our preparations.

THE WESTERING SUN HAD ALREADY touched the red cliffs by the time we trudged up the steep hill toward the Prince of Mancibar's palace. Though positioned like a fortress, the building appeared more like a temple, its stately facade of columns and beast statuary facing the sun's rising. The final approach did not creep timidly under guard towers and battlements but divided into two sweeping curves that embraced an expanse of terraced gardens that made Castelle Escalon's look primitive. Water cascaded through stone-lined channels to feed the myriad garden beds and fountains.

Elegantly dressed people on foot, horses, or litters thronged the road above the terraces where its two arms rejoined to form a stately causeway. Any unknown to the guards were required to show passes before entering the iron gates.

"Maestro Marco Flamberge and his jongleurs: Mistress Madeleine, Mistress Tasserie, and Sonjeur Dero." Ilario produced the paper he'd been given.

"What's in here?" The guard had Andero drop the large canvas bag draped on his shoulders and proceeded to pull out wads of blue-dyed fustian and veils of black crepe.

"Costumes, my kithara and its case, equipment for juggling. We're presenting a tableau about a maiden whose heart is—"

"Around the right side, third door back. And keep to the waiting room if you enjoy having blood and bowels inside your skin."

Once away from the gates, Andero, wearing a green bedsheet and carrying his bag of juggling balls, slipped into the sculpted evergreens and blooming shrubberies of the inner gardens. While we performed, he would survey guard posts, procedures, entrances, and exits. This occasion was as much for information gathering as for any hope we could steal Portier away so soon.

Harassed factotums herded the press of costumed performers into a great barren hall. The scene inside was chaos. Balls and swords flew through the air. Musicians tuned instruments. Acrobats careened into everyone while practicing cartwheels and pyramids. A dog, absurdly outfitted in a red silk jacket and pink feathers tied to its head, caused havoc among a flock of birds.

Three little dancing girls, lips painted red, cheeks highly rouged, and eyes blackened with kohl, wailed as their trainer yelled at them for mussing their gold-encrusted costumes. "The Spider God will eat you for his dinner," screamed the woman. "Your blood will trickle down his chin."

A bulbous man in red pantaloons yelled from a doorway, "Jugglers!" The flashing swords and flying balls disappeared through the swinging doors.

Ilario, Rhea, and I huddled together and reviewed our plan. A quarter hour we would work until our finale.

The red-pantaloon man called for dancing girls, then fire-eaters. We'd near despaired when he bellowed, "Marco Flamberge!"

He led us down a long passageway, squeezing past servants burdened with wine bottles and clean plates, bowls of fruit and heaping platters of meat and cheese. "The table you requested is set up at the left side of the performance floor," he said between wheezing breaths. "Arrange it yourselves."

Rhea fastened a veil across her face in the Syan style. Ilario had greased her hair into curls again, and we had all applied kohl to eyes and brows.

Neither Jacard nor Dante should recognize Ilario or me. At the factotum's nod, Ilario tugged his hat low and shouldered a decrepit kithara. Then, Rhea and I danced into Jacard's hall.

My first impression was naught but light and shadow. Great wooden beams holding hundreds of candles hung from the tall ceiling, illuminating the empty center of the hall while leaving the crowded peripheries dim. The dancing required a concentration I regretted, leaving me only vaguely aware of the clattering dishes and noisy conversation that surrounded us.

Dante could be here in this room. Jacard almost surely was. And the woman, the enchantress who spoke in macabre dreams, she could be here as well.

While Ilario strummed and sang of a maiden whose lover had gone off to fight the witchlords, Rhea and I moved the table into the center of the light and draped it with the velvety fustian. We thrust our tall walking sticks into loops we'd sewn onto the heavy fabric and let them hang so they paralleled the long side of the table.

I paused my steps, hand above my eyes as if I were sighting down the road for my returning lover. Rhea played my friend on whose shoulder I leaned, and also my mother who brought in Ilario as a new suitor. Our wordless dancing play was obvious and dreadfully sentimental. Only the purity of Ilario's singing raised it to a worthy height. When Rhea, swirled in enormous lengths of black crepe, brought word of my lover's death at the hands of the witchlords, I lay on the table and plunged a wooden dagger toward my breast.

Now for the dangerous part. Ilario laid down the kithara. During his unaccompanied lament, he and Rhea draped me in metres of billowing crepe and fustian. Well hidden, I downed sixteen drops of Lianelle's potion. By the time my smearing vision had settled enough that I knew I could not be seen, Rhea had joined Ilario in his song. Her rich contralto was a fine complement to his tenor, what I could hear of it through the layers of fabric and the thumping of my heart. Obscured by their activities, I slipped out from under the mounded draperies, crept under the table, and huddled there to wait.

Ilario strummed a few final bars on the kithara and sang of the wounded soldier who arrived to find his beloved lying dead. Humming a dirge, he and Rhea lifted our makeshift litter by the poles and marched slowly toward the door.

When the last trailing draperies fell away from the table, I felt dreadfully exposed. But the faint tinge of blue that limned the table and my departing companions assured me none could see me.

Scant applause burst out here and there. The buzz of conversation increased as a troop of acrobats raced in leaping, tumbling, and doing cartwheels.

Now to action. I crept out from under the table and rounded the room examining faces. Nervous, hard-faced women, and men with swiftly darting eyes, who laughed too loud and drank too much wine, peopled the crowded tables. Their silks and satins seemed faded, the jewelry tarnished, the good humor feigned. No eye took note of me.

Dodging scurrying servants and a man doing backflips, I moved toward the table at the apex of the great horseshoe. And there was Jacard.

He'd added weight these two years. Gray pouches drooped beneath his eyes. His dark beard, fuller than the sharp wedge I recalled, could not disguise a jaw gone soft, nor could a gold circlet hide the gray threads in his hair. Clothed in elegant dark blue brocade and a velvet cape, he was whispering asides to a small, strikingly beautiful woman. She was like a character in a book come to life. Her deep-hued skin contrasted dramatically with a sheer white gown and a cloud of pale hair that floated free, scarce touched by the forces that hold us to earth.

No other familiar figure occupied their table. Crushing disappointment, I stepped close enough to hear their talk.

". . . could not find a fortune-teller as you asked," Jacard was saying to the woman. Xanthe, John Deune had named her.

"You should scorch his naked feet," she said, popping a grape in her mouth. "It always works to get a servant's attention. Though I'll say the singer's voice was pleasing. Perhaps I'll have him brought to my bedchamber without those awkward women."

"We'd have to blindfold him." Jacard traced the long line of her neck with a finger. Disgusting. He looked ready to lick her face.

"All in all, I'd rather have a seer." She ignored his attentions. The guests on either side of them kept their eyes on their food.

"To remind your mentor of all he's forgotten?"

"For a number of things."

After a quarter hour of such unrevealing nonsense, I decided to move on. Neither of them wore any green jewels.

As I was deciding which way to go, the acrobats tumbled out the door, and fifteen costumed dogs burst yipping into the hall. Xanthe stood abruptly. "Enough of this. I hate dogs. Costumed dogs the worst."

Jacard's hand brushed her waist. "Will you not reconsider my offer?"

"I've no wish to spend the rest of the evening hearing you argue with a dead man, Regent Iaccar. It doesn't amuse me. I'm not yet desperate enough to let a corpse teach me what I want to know."

A *corpse*. I'd thought Dante was teaching her. . . .

"Then why do you do it, vixen?" muttered Jacard. He reached for his wine goblet. As his glare was fixed to the lady sweeping through the doors behind the dais, his hand tipped it. Wine splattered all over him, the tablecloth, and the woman next to him. I thought the overrouged, overjeweled woman might prostrate herself.

"Clumsy cow!" snapped Jacard, jumping to his feet as if the hapless guest had done it. He turned to the rest of the guests at the head table. "Excuse me while I retire to remedy this mess."

Meanwhile Xanthe began dispensing orders to the train of servants and aides on the far side of the doorway. "Wine in my apartments," she told one. "Draw me a bath," she told another, at a volume guaranteed to be heard by every person at Jacard's table. "I wish to get this graveyard stink off of me." Brushing her fingers on the gawking face of a fair youth no more than seventeen, she winked. "Stay tonight after the others leave."

I'd never witnessed a display so perfectly natural and yet so knowingly crafted to enrage.

Jacard knocked over his chair as he bulled his way after her. I slipped around and exited the same door while it yet swung open with his passing. The lady was already vanished.

Portier's prison would most likely be somewhere in the heart of Sirpuhi—the oldest part of the palace, surely downward and west toward the cliffs. Unfortunately, Jacard went up. Two bodyguards accompanied him up a grand stair and through brightly lit passageways to apartments of exactly the tawdry grandeur I would expect of him. Abandoning his attendants in a gilded salon the size of an amphitheatre, he moved on to an equally sizable bedchamber. Perhaps he intended to change his stained garments, as he said. Like a guardian wraith, I followed.

His first move was to lock the door behind us.

I froze in place between an armoire and a boot chest. Had he heard me?

He threw off his cape and doublet and donned a mud-colored tunic right over his wine-splotched shirt. With quick, silent movements, he opened a small door in the base of a marble statue of a man with a goat's lower body and pulled out a polished wood box. Sliding its lid aside, he pulled out a heavy silver chain bearing a single . . . huge . . . green Stone in a cage of silver wire.

My breath caught. Size alone named it worth a city. But who knew how to value a gem of such power? Yet . . .

A probe of the aether, as Dante had taught me, came up empty. Why did I perceive no enchantment? Surely this was one of the Seeing Stones.

Jacard threw his purple velvet cape over all, hiding the Stone and his plain garb. I followed him into the outer passage. Again I was torn. Follow Jacard and his gem or seek out the lady? No doubt her apartments were nearby . . . and her daemon mage. Her teacher. Surely she kept him close. I had to know.

I had to traverse the entire upper floor of the palace to find Xanthe's rooms, yet it was strangely easy to find my way. Around every corner was a statue or table or arch that seemed familiar. When there was a choice of turning, one way would sing out, *Take me.* The lady had demanded a bath, and sure enough, off the middle of a passage in exactly the place it ought to be was a servants' stair and a parade of serving girls lugging steaming water jars. I took up with them like a spare shadow, following them into a great bathing room, lined with richly colored tiles, arranged in erotic designs.

A short passage took me into a large, candlelit bedchamber. And there, in a velvet-lined box on a bedside table entirely exposed to anyone who passed, lay two faceted green Stones, locked into a cage of silver wire. I had just bent over to study them, when a male voice from the next room set my heart thuttering. I scurried to the bedchamber doorway.

"Your hair is the moonlight's mist; your feet the rosy color of spring dawn. . . ." The gawking youth Xanthe had invited to stay groveled half-naked at her feet, uttering inanities. But my attention was captured by the white stick leaning on the wall across the room, beside a curtained doorway. Dante's staff.

Saints' mercy, did he live in these apartments with her? I'd never considered . . . Two years he'd kept himself in our guesthouse. Yet Xanthe was extraordinarily beautiful. Fascinating. Sensual. Perhaps she was a more devoted student than I. . . .

"I've changed my mind." The lady's naked foot shoved the youth onto his backside. "You're not at all to my taste."

Wide-eyed and gasping, as if he teetered on the verge of a cliff, the youth scrambled away, snatched up his wadded doublet and shirt, and scuttled through the curtained arch.

The lady called to the servant girls to keep the hot water coming, and then hurried through the arch after her failed lover.

Emotions in foolish disarray, I followed them out. The bells had rung tenth hour. I needed to be back with Ilario in three hours, lest we be summoned to repeat our performance. I'd best be off to find Portier.

Xanthe had gone only a short way down the main passage. A red-haired man in green livery stood beside another curtained door. A well-armed man . . . a guard. I paused, the prickling sense of familiarity luring me after her.

"Is he here?" said Xanthe.

"As ever. No change." The guard held back the draperies. I slipped through right on her heels, taking care not to brush the guard or the curtain.

A single candle glinted in a great window. The dark chamber seemed spacious. Uncluttered. A few darker bulks could be chairs, a couch, a table. Thick carpet caressed my bare feet.

"Why have you no light here?" asked Xanthe, irritated.

"It does not seem necessary." The voice rattled my heart. Dante's voice, no question. As I focused on the shadows rather than the soft candlelight, I made out the still figure in a chair, facing toward us, his back to the windows. He chose the dark, though he could see. . . .

I wrapped my arms about my aching breast.

"I've given you sight. You should use it."

"So you say." No anger, no passion, no kindness, no contempt. Never had I heard Dante speak so entirely without emotion. Save for its distinct timbre, the voice could have been any man's.

Xanthe circled the room like a stalking cat. "How can you not remember such a gift?"

He didn't answer.

She planted herself in front of him. "You do nothing to restore yourself. Nothing to make yourself useful. How am I to justify your life? Iaccar insists I hand you over. All your rants about keeping the Stones from him . . . our partnership . . . my independence. You swore me an *oath*, you devil."

"I seem to have sworn oaths to everyone I encounter, living, dead, or . . . whatever. Kill me, if you wish."

With a lightning crack, her hand met his cheek. "It is *not* my wish!"

He didn't move. Didn't grab her hand. Saints, what was wrong with him?

She dropped to her knees. "I want you back, mage. All these spells you've taught me, but I've no idea which one might reverse this change. *Tell* me. You're leaving me no choice but to partner with Iaccar."

"He won't like what comes of it. Nor will you."

"Then to the seven hells with you!" She leapt to her feet and stormed out of the room.

He sighed and rested his chin on his ruined hand, staring into nothing. "That is already accomplished."

I knelt to get a good look at his face. Gaunt, fleshless, and pale. An angry scar on one cheek. And his eyes . . . even when sightless their green fire could scorch. But now they were cold, dark, dead.

In that instant, all my girlish imaginings were laid waste. Like the green leaf hidden in a hard, brown bud, hope had named him an *agente confide* again, or a prisoner, kept in some state of unconsciousness or stasis. My friends and I would break the locks of his dungeon and restore him. I had never dreamt of this. He lived but was not the man I knew.

No question what I wanted—to do anything that would restore his unruly spirit to the aether. But I could not risk betraying Portier. This stranger might warn Xanthe or Jacard about me.

He rose and wandered through the room, first to a table piled with books. He thumbed through them idly, moved on to a mahogany cabinet where he poured a glass of wine, and then drifted through a glass-paned door that led to a small balcony. The rising moon showed him rail thin. Strands of gray, new these months, threaded his dark hair, cut brutally short.

Leaning on the balustrade, he peered upward to stars faded in the moon's brightness. Then his gaze dropped to the rocky slope far below.

Despair flooded the aether. Overwhelming. Suffocating. Unnatural. The longer he stared into the depths, the more afraid I became. *Dante, hear me.*

He did not react at all.

"The door is a better way out," I said softly.

"Perhaps. Perhaps not," he said, unmoving.

"You can walk back through it if you don't like what's on the other side."

"Doesn't matter. The scourge forbids easy solutions. It cannot compel me to do the impossible. But it can . . . discourage . . . all else. Eventually I will—" He turned around and peered into the gloom. "Who's there?"

"No one. I am part of you."

"I doubt that," he said, shaking his head. "And Xanthe does not allow me to speak to other women, even disembodied ones."

He exhibited no hint of recognition. When he was blind, he could recognize me by smell alone.

"What's happened to you?"

"If you're part of me, you should know, should you not?"

"I've been asleep."

"Ah." Glancing about once more, he made to return inside. I let him pass. He picked up the glass of wine and returned to the chair where I'd found him. "That I believe."

"Can you not remember?" I said. "Perhaps I can help."

"I'm lost."

"You don't know where you are?"

"I exist in the Regent's palace in the Principality of Mancibar." He said it as if reciting a schoolroom lesson. "But I don't know how I come to be here. Or where I might have been before. Xanthe says my name is Dante and that I'm in love with her, but neither fact has any meaning. She may as well tell me that I am Arsano of the Broad Shoulders and I hold up the bowl of the sky."

Without even a sip, he set the wine on the table beside him.

"Nor can I recall why this Regent Iaccar bears me such animosity. My *true* master, who is much more terrible than Iaccar, also believes I deceive him and applies his scourge to dissuade me. Though I don't bleed from it." He gazed quizzically at his outstretched arm as if it were alien to him. "I think perhaps I'm mad."

His true master? Scourging? Winter's breath wafted over me. Dante had ever claimed madness was his likely end. But never had I imagined such a quiet horror.

"Xanthe tells me I'm a sorcerer, but I can construct no spells. I don't even know where to begin. Yet neither can I doubt that part entire. . . ."

Sparks spilled from his scarred fingertips, flowing down his fingers, and pooling in the clawed cup of his hand. He smoothed his good hand over it, dousing the eerie glow. My knees jellied, the taste of death in my throat.

"When I sleep I do not dream—unless the scourging is a dream, which I've never quite decided. Save me from more dreams like that! And now I sit here and talk to myself, but I've naught to say that I've not repeated a thousand times over. And beyond all is the abyss."

He shook his head as if to rid himself of the vision. "My master assures me I will fall. He says I am his Hand in the Living World. Sometimes I believe I'm dead. Sometimes I believe . . ."

He burst from his chair and threw his wineglass. The glinting glass shattered and clinked to the floor. The bloodred wine dribbled down the wall. Dante yanked something from his shirt and gripped it tightly in his trembling fist. ". . . I need to fight . . . destroy . . . rend. It is my only purpose."

More sparks, blazing white this time and so hot they seared my cheeks, spewed from the fingers knotted at his chest. He sank to his knees. "I need to die."

Clanging bells jolted me awake. Eleventh hour. I had to go. Whether this *true master* with a flaying whip was real or a product of madness was beyond my skill to judge. But Portier was in more immediate danger.

I wanted to comfort him, to tell him everything I knew, everything I loved about him. I wanted to say the world felt broken without his gruff, demanding, ever-tempestuous presence. I rose, bent over him, and whispered in his ear, "I am your memory, Master Dante. I know who you are and who you have been. One day I'll come back and tell you all. Do not despair."

He likely didn't hear. He had begun shaking violently and mumbling. "Master . . . no . . . no more. I cannot . . . I *will* not . . ."

Blotting tears and crushing grief, I left him and set out in search of Portier. An agonized cry seared the air behind me, threatening to split my heart. But I kept walking.

CHAPTER 34

MANCIBAR

I ghosted through the halls and passages of Jacard's palace, heading ever downward. Palaces and fortifications were always built upon the ruins of what had come before. Whatever confluence of trade routes, rivers, mines, or other resources had drawn someone to settle in a place would draw others until the rivers ran dry or the mines petered out. Legends of holiness were even more persistent. Somewhere in this fine palace, aged perhaps fifty years, I would find a path to a much older dwelling, which would connect eventually to the resting place . . . or one of the resting places of Sante Ianne . . . Altheus. His fellow saints grant that it was not the burial place of Portier de Savin-Duplais, either dead or living.

Yet it was less analysis and more instinct that guided my steps—this persistent sense of familiarity, as if my history with Portier would not allow us to be kept apart. He was easy to discover if I but set my feet in the right direction.

At the base of the third downward stair, a gang of three sweepers pushed their brooms about a small rotunda. The chamber's thick, straight columns and elongated, unlifelike mosaics bespoke a style at least five centuries past. Encouraged, I paused on the bottom step, waiting for the sweepers and their dust cloud to pass by. Instead they blocked the stair while arguing about whether to make another round.

My nose itched. My chest spasmed. Swallowing the sneeze, I willed the men—ghostlike themselves—to move on. I could not retreat. This was the way. I felt certain of it.

The second sneeze sneaked up on me. Babbling about haunts, the sweepers barged past, fighting to get up the stair. Though I pressed my back to the wall, the last man bumped my breast. He moaned and dropped his broom on my foot, hurtling up the stair without it.

I raced onward, hunting through dark, empty rooms, backtracking three times at one point. A few steps in each direction and my spirit jarred. On my fourth try I discovered another descending stair of undressed stone. The rooms below were far, far older. Low ceilings. The air was chill and musty, the layer of damp sludge beneath my bare feet unmarred. Only the blue wash of Lianelle's enchantment allowed me to see the way.

A brick arch led me into the lowest, narrowest passage yet. The height forced me, a short woman, to bend over, which said it was more likely some ancient drainage passage than a place where people walked. I tried reversing course, but instinct screamed that I was wrong to go back.

A few steps farther forward and a moan echoed in the tunnel. The sound quickly shaped itself into mumbles. ". . . coming . . . they'll be coming. Not feared. Not feared. Is't you down here, Gammy? Gappa? Won't disgrace you. Won't scream. Won't piss. Won't shit. Best not sleep. Not feared. Aaaaaa . . ." The keening rose until it was abruptly cut off, and the litany began again.

The drainage tunnel led into the dusty corner of a half-collapsed dungeon cell. Two more cells remained intact. One was empty, save for damp and mold. A dirty young man huddled in the other. He didn't seem to have suffered abuse, save for prisoning in that dreadful place. Nor had he been there long. His beard was scarce sprouted.

No keys in evidence. It wasn't just my distaste for magic working that prevented me from shearing off the cell door with raw magic. The fellow would be sure to set up screaming at explosions and invisible hands. And John Deune had warned of watchers. I couldn't afford a fuss before I'd found Portier.

The young man emitted a choked sob as if he saw me pass him by.

Two more turns and faint light illumined a wide arch. *Yes. This was right.*

Incense and smoke, hints of an ancient grave site, drew me forward. But it was wonder and horror that propelled me into the great cavern.

Stars and Stones, what went on here? The hall was deserted, yet the lingering smoke was not so old as to claim that the chamber's grim tale was centuries past. Leather bindings dangled from a splattered wall. Painted words covered walls and floor—Aljyssian words, implying spellwork. *Vile* spellwork, for the sticky brushes and the clotted gore in a square bowl told me what ink scribed them. Cascades of stiffened wax hung from a thousand candle niches. An altar weighted the space between four towering angels. No, not an altar, a catafalque . . .

I pelted across the great chamber, descended a few steps, then scrambled up the stepped marble of the bier. "Portier!" I cried softly as I grabbed the bronze handles of the sarcophagus lid and dragged at its monstrous weight. "I've come to fetch you. Angels mercy, tell me you're not in this cursed box."

"Not." A quiet echo. Even my soundless passing, unmarred by boots or rustling fabric, caused whispers in the stillness.

I yanked again at the awful weight. Again I felt the jarring wrongness.

"Here."

Clinging to the heavy lid, I spun, gawking wildly at the yawning cavern.

"Portier?" My voice bounced here and there, much too loud.

"Spirit?" The word was scarce a breath.

Toward the left end of the splattered wall, a barred pattern of wavering yellow light lay across the floor. A *grate in the navel of the world* . . .

Without thought, I was there. Beyond the crosshatched strips of thick bronze lay the strangest prison cell that could be imagined. On one side were a pallet, a stool, a small writing desk, where a guttering candle sat in a pewter holder as it might in some gentleman's library. A man wrapped in a gray blanket sat hunched over the desk, his head drooping, a pen fallen from his trembling hand. On the other side of the cell was a bleeding-chair, rigid, skeletal, and sturdy, equipped with thick straps to bind a prisoner while a sorcerer drained his blood. Dark stains blotched its white paint.

Deadly could not begin to describe my fury. The grate was set into the stone, its hinges thick and unbreakable. No bolt, no latch, and no keyhole were visible. A survey of the cavern revealed nothing that might pry the solid bronze. It would have to be magic. . . .

"Are you ready to get out of this place?" I said softly, gripping the bronze grid. "You might want to cover your head."

His head dropped a little lower and his shoulders jerked. It took me a moment to hear the soft laughter. Portier's laughter. "Anne de Vernase . . . as I live."

Which looked to be a temporary condition. When he shifted around, the candlelight revealed his already slender face all bones and hollows. He squinted. Blinked. "Madness . . ."

His crestfallen expression near broke my heart. "No, no, I'm truly here, Portier. Stay back.

Raw, ugly power flowed from my roots like molten iron, boiling through bone and sinew. . . . *Control, Anne.* Dante's teaching was blazoned on my spirit. *Build the channel. Release only what's needed.* The bronze grid spat hot blue sparks over my grasping fingers and swung open, near breaking my fingers before I could get them loose.

"You've progressed," he said. "Excelled."

"Only for you, friend."

I ducked through the low opening and crouched in front of him, laying my hand on his cold, palsied one. "We're going now. Any watcher in the city will have felt that. Can you walk?"

"Won't be fast." He lifted my unseeable hand and grinned. "You're not dead?"

"No. Though handsome gentlemen keep inquiring." I helped him to his feet.

"A small problem," he said, fumbling with the blanket. Beneath his sparse beard and his horrid cuts and bruises, his complexion blazed. "I've not a stitch. . . ."

What a vile humiliation for such a private man as Portier. "Honestly, Jacard is too stingy to clothe his prisoners? At least the other fellow isn't quite such a mess as you are."

"Another . . ." He pulled me to a stop. "Get him out, Ani."

"You first."

"He'll die tonight. Horribly." He tried to pull away, his trembling more pronounced. "Can't allow it."

Bile stung my throat, but I held on. "I'll do my best for him. But if I take him first, they'll know someone's been here, and I might never get back. They might move you. We go now."

"We can't leave—"

"I *need* you, Portier. Dante's lost his mind." I snuffed the candle and closed the grate behind us.

"Ani, I've got to tell you about Dante—"

"When we're out."

Portier tried to hurry, but he was terribly weak and his game leg pained him. We were still metres from the arch when we heard footsteps from above, where a gallery stretched the length of the cavern.

I had hoped to preserve Lianelle's potion, as I'd only a few hours' worth left. But we weren't going to make it. Torchlight danced from above.

"Take this," I whispered. "Trust me. It will hide you." I poked a few drops in his mouth and kept him moving while it took effect. Only it didn't.

"*Sante* Duplais!" Jacard bellowed from somewhere above my head. "Crawl into your chair! I needs must borrow another portion of your life tonight." He couldn't see us yet.

"I'll do you no good dead," Portier called, breathless, as he ducked behind one of the angels.

"But you'll not die, will you? Not yet."

Portier's sunken eyes inquired as he held out a hand.

"Try more," I whispered, pressing the dropper to his lips.

He brushed it away. "Maybe this . . ." He closed his eyes, clenched his outstretched fist, and shaped a sigh into a word.

A surprised screech blasted from above us. The torchlight wavered wildly.

While Jacard's cry yet slammed the vaults and walls, two men pelted into the chamber from the very direction we were headed. "Lord Regent? What's wrong?"

One of the men pulled up, yelling at his fellow, pointing our way. "Look there, Soder—the bleeder's out of his hole. . . ."

Jacard's torch winked out as did the one his men carried. Absolute darkness fell. Portier laughed aloud. I would have silenced him, but sounds had no direction in the cavern, and it seemed to give him strength. I dragged him past the groping guards, my enchanted sight showing the way.

"Been waiting . . . long time . . . to do that," he said, when I pushed him against the wall inside the arched passage to let him rest.

"*You've* progressed." I counted to ten. "Now, onward."

The prisoner's retching fouled the stale air in the cell passage. Portier's hand kept me from passing him by. "Please, Ani."

I couldn't let myself think about it. Another focused blast of power broke the lock. The door sagged open. The prisoner screamed.

The rush of magic left me dizzy. "Hear me, prisoner," I said. "By Sante Ianne's mercy you've a chance to live. Be absolutely silent and go left, not right."

Portier and I crept through the drainage channel. We were almost through when we heard the prisoner's harsh breath just behind. At a Y-shaped cross-passage, I pulled Portier to the side and let the young man pass. "Run for your life," I called after him. "Up and out." Throttling a moan, he vanished into the gloom.

Would we could move so fast. The bellowing behind us was furious. How in the name of grace was I to get Portier out if the potion didn't work on him?

"Wait," I said, halting after a single step. "Not that way." Praying I wasn't squandering our head start, I chose, not the way I'd come, but the stem of the Y. Surely two branches of a drainage system would merge in a channel that took the water *out* of the palace.

"You can see in this tarry labyrinth?"

"Magic is all about seeing." Dante's insistent lesson came out of my mouth without thought.

"He's in dreadful danger." Portier's worry swelled large enough to choke the drainage channels.

"Don't talk," I said. "I can't carry you."

"SSST, DERO!"

Saints bless the man. As the tower bells struck half past the first hour of the night watch, exactly on schedule, he was waiting in the pergola where we'd left him.

"Spirits, lady! There's been an uproar such as I've never seen! They're still searching. . . . Had to show papers ten times over. Had to stick my finger down my throat to convince 'em I was too sick to juggle. Even so, I spent the last hour up top of this arbor. Was it you?"

"Yes. Come with me." Torches blazed in the direction of the gates and shouts rose from every corner of the grounds, checking off that this or that section had been searched. I dragged Andero through the gardens around the palace to a steep slope of rock and dirt. Ten metres down the slope was a stone-lined cistern and the outflow ditch for the ancient drainage system. I'd left Portier collapsed in the outflow ditch, tucked just behind a rusted grating that had once protected the palace from infiltrators. Wrapped in his filthy blanket and my bangled scarf, he couldn't crawl another centimetre.

Andero and I slipped and slid down the treacherous slope of iron-hard rock slabs, loose dirt, and gravel. He caught me once when my knee gave way and I came close to tumbling down into the cistern—a nasty pit from what I could see and smell of it. I was visible again and navigating by starlight.

"Told you I'd bring help," I said, scrabbling across the rubble to Portier.

"Sorry." That's all he'd said for the last hour of our journey through the bowels of the palace.

"This is Dante's brother, Andero."

That brought Portier's head up.

"Andero, this is—"

"Feel as if I know ye aforetime," said the smith. "Traveled halfway crost the world with my little brother, and heard naught but good of ye."

"No *self-righteous little prig*?" said Portier, moonlight painting his face a ghastly landscape.

Andero chuckled quietly. "Indeed. That, too. Come, let's get you away from this den of villainy. Though I'm not sure how we're to get you out the gates."

Ignoring Portier's protest, Andero hefted him across his shoulders and began the ascent. "Hold tight."

"I was hoping you'd found an exit that wasn't the gates," I said, planting my feet carefully as we scrambled upward.

Andero didn't reply until we'd reached the verge and he'd set Portier on his feet. "Might have had a couple ways out earlier—service gates or such. But not with this row. He's a scrawny thing. I suppose we could wrap him tight and stuff him in the big bag with the clothes, balls, scarves, and such. I could carry it crost my shoulders. 'Tis only for a bit."

"They'll be searching everything large enough to hold a man."

"Well, then, only one way as I can see. Our permit's for four. Your friend must pass in my place. I can likely get all the way down that cliff we just come up. Grew up in the mountains, didn't I?"

"No clothes," said Portier. "And noticeable marks." He bared one arm, a horror of crosshatched lacerations.

I couldn't see a good alternative. "We brought extra costumes. No one's going to be judging the fit. And we brought face paint and kohl. . . . We'll mark you up like a Fassid warlord—a proper juggler—and you can walk out."

Dodging searchers and departing guests, we trudged through the gardens to a grove of prickly juniper just outside the entertainers' doors. The bells had just rung second hour of the night watch, and from the line of guests waiting to exit the gates, no one was going to be demanding a second entertainment from Marco Flamberge and his women.

Portier drowsed as jugglers, dancing girls, and dog trainers straggled out. At last, two tall figures were silhouetted in the lighted doorway. They called farewells to several people and ambled down the walkway. I slipped out of the patchy shadows and joined them, grabbing the kithara as if I'd been with them all along. "Done for the evening?"

"Oh, Anne," whispered Rhea, glancing around at the other entertainers streaming before and behind us, "we were so worried."

"Saints and angels," said Ilario, raising his face to the heavens. "I very much disliked leaving without you. From the yelling and the guards barreling in and out the last two hours, I'd say you've had some success?"

"A new member has joined Sonjeur Flamberge's singing players," I said, exhaustion making me fey. "We need to get him into costume."

Rhea's steps slowed. "You brought someone out? I thought tonight was just to learn. . . ."

"It couldn't wait," I said. "Portier's with Andero."

"One moment." Ilario darted away.

While the chevalier had a boisterous exchange with the master of the dogs, I grabbed the costume bag from Rhea and scooted across the grass.

Before my eyes could adjust to the shadows, the chevalier was beside me, waving a flask. "I had bet Groubert the juggler a flask of beer that my dancer wouldn't spend all night with the smarmy suitor who grabbed her on our way out. And he paid up! So where is he?"

I parted the juniper's spiky branches.

Ilario took a hard breath, dropped onto his knees, and clasped Portier's shaking hands in both of his. "Ah, merciful Creator . . . my brother."

A drowsy grin lit Portier's face. "Knew you'd come rescuing. Expected the swordsman. Black mask, not frost-faire clown . . ."

"Best go," said Andero. "You're safest if you're not straggling. He'll need your strong arm, lord."

"Aren't we two fine men?" said Ilario, as we decked out Portier in pantaloons and Andero's full-sleeved shirt, which near swallowed him. "Having these women save us. My black mask is lost, and my captain"—he swallowed hard—"is not here. Good Andero had best watch himself or he'll get in a pickle, too, and the ladies will have to do for him." He fed Portier a few swallows of the beer and then sprinkled it liberally over their clothes.

"Ladies?" Portier's brow creased.

"Introductions later." Yet I couldn't see Rhea anywhere. "She's probably keeping a lookout."

Andero stuffed the voluminous costume bag in my arms.

"Are you sure you can get down that cliff?" I asked.

"It's like to take me a while, but I'll be safer than you. Godspeed, damoselle, my lord, and you, my new friend."

"Divine grace, Andero." We said it together. "And mind your feet."

The crowd had thinned a bit, but there was still a long line of performers queued up to get through the iron gates. We took it slow, as if we were enjoying the night. Ilario hooted and waved his flask at his new acquaintances, while watching for Rhea. "Where in Gedevron is she?"

Ilario and Portier were ahead of me, Portier's arm draped over the chevalier's shoulder as if they were drunk. Ilario interspersed his commentary with snips of tavern songs.

"Who are we looking for?" said Portier.

"My physician," said Ilario. "I had a run-in with a sword a few months ago. You and I can compare scars. She's a Temple— There she is. Saints, woman, I thought we'd lost you."

Rhea slipped into the queue behind me. "Had to . . . go . . . you know," she mumbled.

"Temple healer?" Portier craned his head around. "Ani . . ."

Ilario burst into song.

Fa-de-la, and hey and ho. To the deadhouse we shall go.
Seest thou, my ladies fair? This bold lad shall certain dare.
To venture realms none live should know.

He nudged Portier. "Come, partner mine. Marco Flamberge's players are talented in all aspects of entertainment. Especially the delights of beer and ale and the magnificence of spirits!"

Portier appeared to be wriggling out of his embrace, but Ilario only clutched him harder, spewing drunken nonsense and bumping into everyone nearby.

The iron gate loomed over us. The guard closed in. I pushed forward, fumbling with the pass Andero had left with me, trying not to drop it or the cumbersome bag. "The Mysterious Marco and his players," I said, no need to feign my weariness. "Four of us. Only two drunk."

The guard examined our paper, looked us over, and then, without a word, stabbed a short sword into the canvas bag. The tip pricked my shoulder.

I staggered, but Rhea grabbed me and kept me upright. Her eyes were like bronze shields.

Portier gasped. But the guards' words played Heaven's music. "Be on your way," the guard said. "Put that screecher to bed else I'll gut him."

"Aye, your honor."

They moved on to the next in line. We quickened our steps across the causeway and onto the divided road that descended through the terraced gardens. The blaze of torchlight faded behind us, only a few hanging lanterns showing the way. As soon as we were out of view of the gates, Portier shook off Ilario's arm and stumbled to the shadowed parapet. Propped on the marble rail, he caught his breath and glared at me . . . no, not me. . . .

"Introduce me to your physician, Ilario. She'd not be a Temple girl newly converted to the Cult of the Reborn, would she? Troubled? Shy? Scintillating intelligence? Oh yes, and a betrayer?"

"Please, Duplais," she said, "you've got to listen. I swear—"

"Betrayer?" Naught could measure my dismay.

"Did they pay you well to turn me over, girl? A nice stipend to the poor Temple girl in exchange for the heretic, the naive blasphemer who confided that his own nature confused him. And who cared what end the Regent of Mancibar had planned for such a one, for the world would be purified, yes? Rhea Tasserie, I never thought to see you in this life again."

CHAPTER 35

"You were ready to go back to Sabria . . . to the necromancer," said Rhea, backing away down the slope. "I had to keep you away from him."

"You gave Portier to *Jacard*?" I said.

But Rhea spoke only to Portier. "The man said the Regent of Mancibar wished to hire a resident scholar who knew both of magic and the Cult. You needed money. I thought you'd be *safe* with them until I could fetch the tetrarch to speak with you. So I arranged the meeting. I never imagined the Regent *knew* you or would take you by force or— Creator's grace, how could I imagine what he planned?"

Every word we'd spoken since Pradoverde scalded my memory. About Dante, about magic, about Mont Voilline and necromancy and Ixtador. I had lost all caution, allowed her to know everything. I believed myself a woman of the world who had survived a mystery beyond imagining, and I saw Rhea as the naive, sheltered girl I had once been. Only she wasn't. She was a spy.

"So you learned what Portier could tell you, disposed of him, and then were assigned to dupe Ilario. All so your true master could get evidence against Dante, so he could gut and burn him in Temple Square."

She didn't deny it. How could she? Gods save me, after hearing Dante's cold voice, learning what I had of his deeds, I couldn't even say they were wrong to do it. But the tetrarch's motives surely extended beyond one savage show.

"Dante's fall would damage the king, too," I said, "and tarnish the Camarilla beyond repair. The Temple would rise triumphant, and Beltan de Ferrau, the commoner holy man, would become the youngest High Tetrarch in living memory."

"No! You're wrong about him. It's what he *sees* beyond the Veil."

Ilario glided around behind Rhea and blocked her retreat. Night shadows masked his face. "We can't stay here," he said, entirely without emotion. "Portier needs care. You will give it, damoselle, taking a full measure yourself of anything you put in his mouth. And then we'll have explanations all around."

"Lord, please. I told you—"

"Later," he said.

"One problem with that," I said, recalling green scraps scattered along the roadside and Rhea's increased agitation as we approached Mancibar. "Think carefully before you answer, Rhea Tasserie. Did you lead Tetrarch de Ferrau here?"

She drew a shaking breath. "I need to explain—"

"Yes or no."

"Yes."

My hand trembled with power and fury. "Does he know where we're lodged? Consider carefully. Yes or no."

"*No.* I decided to tell you first. To convince you to listen to him. To convince him to listen to you. He's a Reader, the most sensitive there's ever been. You carry your sister's tessila, so some part of you believes a Temple Reader can touch her soul beyond the Veil. He believes your mage to be a daemon walking the living world."

The crowd was scattering quickly. With so little resource and so much need to be out of the streets, we had to move. "Is she lying, Ilario? If she brings that bloody-minded holy man down on Portier, I'll kill her myself."

"I'm no fit judge," he said, persisting in his strange flatness. "She scraped herself to the bone to keep me alive. When Ferrau questioned me, he knew only the fool. She is exceptional in so many ways, but perhaps lying is one of them after all."

"No," she said, softly, eyes fixed on the ground. "Never to you, lord. Never once."

"Portier?"

"Women have ever made me an idiot, Ani. But, the gods' truth, my knees fail me."

We dodged squads of Jacard's guardsmen all the way. They hammered on doors and rousted people from their beds, hunting an "escaped prisoner who consorted with daemons." But by the time we arrived at the Street of Beggars, the shacks and dens had already been tumbled and the district's denizens retreated into their squalor. Even so, Portier, Rhea, and I held back while Ilario scoured the neighboring lanes.

The wind whined and howled down the streets of Mancibar like a pack of wild dogs. Or perhaps it was in the aether I heard the wailing. Neither moon nor star shone through the blackness, yet the night seemed alive. Flesh and bone pulsed with the beating of my heart.

The last few lamps of the district winked out. *Saints bring Andero back soon*. We had to decide what to do about Dante. . . .

Andero had told me of Castelivre and of Dante's fear of losing control as he healed the foolish shepherd. What daemon feared his own wickedness?

"Didn't see anyone untoward," said Ilario, gliding catlike into our refuge. "Even the rats are hiding."

ONCE WE'D SETTLED PORTIER ON Ilario's pallet, Rhea brought out her medicine box. She insisted I feed Portier sips of ale while she prepared wound dressings. "He needs drink more than sleep."

I bit my tongue. Naught but jibes and hatefulness came to mind.

Ilario watched her brew a tisane over a small fire in the alley. She tried several times to speak to him. Each time he shook his head. Without prompting, she drank the first cup when the tisane was ready.

Portier scarce woke as we poured the tea down his throat. As he settled into a deep sleep, Rhea dressed the fresh bleeding cuts on his back, and some on his thighs that had festered, always explaining what she did and why. She offered to dress the nick on my shoulder, but I refused. Silly of me. Even I found no fault with her care.

Somewhere near fifth hour, Rhea said she'd done all she could. "He needs to rest, drink, and eat." She glanced up. Gray pouches circled her eyes. "We can talk now."

"Sleep," I said. "We'll settle accounts in the morning." Ilario was watching.

She curled up under her blanket, but I wasn't sure she slept. I sat in the doorway, tending our little fire till we'd naught left to burn.

On one of his passes through the alley, Ilario sat with me a while. I told him of Portier's rescue and of my encounter with Dante. He let me weep on his shoulder, before setting out for another circuit of the neighborhood.

My eyes drifted shut. Waiting behind my lids were the boiling aether and a cavern painted with blood. Images of Dante holding a burning iron over Portier and screaming vengeance. Of a madman incinerating those who crossed him. Of a madman with dead eyes and flames leaking from his skin, screaming to an unseen scourge. Of a madman.

"ANI . . ."

I blinked and sat up, finding a crick in my neck and a gouge in my back from the bare timber of the door frame. I grabbed my knife, fallen from my hand.

". . . could use a drink." Portier had got himself up on one elbow, but the ale flask was a long reach.

"Some protector I am," I said, as Portier swallowed the weak ale like the king's prized vintage.

"I've been watching," said a bulky figure occupying the doorway I'd just abandoned.

"Andero! Blessed angels," I said, relieved beyond measure.

"Haven't seen folk sleeping so sound since the Norgand coast, when my cadre fought four days straight. Not a man could move for two days after. The chevalier's gone up to the roof to keep a lookout. And Rhea popped up when I fetched a bit of cheese so my belly wouldn't cave. She said go ahead and eat all of it, as she'd bring more from the market. Don't know how you scrawny folk keep going on so little."

"Rhea's gone?" I spun around, engulfed in forgotten fury. "How long ago?"

"Not half an hour yet," he said, his wide brow crinkled. "Why?

But, of course, he didn't know about Rhea the Betrayer. How stupid we'd been not to bind her.

" 'Tis only an hour past first light," said Andero, "though it don't look as if we're to get all that much light today. Never saw such clouds. Or mayhap it's smoke. The whole city stinks of it."

Indeed, I could have believed we'd slept the clock around till dusk and that our little dung fire had incinerated the entire city. How could Ilario let Rhea get away?

"We need to get Portier out of here. Rhea will likely have Ferrau and his bailiffs here in moments."

"Looks like John Deune she's fetched." Andero squinted down the alley. "And he's found Will."

I'd wholly forgotten about Will Deune.

"Get out of sight, Andero. Behind the roof stair. I'll distract them." I hurried off to meet the approaching party, while the smith slipped off unseen.

John Deune was twitching and working his mouth, his seed-like eyes about to pop from his head. Rhea's tatty basket held a blood-soaked straw packet and a small wheel of cheese.

"You came back," I said to Rhea. "Where is your tetrarch?"

"Portier needs meat to build his blood," she said. "I went out early so as not to be seen. But John Deune was hunting us and making a noisy show of it. Figured I'd best bring him." Her mouth was tight, and she wouldn't meet my eyes.

The smoky gloom prevented me seeing much of the street beyond the alley. But I caught no sign of anyone. Rhea pointed to the door. "Andero's likely inside, Will."

A lank-haired youth in filthy slops barged around all of us, following her direction.

"Da, he's not here!" His wail could have been heard for a kilometre.

"Found my Will wandering the streets yesternight," snapped John Deune. "Crazed like this, wanting to talk to the smith. They had him jailed till all the guards ran off last night to search for whatever madman escaped from the palace. You best fix Will's head, else I'll lead soldiers here."

I was almost as agitated as John. Not from fright, however. His elder son's report about the *cage in the navel of the world* had taken me straight to Portier. "I'll hear what he has to say."

"But he won't *say* it to you, no more than he will to me. He'll only speak to the smith."

The wild-eyed boy, his blotchy face the image of his brother, held the doorposts as if to keep himself from flying into the beyond. "Where is he, Da?"

"Andero's not here," I said. "You can tell me. Maybe I can help."

The boy jerked as if I'd slapped him. "Don't let her witch me, Da. I'm already ruint."

"The mage came after him a second time," said John, accusing. "The very morning after the first. Tell them, Will."

The boy sniffed and moaned. "He clamped his hand over my mouth and shoved me into the wall. He says, 'Look at me, Will,' and his eyes burnt just like a daemon's would. I was hot all over, like I was burning, too. Then it felt like he burnt a hole in my head and stuffed nettles inside."

"Then what? What did he say?"

"Swore at me and run off. There was a ruckus in the kitchen and Captain Hosten was yelling about the daemon mage. A guard grabbed me and I fought him crazy. That's when they popped me in the nick." His hand beat the doorpost. "Gotta see the smith, Da. Gonna burst if I don't."

Was this a compulsion? Dante had told me he could do such if the subject was weak-minded. He'd tried it on Portier when they first met, only to realize Portier was anything but weak-minded. I waved my hand where Andero would see, summoning him.

"You were right to come, Will. They couldn't know how you had to come."

"What do you mean?" asked John Deune. "What's the blackguard done to my boy?"

"I think he's laid an enchantment on him—a compulsion to speak to Andero. Once he's delivered himself of whatever he carries, he should be fine." I wasn't exactly sure of that.

"If the sorcerer has harmed my boy, I'll kill the murdering daemon. I don't care what powers he has or who he consorts with."

"Da . . ." Will's chewed fingers gripped his hair as if he might pull it out.

"I think Dante's put Will under a compulsion to speak to you," I said when Andero came around from the stair. "The boy's about crazy with it."

"So I heard. Daemons, I've never been stared at so. What should I do?"

"I don't know. Ask him questions. Command him."

"Have you aught to tell me, Will?"

"Alone!" Will spoke through gritted teeth.

Andero glanced at me. "There's none here who cannot hear. Say what you've got to say."

Will relaxed a bit and began to speak, his eyes never leaving Andero. The hairs on my neck rose, and a chill that had nothing to do with weather swept through the stinking alley. It was the voice of Will Deune that spoke to us, but the words . . .

Andero, my brother. My time is short and I am desperate to get the knowledge I now possess to those who can use it. I've no time to explain all that's happened to me here. I have failed my friends. Failed my calling. Failed in seeing. But if I can, through you, enable someone else to finish what I cannot, perhaps, in some small part, I shall stand redeemed for the evils I have wrought.

Jacard, my onetime adept, the Regent of Mancibar, has secured one of the three Maldivean Seeing Stones. Though no enchantress, the woman of the dreams holds the other two. But neither Jacard nor Xanthe yet understands the Stones, nor did I until this night.

The three together comprise an object indescribable save in the language of myth. They are fragments of the aether—the very essence of the universe. They form a conduit through which this same essence, divine or naturally marvelous as it may be, is channeled into the living world. Think of a water conduit made of ice. It is the very stuff of magic. Unfortunately, this conduit is hopelessly corrupt.

Of paramount importance: The three Stones must be destroyed before they can be wielded as one. Jacard must not use them. Anne must not. I most certainly must not. The thought of their destruction is as painful to me as would be the destruction of the sun or moon, and I cannot deny that it will damage the world irretrievably. But if we do not act, the very souls that allow us to live as humans, to yearn, to strive, to create, and to care for each other, lie in peril.

I have never been a believer in anything of the divine. But our friend Portier and another, whom I have met this night, have convinced me that my prideful ignorance of what lies beyond this world we see has brought us near disaster. Lurking in the three Stones, inseparable from their crystal structure, haunting the visions and dreams that have plagued me across half the world, is one Dimios—yes, he who is named the Souleater. And yes, he feeds on the souls of the dead. The creation of Ixtador during the

Blood Wars, an aberration that prevents souls from passing from this life to whatever awaits us in the next, has provided him a feast, and thereby grown his might. Now he hungers for the souls of the living.

My rending of the Veil at Mont Voilline set Dimios free to inhabit this conduit of magic, and on the day the Stones are joined and used, he can walk free in the living world. The reign of horror Dimios plans will make the Blood Wars look like acolyte's practice, and there will be no sorcerer, mage, king, or tetrarch who can oppose him.

And so we come to my own part. Though we have only just met as men, you know me as well as any. My history. My murderous temper. My disdain for all men, and my arrogance of intellect and skill. My pursuit of magic has ever drawn me to tread the boundaries of reason. Castelivre demonstrated how near I am to corruption. Indeed, Dimios has long reserved a place for me at his side, and several who walk in harmony with the unexplainable, from that old shepherd who reads the stars to my blessed friend Portier, have tried to tell me . . . to warn me . . . that my life's journey leads me there. I can shape the power of the aether as no human has in generations, and Dimios is determined that I will do so in his service. He will use the skills and power I have so valued to implement the ruin he plans. I cannot, will not, allow this.

Though I cannot resign myself to her danger, Anne must come. She will not shrink from whatever must be done. And she is stronger than all of us.

Dimios's first assault on this world is through Jacard. The fool raises his uncle Kajetan from the dead to teach him the secrets of the Seeing Stones, and he plans to use them and our friend Portier to endow himself with immortal life, as well as incomparable magic. In this rite Portier will be ripped asunder, his immortal being enslaved. Jacard does not know that Kajetan has linked a spell to his stone, Tychemus, that will transfer the uncle's soul into the victim's body instead of the nephew's. But Dimios intends to upend both uncle and nephew, using the rite to give himself a physical presence in the living world. If this fails, he will find another way—or force me to make one for him.

Xanthe is the cipher. As long as she holds to her purpose, we will have time to act. She is not the easy mark that Jacard believes, but never mistake her motives. She was imprisoned for seven centuries and desires to make up for it with power. If that means letting Jacard use the Stones, she'll let him. And once Jacard and his dead uncle have the three Stones in their control, there will be no stopping them. The Souleater will walk free in the living world.

As to what must be done. I have altered Kajetan's spell so that it will not work as he plans. I pray it is enough to foil Jacard's rite. I've also done what I can to help you or Anne find Portier. His rescue is imperative, not just for his own sake and to foil Jacard's rite, but because he and Anne must discover what to do about Ixtador and the Seeing Stones.

The Stones are difficult. It is impossible to take them by stealth or purposeful murder, overt or covert. They are enspelled to prevent it. But remind Anne that the compulsive working of a spell structure acts on thought, desire, and emotion. If a person can discipline himself to strip away these things, it is as if he becomes transparent to the spell. Such a one could steal the Stones without falling prey to their protections. Dangerous, yes, but possible. Anne has the skill and discipline to do it. I would take on any consequence to keep this task from falling to her, but I've run out of time.

As to how the Stones may be destroyed, I've no idea. They are of the aether, thus it must surely require enchantment. A human wizard named Tyregious split the original into three. So I'm thinking it will require nothing Anne cannot learn if she remembers our lessons and gives all of herself to the task.

Earlier this night, so that I might gain Dimios's forbearance long enough to do these few things, I took the place ordained since my birth in Grymouth Caves, binding myself to Dimios as his Chosen, his Hand in the Living World. But I'll not serve him for long. It is imperative that neither my new master nor Jacard nor Xanthe find out what I know, or what I've done these few hours. And I will not risk compromising Anne, the one weapon we have that might oppose him. So I've worked a small enchantment to ensure I cannot divulge my secrets. Dimios will have his instrument, but, I hope, a most ineffective one. I swear that I will fight him for as long as I can. But you *must not* count on my help.

I thank you for my life, my brother, and cannot find it in me to regret any circumstance that brought us together. Now, before I can even repay my debt, I have laid this new burden on you. And I am not done even yet, for I ask one more boon. Tell Anne exactly this: I know her. I see her, no matter if I am blind or lost or halfway across the world. And everything I see, I treasure. She is, and will always be, my only light.

No torturer could have contrived a more bitter torment than Dante's message. To hear the words I'd yearned for in such dreadful context near burst my heart with grief and guilt.

"A double life," I said. "Gods save us. All of this—the subservience, tormenting Portier, burning houses, teaching this Xanthe—Dante *was* playing *agente confide* again. Now he's tried it yet a third time with a daemon. . . ."

I did not question what we heard. I had felt the agony of his yielding. And I'd seen the consequence of his determination. "He did what he said. He didn't recognize my voice. His own name was strange to him, and he said he could not recall how to work magic, though enchantment leaked from his hands."

"The Kadr well . . . 'Tis sure that's the magic he's used." Andero's quiet horror set spider feet pricking my flesh. "He described the poison spell exactly as you say. Said it left no person at all and that trying to repair the damage would only make it worse. Curse these jewels and all sorcery." Andero's sinewed arms and clenched fists could have twisted a man's head off.

John Deune saw it, too. He grabbed a giggling, grinning Will and bustled him away, mumbling oaths to set Jacard on us if Will had gone loony.

"He told me. Blessed Heaven, he tried to tell me." Portier leaned on the doorpost, arms wrapped about his chest. "*Think on the life you made me lead and you will understand what I do.* On so many wretched nights, I imagined I heard him calling my name, swearing to come for me. When I saw him, I bled hope. But they had given me some potion. . . . I could scarce speak, much less think, and then he waved that iron around. . . . I was so confused and so afraid for him, afraid he wouldn't hear what I'd learned . . . I blurted out that he was the Daemon but didn't explain what that meant."

"He heard your warning," I said. "Stars of night, he's told me to destroy the Stones, to destroy magic itself."

"It wasn't meant as a warning," said Portier, "but a plea. How many in a generation have his gifts? Even you, Anne. How many can walk the boundaries between worlds? I found a scroll in Abidaijar, a very early version of the myth of the Beginnings, telling of the Defender and the Daemon. Whatever its underlying truth, I believe Dante to be the living embodiment of it. He was born with the strength and talent to champion the souls of the dead at the Gates of Heaven. Only the Daemon . . . only Dante . . . can fight this battle."

"But he has fought the hardest battle already!" The newcomer's voice brought me to my feet.

Four men approached from the roof stair. A shrill whistle brought two others to block the open end of the alley. Leading the four was Beltan de Ferrau.

"Why do you despair? Prophecy is not a sculptor's chisel. Did you not hear this marvel just unfolded?"

Beside the tetrarch, sword sheathed, not a prisoner, not reluctant, and not at all surprised, walked Ilario de Sylvae. Shock robbed me of sensible words. "Ilario?"

Rhea would not meet my gaze, but Ilario did, as sober as I'd ever seen him. "It's time for us to talk with one another," he said. "Time to stop working at cross-purposes. A most courageous young woman has gambled her life to force us to it, and a most courageous mage has just confirmed that she was right."

I backed away toward Portier, fondling my knife through the slit in my pocket. But my eyes did not leave Ilario. "You've been working with this tetrarch all along? A man who chained and beat you when you were half dead, who wants to *burn* Dante?"

"No." His denial was firm. "Though our several meetings in the hospice led me to a less harsh view of his motives than yours, it's only since that night in Kadr when you felt Dante's change. That's when Rhea told me she'd left telltales for the tetrarch. She gave me reason enough to keep her secret until we knew more."

I was wholly at sea. Faithful Ilario . . . "She's a *betrayer*! She gave Portier to *Jacard*!"

Portier held on to the doorpost, but his eyes were closed and his brow creased as if only by concentrating furiously could he remain standing.

Ilario stepped away from the tetrarch and Rhea but kept his distance from me. His wariness but twisted the knife of his treachery.

"I'll confess, I named myself the world's greatest idiot for a few hours last night," he said. "But I heard her out after you were asleep. Ani, you love Dante so fiercely. Our friendship—yours and mine—is forged in the deepest of fires, but would you have listened to Ilario de Sylvae, longtime fool, if I'd told you I believed Dante irredeemable? If I'd told you that I'd sworn to myself to see him dead if what Ferrau feared proved true? You cannot conceive of the destruction Dante wreaked on that night in Jarasco—in an age when other sorcerers can scarce get candles lit."

"But you were wrong. All of you were wrong." In one wrenching message, Dante had proved himself, and destroyed himself, and laid the world's safety in my lap. I wanted to bury myself in my chevalier's embrace and have him tell me that he would shield me from what lay ahead. Now he had betrayed us, too. How could I trust any of them?

"We must get out of this alley." The tetrarch's quiet urgency snapped the overstretched moment. "Damoselle Anne, Sonjeur de Duplais, and you, sirrah, whom I've not met, please come with us. One of our resident scholars has abandoned his house to me. Though not large, it will be more comfortable than this place and more secure, if anywhere in the living world could be named secure just now."

"Do we have a choice?" I asked, bitterness tainting my every thought.

"Always," said Ilario. "If you choose to walk away, so be it. I will defend that choice with my every bone and sinew, and I will remain at your side to do whatever you ask of me. But I beg you listen first. *No one* here doubts what we just heard. And time is of the essence."

"Portier?" I said, crumbling.

"I'll listen," he said softly. "But we must be quick. Feel the world, Ani."

Above us the charcoal sky bulged and shifted. Perhaps it was just a storm, the onset of the rainy season. But inside me the aether boiled with wails of malevolent hunger. I'd thought my shivers were shock and emotion, but the brisk breeze cutting through my thin clothing and into my heart was keen with ice. Dante had destroyed himself because he believed I could do what was needed. I would not betray his trust.

I turned to de Ferrau. "Show us where to go."

Portier

CHAPTER 36

"We're here to listen, Tetrarch de Ferrau. So speak." Anne refused to take one of the floor cushions scattered about the absent scholar's small library.

Ilario and I had once speculated that it was Anne's small stature that kept her on her feet whenever the talk got important. But I'd come to think it was the steel in her spine. Who'd have thought the reticent, shattered girl I interviewed at Montclaire so long ago would come to hold the fragile world in her hands a second time?

And Dante had set her in the eye of the hurricane—sacrificing not only his mind and his life, but his heart. He'd ever sworn to me he didn't have a heart. The worst was that he'd done it believing he had failed us. If only I could have gotten out a few more words that night in the pit. If we needed any evidence of our desperate state, it lay in Dante's choices. The Souleater lived. . . .

"Indeed, every passing moment increases our risk." Rhea's superior, the ambitious young tetrarch who had reached his office through unrelenting pursuit of daemon influences in the world, could be no one's image of a high-ranked cleric. Blocky, sharp eyed. More badger than wolf. I'd not have chosen to end up in his clutches. He didn't sit, either.

I could not join the joust of precedence but settled on a cushion in a corner where the wall could hold me up. Months of bleeding had left me a husk. Despite Rhea's marvelous tonics, a strong east wind could have blown me back six years to my quiet library at Collegia Seravain.

I wished it would. I'd waked in the dark hours, thirsty and frantic that I needed to do something vitally important. I'd had the same obsessive certainty since I was a boy, and I still didn't know what it was. Every glance at the charcoal sky set my heart rattling. Faint streaks of purple and indigo that laced the grim overcast were not lightning, but more like glancing reflections. Like torchlight through deepening water. It was not mere lack of blood that kept my hands shaking like an old granny's.

"We must first establish trust," said de Ferrau. "I came to the Street of Beggars intending to persuade you to sit down with me and share our beliefs about Ixtador and the necromancer Dante. The sorcerer's message has preempted that conversation. But if I am to be of help to you, damoselle—and I believe I can—you and your friends must be assured that I am not the same man who visited your parents' home."

Anne's scorn could have shriveled a stone. I didn't know enough to judge de Ferrau. It all came down to Rhea. Her quiet ways and incisive mind had made her a boon companion in a time when my isolation in Abidaijar weighed heavy. I had confided in her, unwisely it seemed. Had she truly been so naive as to believe Jacard de Viole just wanted to consult me about magic?

The word *saint* disturbed me for many reasons. It most certainly didn't fit a man who had spent several months in a bleeding chair wanting to strangle a gifted young woman of nineteen.

De Ferrau plopped down at the low table, not graceful, but easy with himself. He poured tea for Anne, Ilario, and himself, then passed the pot on to Rhea and Andero.

"Prophecy is a troublesome thing," he said. "It is not magic. It is not absolute. It does not prescribe a destiny for any person. That's one of my persistent arguments with the Cult, which wants to give us all roles in miracle plays—good versus evil, angel battling daemon, saints to champion us incapable humans."

Well put, I had to confess. Everyone in the Cult, including Ilario, liked dressing up their beliefs in mythic drama. The conclusions of evidence and logic were much easier to live with.

"The truth of prophecy lies in the human heart and hand," de Ferrau continued, his earnest delivery belying his body's stalwart calm. "Some of us are strong, some generous, some devious. Our skills vary from swordsmanship to magic to logic to healing. What is the *Daemon of the Dead* or a *Souleater's Chosen* but a name for a collection of such qualities and skills imbued with intent? The true prophet sees a coming storm and tells us what qualities and skills we need to weather it. Those who *heed* prophets, alerted, seek out those who possess these qualities, trying to lure them into the path of the storm by naming the fulfillment of our need *destiny*. Sometimes, they frighten our champions away."

Then again, sometimes one felt the call to destiny, but no prophet came forth with the need. My youthful dreaming had fed my yearning for great deeds: to be a scholar of renown, perhaps, or the mage who revived the lost glories of magic. Over and over again, I had failed. But then Dante had exposed truths about my past. And I had died three times on Mont Voilline. Belief began to nag at me that something extraordinary was going on. Thus, Abidaijar.

Two years I'd spent there, comparing my dreams with the texts, histories, and legends of the Cult of the Reborn and, indeed, I'd found an astonishing correspondence. Yet, the exercise triggered no memory. I abandoned the sainthood silliness and pursued other inquiries . . . until I found a dusty little scroll that tied everything together and made me believe that Dante was far more important in the scheme of the universe than Portier de Savin-Duplais, reborn or no. Rhea was right that I had been ready to run to Dante. I had hoped his acerbic view of the divine could put my feet back on the ground.

"You weren't seeking skills when you came to Montclaire, Tetrarch," snapped Anne, interrupting the mesmer of de Ferrau's logic. "You hunted evidence to convict Dante of blasphemy."

She kept her vision fixed to the window, which had a fine view of the palace where Dante and the green Stones waited. Whatever else Dante had learned these months, at least he had come to understand what I had known for so long. It was a measure of Anne's strength that his profession of love had not wrecked her completely.

"You're correct," said de Ferrau. "I believed Master Dante the cause of what I saw happening in Ixtador."

His simple phrasing snagged my attention like a meat hook. "What you *saw* beyond the Veil?" I blurted. "You're a Reader. . . ."

"A skilled one," said the tetrarch. "Since I first inhaled the smokes of a Temple reading room, I've seen Ixtador's blighted fields as clearly as you see Sirpuhi's cliffs outside that window."

Dante had always believed that talent for magical practice was far more widespread than the Camarilla, locked into family and bloodlines, would admit. He used himself as the prime example. But he also pointed out Temple Readers, those who claimed to assess the progress of souls on their Veil journeys. *Just because the cretins are attached to fancies about gods and angels doesn't mean they can't touch dead souls. Whyever not? It's just another aspect of the aether.*

"For that same eighteen years," the tetrarch continued, "I've lied to every petitioner who's brought me a tessila to read. How can I tell them that their loved ones begin their Veil journey as hopeful as a bride on her wedding night and as eager as a bridegroom, only to starve and wither along the way? Every blasted one of them."

Exactly as Anne, Dante, and I had posited! Though more skeptical of their skills, I had interviewed a few Temple Readers. None had ever confessed to see anything of the hunger and despair we had witnessed on Mont Voilline. They blamed time's murky barrier or lack of information to make a proper link with certain souls. "You *saw* it!"

"I saw it clearly. Did you never wonder why most Readers limit their scrutiny to souls less than seven years dead? Two years ago this deterioration accelerated, taking nearer three years than five or seven. Ixtador has become a seething morass of human refuse. At the same time, rumors flew through the Temples about certain events at Mont Voilline. Master Dante already loomed large in my suspicions. Yet, I also heard disturbing rumors of the man who first brought the mage to Merona. Some said the man ought to be dead but wasn't. . . ."

Anne bit. "And you sent Rhea to worm her way into Portier's confidences to expose his heresy and Dante's."

Had a lioness's tooth marks appeared on de Ferrau's face just then, I wouldn't have been surprised.

"But my faithful spy was changed." The tetrarch didn't shy away from the word as the others did, nor from Anne's accusations. "On her return Rhea tried to give me *convincing evidence* that the world wasn't as I believed. But by then I had a city gate collapsed and a dozen bailiffs dead, and I wasn't listening. I needed her to keep the fool of a chevalier alive so I could get answers from him. When she and the fool, who was evidently not so much a fool, vanished, she left me a letter, detailing her reasons, her horror at my actions, and the urgency she felt that all our skills would be needed in this battle."

He tossed a little bundle onto the table. "She also left me a small gift she'd brought from Abidaijar—one discovered by you, Duplais, I believe."

The small yellowed scroll, tied up with a green ribbon, sat on the table like the blood-soaked evidence of a crime—or of marvels too huge to face.

"It is the first chapter of the *Primordium*," said the tetrarch, "the tale of the Creation, a tale as familiar as the alphabet. But this is a unique translation, the oldest in existence. It uses a very ancient word for the first of the Pantokrator's creations—*sandaemoni*. A notation gives its meaning as—"

"Guardian," I whispered, though my throat was a raw knot. I knew the text from memory.

"It gives a whole new meaning to the term *Daemon of the Dead*, does it not? We who heed prophets must get our terms correct before searching for the fulfillment of our needs. A passage in this text tells of the great war between Dimios and those *sandaemoni* led by Panthia and Celeres, these guardians of humankind. And it tells how Dimios learned he could increase his own strength by—"

"—draining the energies of the human dead." Again I completed the tetrarch's speaking. "Eating their souls."

"Indeed so," said the tetrarch. "So I asked myself, was this Dante himself the Souleater or his chosen champion, or was Rhea correct that the measure of a man must be discovered in his friends? If these exceptional friends were to be believed, something terrible was about to occur in the southern deserts. And so I came here, willing to listen. I never expected to find events so far advanced . . . or to discover truth laid in my lap so clearly as it was this morning."

He sipped his tea, then plopped it on the table and shoved it away as if it had gone bitter. "I committed crimes in my pursuit of a man I believed an abomination. Be sure, all of you, that if Temple or king yet stands when we are done here, I will resign my office and submit myself for punishment. But today, I offer my service to you, lady, and to you, Duplais."

Anne was no longer looking out the window, but propped on the window ledge, examining the tetrarch in that way that made you believe she was counting the hairs on your chest. "How do you think to help us?"

Ah, yes, the tasks of the day. I grasped mundanity. But my gaze flicked to the boiling sky and found no relief for the gaping hollow in my gut.

"Your first mandate, now you have secured Duplais, is to obtain the Seeing Stones before they are used and to destroy them."

"Only we don't know how," said Anne.

"One of us might," said de Ferrau. "If, indeed, he received them from the hand of the Creator."

And in a single instant, he gave my dread a name. Several names: Ianne, Os, Vicorix, Altheus . . .

"I make no claims here," I said, trying not to sound beggarly. It was one thing to believe. Another to produce evidence of that belief. Logic, intellect, science, study, had failed me. "There's naught in me to answer such questions. I've tried—believe me, I've tried."

Unfazed, de Ferrau jumped to his feet. "If I'm to humble myself before a group willing to take on the Souleater, then none of my nattering arguments with the Cult must get in the way."

A few steps around the table and he crouched beside me, gathering my trembling hands in his own. Calluses . . . That surprised me. His nails were blunt. Clean. Consider anything but what he meant . . .

But the young tetrarch's eyes bore the color and clarity the desert sky ought to display. And no little sympathy, besides. "Sonjeur de Duplais, if you are who and what some of your friends believe, then your soul has repeatedly passed beyond the Veil. Eighteen years I've spent making connections with souls that have undergone this change. It's true I've considered only the soul's current state, believing that its progress through Ixtador toward the gates of Heaven was all that should concern me. But souls beyond the Veil—those that remain whole—are not constrained by age or time. Neither should their essence be restricted to the life associated with . . . a current existence . . . if that soul has truly experienced more than one. It occurs to me that I might be able to touch memories that you, confined to this body, cannot."

"Read my soul. . . ." I squirmed as if a scorpion crawled up my leg, heading for my nether parts.

"Do you believe you have crossed the Veil or not?"

His clear gaze would not let me turn away. "Yes. But I—"

"And do you believe that prior to one of those crossings you might have held the knowledge we need?"

Logic had foresworn belief and yet . . . "Yes."

"Well, then, the choice is yours. If you say no, we'll find some other way." He sat there like an impenetrable wall. No tic, no smirk, no doubt or hesitation gave me cause to deny him.

Anne's gaze flicked between de Ferrau and me, as if expecting one of us to launch an attack. Ilario's eyes were closed; he was a prayerful man. But we had no time for quibbling, and this de Ferrau— Curse it all, I believed him.

"Unless someone has a simpler way . . ." I swallowed hard. "Though I suppose it's not so simple."

"It shouldn't hurt," he said, the corners of those eyes crinkling. "None of my subjects has ever complained."

Before I could answer . . . or laugh . . . or have a second thought, he dropped my hands and whirled into action. "Rhea, your medicine box. Our friend will need a sedating potion. In half an hour, I need him conscious, but wholly incapable of directing his own thoughts."

"An hour," she said, firmly, not looking at me. "I can do it more safely, and he needs to eat."

"An hour, then. No more. Goodman Andero, perhaps you would assist Sonjeur de Duplais into the small chamber adjoining. I'll have a meal sent in. Lord Ilario, Lady Anne, once I've gathered the materials I need from Scholar Agramonte's cabinets, I'll need to speak with you outside Duplais's hearing." He raised his open palms as if to quell my concern. "This is only to learn what details of your person and . . . history . . . might enable me to make this connection. Just as I would do in the deadhouse."

I nodded, the terror lodged in my throat preventing speech. Drugged again. Helpless again . . . holy night. I should be glad he hadn't suggested killing me. Nothing in Beltan de Ferrau's face or manner suggested he was incapable of that.

"Until then, Lady Anne, perhaps you would consider writing down the message we heard this morning. There's ink and paper on the writing table. We'd best not lose a word."

Once they'd shown me to a pallet in an otherwise empty room, Rhea brought in a vial and a glass dropper. "I'll give you only a little at a time," she said. "That way, I can judge better when it's enough. I'd take a dose myself—double even—but—"

"I'd prefer you stay clearheaded," I said and swallowed her bitter drops. "And please don't apologize any more. When we've time, we'll sort it out. Besides, I've a friend here to protect me." Andero remained in the doorway, neither in nor out. He'd said not a word since de Ferrau's arrival.

Biting her lip, Rhea touched my arm and hurried off.

"Come talk to me, Andero, if you would. I never knew Dante had a brother. . . ." I surely didn't want to stew for an hour.

Andero was good company, once I convinced him I was neither on the brink of death nor a god. "Honestly, I've had limited success with everything I've done," I said as we shared a glorious hotchpotch of veal bone, dates, and lentils. "I was a decent librarian but a terrible son, a fine investigator who convicted the wrong man, and only by your 'little brother's' grace can I do a lick of magic. As to this other thing . . ." My spoon paused. I blew a long sigh in an attempt to calm my gut. "That could be but one more grand delusion."

"You're the first man ever made a friend of Dante," said Andero, attacking his bowl as if he'd not eaten in a decade. "Even his teacher—this fellow Salvator—was a brute, forever trying to bind his wildness, more than half scared of him."

"I don't know anyone who wasn't—isn't—more than half scared of Dante. Every time I'd start to believe us friends, he'd get angry with me about something. But we partnered well."

The smith told me of their grim childhood, of playing together and growing apart, and he shared the tale of their journey south—their father's death, Adept Denys, Jono the foolish shepherd, and the settlers of Hoven. Between the times Rhea arrived to drop her bitter potion on my tongue, I came near forgetting what we were doing. Almost . . .

When my eyes grew heavy, my tongue thick, my fear swollen, Andero crouched close to my face, his broad face grave and thoughtful. "Most of this morning, I've felt the need to break your neck for dragging Dante and me into this. The life we were born to was no place a divine hand would nurture a favored son. But telling the whole of it . . . That tetrarch made sense with what he said about prophets and gifts and looking for the right person. That's what you did. You found him." A grin creased his face, and he gave a rumbling chuckle. "Guess that's what your king did, too, way back at the beginning. Went looking for what was needed and found you."

Maybe Andero left then. Maybe he didn't. But I laughed until Rhea's worried face appeared above me. Her features swirled and flowed like the reflection in a poor-quality mirror, and I tried to answer. "Sorry pair . . . Dante and me . . . prophet's nightmare . . ."

My lips grew numb and refused to convey anything more of sense, and

I slipped into that swirling glass as a sleek longboat into a current. Candles bloomed in the swelling grayness. Vague shapes came and went. My thoughts dissolved amid the scents of incense and burning herbs and whispered invocations. Names fled, and time and logic. I drifted. So pleasant merely to exist . . . until the world dropped out from under me.

I plummeted through a waterfall of smeared images: books, knives, fire, and blood, chains, drowning, and desert peace. . . .

A javelin of green flame tore through me in fiery agony, pinning me like a butterfly to a biologist's display. . . .

"Go 'way," I said to the man slitting my lost flesh with a silver knife. A green jewel was suspended on his breast.

He smiled and pressed the cup to the shallow cut to draw out my blood. "Sorry, no. We're going to spend eternity together, you and me. You'll make a fine slave. . . ."

As quickly as it had struck, the green javelin was withdrawn, and I plummeted downward again. Another pause . . .

A battle raged, as I stood atop a grassy hill of brilliant green, my wand held high. . . .

Another gut-hollowing descent. Then the fiery weapon pierced a green jewel on my own breast. . . .

The tent billowed in a dry breeze, the sweet promise of desert sunset. The tents of my soldiers spread across the rosy landscape like the santorillium that bloomed when the rains came. How I loved this land. But my bones were weary, my skin dry as the sand.

My dusty, scarred hand smoothed the polished facets of the holy jewel. How could I possibly destroy the Fire of Heaven? Tyregious warned my sons would fight over it and ruin everything we'd built. But how would they survive Aroth's onslaught without divine aid, given for this purpose? Garif was everything I'd hoped for in an heir, but he would not exile the brothers he loved. Nor would I. I should never have sired children. The gods had warned me, but Kassima was so dear, so lovely. . . . The wizard had not gleaned how to destroy the Stone but said he could split it into three, give each their own power . . . protect them from one another. . . .

Another withdrawal. Another plunge into the abyss. Again and again, smeared voices, elation, fear, victory, defeat, love here and there, and with no constant save the green spear. A piercing agony . . .

Naked, purified, empty, my heart lodged in my throat, I crawled through the worm's passage into the lightless cave. Eight, ten, perhaps twelve passages of the sun I lay there in the dark . . . faint with hunger . . . shivering with cold . . . every drip of moisture a thunder, every scurrying beetle trampling on my emptiness. A vain spirit I was to beg such a gift. But the war in Heaven raged. The shadow was growing as daemons' blood damped the holy fire. Tales of wonder would sustain hope.

Only when reduced to nothing did I fumble for the pots. Feel the marks—circle for red, cross for yellow, two lines for black. Stir the ground pigment and the water. Dip the brush. Let the daemon guide my hand to paint the story of our need. Then I lay down again to wait, until the body grew numb and thoughts vanished. . . .

"Wake, Os!" Flame's heat bathed my frail skin. The vault of stars filled my eyes and then the painted face of the modran who had sent me into the cave. "Have you brought an answer?"

My hand ached from clenching hard, sharp edges. When my fingers uncurled, the light of Heaven, the color of rich grass, spread over the gathered clan, drawing sighs and songs of joy.

In gratitude I closed my eyes and touched the mystery again. "I vow . . . yes, to learn always, to care always, to mind duty by sharing the light, and to return this gift should it be damaged by your kind or mine own. . . .

A plummeting descent; another skewering . . .

Another winter coming. The wind of year's end carried a knife-edge as the sun settled beyond the white cliffs. I licked my dry lips and prayed the woman came tonight to bring me mead. Its heat would warm my belly against the coming storms. The daemon had chained me near the top of the mount so I could look on the lands of men beyond the Ring and see the life forbidden me: hunting and herding, coupling and birthing, walking vineyards and fields. He of the gold and gray hair and beauteous face said I had stolen what was meant for greater beings.

"Out there is your proper place, Ianne, groveling in the filth with other beasts."

But I told him, "Celeres taught us the stories. The Creator holds us in his heart and wishes us raised up. If our daemons will not, then we must do it ourselves."

Which did nothing to soothe his anger. And so was I chained and abandoned, allowed neither to cross the Veil nor to live as mortal man. But as the sun fell, I watched the green fires blossom against the night and knew I had done right. A stone house snug against the wind. A knife kept sharp enough to carve a vine on a shepherd's staff. A frightened child soothed with a hero tale that took shape in the flames. Magic . . .

"PORTIER, SWALLOW THIS." SWEET SYRUP seeped into my dry mouth. "Rhea says it will help you wake."

"We need you to look at—"

"*Hush*, Tetrarch. Have you no shred of mercy?"

I smiled—inside, if not without. Only Anne de Vernase would hush a tetrarch.

The effort needed to open my eyelids suggested that someone had glued them shut. I could feel nothing, save the uneven warmth of a hearth and the hovering presence of those beside me. Anne and Tetrarch de Ferrau, the Reader.

With a lung-searing gasp, I sat bolt upright, head, body swelled to bursting with images, voices, names, faces, battles, dancing, horrors, grief, joy, mystery, magic. My heart galloped; my lungs pumped as if trying to breathe for a thousand lifetimes. . . .

No—nineteen. *Nineteen* lifetimes, and more than a hundred deaths shared among them. Impossible. Impossible. Impossible.

"Easy, my friend." Hands grasped my arms, held me still lest the swelling propel me through the ceiling. A tall man, lithe and fair. Hair should be pale, not false black. Friend. Swordsman. I gawked at him, grappling with five thousand names. Panic set in.

"*This* life," he said, firmly. "Concentrate on this life. Portier de Savin-Duplais. Scholar. Investigator. The librarian who hid his light for so many years. My good friend." He glanced over his shoulder. "Rhea!"

"I'm here, lord. Slow your breathing, Duplais. Think about it very hard. Slow your heart. You're safe . . . and exactly where you're supposed to be. Surrounded by friends."

She was quiet but commanding. Tall, too. And so young. She acted plain, but hers was a deep and quiet beauty. Rhea. The big, quiet man in the corner saw it, too, his wondering eyes on her, not me.

I thought very hard. It was quite like putting on my spectacles when reading. The blurred, overlapping letters on the page settled into one orderly line of text. Portier de Savin-Duplais. Librarian. Investigator. Reborn . . . I refused to look back at the previous lines.

"Tell me I'm not mad or dreaming," I said, my throat constricted. "Tell me"—the sky beyond the window was boiling tar—"Creator's hand, tell me the hour is not *day* with a sky like that."

"You're not mad, unless we all are," said Anne, sitting beside me on the bed, holding my hand. Her calm was soothing, though her flesh felt fevered beside my chill. "And it's just past midday. The reading took two hours and you've taken a while waking up."

Ilario sat on the other side of me, his eyes alight. "Seems you've been a very busy man through the years."

"Did you learn what was needed?" I said, feeling naked again.

"You must look at the notes," said Ilario. "The tetrarch dictated for three hours, and we made a sketch from what he saw in one of the last . . . memories."

"Don't know if I can. Lost my spectacles." Though, indeed, scattered images lingered in my skull like tea leaves in the bottom of a cup.

Ilario unrolled a parchment on my lap. "We think you painted this on the wall of a cave, in some kind of prayer ritual."

Memory filled in what faulty eyesight missed. Horses, bulls, goats, wolves, vanishing into a great blackness. A village left starving . . . mothers laying infants out to die for lack of milk . . . the fields barren, the sun darkened. So life had been in this land during the Daemon War. But here and there a dab of red or yellow—on a pipe that blessed a marriage with mystical music, or surrounding a fruitful field, protecting it from ravaging beasts, or on the potion pots of a healer who kept wounds from requiring amputation. Extraordinary skills? Magic? The line between was ever blurred.

He unrolled a second page. "But the hand that painted these other scenes, Anne judges to be different."

I closed my eyes and flexed my fingers, which insisted they held a bundle of twigs. Tied together, chewed and beaten to separate the fibers at one end, twigs made a decent brush for painting. "It wasn't the differing hand that was the marvel," I said, softly. "It was the green pigment. We had no source for green."

"Holy night," whispered Ilario, "you truly remember."

The right-hand side of the drawing displayed three panels. The first showed a great hand reaching down from the heavens to place a green crystal in the palm of a naked man, a very cold, hungry, bewildered man, surrounded by his joyful clan. The second panel showed the same man, holding the green gem high as he walked an endless road, scattering its beams across fields and vineyards and the beautiful, glorious herds. And in the last, the man, now ringed with six fiery green symbols, stood halfway between the ground and the heavens bearing a sullied gem. Blood drops trailed from his heart.

"The green ring means enchantment," I said. Knowing. "Using the god's fire. The symbols are enchanted objects that must be used for the rite. The person here"—I touched a lone figure outside the ring—"would be the modran—the shaman, the magus. The others outside the ring are members of the clan."

"And the one inside the ring?" said Ilario.

"That, I believe, is me."

"So I'll need to work the world's last magic," said Anne, cracks appearing in her calm. "Enabling you to take the Seeing Stones back where you got them."

"But not to that dreadful cave. Gods, that was cold. Yet I would choose it instead . . ." I glanced up at Anne and Ilario and wished I could say something to ease their pain. A calm certainty had settled over me. At last I knew. I—Ianne/Altheus/Os—had returned to the living world for the simple purpose of dying.

Anne

CHAPTER 37

"So this mark is for the seasons, this one for the elements—"

"Earth, air, fire, and water," said Portier. "Not the Camarilla's five nor the alchemists' thirteen."

"The classical elements," I said. "I'll need an object to evoke each one."

Portier, Ilario, and I sat on the floor at the low table where we had begun, the sketch spread out before us. I had to keep my mind fixed to the problems we faced and not to the end result. Nothing in the lengthy transcript of the tetrarch's reading suggested an alternative to the simple solution. Portier had to die, and he believed this enchantment, painted on a cave wall millennia in the past, would enable him to take solid matter across the Veil.

When I suggested he had painted the cave wall himself in the throes of delirium, he reminded me about the green pigment and the crystal in his hand when he was dragged out of the cave. When I suggested that the enchantment might allow him to cross the Veil with the Seeing Stones and then return, he pointed to the blood drops on the figure in the drawing and wrinkled his nose, as if it were something only slightly distasteful. Why wasn't he angry? He wasn't even forty years old. He'd spent half his life in a library.

While my grief was tempered with rage, Ilario's was all wonder. "Can you remember *everything* now?"

"Blessedly, no. Only for the bits of time de Ferrau selected. I can tell you what I smelled in that moment, what I heard, what I knew, what I was thinking. The man who dragged me from the cave was named"—Portier's eyes shifted, losing their sharp focus—"Vit. He was a modran—a shaman.

My uncle." Information from so deep in his past took a noticeable moment to retrieve. "But I couldn't tell you what I did the day before crawling into that cave or anything after that waking."

"We need to move on," I said. "I don't know enough yet." I'd no idea if I could even work such a spell. What if we'd missed some critical detail and Portier died for nothing? And time was racing by. Jacard wanted Portier for his own rite. He could be at our door at any moment.

I tapped the third mark, near hard enough to poke a hole in the paper. "The third you say is a shaman's mark—so I need something sacred. Would a tessila do? I've carried Lianelle's all this way."

"Sanctified by a verger, by your love and belief, and by use, I should think so," said Portier. "It could almost do for the fourth as well. The upward arrow with this knot on the bottom means something that belongs to one of the dead, yet remains here in the living world—an anchor, so to speak." He nudged me with his elbow. "Ani, it will be all right. You'll know what to do."

"Not all of us have divine friends to instruct us," I snapped, eyes fixed on the sketch.

"Dante is a masterful teacher." When Portier's hand touched mine, I felt like I'd whipped a child.

"Oh, gods, forgive me. . . . Something of yours, then."

"I don't seem to have anything of my own. So something belonging to someone else dead . . ."

I pulled Lianelle's frog pendant from my shirt. "This was Lianelle's."

Ilario touched it. "Dante wore one very like this on our journey from Pradoverde."

"He brought it with him?" *My only light.* The stabbing remembrance raised tears I had no time to shed. And now to lose Portier, too . . . "My sister made both of them."

Lianelle was there in Ixtador. According to de Ferrau, she might be whole as yet. Every thought of her surrounded by a *seething morass of human refuse*, knowing such was her only future, had me swallowing stones. "Portier, is the Souleater destroyed once you've taken the Stones back? Can he still devour souls?"

"I don't know. As long as Ixtador remains intact . . . Honestly, Ani, I'd say there's risk. I'll try, but I've no idea what . . . happens. One thing at a time. The fifth symbol is the means of death. The blood drops tell . . ."

Dante had not known how to destroy Ixtador. And we were to be left without magic.

". . . and the sixth . . ."

"The snake has forever been the symbol of reversal." De Ferrau had come up behind us. I'd swear the morning's experience had aged him, grooving his brow and shrinking the flesh of his face from around its bones. He had slept for the past hour, exhausted from the reading and his frenzy to get everything recorded while it was fresh. "I'd say you need something that is the antithesis of death, as if to fool whoever minds the Veil. Agramonte has a cat here."

"We'll not want to carry a cat with us, no matter how we decide to get inside the palace," I said. "Would flowers do? Roots?"

"More in the line of healing," said Portier, raising a hand. "The mo-dran used snake venoms in medicines and took small amounts throughout his life to induce visions. Rhea can give you a medicine to use."

"But you said the objects themselves need to be enchanted?"

"This can't be overly complicated, Ani; we were not a sophisticated people. And the spellwork . . . just think of how Dante would approach it. My uncle Vit would say *choose sacred objects.* Dante would say *choose objects for their keirna*—like the nireal and your sister's tessila, or water from the fountain of this house, where the tetrarch and his shy friend Agramonte have given us refuge."

"Perhaps the medicine Rhea used to heal Ilario. Something vital."

"Exactly so."

"Rhea's just returned from the market," said the tetrarch. "She and Andero found a charm—a door or fence ward that seems to work. We'll set it up so you can practice snatching the Stones."

"Good. That's a grand idea," I said. I had been so worried about the spellwork, I'd given little thought to getting the cursed Stones to begin with. How I was to empty myself of thought and desire so completely as to avoid the consequences of a spell, I had no idea.

Portier excused himself, mumbling about a latrine. Rhea took the ni-real and the tessila and said she would see to collecting the other things on my list. When I explained how each object should bear as much meaning as possible in the context of our work, she understood immediately.

She scanned the list, biting her lip. "You've not put down anything for the killing weapon. I've medicines would do it."

My heart was black as the day. How did one ask a friend how he wished to die?

"I'll do it," said Ilario. "I can make it quick and near painless. So, my dagger. Come, let's practice snatching the damned Stones. Nothing matters if we can't do that."

THE WEAK LITTLE CHARM DESIGNED to protect one's doors and windows from thieves did little but make one's palms itch, little to discourage a determined thief. But even a weak enchantment would give me a way to practice Dante's technique for avoiding a spell's compulsive working.

After an hour's concentrated quiet, alone in a room, using every mental discipline I knew to clear my mind, I walked through the warded doorway, retrieved a cup set on the far side, and returned it to Ilario. My palms did not itch.

"Good," he said. "Now try it again."

Closing my eyes, I swept aside the sound of his voice, my moment's satisfaction, and my fears that this charm was so minor a deterrent compared to the protection of the Seeing Stones that the exercise was ridiculous. Then I walked through the warded door again. By the time I retrieved the cup, I had to clamp my hands together to keep from scratching.

"Again," said Ilario. A man who had spent a great deal of his life training in swordplay was no easy taskmaster.

Three more times I made it through—just barely. But then Ilario jumped out at me right when I moved into the charm's influence. I had to back away before my palms bled. An hour we practiced, Ilario pelting me with nuts or yelling or breaking a plate behind me, until I was ready to strangle him. I succeeded no more than half the time. Wholly unacceptable. The Stones' protections could kill me.

When Ilario advised I try harder, fear and frustration overflowed. "*You* do it if it's so easy!"

"All right."

A twitch rippled from the top of his dyed hair, down his length to his toes, as if a shower of fleas had bathed him. And then, blank-faced, he walked through the doorway, picked up the cup, and returned it to my hands. Four more times he did the same, without a blink, without a scratch.

As he began again, I picked up a handful of almonds from the basket on the table and threw them at him all at once. He didn't flinch. Didn't stop. Didn't scratch.

The next time I yelled, the next I whacked his shoulder from behind with a fire iron. He grabbed the iron and yanked it from my hand but continued on his mission to replace the cup beyond the door.

"How do you do it?" I could scarce comprehend such focus. "Was the twitching some sort of charm?"

He grinned. "That was just for show. Think, dear lady, how have I spent my life? Do you imagine I could play Ilario de Sylvae, court jester of Castelle Escalon, for some seven-and-twenty years without a great deal of practice ignoring distractions, without training my reflexes to kick in when needed and only without breaking discipline?"

I sagged onto the stool. "Then why in the name of sense didn't you tell me? Why waste an hour on my failures?"

"Because you believed the mission yours, and it was not my place to say you had too much to worry about already. I wanted your confidence, not your reluctant yielding. I cannot help you with the magic, but empty-headed thievery and killing, yes."

When we returned to the library, Andero was regaling de Ferrau and Rhea with grim tales of the city. ". . . a riot at the gates. Some are trying to get inside the walls for fear of this storm coming. None's ever seen the sky like this. More were trying to get out, though. Fires are springing up here and there. One's burning in the Street of Beggars. Walls are weeping blood or collapsing. It's astonishing half the people in the city aren't dead. The water in the wells and the channels has turned dark. Everywhere you look there's spiders. Every story's wilder than the next. All blame the daemon mage."

"But he can't—" I stopped short. Dante had said he would fight the Souleater as long as he could. After that, if the Souleater could force him . . .

"We hold to our plan," said Ilario. "We get in. We wait until Jacard and the lady are abed. While Anne and Portier prepare the spellwork down in the cellar, I'll nick the Stones. Rhea and Andero will ensure I'm not interrupted."

Portier believed that we had to work the rite in the heart of Sirpuhi.

"Jacard won't be putting on entertainments tonight," I said. "And even assuming the invisibility potion works on everyone else, it didn't work for Portier. We'll have to go in the way Portier and I came out. The drain."

"Can't," said Andero. "It's blocked. Saw an explosion on my way down yesternight. Thought it was going to bring the cliff down on my head. We could fight our way in and then vanish. None would believe—"

"I've a most certain way to open the Regent of Mancibar's gates," said de Ferrau from the doorway. "It risks drawing him from his bed, but I doubt he'll don his magical Stones to meet a Temple tetrarch."

Despair threatened. "*Meet* you?"

"I'll knock on his door and tell him that I've the false Sante Ianne in my custody. My payment for turning him over will be the necromancer, whom I plan to gut and burn in Temple Square to make myself the youngest High Tetrarch in Sabria's history. Do you think he'll believe me?"

The idea revolted me. "Jacard would demand to see Portier," I said. "He knows him. And your bailiffs can't protect you from magic."

"Ah, but I shall inform him that I've, first, given Duplais a poison that will surely kill him before any use can be made of him and, second, laid a Temple curse on him that will abort his saintly revenance—an ancient Temple secret. If the librarian's immortality is the key to Iaccar's desires, he'll not pass up my bargain."

"Once the bargain is struck, you'll have to hand Portier over," said Ilario. "Then you're dead."

The tetrarch shrugged. "Naturally we must adapt to the circumstances of the meeting. But with a clever use of Temple regalia—hooded robes, to be precise—as well as my usual insistence on proper protocol, and plenty of distraction from you four, you will spirit Duplais away long before the bargain is consummated. Win or lose, our forces shall be in place inside the palace. My bailiffs and I are not wandering minstrels, but warriors sworn to combat the Souleater and his works in all ways. And if the worst comes to pass, then in some small measure our deeds might make reparation for Captain de Santo."

De Ferrau's clear gaze lay square on Ilario. When the chevalier's visage hardened, the tetrarch did not avert his eyes; nor did he offer any excuses to give himself quarter.

Ilario nodded slowly. "It might work. . . ."

An hour's argument found us no better alternative, and we adjusted our plans to suit the new arrangements. The city bells rang tenth hour of the evening watch. "So be it," I said. "Let's go."

THE UNDERSTEWARD SWEPT OUT OF the palace waiting room to fetch Jacard's steward, leaving Tetrarch de Ferrau, his four bailiffs, Andero, and Portier, all of them draped in hooded green robes. The man hadn't noticed that Rhea, Ilario, and I were there as well. I had mixed the last of Lianelle's invisibility powder and divided the potion between us to give us the time we needed. We would have no second chances.

Rhea had supplied one of the smaller bailiffs with a mild sweating potion. Shortly after Jacard arrived and verified Portier's identity, the young bailiff would feign a collapse. Under cover of the illness, Andero's guardianship, and enough ghostly distractions to allow it, Andero and unseen partners would get a hooded Portier out of the room while the negotiations for de Ferrau's bargain proceeded.

It had taken us almost two hours to get to the palace, avoiding crowds trying to quench the raging fires and gangs of rioters tearing into homes and shops. But de Ferrau had gathered his own followers as he proceeded up the palace road, announcing that he had caught the Regent's missing prisoner and was planning to trade him for the fiendish necromancer, who would burn at dawn in the heart of Mancibar. Trust came very hard amid such rhetoric—and the cheers that followed.

The tetrarch's most arrogant manner, plus a great deal of persuasion and perhaps some gold coins, had been required to gain us entry. And once we were ensconced in the palace waiting room, the understeward warned of a long wait.

The moonless, starless heavens boiled. The aether was a wordless tumult. My nerves quivered like plucked lute strings.

I tapped twice on the back of Rhea's hand—the signal that Ilario and I were off to retrieve the Stones. Holding hands so as not to get separated, the two of us slipped out of the room and up the stair. Rhea and Andero would bring Portier to the cavern, Rhea invisible, Andero posing as a guard taking a prisoner down. I'd sketched them a map of the way.

Lamp boys and sweepers hurried through the corridors, eyes to the floor. Footmen stood at the bottom of the stair and at the intersection of the larger passages, looking as if they'd take off running if someone blinked at them.

The Regent of Mancibar was not in his chambers. The polished wood box in the base of the man-goat statue was empty. Gods save us. . . . Paralyzed, I stared at the evidence of our ruin. Wherever Jacard was, he had Tychemus with him.

Ilario tugged at my sleeve. "So we try for the woman's."

Despair predicted what we would find. A lamp burnt in the lady's sitting room, but, indeed, no one was there or in the bed, bath, or wardrobe chambers. No green Stones lay in the velvet box.

"So we hunt," said Ilario, turning down the passage, back the way we'd come.

But I dragged him the opposite direction. "No, we have to see—"

He gathered me close and whispered in my ear. "Ani, Dante is not part of this plan. I'll come back with you after. I swear it."

"We have to know if he's destroying the city." Dante had warned us to beware of him.

No guard stood outside the doorway. No lamps burnt. My hands bade Ilario wait, and I crept across the room toward the balcony. My knee whacked an obstacle—a straight-backed chair on its side. The balcony was deserted.

"Over here," whispered Ilario. "There's been quite a row, and not so long ago. Careful where you step. Everything's upended. There's glass. . . ."

The rug was cold and wet under my bare feet. The armchair where Dante had been sitting when I spoke to him was overturned. The mahogany cabinet with its carafes and glasses lay in splinters. And the night breeze wafted through a dark section of wall where no openings had existed the previous day, stirring the scents of char and ash. Andero's images of Castelivre were ever vivid.

Something hard gouged my foot. Not glass. Metal . . .

I retrieved a thin chain—a neck chain, broken, as the clasp was still hooked.

My breath caught. I patted the damp rug. No mistaking the enchantment that prickled my fingers when I found the gleaming oval. A few centimetres away lay a torn scrap of paper and a ring, also bristling with familiar enchantment. Portier's ring.

"This isn't Dante's doing," I said. "Someone's torn my pendant from his neck. We may already be too late!"

Lightning split the oppressive sky outside the windows. Not two instants later, thunder trembled the palace foundations. A wind gust banged the balcony doors open. I slapped my hands to my ears to shut out a growing polyphony of terror. It did no good. The storm was inside me.

We streaked from the room and down the passage. As we reached Xanthe's door, I pulled up. "Wait."

Dante's staff stood inside the door, exactly where I'd seen it last. I wrapped my cloak about its middle, which seemed enough to make it unseeable. And in the lamplight I examined the scrap of paper. Two short sentences in Dante's left-handed script.

Wear it always.

Fight.

A message to himself, perhaps, scattered in the wreckage as it was. Stuffing the scraps in my pocket with the other things, I returned to Ilario. "Now we go."

Hands clasped tight, we ran. We reached the waiting room just as Jacard barged in, a green prism gleaming at his breast.

I drew Ilario back around the corner. "I'm going on down," I said. "We're going to have very little time."

"Godspeed, Ani." Ilario kissed the top of my head. "We'll be there with Stones and saint as soon as may be."

I hated to leave them. But Portier could wield enchantment, Ilario and Andero could fight, and Rhea was strong, intelligent, and invisible. I had to trust them. Only I could prepare the spell.

Gripping the staff and canvas bag that held the elements for the spellwork, I raced down the stairs and passages I'd followed the previous night. Dante's magic had guided my steps to find Portier. I was sure of it now. An unlikely animal fervor rose from my toes. *We partner well, my friend of the mind and heart. And our friends are exceptional. We'll win this night yet.*

CHAPTER 38

Smoke, yellow light, and the eye-watering scent of incense pouring through the brick arch from Sirpuhi's heart had warned me the cavern was not deserted. A man's thready wail but confirmed it. Yet nothing could have prepared me for the sight awaiting.

The air trembled with candlelight; the blood-painted words on floor and walls shivered. Across the cavern, beyond Altheus's bier and the four angels, two naked men were suspended by their wrists from pegs fixed in the stone wall. The one moaning in terror was a sturdy, healthy young man, very like the prisoner I'd set free. The other was Dante.

Did Jacard think to use *Dante* instead of Portier? It made no sense. Dante could not provide rebirth.

He was so still. . . . Only after a moment did a violent shudder declare him living. I breathed again.

The woman, his mistress, this Xanthe who teased Jacard so unmercifully, paced the length and breadth of the rectangular pit bounded by the wall and the towering angels. She fondled the green Stones at her breast.

". . . no notion what to do," she said. "You've ever advised me not to trust Iaccar. But I won't run away, either. I waited seven centurias to wield the Maldeona. This could all be your trick to steal them. You detest Iaccar. You think us both stupid."

Dante lifted his head. His eyes were sunk into his gaunt face, his lips bloody. Rivulets of sweat coursed down his flanks, pain stretching his skin across his bones. Though he, like the other man, was strapped tight to the wall at ankles, chest, and neck, I could see no mark on him. He jerked again, his every corded sinew twisting and knotting.

"Kill me," he said, harsh and low. "Please, lady—must fight—" He clamped his mouth shut as he spasmed yet again. Harder.

"No," she said, half angry, half grieving. "Tell *her* to save you, whoever she is."

Her? Saints, did they know I was here?

She climbed to the low step beneath his feet. "I don't *want* you dead. But you're no good to me like this. The market burns. The roads and riding paths crack. What pleasure in being queen of ruin? The ghoul says it's your doing."

"Need to die—" He slammed the back of his head against the wall.

The stone beneath my feet quivered. Great gods, what was happening to him?

"You told me that none can command a magus to work magic." The woman's rising desperation made her shrill. "Or was that just another lie?"

Dante snarled as he shuddered yet again.

Thick gray smoke hung in the vastness above the shallow pit. Cloudy tendrils brushed the flesh of the bound men, drawing wordless whimpers from the prisoner. Dante didn't seem to notice.

A gray finger of smoke twisted through the tremulous air exactly in my direction. I retreated, slamming my back to the wall of the prison passage, heart hammering, the taste of vomit in my mouth.

I'd thought Portier's absence would halt this business. Yet Jacard had clearly been interrupted. However hateful it was to leave Dante as he was, our plans were already askew. If the others brought Portier, and *if* we could somehow snatch the Seeing Stones, we'd have very little time to destroy the Stones. By Dante's own judgment, that came before all. I had to be ready.

The cells in the dark little passage were empty. The blue-limned light of the potion enchantment guided my eyes, but Dante's teaching guided my hands. Using his staff, I traced the boundaries of one cell for my spell enclosure, giving me the largest possible field. Circularity was unimportant, but closure was critical. I used the order of the symbols in the cave drawing to lay out the objects from the canvas bag: representations of the four seasons and the four elements, the sacred tessila, the anchor . . . Ah, I now possessed something belonging to Portier. I returned Lianelle's pendant to my neck and pulled out the ring I'd found in Dante's chambers. Leaving an empty place for the weapon, I placed the vial of Ilario's stomach medicine—our representation of the healing snake.

The arrangement felt awkward. *Selection of the objects is primary,* Dante had instructed, *but never underestimate the importance of balance and positioning.* The piled branches, flasks, fan, and candle for the seasons and elements weighed heavy against Portier's ring and the small chunk of rosy marble that was the tessila. So I placed the four elemental objects at the corners, the four reminders of the seasons halfway down each boundary of the rectangular space. The weapon, the medicine vial, the tessila, and the ring would define a second rectangle inside the first. Better.

Assuming we somehow managed to wrest the Stones from Jacard and Xanthe, I must draw together the keirna of these objects and shape them into a spell structure as Dante had taught me. Portier would lie in the center, holding the Stones. And then we would kill him, and I would bind my spellwork.

How in the name of sense would I have time? How in the name of the holy could we murder our friend?

Slumped in the passage outside the cell, I worked to refine the spell structure I had devised earlier. I had envisioned a vessel woven of enchantment that could contain Portier's soul and the solid Stones, keeping them together as his soul left his body to pass the Veil. The objects specified in the painting lent themselves to the idea. The warp would be strung with the keirna of the four seasons, the four elements of earth, air, fire, and water, and the ring that anchored Portier's passing soul specifically to the physical world. The weft would be the keirna of those things that touched the world of the spirit: the sanctified tessila, the intangible mystery of life and healing, and the weapon that brought release from mortal life.

A fierce concussion set the iron doors swinging, disrupting my concentration. The rubble at the end of the passage clattered as it settled. Not long after, the woman let loose a siren scream. I raced back to the cavern.

Xanthe was backed up to the catafalque. Tongues of smoke . . . licked her. Her pale hair floated outward from her contorted face as she stared into the cloud above her, where a half-formed phantom the size of a house bulged and shrunk amid the turbulent fog.

"Sshall you, too, writhe for my pleasure thisss night, girl?" The throaty whisper hissed with malevolence as Xanthe sank to the floor. "You belong beneath my feet. Ignorant, crude. My nephew tells me you value tin over silver and cannot distinguish coal from ebony. Of course he is a beetle like you, too weak to bend a woman and a cripple to his will."

Nephew! I peered into the fog. The spectral features were unmistakably Kajetan's. Would that I could murder the fiend again.

Xanthe squealed as smoky fingers twined her hair. "You dare trespass holy ground wearing the objects of my desire, little trollop. Give them over."

"Leave her be!" Dante clamped his lips and groaned. Candles flickered. Implements on the bloodstained table rattled.

The spectre's attention snapped to Dante. "Does mindless vermin think to command *me*? Does not our sovereign master teach you your place even now?"

Our master. I didn't think he meant Jacard.

With Kajetan's focus elsewhere, Xanthe scuttled toward the stair to the upper gallery. I could not allow her to escape with her Stones. As the revenant heaped scorn and malice on Dante, I raced ahead and blocked the stair. I picked at her gown and blew on her face, making sure she couldn't touch me and discover a living human.

"Oh, no," I whispered, forcing my voice harsh and sexless. "You'll not leave until you drop your useless trinkets on Altheus's coffin. Perhaps we shall strip you and add you to yon display of flesh."

Wide-eyed, she backed away, gripping the green crystals at her breast. Hurrying footsteps clattered on the gallery above our heads. Her eyes flicked upward.

"Back upstairs, Hosten," Jacard screamed. "Find that god-cursed librarian, so I can cut out his heart atop his own tomb. We'll see if he recovers from that. Gherok is going to nip the fingers off those Temple bastards one by one until one spills who's put them up to this."

Breathing a prayer for de Ferrau, his men, Andero, and Rhea, I quickly got out of Jacard's way.

"Your ghoul torments me, Iaccar," said Xanthe, hurrying her steps to keep up with Jacard as he crossed to the pit.

"We must work together, dear lady." Jacard presented her a rictus of a smile. "My uncle is jealous of our life and the grand vision we share. Any blood will satisfy him. But I'll not allow him yours."

"Get this done before Dante brings the palace down," growled the spectre. "You've dallied long enough. The rite will grant you all the power you deserve, and this daemon bound to him will make you a true immortal."

"I'll not rush the rite, uncle. This shall be my body, my power. Dante is a mindless husk who can't speak his own name."

"Tell me why your city is collapsing, fool. His daemon grows stronger by the hour."

"Accept that you are *dead*, uncle! In *this* world we have more than whining spectres to deal with. This is but a spring storm and a plague of earthshakings as happens frequently in Mancibar. All will be well when my beloved and I are joined in power, body, and mind. The Stones shall control both the slave and his daemon master."

Jacard stroked Xanthe's hair, drawing his hand downward to bare her shoulder. He kissed the curve of her neck, the swell of her breast, and then moved to her lips. She clung to him like an infant, more terrified than enamored. "Dante never recognized the beauty and cleverness right in front of him," he said, softly. "It drove me wild. We shall make a magnificent partnership."

Kajetan's black glare might have shriveled Dimios himself. "You are a cretin, nephew. There are forces of magic in this house—"

His diatribe halted abruptly when Jacard held a plate of rock over a small brazier—the source of the incense-laden smoke. "Manners, uncle, or I shall silence you. Your guidance is valuable, but not imperative."

The phantom snarled and retreated into the boiling cloud. Deception . . . double-dealing. Kajetan had to be present if he was to take Jacard's place. Did the dead sorcerer imagine Dimios would allow him to share this prisoner's body?

Jacard laid the slate aside and took Xanthe's arm. "Now, my sweet, we need some fresh blood. Fortunately our great magic no longer requires the librarian's carcass or his blood to bring us an everlasting empire. I've a hearty lad occupying his bleeding chair. Will you join me? The refinement of the torment should please you."

The two vanished into Portier's old cell.

I stepped up quickly to stand beside Dante. Rills of flame cascaded from his hands bound above his head, dissipating in bursts of freezing air.

"I am your memory," I whispered. "You are stronger than they know. The one who scourges you underestimates you in all ways. Neither he nor this bombastic spectre nor his thick-skulled minion have any idea of your gifts."

"Please . . . whatever you are . . . kill me." Agonized gasps punctuated his words. "I've lost the light . . . fighting blind . . . Need to see. Need to die. Need to fight."

Tears stung my cheeks. "Memories cannot kill, but they speak truth. The light is inside you—the fire of your gift. Of your heart. Of your passion for right. I see it, and I *will* help you. You've many things to do before you die."

"There is no help." He bared his teeth, snarling. "I am his *Hand*."

"Not yet. Not ever. Hold, Dante de Raghinne. Fight. Do not yield."

It twisted my heart to abandon him. But I dared not let Kajetan suspect my presence.

I slipped across the cavern to the prisoner's passage. "Ani?"

Never had I been so happy to hear a voice. I ran to meet Ilario and Portier as they climbed through the rubble blocking the drain tunnel. "What of Rhea? Andero?"

"On our heels," said Ilario, helping Portier to sit. "As is Jacard. The switch worked like a clockwork, but there were no negotiations. When Jacard's men surrounded the tetrarch, we were scarce along to the first stair. Rhea stayed to make sure Andero got away, but alas, I'd no chance to touch the emeralds and saw no sign of the lady."

"Both Jacard and Xanthe are here," I said. "And she's near giving up the Stones. And we've worse trouble. They've got Dante strung up out there. It's Dimios's torments and Dante's resistance causing this destruction. He begs to die. I . . . I could do it."

Portier's hand near crushed mine. "*Don't*, Ani. Dante chose this path deliberately, and then destroyed the memory of his reasons. We must have faith that he did what he believed necessary. The tetrarch would say I picked the person who could do what was needed, yes?"

I couldn't answer. Not when I felt the earth continue to spasm. But I did recall Dante's scribbled message. *Do not yield.*

"So they're planning to use Dante instead of Portier for this soul switching?" said Ilario.

I raked fingers through my hair. "Kajetan believes that because Dante is daemon possessed, he will take on full immortality instead of rebirth. I don't think he's told Jacard who they're dealing with."

"They're mad!" said Portier, breathless.

"It makes no difference to us," I said. "We have to destroy the Stones before they try it."

"How do we get the cursed things if we can't yank them from their necks?" Ilario wrenched the cell bars as if to uproot them.

"They'll have to take them off to fit the three together. As soon as they begin, you go, while the rest of us make some outsized distractions. . . ."

"I can wreak a bit of havoc," said Portier. "Even if I've fallen out of favor ritual-wise."

And so we watched and waited. Jacard and Xanthe emerged from the bleeding cell. They were laughing as they spoke of traveling their new demesne from Mancibar to Norgand, of coaches and legions, and ordering their empire. Xanthe commented on the beauty of the suspended prisoner's body. "No grueish hand, and every part so much more firm and powerful than"—she giggled—"yours, dearest Regent."

"The mind that rules the body is of most importance," snapped Jacard. "Now, to work . . ."

Jacard dabbed his brush in his gory medium, explaining that he painted the words in blood because he had no partner sorcerer to read his ritual books. He painted two lines on a whitewashed space next to Dante.

Vosi Dante de Raghinne au recivien, Zevi de Opere.

Vosi Jacard de Viole au recivien, Zevi de Opere.

From Dante to the vessel, Zevi the laborer. From Jacard to Zevi. Saints mercy . . .

Once he'd thrown down his brush, Jacard reached into a crockery urn. A handful of its contents, dropped into his brazier, produced a plume of black smoke. While one hand gripped the Stone Tychemus, he gestured in a circle above his head, and a band of candles, higher than the ones already lit, sprang into life with purple flame. "Uncle, spectre, prisoner of cruel Ixtador, answer my summons. Show us your face and tell us how best to join our three treasures."

Kajetan's tarry eyes glared, as his colorless mouth took on more definition. "Your future moves away instead of closer, boy. Shadows draw nigh. Let this be done."

"With my lady at my side, I fear no one. And as long as one of the shadows is Duplais, I'm happy to hear it. He will die beautifully, and so slowly he'll never wish to return to humankind."

Portier's face was unreadable in the gloom, but his hand, already icy, was trembling again. I enfolded it in both of mine. He had been so calm and deliberate. To feel his human fear reassured me that he was not in some ecstatic trance.

"The Stones were cut to accommodate each other like male and female. Turn them until they fit." The spectre's mouth gaped wide, and he licked his gray lips. Bottomless blackness yawned behind the colorless tongue. "Ensure your lesser spells are bound before invoking the three. Everything will happen very quickly."

"Are you ready, my love?" Jacard touched Xanthe's exposed breast. "My uncle is most impatient, and his touch is"—the prisoner screamed as a finger of cloud entwined his nether parts—"uncomfortable. Trust me and you shall rule Heaven and Earth at my side."

I caught my breath as Xanthe unclasped the slender chain holding the two Stones. The baubles shot green light beams through her clenched fingers.

Ilario's spirit went still. He released my hand, and I felt him step away.

As if to prove he was not lusting after her treasures, Jacard turned to his work. Raising Tychemus, he intoned a litany of Aljyssian phrases, pointing at the words he had just painted. As ropelike curtains of smoke obscured them, he stepped up beside Dante and the prisoner, Zevi de Opere.

Without warning, Jacard raked a knife across Dante's breast once and then again. Dante gasped and shook violently. The air of the cavern darkened. Was it imagining that I saw flames in his glare?

Jacard stepped back and admired the bloody *X*, while sucking Dante's blood from his fingers. "That's where I'd cut your heart out did I not have better use for you."

Dipping his finger into a silver dish, Jacard began to anoint the panting, wide-eyed Zevi. Portier drew me closer and whispered in my ear of ruses and distractions.

Noise from behind us spun me around. Andero loomed from the shadows and then Rhea beside him; her dose of the potion had run out. We were in dire straits, if our time was already expiring.

I made sure Rhea knew we could see her, then told the two quickly of Portier's plan to distract Jacard.

"Ssst!" Portier's signal set my blood into a fever.

Jacard returned to the catafalque and removed his own neck chain. He swept a courtly bow to Xanthe. "All is ready, my lady. Shall we seal our partnership?"

The two removed the Seeing Stones from their wire cages and laid them atop Altheus's coffin.

Portier and I moved. He slipped out and ducked behind one of the angels. Unable to see Ilario, I had to fight the urge to run to the bier. Instead, I grabbed Dante's staff—he had tuned a few of its spells to my hand—and took my place at the table holding Jacard's books and implements. Time slowed and stretched. . . .

"I see the joining edges, uncle. Are there words that must be spoken?"

"Don't do it, Jacard." Portier stepped out from hiding. "You'll rue the day your uncle set you to this work. Look at Dante. Do you want his tormentor inside you?"

Jacard stood transfixed for a moment, as if Portier were the true revenant. Then he stepped down from the catafalque, a smile blooming slowly, until malicious glee beamed from him like shafts of candlelight. "Oh, foolish, foolish holy man. I know how little blood flows in those veins and how weak it is to begin with. Do you think you can outmatch the power of any healthy man, much less the power of sorcery?"

"There are things you don't know about me." Portier raised a hand and snuffed half the thousand candles. At the same moment, I upended the table. The bowl of blood shattered and splashed gore across the paving amid a cacophony of cups, tins, candles, and spoons.

"Nephew!" screamed the phantom. "Ignore the weakling. Proceed with the invocation now!"

I pointed Dante's staff at one of the angels and released a focused blast of power. The statue shattered.

"Iaccar, the Stones!" Xanthe cried.

Only scattered shards of marble topped the coffin. No green. Exultant, I blasted another angel, just as Kajetan bellowed in outrage. Together we drowned out the cries of warning. Jacard himself dashed toward Portier.

But Andero appeared in front of Portier as if by magic himself, his blood-streaked sword drawn and raised.

"Who are you?" Jacard skidded to a halt a few metres away.

"I'm this fellow's friend," said the smith, "come along to see he's not harmed. You've already harmed a number of folk I care about."

Jacard snorted and raised his hand. . . .

I blasted a third angel, scooting away as the marble head struck the catafalque and bounced my way. But when I glanced back, Andero lay sprawled on the floor, blood pooling beside his head. Portier tore at Andero's clothes. I couldn't tell if he was injured, too.

"Aieyy!" Dante bellowed in agony. The earth rumbled.

"Get the Stones, fool. The harlot's snatched them back!" screamed Kajetan. "She has allies here. Did you not feel the bursts of magic? She never intended to give them to you."

When Jacard whirled around, he held Tychemus. Hope disintegrated.

"Where are they, lady?" he said, soft as a cat's purr. "All depends on the three together. On our agreement."

"They vanished," said Xanthe, quivering. "Believe me, lord. Lover . . ."

Eyes wide, lips colorless, she retreated before Jacard's wrath. Tychemus's green glints stained her face and her white gown.

Where was Ilario? Was he waiting to seize the third? If he became visible, it would spell disaster.

Xanthe threw her hands in the air. "The smoke ate them. Iaccar, my darling. . . ."

He touched her tentatively. Then gripped her shoulder and shoved her to the ground. "You pissing, teasing little whore, you really don't have them. Where did they go?"

Spewing short, desperate bleats, Xanthe tried to scramble away, but Jacard kicked her flat and stomped on her back.

"Magus, help me!" she screamed. "Dante, lover!"

But Dante was fighting even to breathe. Faster than an owl takes a mouse, Jacard plunged a dagger into Xanthe's back. He snarled as he yanked it out again. "Good riddance!"

Turning to the catafalque, he kicked at the debris. "Where are they, uncle? What did you see? Or have *you* hidden them?"

"Hands of flesh have taken them, fool. Muster your own power, you puling little weasel. Use Tychemus. Once we've done the switch, the other Stones won't matter. Hurry!"

But Jacard's fury spun him to face Portier. "Is it you, librarian? You and Dante again. And that woman . . ." He inhaled sharply. "Anne de Vernase, the Mondragon witch. Did *she* set you free? She and this damnable, cursed mage. Xanthe said she'd found a woman's trinket on him."

"Nephew! Attend!" Kajetan was panicked now. "We must do this before they invoke the power of the two! Tychemus can accomplish the switch alone if you but focus! The rite to free our master can come after."

Jacard bared his teeth and raised his Stone to the wall. *"Conforme desiti novae!"*

"No!" I screamed. The surge of power through the Seeing Stone near knocked me from the step.

The phantom Kajetan bellowed in triumph.

Jacard wasn't using the three together—a partial victory—but success or failure could kill Dante. I drew my zahkri and cut the straps holding him to the wall, letting his weight slump onto my shoulders and slide to the ground. I freed the wailing Zevi, who flailed his arms and backed away crabwise. Once disentangled, he scrambled to his feet and bolted for the stair, sobbing.

Dante shuddered and the trembling earth shook beneath us. I threw my arms around him as if I could shield him from what was to come. His flesh was cold as a dead man's. "I know you," I said, drilling the words into his head. "You will not be what he wants you to be. You are mine, Dante de Raghinne. Mine!"

Kajetan roared in fury, "No, no, no! You incapable runt, what have you done?" There followed such an ode of malediction as I had never heard, wails and screaming and bellowing, until they all faded into one extended scream that was the very sound of madness.

When I looked around, I saw Jacard's terror-filled eyes bleeding and his swollen body shaking violently. The Seeing Stone dropped from his hand and clattered down the steps. His eyes went entirely black . . . and then entirely white, again, and then again. Holding his skull together as his skin wept blood, Jacard screamed and staggered in frenzy, until he followed the course of his Stone and tumbled into the pit to lie still.

The gray smoke thinned and dissipated, and as I cradled Dante in my arms, I began to laugh and sob together. The blood-painted words on the wall had changed. They now read: *Vosi Kajetan de Saldemerre au recivien, Jacard de Viole. Vosi Jacard de Viole au recivien, Kajetan de Saldemerre.* From Kajetan to Jacard. From Jacard to Kajetan. Not only had Dante switched the original receiver to Jacard himself, but every time Kajetan took control of Jacard's body, the enchantment had replaced him with its former owner.

"You had your little joke on them after all, didn't you?" I said. "And it *does* matter. . . ."

Across the cavern a tall, slim form rippled the air like a child behind a bedsheet. Ilario became visible. Oblivious, he carried Xanthe's two Stones into the dark maw of the prison passage. My own enchantment faded as I laid Dante on the step and retrieved the Stone of Reason from the floor.

Unspeaking, Dante curled into a ball. Spasms racked him continually. The walls trembled. Candles toppled from their niches. I stroked his sweat-soaked hair. "We'll solve this," I said. "But first the Stones. As you instructed me."

Perhaps destroying the Seeing Stones would set him free—one way or the other.

Rhea knelt beside Andero. She pressed a clean cloth to a nasty laceration on his scalp, where Jacard's blast had thrown him against a shard of broken angel. To my relief, the smith was slowly coming around. "Stay still," she said, "at least until you can hold this yourself. You're going to have a wicked headache for a month most likely."

I stuffed a lit candle into Portier's hand, helped him up, and we made a slow progress into the prison passage. Ilario sat in the last cell, the one with the collapsed wall, clutching Xanthe's Stones close to his breast. His eyes were closed, his slender face drawn and creased as if he'd aged fifteen years.

"Stars of night, my friend," said Portier, crouching beside him, "are you all right?"

"Makes a skewered gut seem like a holiday." Ilario rubbed his forehead. "I need a nap. I need to give these infernal things to someone. And I need to get away from here and never see—" His eyes popped open. "Ah, gods' teeth, Portier."

"We did well, all of us," said Portier, shaking off Ilario's anguish. "We need to finish this quickly. For Dante's sake. And Mancibar's . . . and everyone's . . ."

The newest tremor dislodged dust and pebbles from the ceiling.

"We oughtn't leave Dante out there alone," I said.

"I'll go." Ilario held out the Stones to Portier. "I believe these are yours."

Portier smoothed the polished green facets and perfect edges with his thumb, then glanced up at us with a sheepish smile. "It's so strange I don't remember them, save in those fragments Ferrau dug out of me. We need to see to the tetrarch and his men. . . ."

But we couldn't. Not yet. We needed all of us to make this work. Once begun there would be no second chance.

"After," I said. Only for Portier there would be no *after.* Not here.

Ilario was back in moments, followed by a bandaged Andero cradling Dante in his arms. "Couldn't leave him out there naked, could I?"

Rhea held Dante's ancille gingerly in two fingers. I snatched it away, as her hand was shaking. She said she had seen to the youth in the bleeding chair and sent him running.

We laid Dante in the other cell. Again he curled into a quivering knot, his breath coming in strident gasps. His eyes were open but looked on nothing we could see.

Ilario and Andero moved down the passage to stand guard. Rhea sponged Dante's face and said she would watch over him. And so it was left to me.

I whispered in Rhea's ear that when she heard me call Portier into the cell, she should fetch Ilario. Portier was watching from the doorway when I rose.

"Are you ready for this adventure?" I tried to smile but didn't think I made a good job of it.

He drew me into his arms and squeezed much too tightly. "It's all right, Ani. To be honest, yes, my gut's in a knot. But also"—he stepped back and held out his hand, which was now as steady as my father's love—"this is why I'm here. Had I never heard mention of Ianne or saints or the Souleater or the Seeing Stones, I'd know it. When I heard the stories of how Altheus came down here and lay down to die, I assumed them metaphorical. But now? I don't think so."

"I'll do my best for you. You understand I've never woven a spell completely. Pieces. Small things, but . . ."

". . . but we had the same teacher, so I trust you. Tell him . . . I've never known anyone with his courage or his strength or his goodness. Tell him I never had a true friend either until him. And tell him I will never forget him . . . or you . . . or our magnificent chevalier. I'll likely come haunt you all, just to see how you're getting on, as you're the only people I know who wouldn't be at all surprised."

I opened my mouth, but no words came.

"I know. You'll think of what to say tomorrow. I promise I'll listen,

Ani, no matter what the rules are. I think I was done with rules a very long time ago."

I laughed at the imagining, ignoring the dark things he must surely encounter along his way. Time enough for that as I wove. "You'd best wait out here . . . and you'll need this. . . ." I pulled out the third stone.

Something fell out of my pocket and chinked on the floor as I gave him Tychemus. Dante's nireal. On his bit of paper, Dante had written: *Wear it always.*

"Would you put this on Dante? He brought it all this way."

"Certainly."

Kneeling at the door opening, just outside the boundaries of my enclosure, I ran through a series of quick exercises to clear my head. Then I heeded my teacher's instruction. . . .

Begin with intent and hold it in mind always, the core of any spell: mortal death, a natural passage, one we humans feared but should not. But the Veil had been damaged, torn repeatedly, and to avert further damage I must use its aberrant nature and shove these mystical bits of the aether back through the hole, carried on the wings of Portier's soul.

And then construct the shape of the work: Piece by piece, I wove my containing vessel, warp and weft . . . physical and spiritual, as I had planned. Then, I wove in Ilario's dagger, keen, light, to be wielded by a skilled hand, moved by grief and love, duty and mercy.

Only when the construct begins to glow with light, bring in the focus: first the Stones—which I knew from history, from Dante's tale. They did not have keirna, for their essence was the aether itself, with which I was very familiar. And then I wove in Portier . . . the man I had loathed and come to respect and then to admire and then to love as a brother. His talents, his failings, his shyness, his muddleheaded approach to women, his own difficult family history, his friendship with a man who had no concept of friendship. Portier and Dante had saved each other from things far worse than death . . . and given each other gifts beyond measure.

Pausing. "I need you in the circle now, where I've marked your head and feet," I said. My voice existed somewhere outside the aether where my great construct shimmered with the light of magic, the blue and green and yellow fire of Heaven.

I didn't open my eyes. Instead I felt the shifting warmth as he passed me, but heard no footsteps. He must have removed his boots. He grunted softly as he lay down—his leg, of course. And then stillness, and I began again, encompassing his keirna with that of my enchanted vessel.

Behind me Ilario waited, but I wasn't ready. My stomach churned with familiar disgust. I hated spellwork . . . or was it merely that something wasn't right? Dante's constant warnings blared: *Think deeper. Don't assume that everything's right because it fits. Think about what does not fit; dig deeper for what you've not considered.*

The pieces were well chosen. Their woven keirna shone like strings of drawn glass. I parsed through them, one by one. One particular piece felt awkward, as if the weft had collapsed, leaving a great hole in my vessel. Healing . . . the snake symbol. What was I missing?

All my doubts crashed in on me. Ixtador. The starving dead. Lianelle, perhaps devoured already. Captain de Santo, condemned. Could even Portier's soul escape the Souleater now the daemon was so strong and emboldened? There would be no true healing unless we destroyed Ixtador. And once this spell was bound, there would be no magic in the living world.

And of course, now I saw the problem, the answer came clear. What had de Ferrau said about the snake symbol? *Reversal. The antithesis of death.* Not healing, then, but something to represent life itself—strength and passion and determination. The gifts we needed to accomplish our purpose. I touched the scrap of paper in my pocket . . . then turned to Ilario and told him what to do.

"Ani, are you certain?"

"As anything in this world. Right beside Portier—touching. Otherwise, exactly as we planned."

Ilario did as I asked, removing the vial of his medicine and replacing it. I wove in the new element—so familiar—and went through it all again. And then I was ready.

"Now."

A small grunt. As the smell of my friend's blood flooded the stale air, I focused my will on the shimmering structure and released every spit of power inside me. No use holding back when this was the world's last enchantment. Magic boiled through my limbs, fueled by grief and anguish and rage at the loss of those I so loved. The spell structure grew luminous. Huge. Cruel. Glorious. Only here at the end did I understand Dante's love for magic . . .

. . . and when I felt like a plummeting kite, or a wineskin when the final drop has fled, I bound the spell and opened my eyes.

Portier lay still, a faint smile on his lips. One hand was yet cupped at his breast. Empty. The other hand lay beside him where Ilario had laid the replacement for the snake symbol. Nothing was there, either. Along with the Maldivean Seeing Stones, Dante, the Daemon of the Dead, had vanished. For the first time in ten hours, the earth was still.

Dante

CHAPTER 39

Reach, Dante. Extend the staff. Your arm won't break, else it would have done so a lifetime ago. Scribe yet another circle of power in the dry, grassy hillside that is neither grass nor earth nor even dry. How could a place *lack* water if none existed anywhere? There was no growth here, no replenishment of any kind.

The feral howl rose from behind me, traveling up my spine even as it traversed the chill wastes. Purposeful. The hunter was very angry. Hands and spirit trembled at the memory of his fury.

Raise the fire now; instill it with safety and warmth and the promise of protection. Circles of fire had ever been the best defense against predators. How did I know that? Even were I in possession of the mind I had lost, I could not have said, for there was room for nothing in me save magic and will—to endure, to fight, to destroy, to protect . . . what?

I had glimpsed an answer just after the world ended, erasing light, stone, smoke, color, blood, voices, and . . . blessedly . . . the pain that had left me mindless, quivering wreckage. What remained—this existence—was a chill, vomitous chaos, a dense whirlpool of hunger. Formless fingers pawed at me; gaping mouths wailed, begging, whispering of loss, anger, hunger, and lust. My mind and body came near exploding in the search for solidity. A creature of flesh, I needed walls, floor, tree, earth . . . anything I could grasp.

Then, for a single moment, a glare of white had enveloped me in calm stillness. "Time for only one lesson, *student*," said a dry, familiar voice. Teasing? "Close your eyes."

The whisper dissolved into my bones, a warmth that spoke of existence that was not pain, of common purpose and resolution, of trust, of a *friend* whose name was long lost in the abyss, but who bound me to other friends and a life. . . .

As the words and the brilliance faded, I was plunged back into chaos. Yet I did as my unknown friend advised and, in the dark, found clarity. No longer hampered by the confusion of shapes and colors I could not name, I created my own order. I knew how to do this. My feet were *down*, a grassy hillside under them. My head was sheltered by a colorless sky. A heated spark burned on my chest, centering me. Now the ravening spite of the approaching scourge—my cruel and comely master—stood out from the starved terror of these other beings as distinctly as a thorn among rose petals. I fixed him as the focus of my world and set my arm and the *poulon*—this white staff that seemed an extension of my hand—between us. The heel of the staff dug into dry soil. Did I not stop him, he would eat us all.

Ten circles . . . twenty . . . a hundred had I raised already.

The lash struck, ripping through nerves and sinew. *Daemon! Servant! Your punishment has only begun. Do you think you shall escape the caves of Gedevron? Your chains wait. My scourge waits. Eternity waits. . . .*

"Here. In here. Come." Eyes squeezed tight, I drew them into my circle of fire, those beings I could not look on without madness. "He cannot reach you here. When he's gone, I'll set you free."

Those who could yet comprehend words crowded in around me. Fluid shapes brushed my naked flesh like veils of cobweb. When the circle was filled, I stepped through the flame and looped the staff to raise the barrier high, until it was a dome of fire. I moved on and scribed another. . . .

A firm touch on my chest. I jumped backward and squeezed my eyes tighter lest I lose myself in the maelstrom. But unseen fingers gripped the bit of silver suspended from my neck. And other warm fingers touched the silver band around my throat, tapping on it softly.

We know you, mage. The man's graveled voice sounded in my head, not my ears. Yet it seemed right. *All who remain whole will help. Even the Empty Ones know who contrives our ruin.*

The lash jarred me again . . . colder, sharper, cutting deeper.

The bit of silver . . . the words in my head . . . in the *aether* . . . memory just beyond reach. Phantom images of a wild-haired girl and a sturdy-built man with black hair drifted through the darkness behind my eyelids like smoke shadows. These two were a part of the life the teasing voice had waked. They should not be here. And these others . . . my master would steal their immortal being. . . .

I'd thought I neared the last of my strength, but a cold, tarry rage surged slowly through my limbs, through my chest, into my arms.

"Can you bring the Empty Ones?" I said.

Yes, said the girl. *But they've naught to give. Once he's stripped them dry, they fade.*

"I can't restore them," I said, "but I can give purpose to their loss. I need their help, and yours."

So I spread my arms and planted my staff, and as the starving spectres gathered round, I let my anger enfold them, engulf them, drain their incoherent fury to add to mine, and when my power was swollen so huge, I thought my soul must shatter, I shot flame from my staff and cried, "Begone, Dimios Souleater, back to your ice caves. Face me, if you dare. . . ."

Ilario

CHAPTER 40

"You don't know where he's *gone*?" Andero stared down at Portier's naked corpus and the empty place where I had laid Dante. The good smith was near tearing his hair at Anne's declaration. "Chevalier didn't say he'd be *vanished*."

Well, it wasn't as if I'd actually known what Anne was going to *do* with Dante. She just said to put him in the enchanted circle with Portier and make sure Portier was touching him. She'd had that look on her face that was so much like Dante's when he was working enchantment—absolute certainty. *Open a path through the eternal Veil? Raise the dead? Explode a mountain? Of course I can do that.* Or, *I'm going to live with a murderous blind sorcerer who can skewer a man's heart with a thought, but deep inside all that crust and anger, he loves me dearly.*

I'd never been that certain about anything in my life. But Anne de Vernase had always proved her certainties, so I had laid the poor devil Dante beside Portier, who lay on that dirty stone floor waiting to die, and we both shrugged and yielded to a woman like none other in the world. If Anne had told me that Dante was going to walk back out of Heaven with the Pantokrator's scepter, I had no doubt he would. I was surprised to hear she didn't know.

"He's in Ixtador, I suppose." Still she held her grief in check. "He was in torment here. He said he was the Souleater's Hand in the Living World. He was being driven to obedience with pain, readied for the moment his master would walk free. But he was fighting it with everything in him. Why do you think this roof is still intact? You told us how amazing it was that half the population of Mancibar wasn't dead. Why so? Because Dante deflected and diverted and did whatever he could to mitigate the violence of their conflict. He was trapped here where he couldn't fight freely. He needed to be in Ixtador. That's why he wanted to die—not in despair, but in frustration because his body, his instincts, everything he was, told him he was supposed to fight, to destroy, to wield wild magic . . . but not here. If he prevails, then Ixtador will be no more, and the Souleater will lose his feast of souls. If not . . . I can't think it would be worse there than what he was enduring here." That's when her voice broke. "Gods save me, Andero, I didn't want to lose him."

Not even I wanted to lose him. She'd been right about him all along. Dante was her completion, her joy . . . and I would do anything necessary to bring joy to Anne de Vernase.

Andero cared a deal about Dante, too. I never would have picked that gentle man for Dante's brother—especially after hearing about their upbringing. Then again, I'd seen him put a few of the palace guards down with a move that near snapped their spines.

"No, no, I understand you didn't," he said, "but spirits and daemons, lady, he wasn't dead! What does he do there? Have you a spell to get him back? Can you talk to him in your way? Touch him as you do, to know if he lives?"

"There are no spells anymore. No aether. No voices. No sense of him. The Seeing Stones are no longer in the living world, and magic's gone with them, and I don't know that he can ever get back." And she had known it when she sent Dante beyond the Veil. "It means we won," she said, though never was victory pronounced with such sorrow. "Portier did what was needed—dear, blessed man. The Souleater won't walk free in this world. It remains to be seen about the next. . . ."

Ah, Portier, I thought. *There's a hole in the world where you ought to be. We'll not forget.* My chosen life had forbidden me many friends. That one should be a Saint Reborn must serve a lifetime's wonder. It near left me grinning to imagine him—so slight, so intense, so reserved, yet bold enough to challenge the Creator of the universe and steal his holy magic.

"I understand your grieving for your friends," said Rhea, packing up her kit. "But there are others who may need us. I'm going to the tetrarch."

"Damnation!" I yelped. Lost in thoughts of the dead and missing, I had entirely forgotten the brave men who'd gotten us here. "The palace guard don't know Jacard's orders aren't in force any longer. Will you come, Andero?"

"Aye. Could use a fight."

I, too. I turned to Anne. . . .

Her eyes darted to Portier; her hands fidgeted. "I'll come," she said. "I just need something first. . . ." She glanced around, then visited the adjoining cell where we had laid Dante. She emerged with empty hands, agitated beyond reason.

Rhea picked up something from a stack in the passage. "Use his shirt," she said, handing Anne a wad of cloth. "He was a tidy man?"

Anne laid the shirt over Portier's face, and his hose across his privates. It wasn't all that dignified. I looked at her askance, and she colored a bit. Even laughed a bit. "All right. It makes *me* feel better," she said.

Indeed Portier had been a tidy man. He had removed his clothes, folded them, and left them in a stack. And just like Altheus, he had stopped breathing just before I stuck my knife in his neck. I hadn't had to kill him. Blessed saints . . . Grief unsheathed its blade and plowed it into my gut.

"When we come back we'll dress him," said Rhea. She brushed my hair with her fingers. Rhea had a gift for comforting. All these days . . . years . . . not even my sister, Geni, had guessed how I felt about Anne.

Anne still wasn't done, though. "Where's Dante's staff? It's not enchanted anymore, but it would make a decent fighting stave."

I waved my hand. "Uh, I kept it with him. You didn't say not. He didn't look right without."

That got a genuine laugh out of her, no matter that it was laced with tears. "It might do him more good there than it will here. If Ixtador is formed of the aether, perhaps his magic will work."

"And if Dante de Raghinne can work enchantments beyond the Veil," I said, "then he'll find his way back to you." No brighter beacon existed in the universe.

"Aye," said Andero. "I'd say he would. His is the stubbornest head and heart was ever born to woman."

I prayed we were right. I had heard the message he'd sent her through Will Deune. For the first time, I knew Anne's certainty about Dante was the truth. I was content.

RHEA HAD NO ONE TO HEAL. Tetrarch de Ferrau lay dead in the waiting room along with two of his bailiffs. The other two had vanished along with the guards who had held them captive. The whole place seemed deserted. Servants, guards, and courtiers must have gone to see to their families amid the terrors of the night. To our astonishment, dawn was breaking. A clear, silvery desert dawn. We saw no signs of fire down in the city.

We found a buttery and drank gratefully. Then we returned to the navel of the world and placed Portier in Altheus's—his own—tomb. We didn't think he'd mind mixing his bones. He wasn't truly there.

We left the vile mess that was Jacard where it lay, but Xanthe was missing. We found the blood pool where she'd fallen. Mayhap she crawled away. Mayhap she'd dissolved to dust and mingled with the rubble from the shattered statues.

Rhea spotted me kneading my tender gut and suggested we burn the tetrarch and his two men. The palace sat on rock, too hard for digging, yet we couldn't leave them behind. De Ferrau had helped us find the answers we needed, difficult as they were to hear . . . and to live with.

We built the pyre in front of the palace, searched out lamps and oil, and waited until we were sure the flames would take our comrades. Likely all in town could see it.

Then we left. The red-haired captain was manning the gates. As none of us were Portier or Dante, he let us pass.

"Hosten, isn't it?" said Anne, once we were outside. "We're messengers from the saints, sent to free Mancibar. The Regent is dead, as is the Lady Xanthe. Go to the crypt and you'll see. There will be no more vanishings. No more bleeding. The daemon mage is no longer in this world. Have mercy on your citizens and keep order. You're in charge here."

He might have believed us; he might not. To my mind he looked relieved as he charged off toward the palace.

We returned to the scholar's house and slept the clock around. Two days later we rode north.

WE WERE A QUIET COMPANY. We had won such a victory as no cadre of soldiers ever had. But each of us had left a piece of the heart behind, even Rhea. She knew the two dead bailiffs well, and de Ferrau had been her master since she was twelve.

We chose a route that bypassed Hoven. Andero's honor demanded he return there to finish out his bargain, but I wouldn't hear of it. "We need you," I said, pulling him aside. "Anne has no magic, and to be honest, my insides are still as tender as a rabbit's kit. Once we're through the wilds of Kadr, you can head back for Hoven if you feel it right. But be prepared. Rhea will likely insist on going along to look after your head. I don't think she's ever seen one so hard, as she never got a chance to tend your brother."

"She's a marvel," said the smith, watching her riding beside Anne. "So wise. And she's a quietness about her as I've never seen. . . ."

I muzzled my grin. Rhea had confided that she found the smith's quiet ways a *marvel*, as well. "He's the gentlest man I've ever met, especially for one who's gone soldiering, especially when one considers what his brother is . . . was. And smithing is such a stalwart profession. . . ."

Which being a gentleman in the queen's service—and occasional swordsman and *agente confide*—was most certainly not. She had spent a great deal of time during my recovery trying to persuade me to become a Temple scholar. When I told her that my wardrobe would just not support that shade of green nor my reputation support any designation as *scholar*, she had left me eating porridge for three days running.

Of course, that was before I had told her that it was the Cult had claimed my loyalty when I was a boy and our converse grew more serious. I didn't think she'd be going back to the Temple right away, if ever. Over our last game of stratagems, the previous autumn, my royal brother-in-law had told me of a plan to build a new kind of hospice in Tigano. I had a notion he might be interested in a fine physician once Andero's time in Hoven was done.

It was Anne worried me. She didn't want to go back to her parents, yet without Dante . . . I wasn't sure anywhere would feel like home for a good while. It was not a place I could fill. Not this time.

As we traveled, it seemed to me a peace settled over the world. I didn't dare suggest what that meant. Anne assumed the quiet was merely the absence of voices in her head.

On our tenth day out from Mancibar, our track from the southwest rejoined the ghost road near the village of the shepherds, the impoverished little place where people spoke of the Pantokrator and the guardians as personal correspondents and the War for Heaven as if it had occurred last month. Comparing the scholar's map to Andero's, we judged we'd come out to the north of the village, which meant it required a backtrack to go there.

Anne was of a mind to pass it by. "I'm tired of the road," she said. "I need to be home." She didn't say where home might be, now Pradoverde was ash.

"I want to contract for some of their woolens," I said. "You know how I adore such fine colors, and, saints know, they could use the coin."

But it wasn't that entirely. These people had shown an uncanny connection with the sublime that I believed all four of us could use. The old man Otro had called Dante the *Daemon*, and spoken of him as wrestling daemons, fighting for his soul. And so he had been. We had come full circle on this journey, and I felt the need to acknowledge it.

"All right, then." Anne had no vigor to argue, which told me much of her state.

THE WHOLE VILLAGE, SAVE THOSE off with the sheep, came out to greet us. They honored Andero, especially, saying he had *wrestled the cruel spirits* possessing their man Jono while Dante cast them out. Young and old begged him to tell stories of his journey and the fate of the great and noble mage he served. He deferred to Anne.

Thus, on that night after feasting, Anne told the story of Portier and Dante, Jacard and Xanthe, of the rent in the Veil and our narrow escape from having the Souleater free to ruin the human world. She crafted our grim tale in the language of myth and legend, holding the villagers rapt for near two hours. And when she was done, she smiled at me across the sea of heads and nodded, and I knew it had been right to come.

"Have you called the great sorcerer home?" asked Ertan, the headman, laying a withered hand on hers. "Surely you've not left him to wander the stars before his time."

"I've no enchantments to bring him, and I am bereft of prayers." The weight of sadness in her admission must surely make the stars weep. "He might be prisoned in the ice caves."

"'Tis only a call, no prayer or enchantment," said an old women. "We call those who are dead and they come to us, but if your healer lives, how much easier for him to hear. A place away from day business makes it easier to hear. We'll go with you. 'Tis a night of no moon, so the stars will be bright enough to guide him." And they began gathering blankets and rugs, children, hats, honey cakes, flasks of tea, and walking sticks.

"Perhaps I could just speak to Otro," said Anne, a bit dismayed. "We talked last time."

"Well, then, you see," said Ertan. "Your voice is clearly heard among the stars. How much easier to call one who shares your heart."

Anne seemed bewildered. So was I, but being of a less scientific bent than Anne, I caught what he meant. "This Otro," I said, "he is not living?"

"Gracious, no," said Ertan. "Otro was my father's father, and I'm so old my bones wither. Otro loves this land and all of us, so he remains close."

Anne was wordless. As was I, which my friends will say is not at all usual.

With the entire village shepherding us, we made a jabbering procession out of the village and onto the rolling meadows beyond. Men sang and women laughed. Children darted about like fleas, forging ahead and then bouncing back as if they rode bowstrings, released from dusky bedtime as though it were solstice night.

When we reached the hilltop place of their choosing, they spread their blankets and rugs on the rocks and grass and shared out the honey cakes and cooling tea, as grand a feast as I had ever experienced. There were no prayers or invocations, only quiet conversation and good cheer.

Andero and Rhea were quickly caught up in a game of chase. Anne and I were left alone on the edge of the crowd. A matter of respect for her grief, I believed.

"It is a peaceful place," said Anne. "No matter their foolish ideas, I'm glad we came. Nice to be somewhere the people honor him."

"But have you called him?" This from a bent old man now sitting beside us. I wasn't at all sure he had walked up from the village. I decided that perhaps I wouldn't look at him too closely.

Anne did, of course. "Otro! Can you tell me where he is?"

"He wanders. Weary and lost. Searching. Call him. They'll bring him if they hear."

I'd swear on my blessed father's dead eyes that the old man vanished or perhaps turned into a star. And I'd swear on my blessed mother's heart that when Anne closed her eyes and began whispering Dante's name, that naught but a sheet of stars topped the next rise, though I blinked and a dark shape stood there. And I'd swear on my own hope of Heaven that he was escorted down the swale and up the hill we inhabited accompanied by a sea of faces that you could see only if you weren't quite looking at them.

He leaned heavily on his white staff and was as naked as a plucked chicken save for the silver chain and pendant I'd put about his neck myself. "Anne!" he called, hoarse as if he'd been calling for a century. "Where are you? Anne!"

All our hearts stopped, I think. Mine certainly. Anne's hand flew to her mouth. Andero halted in his tracks, the game of chase swirling below him like a turbulent river about a rock. Rhea paused beside him.

None of us moved toward Dante. I wasn't sure our feet could tread the swirling darkness between us. He paused and touched the nireal, then straightened his path directly toward Anne. Hurrying. Faster. Shedding his companions. Another hesitation.

"Dante!" she called.

Even when he came within a few metres, he strained to see. . . . Then he touched the nireal and took a few more steps. Felt his way with the staff. Blind again.

"Dante, beloved!"

"Oh, blessed gods . . ." He slumped to his knees and pressed his brow to his staff, rocking back and forth. And then he craned his head back and released a great bellow, of triumph and hurt, of joy and exhaustion, of loneliness and pain and grief beyond a mortal lifetime's measure.

Anne knelt in front of him and stroked his hair, and I could not say what was spoken. But she soon laid his staff aside and enfolded him in her arms. He rested there, his head upon her breast, hers upon his black hair, and never did her hands stop soothing and comforting. After a while, she helped him to his feet, and they walked hand in hand up the hill.

I snatched up our blanket, and though my mouth was full of questions and good wishes, I did not spill them. Instead, I passed the blanket to Andero and jerked my head toward his brother.

"Who's this naked jaybird walked out of the wilderness, my lady?" No crack in his robust basso revealed the tears streaming down his face as he threw the blanket across Dante's shoulders.

"Andero . . ."

A reunion for all ages of the world. Dante was not at all surprised to find me living. "You weren't there."

The experience contained in those three words set me shivering. When some idiocy skipped off my tongue, something about prayers, he snapped one finger in the air. "No more of the peacock, lord. I know the man who saved me. The chevalier. The man of honor."

The villagers, gratified but not surprised, rounded up their children and drifted back toward their homes. The five of us, for Andero caught Rhea before she could escape, sat on that hillock and talked.

We told him of de Ferrau and Will Deune, and how his reworking of Kajetan's spell had worked. And we told him of Portier, and how we had discovered what had to be done.

"So he found what he wanted." Sadness and weariness entwined a laugh. "Knew it was him. He called me *student*. . . ."

Dante had too few words that night to say much of his battle beyond the Veil. But he told a bit . . . and the ending struck both Anne and me very hard. ". . . I drove Dimios back through the gates of Gedevron and set the dead to hold him while I explored the construct of Ixtador. It was a girl of seventeen, dead long before her time, who led them, along with a faithful guard captain who saw one last duty for his noble chevalier. By the time I unraveled Ixtador, the gates of Gedevron were closed and the dead had scattered—all of them. I didn't think it wise to open my eyes. Whatever I might see . . ." He twisted his mouth in wry humor. "Well, I didn't want curiosity to make me stay. I wanted to go home. This"—he touched the pendant on his breast—"told me where I belonged."

The sun kissed the horizon when we decided we could not utter one more syllable. Andero, Rhea, and I spread blankets on the grass, for it was a fair night under the stars. We left the lambing shed to Dante and Anne. Andero and I agreed, we'd allow no more talk of guesthouses.

Anne

CHAPTER 41

"Read it to me again. Please. There's something . . ."

Dante had been restless the entire afternoon, the last before Andero and Rhea set out for Hoven, and Ilario, Dante, and I for Sabria. The two of us had taken long walks. We had explored the joyful awkwardness of love. We had sat with the elders to drink tea and shared more of our own stories with our friends. My heart soared so high, I felt one with the hawks and kites.

Dante's ordeals had made him no more comfortable with politenesses and large gatherings where it was difficult to distinguish one stranger's voice from another. And, after three months of seeing, he found it humiliating to be back to the beginning with eating and drinking and other simple tasks he had once mastered. He hated knocking over things or dipping a spoon outside a bowl. But he would bury his face in my hair and laugh at his own discomfiture. "I have been and will ever be a boorish oaf," he said. "How do you put up with me?"

All I had to do was touch the nireal he wore around his neck and he would wind me in his arms. "Oh, gods, Anne . . ."

While I visited each family in the village, he spent a great deal of time walking in the swales. Sometimes at night, I saw him with Otro. In the sunlight, it was more often with one of the elders or Andero or even Rhea. He said Rhea had examined his eyes and told him the nerves were dead and would not recover.

". . . but it's all right," he added quickly. "Unlike blessed Portier, I live. You are here at my side. And my brother. And my friends. Though I will protest to the gods that it isn't at all fair that I didn't get to see you all when I had both eyes to do so and a rational mind to savor it."

With the elders he talked mostly of sheep and the land. "I'm going to have to find a new profession," he'd told me that morning. "Sheepherding might suit. I like the quiet and the countryside. Though you'd have a dreadful time marking routes so I wouldn't get lost."

"I'm not ready for you to be gone so much," I said, as I worked—very awkwardly—with the hand spindle one of the women had given me. "And I would make a terrible shepherd's companion. I'm all thumbs at spinning, as well as needlework."

"Then, no sheepherding. Perhaps I'll take up smithing, persuade Andero to set up shop in Laurentine and hire me on as an assistant."

We spent an hour talking of various occupations a former sorcerer of good mind and bad eyes might take on. And then he grew quiet. "Ah, Anne, I do miss it so very much. For one moment, the world doesn't feel so very different; then it bludgeons me again . . . no voices . . . no friend of the mind . . . and I can't conjure a feather." He rubbed his fingers over the hornbeam staff and its carved crescents and stars and other symbols. Not even a spark resulted.

Though I had finally experienced the glories of his art, my own small loss was soothed by his presence. Dante had lost his life's work.

That's when he asked me to read the transcript of Portier's memories yet again. I had read it to him at least five times already. Not that I minded . . . anything and everything to do with Dante was a joy. But the transcript had become an obsession with him.

"Doesn't this strike you as something of a violation?" I said as I unrolled the paper I kept carefully in a hollow tube. "Like constantly peering into someone's bedchamber."

"Certainly not! Portier was a man of science and would wholly support—"

His cheeks displayed his acknowledgment of my teasing. "I keep thinking I'll glimpse something beyond the words written. Are you sure you recorded everything the tetrarch recalled?"

"I wrote as fast as I could, and Andero listened, so he could supply the bits I missed. De Ferrau never hesitated. I suppose it's a skill a Reader develops."

"Aye . . . they'll have a difficult change, too. We won't need Temple Readers anymore."

We lapsed into the shared quiet that swelled whenever we considered the implications of our deeds. Sometimes he would hold my hand to his forehead and pretend we could yet feel each other inside, even if the other voices were silent. In the rare times he was out of my sight, I would reach into the void in search of him and imagine I felt some unruly warmth just beyond the range of my senses.

We had walked out from the village to the hilltop where he had returned to me. It seemed a miracle we had come to this obscure little village to find Dante making his way back to living. Yet I decided this case was much like the tetrarch said of prophecy and destiny. To bring him back we had needed a place where one could reach across the barriers of time and memory to call or to hear. A place of quiet, of peace and simplicity, of harmony with the divine. This happened to be one such place. It could have happened at Pradoverde or in the summerhouse at Castelle Escalon. As long as I was there, he said. As long as he was listening for my call, I told him.

Our backs propped against a great rock, we bathed in the stretched sunlight. I scrunched myself into the hollow of his broad shoulder, a place quite near to Heaven, so I had discovered, though he always froze, startled for the first few moments when I took advantage of it.

When he had shifted a bit, exhaled, and snugged his grip on me, I began to read. . . .

> *Transcript of the Reading of Portier de Savin-Duplais. Beltan de Ferrau, Reader.*
>
> *I focused on glimpses of the peculiar deep green color of the Seeing Stones.*
>
> *First probe:* "Go 'way." The man was slitting my lost flesh with a silver knife. He smiled and pressed the cup to a shallow cut. . . .
>
> *First probe discontinued. This was the present, the subject's encounter with Iaccar, Regent of Mancibar, in the bleeding chair.*
>
> *Second probe:* A battle raged . . .
>
> *Second probe discontinued, as the brilliant green that cued my attention was a grassy hillside, not the Seeing Stones.*
>
> *Third probe:* The tent billowed in a dry breeze . . .

Dante had withdrawn his arm and drawn his knees up, forehead resting on his clasped hands. He lifted his head when I finished. "So Ferrau believed that these probes were in reverse time order. Newest first and on through the oldest."

"Yes. He said that was always the way of it."

"Then read me the last two again in the order he recorded them."

I did as he asked. First, Os's journey of the spirit and the cave painting that had given us the Seeing Stones, the key to our victory, and the answer to Portier's long yearning. And the last, Ianne's ordeal on Mont Voilline.

"Did you not think it odd that the order was *Os* first and then *Ianne*?"

"Of course not," I said. "Ianne was his original identity, his first life, and thus the oldest story."

"Would you—?" He hesitated. "I need to be alone for a bit. Think. Without the distraction of . . . companions."

His expression gave nothing away. Each of us had needed thinking time since leaving Mancibar. But this was different somehow. A subdued eagerness gave his muscles life, as if he were on the hunt, tracking down another puzzle.

"All right. Certainly. You can find the path down." His staff, just a walking stick now, would identify the well-worn track and help him down the steep. I knew better than to coddle him.

"Come back at sunset," he said. "And bring the others . . . ours."

"All right."

As I stood, he caught my hand, kissed it, and pressed it to his eyes. "My only light," he said softly, as he did every time we parted.

I puzzled over his odd behavior as I bargained with one of the women about buying one of her rugs to take home. We would rebuild Pradoverde around a reminder of warmth and welcome, starlight and holiness. Ilario had already contracted for their entire year's output of fabric. I laughed inside while watching Ilario consult with Rhea, trying to nudge her toward colors more vibrant than dark blue, while she quietly moderated his inordinate love of yellow.

The three of us, along with every child in the village, gathered to watch Andero's deft hands use oil, stone, and file to sharpen every nail and knife blade in the village while he bellowed a medley of marching songs. Rhea watched him closest of all, and when I looked at Ilario, he smirked at me, waggling his eyebrows in a most self-satisfied manner.

Perhaps I'd been mistaken about the ties of affection forming in our little party. . . .

At sunset, the four of us trudged up the hill and found Dante sitting cross-legged in front of a small expanse of dirt. Laid out on the bare patch of ground were five small piles of dry grass. He hushed us before we could speak. At the wave of his hand, we sat in a half circle like children around a storyteller.

Once we were settled, he pointed to me and said, "Anne. You radiate light like a balefire."

After a moment's pause, he pointed to Andero. "You, my brother by blood and history and giving, you've a forge buried deep beneath an ocean of peace."

Then Ilario. "And you, my chevalier, you who watched my back when I was truly blind, my brother by the faith of our friend who is not here. Your fire shines silver like the steel of your sword and with the brilliance of your honor."

And Rhea. "You, whom I know least, you burn, as well. I sense it when you dress a wound or venture a question. You ever seek the truth behind the wound or the answer you're given."

His hand shook a little. "Listen to this story, passed on to me through the gift of one I called my enemy, drawn from the life of one we all called friend:

"Another winter coming . . . He had chained me near the top of the mount so I could look on the lands of men beyond the Ring . . ." Word for word, Dante recounted Portier's last memory, Ianne's memory, of an hour in his long prisoning on Mont Voilline back at the Beginnings of the world. ". . . *but as the sun fell, I watched the green fires blossom against the night, spreading across the land and knew I had done right. A stone house snug against the wind. A knife kept sharp enough to carve a vine on a shepherd's staff. A frightened child soothed with a hero tale that took shape in the hearth flames. Magic . . .*

"Does it not tease you that this memory came from the earliest of all his lives?" Dante's voice resonated like Merona's bronze bells, like thunder in the deeps, sending heat down my limbs like power in the veins. "Why was Dimios punishing him for *stealing what belonged to greater beings*? It was likely centuries later, at a time when the war beyond the Veil cast the living world in shadow, that Os crawled into that cave and petitioned the universe, only to be dragged out holding the Seeing Stones. What was it our friend *Ianne* saw blossoming across the lands of men from the mount? The *fire* he had stolen. The *fire* Os begged to be renewed. *This*, I think."

The warmth heating my cheeks belied the cool highland night. My neck prickled as Dante felt for one of the little piles and used his scarred hand to trace a circle around it in the dirt. He touched the pile of grass nearest him and did nothing we could see, save smile. . . .

No one spoke. The wind of early summer caressed our cheeks and the afterglow faded. And as the first star came out in the deepening sky, white smoke curled up from his finger. Moments later, a cheery flame of orange and yellow, threaded with dark green, had devoured his little clump of grass. Yet it continued to burn and followed his hand into the air, where it hung like a newborn star.

"Attend, students," he said, "each of you whose fire burns so brightly, your first lesson. The night cools and grows dark. It is the nature of grass to dry. It is the nature of dry grass to burn. The aether is closed off to us, but keirna . . . essence . . . remains. Magic lies not in our blood, not in a random talent, not pouring through the conduit of Heaven's fire, but hidden in this world itself. That is Ianne's gift . . . Portier's gift. To find it is our task—to discover our need, and then to bring will and intent, imagining, and our own inner fire to serve it. All of us here are capable. But we must begin again, here at the beginning. . . ."